ENDGATE ISLAND

Flo Fitzpatrick

www.BOROUGHSPUBLISHINGGROUP.com

ENDGATE ISLAND
Copyright © 2019 Flo Fitzpatrick

ISBN 978-1-951055-00-4

ENDGATE ISLAND

Chapter 1

An explosion demolished the front door, sending missiles of flaming molten glass and bits of metal across the porch.

Black smoke. So heavy. The weight of an iron planter in my hands.

A figure on the floor.

"Fire. Get up."

"Trying..."

Heat. Too much heat. Cloying smoke.

Screams.

Trapped.

***

"May I take your tray?"

I blinked. "Beg pardon?"

"Your tray. I'll get it out of your way if you're finished."

"Oh. Sure. Sorry. I was zoning. Thanks."

The flight attendant piled my tray on top of several others and headed down the aisle.

A vision. A waking nightmare. Something rising from an odd place in my mind. A future event? It hadn't happened and—with any luck—never would.

After locking the tray holder into the seat in front of me, I reached down, grabbed my bag, and pulled out the e-mail printout, which I read for about the tenth time in the past three days. Sent as a mass mailing, as if it were nothing more than a simple job notice to scene designers around the country:

Currently hiring set and lighting designer for dinner theatre. Tentative production of the mystery Blood on the Bayou. *Endgate Island, Louisiana. College degree and professional experience required. No temperamental divas or wannabe stars. Send resumé and reviews via e-mail to J. Harrison at Sugarberry Terrace, Endgate Island.*

J. Harrison. Jenny. My best friend since college. I knew it was her, especially since there were clues I knew signified trouble. The word "stars" had always been our code for "help me out here, *now.*"

We spent three days corresponding but kept the e-mails strictly business. It seemed Jenny was worried someone was going through her private e-mail and she didn't want whoever it was to realize she and I were friends.

It had been about three months since we'd spoken on the phone or texted or even sent an instant message. I'd assumed Jenny was settling into life on Endgate Island with the man she'd married about eight months earlier.

Again, I read her e-mail with the underlying message screaming: *"Teddie, I need you. Please come. Help."*

Chapter 2

Double French doors opened into the main parlor of Sugarberry Terrace. As a theatrical designer, I was hyperaware of my surroundings and the different fixtures, colors, and furnishings used to set a mood. The parlor here at the house on First Avenue was a cacophony of styles that jangled, annoyed, and amused. I sensed Southern matriarchs had, for generations, attempted to provide a magnolia-laden sweetness in their décor with the prominent floral drapes on the windows, staid portraits of ancestors on the walls, a rolltop desk topped with numerous vases and little knickknacks, and the floral sofa and chair sets. The ladies had been thwarted by subsequent generations putting their own stamp with funky paintings of scenes of New Orleans during Mardi Gras, and Cajun gators on the wall gazing down on wrought-iron tables and chairs and Victorian streetlamps.

My first quick scan of the room revealed no hint of Jenny's style. She preferred clean, sparse lines and neutral colors of gray, cream, and soft sage. Not this hodgepodge clash of centuries and sensibilities. Seeing the mix disturbed me. Disturbed rose to agitation when a wave of recognition about the room hit me. I was taking deep breaths, trying to objectively analyze what was familiar and why I felt I'd been here before when my focus was drawn to the trio of men in the room.

Two of the men were standing together conversing about something clearly unpleasant. The shorter of the two, who was still at least six feet tall, and a stunningly handsome man in his early forties, with a weary charm, spotted me and weaved his way around an ornate sofa, a marble coffee table, and two marble end tables until he reached me. He held out his hand. Eyes the color of ripe blueberries held more than a hint of surprise. "*You're* Teddie Grant? Sorry, don't mean to sound chauvinistic, but I'd expected a man."

"No problem. I get it all the time. And yes, I'm Teddie."

"Nice to meet you. I'm Michael Laurent, Jenny's husband."

Apparently, when Jenny mentioned her best friend and ex-roomie to Michael, she'd referred to me as Theodosia. She was the only person in the world to call me by my proper name.

I turned to the second man now making his way toward us. He exuded an almost animalistic vibe mixed with an icy control and sharp intelligence I found a bit off-putting.

"Teddie, this is Zach Prideaux. He's an island native, in the construction business. He'll be helping with renovations at whatever house we end up with for the theater, assuming it all comes together."

Zach took my hand and kissed it, which was way too Southern even for a Texas native, but fun in a corny way. "Please feel free to come to me with any questions on beam supports or knocking down walls, or the best AC and heating systems needed for an old house currently equipped with window units and radiators."

I avoided drowning in the sexy New Orleans accent and the dark hazel eyes holding a mix of mystery and a flirtatious charm.

"Thanks, Zach. I appreciate the offer."

A smooth baritone voice rang out from across the room.

"You can take it up with Zach *after* you and I discuss it. I'm Eric Desmarais. I'll be directing what's currently a tentative production of *Blood on the Bayou*."

Mr. Desmarais was seated at an antique piano in the corner next to a set of louvered windows. There was a timeless quality about him, and I thought, *I can imagine him in this room wearing clothes better suited to two hundred or a hundred years ago.* Yet he seemed much in the present. Sheer blazing good looks and an air of wit mixed with a dash of arrogance and delightful mischief. His dark skin highlighted the lightness of his ivy eyes, and as he glanced up and met my gaze, a flash of recognition hit with such force I had to fight to keep focused on any discussion of theatres. This was the man who'd taken a lead role in the frightening vision I'd had on the plane, I was somehow sure of it. But…there was more. A familiarity I couldn't pin down.

Along with the huge helping of déjà vu or clairvoyance came a medley of tunes over the last sixty years or so about love at first sight, followed closely by images of this man wearing faded and torn work clothes, as if he'd been outside working under the sun, taking my hand in his and whispering something only I could hear. I blinked and forced myself to come back to the present.

Mr. Desmarais didn't rise to greet me. I knew who he was from seeing his name on numerous programs for Broadway shows and hearing how fabulous he was to work with, but this was my first chance to meet him in person. My first thought was, *Great. Another gorgeous but rude director. Can't even get up long enough to come over and shake my hand.* My second thought, based on his comment about checking with him first, was he might be annoyed having an unknown female designer invade his territory. Third and most worrisome was whether he'd heard the rumors started by my ex-boyfriend, Colin Barrow, hinting in a less-than-subtle way that Ms. Teddie Grant hadn't done the design for *Measures of Light* but had stolen ideas from Mr. Barrow himself. The love songs floating through my head quickly changed to sad and trite country n' western ditties about betrayal.

When Desmarais swung away from the piano, I saw the booted cast on his left leg and realized he was sitting for expediency and comfort. No rudeness or chauvinism involved.

I responded, possibly a bit late, trying not to display my angst regarding his comment. "I'm no diva, Mister Desmarais. I'm a firm believer in collaboration in theatre, and I have no intention of designing anything before we've had a chance to go over concepts with Je—with Miz Harrison, and then only if my ideas meet with your approval."

Whatever response Eric Desmarais might have given was lost in the sound of voices shouting, a sound coming from behind the French doors closest to the piano.

There wasn't much point in politely pretending a couple of folks weren't having one whale of a row the next room over. Everyone in the parlor ceased talking and waited for a lull in the drama.

Five seconds later the doors were flung open. I winced and held my breath, hoping the antique glass would miraculously remain intact. A lady in her seventies and a man possibly in his fifties wearing an apron tied round his waist stomped into the room. An immediate tension displaced the last ten minutes of pure Southern charm.

The younger of the two combatants glared around the room. "Ah'm sorry, Mister Michael, but kin you tell me what in hell Ah'm supposed to do 'bout the dinner party tonight? Am Ah cookin' for five or ten or twenty or *none*? This is ridiculous. Not ta mention, but Miz Jenny still ain't back and Ah've got to say, Ah'm not one bit happy havin' a party without the hostess."

Chapter 3

Jenny's last message had been full of enthusiasm with excited phrases, exclamation points, and cute emojis about how she couldn't wait to see me. Yet she hadn't been at the airport in New Orleans to greet me. She hadn't been with the boatman, a Robin Trahan, to take the trip across the bay with me. Admittedly, it's a long ride—an hour to and an hour back. But she hadn't been waiting on the veranda with her husband, Michael, when I'd come tromping through the path. I'd still been expecting Jenny to grab my suitcases, hug me, and lead me inside to plop down somewhere while she pressed a tall New Orleans-style boozy drink in my hand. She knows I'm shy around strangers and wouldn't have left me to cope with a room full of them alone. Oddly, while I was aware of feeling something was wrong, I was experiencing quite a contradictory impression of coming home.

Michael Laurent glanced at me, perhaps to gauge my reaction to the newcomer's comments, then stated, "Miz Grant, you'll have to excuse our chef. He tends to join my wife in his love of the dramatic. Let me introduce Luc Bouvier. Luc, this is Teddie Grant, down from New York."

The chef glared at Michael but crossed the room and grabbed both my hands in his. He stared into my eyes for a long moment before a look of what I could swear was relief came into his own. An unspoken *Thank God you're here* passed between both of us.

"Miz Grant, Ah'm honored to have you in this house."

"Honored to be here, and please, make it Teddie?"

Luc squeezed my hand, then let it drop. He turned back to Jenny's husband and growled, "Mister Michael, Ah maght share Miz Jenny's flair for drama, but you could benefit from even a hint of her 'magination. She's been gone since last night and Ah fail to understand how y'all can take this so calmly."

A response came from Zach Prideaux. "Because, Luc, Jenny is a flake and Jenny goes missing once a week."

The older woman who'd been arguing with Chef Luc about the party added in a sweet voice with barely a hint of a Southern accent, "Sadly, there's a lot of truth to what Zach is saying. Jenny has been acting erratically for weeks, taking off without a word to anyone or holed up in the attic reading bizarre historical novels about the slave trade for hours. It's absurd to postpone the party for even a moment, especially since we're facing bad weather within the week. It's Jenny's own fault for missing it."

I had to literally clamp my teeth together to stop myself from blurting out *Jenny? A flake? She might look like the daffy ingénue in a British farce, but she has the practical nature of a CEO running a multimillion-dollar trading company. No one morphs into a flake in three months without a damned good reason.*

Michael blanched at her words but seemed disinclined to stand up for his wife. "Olivia is right. Jenny will come back when she's good and ready. I'm sure she'll pop up once she realizes her designer is here. Sorry for this less-than-tranquil discussion, Teddie. Let me try to lessen the tension by introducing you to my aunt, Olivia Laurent, one of the owners of Endgate Island."

Zach coughed. "Correction. Of Sugarberry Terrace and two other properties. *Not* the island."

Olivia, a petite, attractive, and smartly dressed lady, frowned at him. "It's still in question as to the ownership on the other side of the island, Zach. You and the others need to remember there are no real documents currently supporting your claims to the Tenth Avenue area and the castle." She turned to me. "Lovely to meet you, Miz Grant. I apologize for all this talk about legalities."

"Nice to meet you, too. Um, I didn't realize so much of the island was privately owned." I tried to lighten the mood. "Could explain why I couldn't track down much about Endgate online."

Olivia Laurent possessed the charm of her nephew by marriage, but there was a strength there I hadn't yet sensed in Michael. I couldn't tell if the strength leaned more toward power and control or a simple self-assurance in her decisions.

It was also evident Michael's Aunt Olivia loved this island. "We value our privacy, Miz Grant. Endgate Island is almost a secret we cherish. Originally settled..." She paused and smiled. "Actually, settled is too tame a word. The first to arrive were French pirates, sometime around sixteen-ninety. They used Endgate as a storage area for goods smuggled into New Orleans and as a hideaway for the buccaneers trying to escape a formidable English navy. You still find tunnels attached to sheds and houses, which is quite unusual for an island."

"What happened to them? The pirates, I mean?" I asked.

"Most of them ended up settling here. Once America claimed independence, legend has it many of the pirates who survived an attack by the British in the mid-seventeen-hundreds stayed and, along with their sons, fought with colonists in places like Virginia. In terms of commerce, piracy was replaced by the planting of rice, sugarcane, and indigo plants. Captain Jacques Chaudret, the original pirate settler, even planted a vineyard on the west side near Tenth Avenue. Although, I believe his descendants were more successful at rum running."

"Not to mention slave trading." The flat statement came from Eric Desmarais, who was still seated at the piano.

Olivia's eye twitched, but she nodded as though she hadn't been interrupted with an unwanted truth. "Yes. Eric is correct. Endgate eventually became part of the Confederacy, though it was sparsely populated by men of fighting age at the time. After the war, the slaves were freed. Miraculously, the island has managed to withstand hurricanes for centuries, so we haven't suffered the erosion the way most of the Barriers have."

"So, what's the source of island income now?"

"Primarily rice and sugar. There was a fishing charter service for years, but sadly the owner passed away about six years ago. My great-nephew Alex is interested in reviving the same business. There are plans to renovate some of the old mansions to become bed-and-breakfast inns, but tourists need a reason apart from a nice beach. We've resisted turning ourselves into an inn here at Sugarberry Terrace—which is why Jenny's idea of the murder mystery theatre is intriguing, *if* she uses one of the currently vacant houses."

Zach Prideaux stated, "Olivia hasn't mentioned *my* option for revenue, which is a casino over on Tenth Avenue."

"Sounds fun," I told him. "Actually, a casino could work quite well with a theatre."

"Possibly. If it were more of a cabaret venue where tourists could gamble and drink then watch a short show and come back and gamble and drink."

"Got it."

Olivia responded, "I'm not enthused about a casino, as I've previously made clear, Zach. But, as noted, the ownership of portions of the island is currently being…verified."

I tried to play peacemaker by smiling and stating, "Well, I'll do my best to create fabulous sets and help make the theatre, *and* casino if y'all get together for a joint business, a major tourist attraction. And hey. Maybe one or more of your pirates left some booty or barrels of rum hidden in storerooms below the theatres and you can all live off their ill-gotten gains."

An awkward silence filled the room. I could tell I'd stepped into territory best not discussed in polite society, but wasn't sure if it was the mention of pirates, their booty, or the theatre. Eric Desmarais saved the moment from becoming too awkward by swinging his cast away from the limbs of the piano, rising, and coming to my side. "Speaking of gains, but definitely not ill-gotten, and adroitly changing the subject, I saw your last show, Miss Grant. It was brilliantly designed." His voice was rich and melodic, and Broadway love songs started swirling in my head again.

I stared into those hypnotic dark green eyes. "Make it Teddie. Please. And thanks for the kind words. I've seen several of your shows as well, Mister Desmarais, and you may count me among your many fans. I was absolutely blown away by your direction of the revival of *Parade* two years ago."

"Call me Eric. And thanks for the compliment. I loved doing *Parade*. One of those shows I personally thought never got the recognition it deserved. Some of the best music composed for Broadway in the last thirty years. But, back to *Measures of Light*. I saw it in previews about two and a half weeks ago, right before I headed down here to the island. Good show in general, but your set was magnificent."

I blushed.

Zach's right eyebrow shot up. "*Measures of Light*? Seriously? No offense, but the title sounds more like a physics project."

Eric turned and glared at Zach, but before he could respond, Luc announced, "Sorry to interrupt you, Mister Eric, but if Mister

Michael and Miz Olivia are determined this party is on for tonight, then Ah'd best be gettin' back to the kitchen and create a little Creole magic for the guests." His volume dropped. "Miz Teddie? We'll chat later 'bout Miz Jenny."

I could have kissed him. "We will. Thanks, Mister Bouvier."

"Luc."

"Luc."

The chef headed back through the French doors to wherever the kitchen was. Zach waited until he was out of the room before asking Eric what was so special about a show with, quoting himself, "a creepy name."

Eric stated, "*Measures of Light* is an interesting psychological drama regarding ghosts... both real and imagined. And the set design really was one of the best I've ever seen. Teddie used flat gray boulders and alternately made the audience believe they were experiencing something resembling a combat zone drifting into the afterlife and lent an air of... I don't know... I'd call it the coldness of death."

Zach, Michael, and Olivia were riveted by Eric's storytelling. I already knew the plot and *I* was riveted by Eric.

"Go on," Michael urged.

"Once the boulders were in place there was a collective gasp from the audience."

Zach chided him. "Eric, the suspense is killing us. Why the gasp?"

"Because the boulders had morphed into the Vietnam Memorial Wall. It was a punch to the collective stomachs and sensibilities of everyone there. I personally saw more than ten people who were unable to leave the theatre after the show ended. Ushers were handing out tissues to folks who couldn't stop sobbing. I was one of them."

The blush turned into a full-blown color change of beet red at the praise. I hoped Eric would leave any nasty gossip from Manhattan regarding my concept versus Colin Barrow's lies out of any discussion that followed. He had to have heard the rumors... the New York theatre community isn't really all that large.

The other three eyed me with what seemed to be a bit more respect. Michael started to ask me something about my design process but was interrupted—again—when someone burst through the French doors, which really were perfect for making theatrical entrances and exits. If either of the other houses Jenny had slated for her theatre had as much ambiance, she could make it the showpiece of the southeastern Louisiana gulf.

I stared at the newcomer, silently exclaiming, *"Wow."* It was as if Michael Laurent had dropped twenty years and added arrogance along with an enticing danger and absolute ladies-man sexiness. The newcomer was perhaps age eighteen or nineteen, but the adult arrogance was evident when he sauntered into the room, pointed at me, and declared, "Fraud."

Chapter 4

All eyes focused on me. I could almost smell the tar burning and hear the rustle of feathers. My worst fears were realized. Colin Barrow's venom reached clear down to the inhabitants of Endgate Island. To hear "fraud" from someone outside of Manhattan was a punch to the stomach. Could I find a convenient hole to drop into? Turn around and run to the pier, then try to swim back to New Orleans for about six hours? Tackle the boatman, Robin, and ask if he would mind dumping me in the bay midway to the mainland so I could sink beneath the water and be done with it?

Michael spoke first. "What do you mean? Fraud? Are you saying this *isn't* Teddie Grant?"

The young man who'd made the accusation snorted in feigned exasperation. "Oh jeez, Dad. She's Teddie Grant all right. But Teddie's a nickname for Theodosia. She's the New York designer you expected, but she's also your wife Jenny's old roomie and bestie forever."

Alex. I recalled when Jenny told me about her elopement with Michael, she'd said Michael's son from his first marriage had been less than gracious to her. It seemed nothing had changed in the months since Jenny had come to live on the island.

Young Mr. Laurent shot me a quick look and spilled all. "Just so you know, Jenny tried to cozy up to me by showing me old photographs from college and told me about her buddy Theodosia Grant and how much she missed her." He fully turned in my direction and smirked. "I remember exactly what you looked like when you were a sophomore in college. You haven't changed."

I responded with some light humor. "Well, it's only been about seven years since those photos were taken, but I suppose I should be giving serious thanks for great moisturizers keeping away any wrinkles... at least until I hit thirty."

Alex's blue eyes twinkled, and for a moment the charm inherited from his dad overcame his tacky comments. Both Eric and Zach chuckled before Eric quickly resumed his less-than-delighted-to-meet-you stance, and Zach zeroed in on what he considered the pertinent part of Alex's statement. "So, you're a close friend of Jenny's?"

"Yeah. I am."

Olivia took up the interrogation. "Why the deception, Miz Grant?"

Because Jenny is terrified of something or someone at Endgate Island and hoped by bringing me here as a stranger I could get a sense of what was happening without anyone following me around and getting suspicious.

I hoped improvising was like riding a bicycle, because I needed to hop on and pedal fast in order not to betray the fear I sensed about Jenny.

I swallowed and tried to talk fast enough to avoid questions. "Jenny didn't want me to come here and start blurting out details about college before I'd had a chance to show everyone my designs. She was worried folks would assume the only reason she hired me was due to our friendship and felt I deserved an opportunity to make it on my own merits. Nothing mysterious. I didn't change my professional name, Teddie Grant, and would have immediately said yes if anyone made the connection between Teddie and Theodosia before Alex brought it up."

Nods all around. All these men, and possibly Olivia too, had worked different jobs and doubtless had run into situations where they needed to prove their worth without relying on nepotism or friendship. Still, a palpable tension remained in the room. The secret was out but I hadn't been the one to tell it, which put me at a disadvantage with—well—everyone.

"Understandable," was Michael's kind comment. Olivia, Zach, and Eric remained silent. I had this horrible feeling Eric was thinking "make it on my own merits" included stealing ideas from Colin Barrow. Eric's expression was hard to read, but I had a swift impression he had secrets of his own he'd prefer not to share with the others in the room...at least not at this time.

Alex tossed off, "Well, I hope you're more talented than your roommate."

I stiffened. I have difficulty standing up for myself, but no problem at all when it comes to defending a friend. "For what it's worth, Alex, Jenny is an extremely talented actress. You should take the time to check out the movies and some of the television shows she did almost immediately after graduating Cal Arts. She can *spot* talent, as well, as is evidenced by inviting Mister Desmarais here, although I'm sure he hasn't been tooting his own horn or displaying more than one theatre award he's received over the last ten years."

Alex didn't respond, possibly because Olivia didn't give him a chance. She turned to Alex and scolded him. "Enough. Quit acting like a spoiled child with no manners, something you've been doing for months for no good reason. Apologize to Miz Grant and go sit in a corner someplace where you won't cause trouble. Or, better still, go help Luc in the kitchen. We're having a party in this house in three hours and he's got his 'too much to do and no time to do it' face on. Hopefully Cici is back from New Orleans and can help."

Alex muttered what seemed to be a sincere, "Sorry," at me before heading for the kitchen, looking surprisingly cheerful at the dismissal.

Olivia threw up her hands in mock despair. "Not the most heartfelt apology, but at least he didn't throw a vase at you and break a door on his way out. I'm personally sorry my great-nephew hasn't quite matured…and is taking out whatever frustrations he has on a guest."

"It's okay. I hope he's willing to sit down with me at some point while I'm here and talk. I don't want him to be my enemy."

She smiled. "You're very gracious. Thank you."

"No problem." I cast around for something to say. "Um, I gather there's a question of island ownership that could affect which space Jenny uses for the theatre? Wait, or am I being too nosy? It seems confusing."

For a brief moment, an odd tension permeated the room. Something was definitely off with the residents of Endgate Island.

The moment passed so swiftly I silently chided myself on my reading. My radar had to be wrong.

"The importance is due to the Prideaux, Pelletiers, Monique Bernard, George Adler, and yes, the Laurents, all claiming ownership of the west beach and *Chateau Sans Frontiers*, and wanting to keep the area for different purposes," Olivia stated. "I understand the desire to bring in commercial enterprises, but I'm more interested in bringing back the kinder, gentler times here."

Eric interjected, "Which would be…when?"

She didn't appear to notice the slightly sarcastic tone in his voice. "I suppose it was when I first married Michael's uncle, Cyril, and moved to Endgate. I recall people coming over to use the beaches and stay in fancy mansions and enjoy photographing exotic birds. It was far quieter then. The island stayed a combination of residential and scenic through the thirty-five years we were married before he passed." Her voice took on a wistful, dreamy quality, as though she'd managed to time-travel to her past and wouldn't mind staying there. She snapped back as fast as she'd zoned. "I do apologize. My manners have all but disappeared. Miz Grant, you must be exhausted from your trip and ready for a rest and an opportunity to freshen up before tonight's party. Michael? Will you see if Robin is still around to show her to her room?"

Talk about time travel. I felt as though I'd landed in pre-Civil War South where servants—or slaves for that matter—were summoned on cue to perform tasks masters and mistresses deemed necessary.

"Please, Miz Laurent," I said. "There's no need to disturb Robin. I'm sure if you give me directions, I'll find the room without a problem."

"Well, it can get a bit tricky. We have staircases leading to other staircases and long halls with too many doorways."

Zach waved his hand at her. "I'll escort Teddie. It'll give me a chance to point out some architectural details. I'm sure as a designer she'll find them intriguing."

He crooked his elbow and I cheerfully fell into the role and linked my arm in his. We left by the arched opening closest to the front doors and, as we walked toward the giant spiral staircase, I sensed the brief silence in the parlor would soon erupt into an animated discussion about me. No premonition or vision… simple human nature.

Chapter 5

Questions about this island were lining up in my mind like kids on a playground waiting to use the slide, but once Zach and I were partially up the front staircase, the question that flew out of my mouth was, "How did Eric Desmarais hurt his leg?"

"Not leg. Ankle. Or, to be more precise, the ligament above. From my understanding he was about to explore the cellar below the house on Third Avenue...Hickory Shadows, which might actually work for your Endgate Island mystery theatre. Anyway, he was halfway into the cellar when one of the steps gave way. I'll bet they haven't been repaired in a hundred and fifty years. He managed to grab a shelf attached to the wall and swing down to the floor instead of falling straight down. Snapped the ligament. Amazing he didn't break his neck—although it's a short drop."

"Thank God. Um, what's in the cellar?"

"No idea. Eric said he was looking for possible trapdoors to use in the murder mystery and for furniture as set pieces. The houses are architecturally ridiculous on this island, thanks to the pirates. Trapdoors in dining rooms and kitchens and probably bathrooms as well."

"I could use a trap in the set for *Blood on the Bayou*," I told him. "Or any mystery we decide to go with."

Zach started to say something, then stopped.

"What?" I asked.

"There's a lot going on here, and it's messy."

I was already well aware of the messiness without Zach bringing it up, but I was ready for specifics. "What's up? Or not up?"

"To begin with, Olivia Laurent is not exactly what you'd call enthusiastic about this whole project. The idea of a theatre in one of the Laurent homes offends her genteel sensibilities. She's been somewhat critical of Jenny. To be honest, I'd lay bets Jenny's disappearing act is to make Michael worry about her. She thinks if he freaks, he'll cave and tell Olivia off since *he's* the actual owner of Hickory Shadows as well as Sugarberry Terrace and Chittamwood Gardens once the bride returns." He shrugged. "Which is fine by me. Because the Chaudret chateau is the real prize."

I was about to ask why but we'd reached the top of the stairs. Zach pointed to the left. "The first hall. We'll make a couple of turns and hit more stairs before we reach what we fondly refer to as the tower room. Watch out for tables and chairs and wardrobes and dressers and tons of other junk sticking out everywhere. It's one big obstacle course."

He was right. Before he finished his sentence, I bumped into a table and nearly fell over what appeared to be an antique spittoon. "Wow. I gather no one has tried the concept of storage and wide-open spaces for the last four hundred years or so?"

"You nailed it. Here I am, supposedly primed to give an estimate on renovating this house, but no one seems to care. Michael's gone most of the time with his own antiques business, so I'm left to deal with Olivia. I try to push for a bit more organization and less junk, but she loves all this stuff and wants things seen."

"But preferably not felt," I stated as I rubbed an elbow that hadn't quite made it around a giant bookshelf unscathed. "I'm sorry to bring this up again, but I can't help wondering about Jenny, whom I have to defend. She's *never* been manipulative, so I can't conceive of her suddenly vanishing as some kind of ploy to get her way."

"Well, people change."

No, I thought. *Not Jenny. Not in three months.*

"Zach, back up a bit. Let me make sure I've got this straight. You're saying the Laurents don't want a theatre under their name? That the whole the idea has turned into one big tug-o-war between the family and Jenny?"

"Olivia hasn't been thrilled about the project since Jenny first brought it up. The idea of strangers coming to Endgate, even though they'd be bringing in money, really bothers her. Alex's head has been on another planet since he hit puberty however many years ago and hasn't cared. This past year he's been surly and opposed to anything anyone suggests. As to Michael? I'm not sure where he stands on this...the theatre. Since he's totally dotty about Jenny, I imagine he'll acquiesce to her every desire." He shot me a look. "Sorry. She might be your buddy, but I'm not a fan of hers."

"And the ownership of the island is also in question. Did I understand correctly?"

"Not the entire island. Primarily the properties from Tenth to Sixth Avenue, which includes the west beach and the castle *Chateau Sans Frontieres*, thanks to a cockeyed will created centuries ago. I'm really surprised no one contacted you to tell you to stay in Manhattan until things are settled. I said the same to Eric when he arrived about two weeks ago and started exploring."

I grinned to dispel what seemed to be a distinct tension about ownership. "So, is the castle haunted? Can we give ghost tours?"

Zach replied, "You and Jenny are in accord on that point."

"Well, people do love them, especially when the spooks include old pirates."

Zach produced a hint of a smile. "I suppose. Not my thing. At any rate, the first members of the families of Endgate, which includes me by the way, are running around debating and looking for documents and consulting lawyers—and you and Eric could be considered…in the way at this time."

Was he threatening? Was he warning? I hadn't pressed Zach about Eric's accident, but my initial impression of Eric Desmarais was that he was way too savvy to go poking around a cellar without making certain every entrance, egress, and means of getting around was safe. Had someone deliberately sabotaged the stairs to keep him away from something in the cellar? Perhaps something that could provide proof of ownership? And why did it matter who owned what?

I inhaled. "Well, I suppose I'll have to wait and see what happens once Jenny gets back. And I'll tell you in all honesty, it's going to take more than speculation to convince me she's pulling some kind of power play by trying to scare Michael. I wish he'd organize a search party or something to see if Jenny's all right. What if she's had an accident and is lying outside somewhere in pain while everyone in the house blithely goes about his or her business?"

Zach seemed to agree. "You may be right. Look, I'll tell Michael this has gone on long enough and it's time to bring Jenny home, no matter my thoughts on *why* she's missing."

"Thank you. As Alex rather pointedly noted, Jenny has been my best friend since the day we met in college. I have no problem admitting my anxiety level has been climbing higher than these crazy stairs for this last hour."

"Speaking of stairs, do you need a break? One more flight and we're at the attic. It's been given a makeover to work as your room."

I squared my shoulders. "I'm fine. No break needed. I'm a good Texan-turned-New-Yorker who walks about six miles a day, climbs ladders for hours on end, has no elevator at her fifth-floor walk-up, and hits the gym every chance possible. So, lead on."

I followed Zach down the first hallway that was free of clutter and up the last set of stairs to the attic.

He politely held the door open for me and I was pleased no creaking sounds issued from the door. Even better, no cobwebs were draped over or around it, and no musty or moldy scents assailed me. The room traditionally considered the spookiest in an old house had been turned into a welcoming space, with touches screaming décor by Jenny Harrison.

Half the attic was a gym. The floor was a refinished hardwood. Mirrors hung from two walls, while large windows offered the option for fresh air or simply an open feel. Yoga mats were stacked in the corner along with two CD/digital-device-enabled players, and two bicycles were set up in front of flat-screens with a rowing machine set up between them. A machine for any exercise one could imagine designed to work every muscle in the body took up a corner space.

I'm big into fitness, but I barely gave the area more than a quick glimpse because my focus was drawn to what would be my bedroom-design studio for however long I was on Endgate Island. A huge table with a stack of drawing papers stood in front of double windows welcoming perfect light. A window air conditioner pumped out blessed coolness from the opposite side of the room while ceiling fans circled above. The queen-size bed had been made up with a light sage cover and cream and sage throw pillows, which also decorated an antique rocker sitting in a corner across from the bed. There was a reading lamp angled toward the chair on one side, and the five-shelf bookcase next to it invited any avid reader to dive in. A steamer trunk sat right against the wall opposite the bed. If Jenny had had a hand in storing goods, I figured the trunk would hold every linen needed, including extra towels for the "add-on" bathroom, a definite plus for a guest who didn't mind climbing stairs but liked having the "necessaries" in her own private space. Another welcome touch was the mini-kitchen furnished with a small fridge, microwave, sink, and a double hot plate.

I whistled. "Nice."

"You approve?"

"Oh, yeah. If the idea for the theatre *does* get trashed, I'll ask if I can design a gazebo or something for this Hickory Shadows place so I can stay for the summer."

"Could be interesting." Zach bowed and added, "Okay, Miz Teddie Grant, I'll leave you to explore your new lodgings and rest. The party is set for eight o'clock this evening, so if you need a wake-up call, it can be arranged for someone to trot up here and guide you back downstairs."

"Thanks. I've got my cell, which has an alarm, and my sense of direction is pretty good, so I shouldn't have to bother any of the family or some poor maid."

"Great. See you in a couple of hours then."

My bags had been dropped in the corner, presumably by the boatman, Robin, but I wasn't yet in the mood to wash up or dig through my clothes to find the appropriate outfit for a party I had no desire to attend unless Jenny returned to join me.

If I didn't sneak in a nap, I wouldn't be sharp tonight, and I needed my brain working at top speed. However, I couldn't help being drawn to the books and a display of an estimated twenty-five paperbacks on the middle shelf, clearly from the 1960s and 70s. All Gothic romances. Jenny and I used to devour these books back in college.

I had a growing, uneasy certainty I was living one.

Chapter 6

It was now midnight, and the party at Sugarberry Terrace showed no indications it would be winding down any time soon. Two teenage girls moved efficiently and unobtrusively through the crowd in the Laurent parlor, dining area, and living room with pitchers of margaritas, mojitos, and sangria, while Luc Bouvier himself provided offerings of Cajun and French dishes as tasty as those from any five-star New Orleans restaurant

I tried to hide out near the kitchen, but folks wanted to meet the set designer and ask questions. I did manage a nice conversation about the current New York theatre season with a woman who was elegant, soft-spoken, and well informed after Manhattan and Broadway. She was dressed in an off-white designer gown I envied without rancor, fully aware I'd never be able to afford clothes that weren't off the rack. She introduced herself as Renee Pelletier and wanted to hear about the shows I'd seen this year on Broadway. When we exhausted the subject of theatre, she asked where I was from and seemed surprised when I said Texas.

I smiled at her. "Because I don't have an accent?"

"Well, I suppose I don't normally associate female set designers from New York with Texas. Do you have any family in Louisiana?"

"I have a couple of cousins living in Shreveport, but no one farther south."

"Ah." She raised a perfectly groomed eyebrow. "We barely consider anything north of Baton Rouge or Lafayette to be part of Louisiana. To be honest, we tend to be a bit snobbish about this part of our state, especially our island." She paused, then added, "I hope you enjoy your stay on Endgate, Miz Grant."

"Thank you. And please, make it Teddie."

"Yes, of course. Teddie."

Before we could make graceful good-byes, Luc Bouvier spotted me standing with Ms. Pelletier near the front hall entrance and came over to join us.

"Miz Renee, how ya doin' tonight?"

"Fine, thank you. Lovely food as always."

Silence. There didn't seem to be a follow-up, so Luc jumped in with, "Thank ya, ma'am. Ah hate to interrupt, but Ah actually came to tell Miz Teddie Ah have some special dishes for you in the kitchen if she wants to follow me."

"Special?" I inquired.

"Yes, ma'am. Miz Jenny told me you're vegetarian, so Ah whipped up a veggie quiche and some spicy rice and beans. Hush puppies on the side."

I impulsively hugged him, then turned back to Renee. "Miz Pelletier? Nice meeting you. Now, if you'll excuse me, I'll follow Luc to the kitchen and check out the delicacies."

I received a faint good-bye from the lady as Luc and I strolled off together. "Luc Bouvier, you're the best. I knew it the minute you walked into the room this afternoon and tried to get... well... various folks in this house to listen when you voiced your anxieties about Jenny."

"Miz Jenny is good people, and the way she talked 'bout you last few months, Ah knew you're good people, too."

"She told you we were friends?"

"She did. Ah think Ah'm the only one in the house she ever opens up to. She adores Michael and doesn't want him to know she's unhappy. And she's been tryin' with Mister Alex, but he's got too quick an eye, plus too sharp a tongue too often this last year. She tried to make friends with him. Ah think she showed him old photos and her college yearbook to get him to open up."

"Yeah. I heard about the yearbook. He told the entire household earlier by calling me out as a fraud." I swallowed nervously.

Luc sighed. "He's a good boy, just needs to grow up more. Mister Michael lets him get away with too much. Not mah place to say anything... although Ah do anyway. Plus, he's been dealin' with somethin' botherin' him since his great-uncle Cyril passed last year." His tone became more serious. "But 'nuff 'bout Mister Alex. Ah'm really worried 'bout Miz Jenny."

"Me too. Didn't I meet a sheriff somewhere in this crowd, or did I imagine his existence?"

"You met one. Only law on the island 'cept for a deputy, who's still in college. But you're talkin' 'bout Sheriff Guidry."

"Do you see him? Maybe if we both ask he'd be willing to start a search. It's been twenty-four hours now, hasn't it?"

"Sheriff Guidry is all about doin' Olivia's bidding, but he might listen to you. Michael is more concerned than he let on this afternoon, and he's ready to do more'n sit 'round worrying." Luc pointed to a tall gentleman taking advantage of the cheese trays on the table closest to the kitchen. "There he is. Tell you what. Ah'll escort you to the kitchen and we can stop on the way and grab Michael. Folks have tried calling Miz Jenny's cell and even checked with a couple of places in Nah'leans where she likes to hang out, but no answer. Somethin's wrong. Ah don' like it."

Luc and I wove our way through tables and people until we were able to reach Michael, who was conversing with an extremely attractive brunette I hadn't yet met. I was trying to figure out a way to get his attention without shouting, *Look, dammit, we need to find Jenny and you need to not be flirting with hot chicks…or cool chicks either.*

Luc didn't share my reticence to interrupt their chat. He grabbed Michael's elbow then whispered something in his ear. Michael made a polite excuse to the brunette, and then turned to me. "Teddie, this is Monique Bernard. Um. Luc and I need to talk to the sheriff. Perhaps y'all can keep each other company?"

Apparently I wasn't to be part of the discussion about my best friend. Instead I was expected to entertain Ms. Bernard, who didn't appear enthused having Teddie Grant made the appointed substitute for Michael Laurent.

"Actually, Ah need to use the powder room. Miz Grant, lovely to meet you and Ah'm sure we can get better acquainted later," she announced in a heavy Cajun dialect.

Monique headed off in the direction of one of the downstairs bathrooms. Michael and Luc headed off to the sheriff's current location, which had changed from the cheese table to the dessert table. If I hadn't been so anxious about Jenny, I'd've gone to my room and grabbed one of the novels for better company. But I was determined to stay and see what the sheriff intended to do—assuming Michael pressed him to track down his wife.

I glanced around the room, looking for an empty chair where I could avoid giving the same answers to the same questions about New York and theatre, and spied Eric Desmarais seated at the piano bench. I didn't stop to analyze the heat zinging through my entire body.

"Not to be pushy, but is this seat saved?" I asked with more than a little hesitancy. "It seems to be the only partially empty space."

He shrugged. "Sit yourself down, Miz Grant."

I sank down on the bench. "Thanks. Do you suppose anyone would mind if I kicked off my shoes?"

Eric glanced down at my feet and smiled directly at me for the first time in our brief acquaintance. "Ouch. Lethal stilettos. Pretty, but doubtless extremely painful. What the heck. I say go for it and give your feet a rest."

"I am *so* totally not used to these demons. I miss my comfy boots and walking shoes."

"But they're perfect with your lovely dress." The words were complimentary, but his tone still came across as a bit frosty.

I blushed. "Thanks." I managed to add, "Warning. Take a good look now since it's the last time I'll be seen in anything other than tees and jeans or shorts for the next few weeks. Assuming, of course, that Zach is being overly pessimistic and Olivia and Michael allow the theatre plans to go through."

"Is Zach still harping on the idea it's a failure before it starts?"

"Well, he's blaming Olivia, but it's clear his focus is on his fancy casino."

"With an idea of keeping tourists away from the caves and the cellars."

"You have a rather cryptic tone, Mister Desmarais."

"You have a good ear, Miss Grant."

"But my brain seems to have stalled in understanding various nuances from people I've met today."

"Well, from my two weeks here I've discovered people take great delight in being confusing…and cryptic. Do you recall the awkward pause that greeted your comment about Olivia being able to retain finances through treasures left by the Laurent pirate ancestors?"

I grimaced. "I tried to ignore it. Was I a bit too blunt?"

"Probably not blunt enough."

I forgot my shyness and anxiety in my delight over his last comment. "Aha. You mean there really *is* pirate booty to be had on Endgate Island?"

"Legend has it half the families began living off ancient ill-gotten gain after the Civil War when they could no longer participate in the slave trade. Easier to dig for pirate booty than get a bloody job."

"I agree. So…who gets the treasure? Legally, I mean."

"Wham. You've asked the big brouhaha question, along with the other dispute as to which parts of Endgate belong to the Laurents, or Prideaux or Pelletiers or Bernards or even the late-coming Adlers. I gather they've only been here since the 1800s." He paused. "I'm sure you've heard the major fight has to do with the ownership of Tenth Avenue and the castle. That's all these people seem to talk about, and they all seem to have plans, but no one's being specific. Personally, I think if it's true about pirates stashing jewels and pieces of eight, there's plenty of loot to satisfy everyone, no matter how greedy."

"So, treasure hunts are still part of the entertainment?"

"I wouldn't be surprised. This is a strange island. Almost miraculous in some ways. It's riddled with hidden caves and tunnels and old houses with secret passages leading to *more* caves and cellars. They shouldn't exist on land this close to sea level, yet they do. As to treasure hunts? Zach freely admits his interest in construction stems from being able to explore old homes and check for pirate gold. Michael sells antiques and gets invited everywhere to check out all the old junk from great-grannies, so it's like a race to find hidden rooms before the other does. Although I think most of the pricey treasured items have long been sold."

I swallowed and hoarsely asked, "Could Jenny have somehow gotten involved in this… contest and be trapped in a cellar or something?"

Eric lapsed into silence for a long moment. Finally, he stated, "Nothing would surprise me. Look, Endgate Island was settled by pirates. Nurtured by slave traders. Not a peaceful beginning. Bad things have continued through the centuries. One reason I agreed to take the job as director for a show I normally wouldn't look at twice… well, it's not something I want to go into right now because it's personal, but Jenny herself called and told me I needed to be here. I'd love to believe Jenny is somewhere in New Orleans partying, but it's stretching imagination. If she *is* trapped somewhere, I don't believe pirate booty has anything to do with her explorations."

My anxiety level continued to soar. "What do you mean?"

"She's been searching for weeks for something to explain the tension and the strange behavior of people on this island. Something possibly as old as the pirates who settled here."

Chapter 7

Luc and Michael stood inside the French doors by the kitchen hall. Neither seemed happy. Eric waved at them to get their attention but only Luc hurried over to join us.

"Boat," I said.

The two men stared at me. "What?"

"Boat. There's a boat missing."

Luc's eyes widened. "Why do you say that?"

"I have no idea. It was some weird intuition taking over my brain."

"Well, your intuition is workin' overtime, Miz Teddie. Sheriff Guidry told me he found one of the motorboats wasn't in its slip on the dock. He's sayin' Miz Jenny took it and he believes she's hidin' out on the mainland somewhere just to be causin' trouble."

I fought the tears threatening to spill. "No way. Jenny would never deliberately hide out. For one thing, why invite me down here and then take off before even greeting me? She's never *ever* been a mean-spirited or mischievous person. Zach keeps claiming she's being manipulative, which is *totally* opposite her character."

Eric frowned. "Zach has no idea what he's talking about."

Luc turned to him. "You right 'bout that, Mister Eric. Damn. Looks like it's up to us to find her."

Eric's eyes narrowed. "Luc, did the sheriff say because they can't find this stupid boat it means they're calling off the search?'

"Yessir, I'm tellin' ya 'xactly what's happenin'. Even Mister Michael agrees there's no point in botherin' the sheriff and his deputy or organizin' some kinda search party if Miz Jenny is off on some lark. Ah'm 'bout ready to slap some sense inta him, even if he fires me for stickin' my nose where some folks believe I shouldn't."

I took a deep breath. "Gentlemen, I'm going upstairs to my room to try to get some sleep so I can help with the search tomorrow. Which is really pretty ridiculous, since I have no idea where to begin. I'm clueless as to where *this* house is in relation to this Hickory Shadows place."

Eric's tone was grim. "I do. And, actually, Hickory Shadows might be the best place to start looking. How're your skills at climbing ladders into ugly dark spaces, Miss Grant?"

"I'm better at climbing ladders to catwalks," I remarked, hoping he'd appreciate a little humor. "But, since it appears *one* member of this search team is injured and can't go scampering down ladders himself, and the other probably needs to stay here and answer any phones in case Jenny calls, it's up to me to try to conquer any claustrophobic tendencies and simply do it. Be brave. It would help if someone were holding a giant light shining into the ugly dark space. What are you planning?"

"I'd like to check the cellar I'd started to explore at Hickory Shadows before the stairs gave way. It's not far, over on Third Avenue, but with this boot cast, I need wheeled transport."

Luc shot him a sharp look. "Why Hickory Shadows, Mister Desmarais?"

"Come on, Luc, we're conspirators. Make it Eric, okay?"

"Ah'll do mah best, but the whole mister and miz thing is pretty much ingrained from childhood, Mist—Ah mean, Eric."

Eric fist-bumped him. "Time to be contemporary, Luc." They smiled at each other and I melted. My pulse beat faster seeing Eric's expression, even though his smile wasn't aimed at me. "As for that particular location? Jenny told me two weeks ago she believed there was more in the Hickory Shadows cellar than furniture for use as set pieces for the mystery theatre, but since I landed on the floor I couldn't investigate. Jenny was getting edgy about going back. Why she'd decide to do so on the day you arrived is weird, but something might have hit her she believed was worth looking into."

A cold sweat swept my body as a flash of something raced into my mind and was gone before I could pin it down and define what I'd seen.

"Miz Grant, uh, Teddie? You okay?" asked Luc.

"Not sure. It's like a proverbial chill grabbed my spine for a moment." I did my best but couldn't make any sense out of what I'd seen. "Forget it." I bit my lip and glanced in the direction of the stairs. "When and where do we meet tomorrow for exploring?"

Luc answered. "Y'all come on down to breakfast in the kitchen instead of the dining room. We'll keep it simple with croissants and coffee. Is eight too early?"

I glanced at my watch. Even the cartoon mouse appeared sleepy. "It's one-thirty now. But we're all young and hale and hearty, so a lack of sleep now and then shouldn't kill us. I'd prefer if no comment is given on any dark circles under my eyes tomorrow morning."

Luc smiled. "You'd be beautiful with circles and bags all over your face, Miz Teddie. And thanks for callin' fifty-three young, though last coupla days Ah'm feelin' more like ninety-three. Anyway, Ah'm one of those folks who gen'rally goes strong on five hours, so Ah'm good."

Eric yawned. "Well, I'm thirty-five and tired as hell. I shall provide my wounded foot as an excuse."

"Okay, gentlemen. While we're 'fessing up to flaws, I'm twenty-seven and exhausted beyond belief, but my rationalization for poopedness is being on a plane trip, a boat ride, and suffering an attack on my character by Alex Laurent. Not to mention extreme worry about Jenny. So, croissants and I'm hoping *café au lait* in the morning? Oh. Eric, if I'm not being nosy, where are you staying?"

"I've been given the carriage house, which is about twenty yards behind First Avenue. Much as I'd enjoy the view, I'm glad you were given the tower room since there's no elevator in this house and if they'd stuck me up there it would take me until tomorrow morning to clomp up those stairs with this stupid boot."

"How much longer do you have to wear it?" I asked.

"Not long. Maybe three or four days. Although the doc did say I could probably chuck it now if I did a tight wrap, which I'm considering since this is not only awkward and clunky but hot."

"I've had more than one broken foot. Not fun. You have my sympathy," I told him. "Okay, guys. Sleep."

I rose, hugged Luc good night, wished I had the nerve to also hug Eric but wasn't sure he'd appreciate the contact, then I headed toward the front entrance to deal with the killer climb to the attic. Unfortunately, I wasn't able to get by Monique Bernard, who grabbed my shoulder. I had to turn to face her as she loudly announced the sheriff had found a boat missing and so it was "obvious Jenny is pulling a stunt."

I stared at the woman. No. "Stare" was too mild a word. I glared, while my right hand itched to smack her face and wipe the smug expression away. Instead, I quietly stated, "Miz Bernard. No offense, but you have no earthly idea what you're talking about. Perhaps your evening would be better spent chatting with the gentlemen in the corner."

Her mouth dropped open. I didn't wait to find out if she took my suggestion about joining the gentlemen, including Zach Prideaux— all of whom doubtless would welcome having her join them. I was fairly certain she and I were not destined to be best buddies, but I had to admit she was a major knockout in the looks department.

I whirled around and stomped to the front hall and started up the stairs.

I didn't make any unexpected detours and reached my room within two minutes of leaving Eric and Luc. The alarm clock and my watch were in sync. It was now two a.m. and I was awake. Exhausted, edgy, and terrified for Jenny...but awake. I headed for the bookcase and debated the wisdom of grabbing a gothic mystery, written in the 1970s, when what I really needed was sleep. I spotted an old hardbound book with no dust jacket.

Endgate Island: A History, by Hannah Chaudret. *Copyright 1940.*

Not the most exciting title even for nonfiction. I stared at the spooky photo of what seemed to be an ancient French *chateau* and wondered if any answers about the mysterious beach and land on Tenth Avenue were to be found within the pages. A quick scan of page one warned me I wasn't ready to dive into heavy reading. I required a sharper and more caffeinated brain if I wanted to cull anything useful from Ms. Chaudret's tome.

I put the book down, found a notepad by the telephone, and tore off the top sheet to use as a bookmarker.

Ten minutes later, even after following the familiar bedtime ritual, I lay awake for another forty minutes or so. It had been a long, confusing day and I needed time to sort through things I'd heard and people I'd met and try to find some sense in the reactions of people on this island. Compounding my confusion and worry were the odd flashes of precognition cropping up without warning.

I couldn't stop my growing fears regarding Jenny. She could be hurt. She could even be dead. Added to the muddle of feelings was avoidance of what I'd swear was love at first sight for a man who seemed to be guarding his thoughts and feelings. Eric had intimated he was also searching for something on this island, and I wondered if his defenses would fall once he found it...or if perhaps bigger barricades would rise in their stead.

Enough. I forced myself to do some deep breathing to help me relax, thanking good yoga instructors for giving me the ability to blot out most of the questions swirling in my brain.

But nothing could knock out the image of Jenny lying in a dark space calling out, "*Stars, Teddie, stars.*"

Chapter 8

Eric and Michael were sitting at the kitchen table sipping coffee and holding a quiet conversation. I was still tired from yesterday's stress and too little sleep, but it hit me I must be rather far gone in the romance department if I was noticing how long Eric's lashes were instead of how much I wanted caffeine.

Michael pulled out the chair next to him and asked, "How's the room? Did you get some sleep, or were you too distracted by exercise equipment?"

"Room's great. I skipped the machines, found a few things to read, and conked out before I made it through a chapter." Not quite the truth, but Michael didn't need to know how stressed I was. He was polite but plainly distracted.

"Good. Um, care for some *café au lait*?"

"Sounds wonderful. Thank you."

"Don't thank me. All Luc's doing."

"Well, my thanks to Luc for making it then—and *you* for offering a chair."

Luc set a plate on the table in front of me and motioned to the tray of hot, homemade croissants. I minded my manners and used the tongs provided instead of maniacally grabbing from the tray, then took a large bite. Once I swallowed and could speak, I sighed, "Luc, you are my hero. Would you either marry or adopt me?"

He winked at me. "Mah wife might have a little somethin' to say 'bout the first, but Ah'll consider the second."

I winked back. "Well, my dad might be upset to hear I was throwing away my inheritance of his vast estate. Of course, the riches primarily consist of a roomful of textbooks and reference books for his college classes, but if I knew I'd be having fresh croissants each morning, it could be worth it to be disowned."

"Luc is half the reason I came back to Endgate Island," Michael told me. "His mom worked here off and on when I was a kid. And much as I love New Orleans and the fancy restaurants, I'm always disappointed their cuisine never matches Luc's brilliance here at home."

Luc bowed. "And you're smart enough to know it, Mister Michael, which is why Ah stay no matter how many times folks try to entice me to the city."

Michael lifted his coffee cup as a toast. I noticed his eyes were red. I had to bring up the subject, even if the light mood darkened.

"Michael, any word on Jenny?"

"No. And since she didn't come sashaying into the house in the middle of the night, I'm not buying this notion she took a boat out for a joyride and was playing a prank. She's not crazy and she's not rude, and not being here to greet Teddie would be both. I've been kidding myself this is some lark because I'm terrified she's in real trouble."

I grimaced. "Why hasn't she used her cell to call for help?"

"Easy. She never recharges the darn thing," Michael answered. "I contacted Sheriff Guidry almost as soon as I got up and told him I want a thorough search of the island."

Eric tried to be reassuring. "Teddie and I will look inside Hickory Shadows after breakfast and see if she got locked in last time she went over to get ideas for the show."

Michael stood. "Thanks, Eric. Well, I'm off to meet the sheriff. And *please* call me immediately if you find Jenny in the cellar or in a closet or anywhere else. She's got to be all right. Got to."

He left, clearly choking back tears. I downed three croissants and two cups of coffee much faster than was good for digestion. We needed to get going.

Luc said he'd stay at Sugarberry Terrace and deal with any questions from Olivia or the possibility of a call from Jenny or someone who'd found her. He suggested we take the small four-wheeler ATV to keep Eric from having to be on his foot too much.

"Can you drive a stick?" Eric asked.

"I can."

"Would you mind driving then, so I don't have to deal with a clutch and a cast?"

"I'd love to. I actually drove some of these babies in college, so have no fear we'll crash. Be a good navigator and we'll be fine."

With Eric providing directions, we reached Third Avenue in about seven minutes after taking a back route through the woods. I was sorry we couldn't spend the day touring the island; the sights were certainly worth taking the time.

Eric leaned down and undid the straps of his boot cast. He laid it down on the floor of the ATV, tightened the bandage wrapped around his ankle, then reached into the backpack lying on his lap and took out a pair of high-top work boots.

"You're healed?"

"Not completely. But remember when I said the doctor was good with me keeping my ankle taped? I should be capable of doing anything other than marathons, including staggering down whatever path is there." He added, "Teddie, before you ask, I don't really want folks on this island believing I'm capable of...uh...."

"Leaping tall buildings in a single bound? Or at least climbing them."

"Precisely."

"Eric, my danger radar has been on high since I stepped onto the island, but it seems you're a step or two ahead in the distrust level."

"I am. Let's walk while we talk. I can do both and I'm sure you're equally gifted."

We headed down a steep path that was less than smooth, but I didn't see any gaping holes in the ground, so felt less worried about Eric reinjuring his foot. He led the way to a structure about thirty yards from the house, which appeared to be standing by sheer determination, since the wood was rotten, the windows broken, and the roof basically nonexistent.

"What was this used for?" I inquired. "Any idea?"

"Luc told me it was built in the 20s as a garage, but the Pelletier family, who owned it at the time, decided it didn't make much sense to use it for cars when the house was so far away. They built a six-car garage with the covered walkway leading to Hickory Shadows so no one would get drenched when it rained. When they sold the property to the Laurents about forty years ago, the garage was part of it. I don't think anyone noticed or cared."

"Is there really a reason Jenny might have come back here?"

"Possibly. Look, I think it's time I backtrack a bit so Jenny's actions make more sense. Teddie, I truly believe there's danger here."

"I do, too. Even having only been on Endgate one night. Sorry, go on."

"Okay. I met Jenny about eleven months ago when I was directing *Twelfth Night* in Los Angeles."

"I remember. I told her I'd seen your *Much Ado About Nothing* two years ago and hoped one day I'd get the chance to design a set for one of your shows. And she told me how working with you had really pushed her farther as an actress."

"Funny. I felt the same as her director. Learning from her. Like an English professor specializing in the Renaissance who's suddenly given the graduate course in medieval lit the day before a semester starts and has to rely on the best student to bail him out when he's stuck."

"Nice analogy," I told him with honest admiration.

"Ah. Well, thanks. Anyway, I'm not spilling secrets when I say Jenny *is* the consummate professional. She was totally focused, even though she was becoming more and more involved with Michael. Not sure why he was in LA, but I'm pretty sure it had something to do with Spanish antiquities. Doesn't matter. Fast forward. Show was a limited run and it closed on time. Jenny and Michael eloped a few months later. She wrote me Alex was being a pain and Cyril, Michael's uncle, was gravely ill and Olivia was totally focused on him and had no desire to take a step off the island. Jenny wanted a drama-free wedding. Or should I say a trauma-free wedding. They moved back here I guess about eight or so months ago. I didn't really expect to hear from her. We all know theatre's an iffy business when it comes to keeping in touch."

"Got it. So, what happened?"

"About a month ago I got a call from Jenny asking if I'd be interested in directing the mystery *Blood on the Bayou*. She told me there were three old vacant houses perfect as theatres and she'd been exploring this house on Third Avenue first, including the cellar. I was in Manhattan, finishing up *A Midsummer Night's Dream*, which happens to be my favorite of Master Will's comedies. Anyway, I wasn't really thrilled about the idea of a murder mystery theatre on a remote island, but there was something odd in her voice. She told me Endgate and its inhabitants held more secrets than a DC hooker's date book. Then came the kicker. One of those secrets concerned me and possibly my ancestors, too."

"What? What did she find?"

"Ah. We get to the dicey discovery." He stopped. "And we're here."

He opened what passed as a door to a shed. It was overgrown with brush and I hesitated for a long moment before stepping inside the dark room. It led to a darker tunnel.

"Oh, joy."

"Are you really claustrophobic? You sounded like you were kidding last night when I asked about ugly cellars. I promise these are *not* deep in the ground. More like passages than tunnels."

"My claustrophobia depends on the brightness of the light in the confined space and whether I have company to keep me calm. I take the subway in the city all the time but won't step into an elevator unless someone else is there."

"Well, this could be nasty. There's no telling what we'll come across."

"I'm okay. Although if either a snake or a rat drops by for a visit, I'm outta here."

Eric mock flexed his muscles. "I shall protect you. Chuck rocks at any overly friendly or curious reptiles or rodents."

"Appreciate it. I actually hope we don't find Jenny anywhere near this cellar. She really *is* claustrophobic and would be a raving lunatic by now. But before we plunge into the creepy passage, can you tell me why things got dicey?"

"Planning to. Let's sit for a second. It's moderately cool here even without windows and my leg could use the rest."

He pointed to an old steamer trunk someone had deposited and abandoned. It had a military 1940s look to it, which gave me a hint as to its age. Eric sat, dusted a space beside him using his hand, motioned for me to sit, then continued his story.

"Back to the kicker... Jenny told me one of my ancestors might have been a slave on the island here."

"Oh man. Not exactly conducive to instilling a love of Endgate. And how bizarre to discover a relationship, since this island is so off-the-map. You're from New York, right?"

"True. But there were always hints floating around the house when I was a kid about some of my family originally coming from somewhere in Louisiana, so I was intrigued and ready to believe whatever info could be found linking me to my Southern ancestors.

Jenny said she'd found a reference in what little of the diary she'd read pointing to something involving the slave of one of the Chaudrets, circa 1865. The slave's name was Desmarais, which could have been a first or last. She said it struck her because when we were doing *Twelfth Night* we talked about Desmarais and how it's not an unusual surname in Louisiana, but not typical for black kids born in Brooklyn. I told her family legend had it we were originally from New Orleans, but no one seemed to have much information regarding when, where, or how part of the family ended up in New York, apart from an old reference to a Desmarais having been a slave on an island."

"I can see why you'd be curious. But so far this sounds relatively normal for a genealogy search. Where does the dicey part come in?"

"Jenny took the diary and the rest of the books she'd found— mostly old novels, doubtless stashed in the trunk for decades—out of the cellar at Hickory Shadows. She brought them to the tower room, which she'd already set up as a hideaway/reading space. She intended to come back down and explore further. Something got in the way of both reading and exploring in terms of time. She didn't say what and it probably doesn't matter. Anyway, two days after the first find, she climbed to the tower and discovered the diary missing."

"Hmmm. Curious, indeed. When did you say the diary was written?"

"Jenny said the diary dates in the front of the book were from 1840 to 1866. The name of the writer was Marianne Chaudret, daughter of Monsieur Henri Chaudret, which I suppose made her part owner of a slave named Desmarais."

Chapter 9

Eric let me digest the whole story for about ten seconds then he slid off the trunk and helped me to my feet, though he dropped my hand as soon as I was up. I wondered if he'd felt the same charge, like a supersized electric current, flowing between us with a simple touch.

"Ready to explore and see if we run across whatever it is someone doesn't want Jenny or me to find and is willing to maim for it?"

"You think the same person who took the diary sawed a rung off the ladder from the house itself just in time for one Eric Desmarais, New York director, to take a tumble?"

"You're quick."

"Or too avid a fan of mysteries. Or…"

"Or?"

"You're going to say I'm wacked."

Eric grabbed my arm. "Stop."

"What?" I froze, terrified.

"Sorry. Didn't mean to stop the explanation of your possible wackiness, but we need to tread slowly and pay more attention to where we're walking."

I gasped. "Snakes?"

"Nope. Nothing slithery. Only a rather large hole two feet in front of us."

"Ah. I see it. Okay. Thanks."

"So, you were saying about wackiness?" Eric inquired.

"You're going to think I'm crazy but, well, since I first read Jenny's job notice when I was in Manhattan, I've had more than one odd flash or feelings of…oh hell, I'm not sure whether to call them premonitions or déjà vu, since those seem to be opposites, but when you were talking about Jenny exploring and wanting you to join her in stumbling across something equally as awesome as the missing diary, I saw intact stairs and immediately saw a shadow move from it, leaving something like a crack in the wood. Not visible, but possibly lethal." I stopped. I considered adding the vision on the plane about what appeared to be a house on fire, but decided one premonition at a time might be best, especially since I couldn't identify the house or know when this burning might take place. I wanted him to like me and not write me off as a lunatic.

"Odd. Maybe you've been gifted with some kind of psychic ability?" He added wryly, "I wish you'd've signaled from Manhattan before I took those stairs."

"Hey, I apologize. Believe me, if I'd had any idea it was real, I'd've made a call. Anything to keep bad juju away. Then again, you'd've thought I was nuts and told Jenny to find another designer."

"Not necessarily. I'm not sure how much weirdness in life I subscribe to, but I do believe such things as second sight exist."

He stared into my eyes. For one brief, insane moment I thought he was going to kiss me. And I welcomed it. The atmosphere wasn't a bit romantic—in fact, the right adjectives were icky and creepy, but I didn't care. I swore I saw the desire in his eyes.

Instead, in a friendly conversational tone with no hint of passion, Eric changed the subject and asked me why my parents named me Theodosia.

I didn't want him to know I was hurt at a rejection—which in actuality wasn't a rejection since nothing had been rejected. "According to several baby books, Theodosia means 'gift from God.' My mom had cystic fibrosis. It was a miracle she lived as long as she did. I was a second miracle to even have been born, but she firmly believed I really was a gift from God." I paused, remembering. "She used to tease me and say I was the most mischievous present a deity could provide since I was constantly in trouble." I swallowed hard. "We used to do everything together when I was growing up. Silly stuff. She'd take me for ice cream an hour before dinner and not care if it ruined my appetite for veggies. We'd stay up watching old movies and sing along with every song in corny musicals from the 30s and 40s. Maybe I'm so intrigued by the whole pirate thing here on the island since we used to play pirates against colonists in our backyard. I miss her so much."

Eric's voice was gentle. "She sounds amazing. And she must have been truly unique to give you such an unusual and beautiful name." He nudged me to lighten the mood. "However, since you entered the tech side of theatre, I understand why you shifted to Teddie."

"Definitely takes less time to yell when someone needs a nail gun. There are times I wonder if I'd even been offered some of the jobs I worked if I'd sent out my resume as Theodosia Grant. Which still does not explain why Jenny wanted to keep our friendship a secret from the residents of Endgate Island."

"If I had to guess, I'd say after someone stole Marianne Chaudret's diary she started getting worried. More than worried. Scared. She decides to contact you through e-mail instead of even phoning in case she was being watched more closely than she even realized. Maybe to make our anonymous thief believe Jenny had nothing more on her mind than her theatre?"

"Eric, I knew there was trouble the instant I read the notice she sent."

Eric's right eyebrow lifted. "This precognition giftee?"

"Nothing so mysterious." I told him about the use of the code word "stars" Jenny and I cooked up back in college. "What ticks me off is Alex blew my whole cover of a strictly working relationship less than an hour after I arrived on the island."

"Alex has a talent for…"

"Mischief? Danger? Brattiness?"

"I was going to say 'poking his nose into everyone else's business,' but you summed up the young Mister Laurent's personality quite succinctly. Although I suspect the real trouble is a combination of boredom and a crush on some girl who, heretofore, has remained nameless." He added, "Our Alex is a heartsick swain pining for his love and being a pill while doing so. Anyway, for what it's worth, I doubt it matters you were outed as Jenny's friend. I'm sure whoever sabotaged the stairs and stole Marianne Chaudret's diary is already well aware there's more on Jenny's mind than checking houses for good exits and entrances for some show." He pointed ahead of us. "Okay. Enough of the spooky, scary tunnel. You ready to get to the cellar?"

"Sure. I'm just hoping it's cleaner and has some kind of ventilating system."

Eric's flashlight projected a lovely beam. Neither the shed nor the first part of the passage had been as bad as I'd feared, perhaps because he'd kept my mind focused on the intrigue swirling on the island. And dreaming about a kiss that never happened.

We reached a door any television house hunting, flip-it, or fix-it-up show would have featured as a rare antique. It was a huge sliding "barn" jobbie with hardware so old the main question was whether one can of oil or two would ease the rust to a level where the door would open.

Eric was way ahead of me. He reached into his all-purpose backpack, pulled out a spray can, and was about to point the nozzle at the hinges when I stopped him.

"Eric, wait. Look. It's been opened. I'd say recently."

He peered at the sliver of space between the door and the wall. "You're right."

We stared at each other. "Jenny? Could it be Jenny?" I breathed. "Unless you were also precognizant about taking a spill down the stairs and had your handy-dandy Tin Man oil survival kit with you. In which case you would have opened the darn thing and gotten out, so that was a stupid idea I had and I'm rambling. Sorry."

"It's okay. Believe it or not, I saw the door when I was lying on the floor in pain cursing the stairs. I figured it had been stuck for a hundred years or more and wasn't going to move without a ton of help."

"I meant to ask, how did you get out? The stairs were broken, weren't they?"

"I called Luc on my cell. Unlike Jenny, I'm great about keeping it charged and handy. He came over with Robin, the boatman who picked you up on the mainland, who also does odd jobs around the island. They scoured the neighborhood for a ladder, found one at a house about two blocks over, absconded with it, lowered it down, and I crawled up and out. They got the ladder back before the owners even noticed it was gone. Later I told Jenny about the shed, passage, and this door. Even Luc hadn't known it was there. The house had been boarded up for a good thirty years before Jenny decided this might be a great location for her theatre."

The door might have been opened recently, but the creak of the hinges cried out for another squirt of the oil can. The sound was almost painful. Eric gave it a last shove and stepped inside.

Eric swung the flashlight around the cellar, as we both hoped we'd spot a weak but breathing Jenny Harrison in a corner. We weren't overly optimistic and consequently not surprised to find the room filled with a ton of inanimate objects and nothing alive. Even so, I bit my lower lip and tried to stave off a threatening wave of tears.

"Damn."

"Yeah. I feel the same."

I began pacing in a small circle., "Eric, where could she be? I'm going crazy with worry."

"Maybe the Chittamwood Gardens property? Although why she'd take off before you arrived is odd. This cellar was my first choice since I knew she'd wanted to get back here after the diary disappeared, but after? It's like playing pin the tail on the donkey without being told where the gamesters hid the big, bloody, paper jackass."

"I keep wondering why someone wrecked the stairs to keep you from exploring. What was down here they didn't want you to see?"

"No idea. But I wouldn't be surprised to discover whoever performed a major piece of sabotage came back through those doors and took away whatever he or she considered a prize of… ah hell, I'm clueless."

I quit my mouse-in-a-maze pacing. My eyes were drawn to a large wardrobe in the far corner of the room. I had to admit it was a cool-looking piece of furniture and could add to the ambiance of any mystery theatre production, but it wasn't the reason I headed toward it before checking one of the trunks Eric was currently sliding into the middle of the room.

"Teddie? What'd you find?"

"We need to search through this wardrobe. Books. More books. One of them is important."

He joined me. "And this insight is hitting you—how?"

"Unanswerable."

"Second sight?"

"Could be."

Unlike the sliding barn door, the wardrobe hadn't been opened in years. My guess was at least fifty. I turned to Eric. "Speaking of second sight, time for the oil can you were smart enough to bring."

He sprayed the hinges. I opened the doors and peered at dresses with skirts so short they almost literally screamed 1960s minis. The wardrobe was typical of furniture built in the early 1900s. It boasted a small railing at the top for clothes and a low shelf for shoes and any apparel better served by folding. But the shelf sat above more doors, which swung open fairly easily once Eric squirted more oil on them. Inside were books. Lots of books. Paperbacks and hardbacks.

I looked up at Eric. "I feel as if one of these books is important—but I am at a total loss in terms of what it or they mean to the island and Jenny and secrets. This is confusing. It may not be the book itself but someone who believes there's something important. Am I making any sense?"

"A little." He gestured at the books. "I say we pile them into a box and get them out of here."

We found a couple of smaller trunks and divided the books into them, then stacked them onto a furniture dolly found lying on its side under a sturdy kitchen table.

"Let's put the dresses on top of the books," Eric suggested.

"Good idea. If anyone spots us moving stuff out, they'll assume we found some possible old costume pieces. Who knows? Several of these might actually work."

I started removing the clothes from their hangers. A medley of emotions swept over me when I touched a designer mini shift dress at the back of the wardrobe.

I sank to the floor.

"Teddie? What's wrong?"

"The girl who wore this…"

"What did you feel?"

"Despair and fear." I tried to breathe. "What the heck is happening?"

He shook his head and tried to lighten the mood. "Do we need to hire a palm reader from New Orleans? A voodoo priestess perhaps?"

I managed to smile. "Might not be a bad idea. I'd prefer Queen Marie Laveau to men in white coats fitting me for a straitjacket."

Eric let his guard down long enough to say, "Don't worry. I'm not sending for either just yet. But it's pretty bizarre you're having these waves of premonitions. Any clue what they could mean?"

"Nope. This whole second-sight-feelings-from-beyond thing is new for me and I freely confess it's freaking me out." I stared down at the floor. "Eric, it's also kind of nuts… I hate not being able to trust anyone on this island but you and Luc. I can't even tell yet where Michael is in all this weirdness."

"My own intuition says Michael truly loves Jenny… but he's been distracted by all this mess about island ownership. Sadly, until we can figure out where Jenny is or why an old diary was stolen or why the stairs were broken or why your spine gets chills when it's eighty-five outside even at midnight, we're stuck hiding books and keeping our mouths shut." He paused for a long moment. He looked into my eyes, turning my bones into mush, before saying, "Teddie, since we're sharing, the other question in the mix is why I've also been feeling déjà vu moments since I arrived on the island."

"You have? Care to elaborate?"

"No." He reached for my hand and squeezed, then let go. "Not because I don't trust you. Really. But I need time to sort things out in my head."

"I get it. Believe me." I glanced at my watch. "Whoa. We've been gone for two hours. If someone *is* watching us, could be time to get back."

Eric helped me get the dresses out of the wardrobe and piled on top of the cartons. Exiting was easier since we had a better idea of the length of the tunnel and what small hazards to avoid; we were able to return to the old shed and daylight in half the time it had taken us to get to the cellar. I was thrilled to have found the books and almost positive answers would spring out at me as soon as I could open the right one.

I was also heartsick and frightened because we'd gone to the most logical spot. And Jenny was still missing.

Chapter 10

We must have appeared as if we were pulling off a heist—tossing furtive glances at the magnolia trees lining the path to the ATV, hoping no one would come racing out from behind bushes screaming, *"You can't take those books, you filthy thieves. They're mine, do you hear? Mine."*

Once we were back in the ATV, with the boxes under Eric's feet—not comfortable for his knees but safe—and no pitchforks and torches waving anywhere near us, I began to breathe like a normal person.

Eric slapped the boot cast back on his leg. "You good to drive? Let's head to the carriage house. I think these will be safer there than at Sugarberry Terrace. I want these locked away before anyone realizes we absconded with anything from the cellar." He paused and then added, "Can you stand a few more minutes without food? I have stuff for sandwiches unless you're aching to get back to the main house."

"My stomach is churning too much to even *have* an appetite, although if I get another whiff of Luc's croissants I might not care if the entire island comes after us screaming for the books and dresses. That being said, I agree, you're right. Let's head to the carriage house. We can call Michael and see if he's heard anything about Jenny. I'm not sure I want to face him if there's no news. At least he did seem genuinely upset this morning."

"Well, I've been pretty ticked at Michael for seeming to side with his aunt Olivia instead of Jenny. Haven't said anything—but there's been more than one occasion during these last two weeks when I've wanted to throttle him and ask him to take a good look at what this island is doing to Jenny's psyche."

"I remember last fall when Jenny originally called to tell me she and Michael were getting married in Vegas to avoid a fuss. She admitted the fuss included Michael's aunt who acted more like

Michael's mother and was not enamored of Michael's marrying an actress. By the way, not to gossip too much, but speaking of maternal types, where *is* Alex's mother? All Jenny told me was Michael was divorced, not widowed."

"The first Mrs. Laurent is lounging somewhere in Switzerland with a hedge fund CEO from Germany. I gather she held no love for Endgate Island and left when Alex was only six. Not a lot of angst there though, thank heaven. Alex visits her often and I've never heard of any major trauma caused when she left. It sounds as if she isn't terribly maternal… but everyone accepts her for who she is and moves on. No nastiness. I got all this from Jenny when she invited me to come to the island and was in one of her typically chatty moods. It seemed Jenny was trying to divine why Alex didn't welcome her as his stepmom."

Eric's tiny carriage house was only a three-minute ride from the Laurent house and almost the same distance from the theatre. There was no driveway and the house was only about twelve yards from the main road.

"Eric."

"Hmm?"

"Is there any way you could stay somewhere else?"

"Why? What's wrong with this place?'

"When I was on the plane heading to the island, I had a vision about what appeared to be a house and lots of smoke. It wasn't terribly specific, but plenty scary. Things were sort of flashing before my eyes in bits and pieces. I can't even say for sure this is the same house. It's more a gut feeling. And heck, the whole thing could have been nothing but bad airplane food giving me waking nightmares"

"So, you don't really know what's real and what isn't. Any idea when this might take place?"

"Nope. Sadly, the only specific was there was a trapdoor in the bedroom."

"Ah… a plus, although it doesn't help since every bloody first-floor bedroom on this island seems to have traps. Um, not to poo-poo the suggestion, but I'm not ready to move over to the main house at this point. To paraphrase a famous actress from days gone by…I'd rather not be around other folks right now."

I didn't press suggesting he move. "Privacy issues?"

"To some extent. After years of living in Brooklyn, I'm used to everyone being knee-deep in everyone's business, but those are my neighbors. Down here I'd prefer not to have my every move scrutinized."

"I get it. I have to admit I'm glad to be in the tower room where I'm away from family."

I finally brought the ATV to a stop. We'd had to leave the dolly at Hickory Shadows but the cartons were lightweight enough so we could each grab one and carry it up the three steps leading to a small deck. I plopped mine on the deck as I waited for Eric to unlock the back door, then turned and eyed the neat rows of vegetables growing only yards from his house. Seeing the bright colors of life cheered me up. They represented order in a world that had become absurdly chaotic in less than a week.

The inside of the carriage house was also a relief after the Southern gothic atmosphere permeating the Laurent house. We entered directly into a combination living room and den, furnished with a new charcoal gray couch and matching chair and ottoman. They faced an entertainment module complete with TV, and every player for discs and videos or even streaming music. Bookshelves framed the center on each side. To the right of the bookshelves was a large opening leading to the kitchen.

"Eric, are there some decent-size closets where we can stash these books?"

Eric set the heavier box on the floor before answering, "One. A nice big walk-in in the bedroom. Although it might be better to leave the books here in the den. Tell you what; let's add them to the shelves. On the off chance any interested parties find a way to break in, it might look less like we're trying to hide something."

I still didn't like the idea of books—or Eric—being in a house I felt certain was going to go up in a blaze soon, but I didn't push. I deposited the lighter box in front of the nearest shelf, leaned down and hoisted out a stack, and plopped the books without bothering to see if the titles were right side up. Eric was right behind me with another pile.

I finished putting several books on the bottom shelf and turned. Eric was standing a few feet away, looking at me. He appeared uncomfortable.

"Problems?" I inquired.

"Not really." He cleared his throat. "Look, I need to ask you something."

"Sure."

"You can tell me to mind my own business but... Oh hell, I'll just come out with it. Are you still seeing Colin Barrow?"

"Oh hell no."

Eric popped out with an immediate, "Thank God."

"Why do you care?" I shot back.

"Because I'm not one to horn in on someone else's territory." Eric appeared totally chagrined. "I'm *so* sorry. That did not come out right and sounded not only rude but sexist and demeaning and I apologize."

"It was pretty bad, but I'm not offended since I probably shouldn't have been quite so... abrupt... in my response." I stared at one of the books in my hand and avoided looking at Eric. "Since we're discussing Colin, I assume you heard his claims about my designs?"

"Oh yeah. Made me want to pick him up and toss him into the East River even before I met you. Teddie, everybody knows he was trying to take credit for something he wasn't capable of doing. And anyone who'd seen one of your shows could see your style all through *Measures of Light*. Folks in New York know the truth."

I exhaled with relief. "Thank you. I've been pretty bummed about the whole thing."

"Hey, I get it. It's tough to be accused of stealing what's yours." His tone turned almost mischievous. "I'd ask why you were crazy enough to date the jerk in the first place, but I've had my share of lousy relationships, some of which have nearly landed me in the tabloids, so I'll repeat I'm damned glad you guys broke up."

"You and me both."

I began to alphabetize the books to give my trembling hands something to do to cover my embarrassment. Neither of us was handling this conversation with any grace.

Eric was quick to pick up on my feelings and desire for a change in subject. "Hey, I'm, uh, going to phone Michael and see if there's any word on Jenny. I'd like to be optimistic and believe he's so busy reuniting with her he forgot to call us, but my own pitiful flashes of insight are telling me she hasn't turned up yet."

Eric grabbed his cell and hit one of the preprogrammed numbers. Michael answered after one ring. Eric put him on speaker.

"Michael? I've got Teddie here with me. Any news?"

Michael sounded tired, anxious, and depressed. "Nothing. Guidry organized a search party but it's sparse since most folks are working, either on the island or on the mainland. Are you guys still at Hickory Shadows?"

"No. We stopped at my place for a moment."

Michael responded, "Ah. So, I'm assuming you didn't find any hints as to where Jenny might be?"

Eric answered truthfully. "We didn't."

"Damn. Just… damn. Look, Luc has made a huge pot of shrimp jambalaya and a small pot of veggie-only for Teddie. My aunt has invited all the folks who are staking claims to Tenth Avenue to come over, although I'm not sure why since there's nothing really new on the ownership front." He sighed. "To be honest, I'm avoiding answering because it's so trivial. Aunt Livvie is first and foremost a hostess who wants to entertain, no matter what else is happening. Why don't y'all head back now? It might not be festive but should prove interesting and it'll keep me from losing my mind with worry about Jenny."

Eric raised both brows in question to me. "I'm good," I silently mouthed.

"We'll be there in about ten minutes," he told Michael.

Eric clicked off. "Craziness upon craziness. I'm getting indigestion thinking about sitting at the dining table with people who actually refer to themselves as the 'first families.' I've been in plenty of situations when I've felt people have looked down on me, but never so blatantly."

I had noticed, and had also noticed Eric handling it with more grace than I ever could. "It is pretty annoying. Well, we can eat fast, then come up with an excuse to head to the tower room. There's a book I saw last night, a history of the island. It might provide a little info about the stolen diary and the Emeric Desmarais named by this Marianne Chaudret. Maybe." I stopped. "Eric, I'm not sure if this is more insight or simple common sense, but I keep getting this feeling about the question of ownership of Tenth Avenue. I'm sure it has something do with Jenny's disappearance. Possibly your accident.

Should we hang out behind the piano or something and eavesdrop in case one of the ownership contestants lets something slip?"

Eric whispered conspiratorially. "It's not the biggest piano in the world. Not even an upright. We'd be spotted. Especially if I got bored and started pounding out a few show tunes." He suddenly stared at me as if seeing someone else.

"What?"

"One of those déjà vu moments I mentioned. Do you play piano?"

"I took lessons until I was twelve and got more interested in hammers and paint. What did you see…or feel?"

"You'll think I'm crazy."

"Really? Can I say…ditto? Remember who you're talking to. The psychic wonder."

"True." He inhaled. "I had this…flash. A girl who looked like you. She was sitting and playing piano. I'm standing a few feet away listening. But she's wearing a long dress more suited for a period theatre piece. The whole thing lasted about one second, so I didn't exactly get details."

"Whoa. It's still interesting."

"Or nuts. I'm going to file it under 'to think about later' in my brain. Meantime, I suppose we need to get going. Finish getting these books out."

We hurriedly stacked the rest of the books onto four rows of empty shelves. I tried to keep from glancing at him, but the tension between us kept simmering and I couldn't logically say why.

I stopped and pointed to the top carton. "Let's take this with us. Not to get into even more weirdness, but I think something in there is important. I'll bring it up to my tower for safekeeping and easy access."

"Sure. If your premonitions are right, we need all the security measures we can get."

We climbed back into the ATV. With the carton balanced on Eric's knees, we took off for Sugarberry Terrace. The silence between us suddenly became as awkward as the box of books. We might have shared a few too many feelings during this excursion. Feelings we weren't ready to examine or discuss.

Michael greeted us at the back door once we finally pulled up at the house. "Guests are all here, already diving into lunch as if they hadn't been fed in months and gearing for a fight. I'm actually hoping having you two noncombatants in the dining room will force everyone to stay civil… at least until dessert is served."

Chapter 11

Olivia, Alex, Zach Prideaux, Renee Pelletier, George Adler, and Monique Bernard were already devouring jambalaya and baskets of hot garlic bread by the time I'd trotted up the stairs to the attic and deposited the small carton filled with books. I still had less of an appetite than normal, but then, for me normal is on the order of an offensive tackle for a professional football team. I slid into the empty chair closest to the kitchen and politely waited for Eric to take a seat across from me before taking a bite of my special vegan jambalaya, which was aptly named. Special.

Michael brought in another basket of bread and plopped it in the center of the table, walked to the other end, and sat down next to Monique, who wasted no time in interrogating Eric and me.

"Ah hear y'all went explorin'?"

Eric stiffened but the movement was so slight I was possibly the only one who noticed. I answered, "If by 'we' you mean Eric and me, the answer is yes. Alex, would you pass the bread my way?"

Monique waited until I'd plopped a slice on my plate then continued with, "Y'all went to Hickory Shadows, right?"

"We did."

Monique was determined to cut through my sparse response. "Any strong opinions about using Hickory Shadows as your mystery theatre, Miz Grant? Ah personally like Chittamwood Gardens, which was Jenny's second idea. It's got a larger living room where Ah 'spose y'all could set up a stage if you knocked out a wall or two. Presumin' of course it could be cleaned."

Renee added, "It's kind of a...mess." She joined Monique in pointedly surveying my admittedly grubby appearance, from the wisps of hair escaping a ponytail to the sleeveless camp shirt, the patched jeans bearing more than one dirt stain, and the work boots that had saved me from more than one errant nail sticking up from boards on a stage, with a mix of amusement and distaste. Clearly all the elegant Southern ladies considered Teddie Grant a mess as well.

Everyone at the table seemed to be waiting to hear my thoughts on a house I hadn't had the chance to explore since I'd spent the morning in the cellar underneath. I glanced at Eric and tried not to let my panic appear obvious. He murmured, not quite under his breath, "May I?"

I almost sighed out loud in relief. "Take it."

He raised his volume and assumed his "brilliant director" persona. "Miz Grant and I believe *whichever* house is picked would be better as an interactive theatre rather than the normal fourth-wall-separation with the audience watching while actors entertain. So, a massive front room isn't necessary since an interactive theatre doesn't require a stage."

"Interactive theatre? What do you mean?" came from George.

Eric continued, "Think in terms of a game. Audience members are given parts to play and clues, from there it's primarily improvisation. Several theatre companies in Manhattan have been doing really well with interactive theatre since the 90s. And Hickory Shadows does have the perfect name and great space." Eric glanced at me to provide backup.

"Eric's right. You need a house with a ton of rooms that could work as different sets for each scene. And of course, professional actors would play leading roles and keep the action going. Tourists really love this kind of theatre."

Silence.

A surprise assist suddenly came from Alex. "It's got my vote. Sounds cool. I'd love to be involved in an interactive theatre. It might also be a really great way to sell folks on how different Endgate Island would be from the other tourist attractions near New Orleans. Add a bird sanctuary a few blocks away from the castle and a fishing charter service and this island would be hoppin'."

Zach's tone was decidedly condescending. "Sounds complicated. Your theatre, I mean. No offense, Teddie, but you and Eric might both be a bit too New York for Southern tastes. I personally vote no."

Michael tapped on the wooden table to get Zach's attention "Not your decision, Zach. Since the Laurents own Hickory Shadows, we can make the house anything we want. As we are all too aware, the jury's still out on *Chateau Sans Frontieres*."

Eric assumed a role of peacemaker. "Well, nothing has to be decided here and now about which house gets the nod. And having brought up theatre... change of subject. It feels stickier than normal outside. Not to be gross, but I'm sweating buckets. Anyone heard a forecast?"

Six voices began chattering at the same time.

Renee raised her hand for silence. "Last I heard, we're in for some pretty fierce storms startin' tomorrow. Could get to a hurricane category, although it's really too early in the season."

Olivia spoke for the first time since we'd started lunch. "Thankfully, the island usually remains surprisingly safe. But we'll begin boarding up the houses early tomorrow morning. I learned years ago to believe the weatherman and go with the adage of better safe than sorry."

The conversation shifted to a contest as to the "worst hurricane or storm I've survived," as the Louisiana natives tried topping each other with stories about flying debris and uprooted trees and flash floods. Eric gleefully told them they were all wimps and they couldn't call themselves storm busters until they'd gone through a real New York blizzard.

At least the impersonal topic allowed me to eat lunch without more worry knots twisting and tying somewhere in my digestive system, fearing someone would yell, *"You were in the cellar and you absconded with books holding clues as to why everyone is jumpy, not to mention old mysterious dresses—and we'll get you, you snoop."* I surprised myself by eating two bowls of jambalaya and three pieces of bread. But when the offer of homemade vanilla ice cream with some kind of brandy or rum sauce was made, I declined.

"I love your cooking, Luc, but I'm close to bursting and it's probably wise to quit before my jeans stop fitting."

Eric also refused dessert. "If you folks will excuse us, we'd like to start working on designs while we still feel moderately creative. Teddie has sketchpads upstairs in the tower room."

Eric walked around the table and politely helped me up from my seat and led me through the dining room as though he were escorting a princess to a coronation ball. A princess wearing torn, dirty jeans, a few mud stains on her cheeks, and badly scuffed work boots, that is. He stopped at the entrance to the living room and turned back around. "Feel free to talk about us after we leave. Or get back to fighting—excuse me—*discussing* who owns which lands and which houses and whether anyone wants an Endgate Island interactive theatre to be the showplace of the Gulf. And Michael, both Teddie and I have our cells, so please call us if there's any news about Jenny."

Chapter 12

I unlocked the door to the attic bedroom and immediately headed for the large floor fan, cranking it three notches up to "high" and taking a moment to enjoy feeling the air flowing around me before turning back around to address Eric, who'd plopped into the closest chair following what for him had to have been a killer climb.

"It's a shame it's late May and already ridiculously hot and a storm is headed our way, because I really would like to spend the next week buried under covers sleeping and hiding. Jeez, what a lunch."

Eric nodded and gave a languid stretch before leaning back. "Yeah. I'd call it somewhat tense."

"Agreed. I have to say, Mister Desmarais, I did admire your ability to tap dance better than Bill Bojangles Robinson himself when asked about the theatre. Thank you for the wonderful assist since I still haven't seen the house itself."

"No problem. And I was serious about the interactive theatre being a great way to go."

"I think it's brilliant. I did find it interesting when Alex Laurent suddenly jumped to our defense. Why the switch to 'let's help Teddie' and, in doing so, ultimately Jenny? Is he mellowing?"

"A combination of things. I got the feeling he likes you, although I'm not sure he's yet willing to extend his sweet attitude to his new stepmother." He reached over and grabbed a small stool sitting a few feet from him, then rested his foot on top. "I'm giving him a break. It's gotta be rough on a kid of eighteen when his new mom is only about ten years older than he is. But I gather he wasn't the only one causing a ruckus about Jenny. Olivia wasn't happy about the marriage and I've heard rumors since I've been here to the effect Monique thought she'd be the next Mrs. Michael Laurent. Consequently, Monique wasn't exactly welcoming Jenny with proverbial open arms. She considers her an island interloper and a man-stealer and generally weird because she's... 'gasp, gasp, a trashy LA actress.' Jenny's words; not mine. I got an earful when she was coaxing me to come to the island."

"Do you suppose this is the kind of garbage Jenny's had to put up with since she moved here?" I grimaced. "I'm so angry with myself for not staying in touch better. Being busy shouldn't be an excuse not to be on the phone or e-mailing one's best friend at least once a week."

"We all do it. Don't beat yourself up. About Alex? He's a smart guy who didn't want a step-mom, but at least there are good reasons he's been less than cordial toward everyone. Not just Jenny. I discovered today, literally right before lunch, that Alex is crazy about Cici, Luc's daughter. Luc told me while you were freshening up. Apparently, something happened last year to keep Cici and Alex apart and he was mad at the world, or at least the world of Endgate Island, and resentful because his dad and Jenny were happy and he wasn't. Latest news is Cici and Alex have made up. Which could be why he was more congenial at lunch."

"Oh good. I'm all for young love, especially if it means Alex quits being a pain."

Eric drawled in a seductive tone, "Why, you sweet l'il romantic, you." His voice made my pulse race. He continued normally again, "Anyway, I've also heard Zach showed more than a passing interest in Jenny when they first met, which pissed Michael off and didn't make Jenny happy either."

"Whoa. It's a soap opera. Or typical Manhattan theatre gossip."

"It is, isn't it?" Eric made a sound suspiciously like a snort.

"Is there more? About the so-called first families?"

"Of course. Olivia doesn't consider either Zach or Monique high class enough to turn Endgate back to whatever she remembers from childhood and wants them to back off any projects on Tenth Avenue in the hopes the Laurents actually own it and can either turn it into some lovely B&B or find treasure in its cellars. George appears quite besotted with Monique and wants to share whatever he owns with her. Oh, almost forgot, there's another player I didn't realize was as rabid about all this until last night during the party."

"Really? Like we don't have enough intrigue and greed by the current players?"

"Always room for one more, though. Ready for this? Miss Renee Pelletier. Turns out the Pelletiers were on the same ship as old Captain Jacques. Or at least one Pelletier. Olivia mentioned it at some point during last night's party. She claimed Renee has to be restrained from toting the old family bible to every party on the island." His eyes twinkled. "I assumed Olivia was kidding but one is never sure with the matriarch."

"What does Olivia think of her?" I asked. "Renee, I mean?"

"She thinks she's classy and would do nothing to hurt the island's image."

"Oh-kay. So Renee is loony on the topic of the first families. Zach seems to be loony on how to make money. George is loony about Monique and Monique is just...loony. So, is this why Michael has been distracted? Too many folks wandering around acting crazy?" I had to wonder how much of what Eric was telling me might be the reason Jenny was missing. My breath started coming too fast. *Missing.* Was she trapped somewhere? Scared? Hurt? I wouldn't let myself even think the final word... dead. I left my spot by the fan, crossed over to the bed and sat on the edge, then focused back on what Eric was saying.

"You could be right about Michael and distractions. He's been pretty beleaguered about all the machinations swirling here, there, and everywhere. He's not thrilled with the constant conflict and craziness, and he honestly feels incapable of dealing with Jenny's disappearance. Then you add whatever has been pushing Jenny to go exploring in dangerous places... at this point I wouldn't give you the proverbial two cents for anyone on this island except Luc. Well, maybe Alex, because he's smart enough to have fallen for Luc's daughter, whom I'm assuming is as awesome as Luc. I suspect Alex also sees through a lot of the trash our luncheon companions tend to toss around."

"Gee, Eric, tell me how you *really* feel," I teased.

"Too much?"

I answered slowly but definitively. "No. I sensed at lunch almost everyone at the table had some kind of agenda. Watch. It'll turn out Jenny is descended from the old pirate Jacques who first landed on this island and she's been whisked off somewhere to keep her from popping up with a document stating ownership she'd have no intention of claiming."

"Shame she isn't. There are a lot of cool things about Endgate Island, starting with a totally unpolluted west beach. I was able to see it before the great cellar sabotage. I'm really not sure if the theatre was a ruse to get the two of us here to help Jenny figure out what else is going on, but it really could be a workable proposition...with, of course, an assist from Miz Teddie Grant and Mister Emeric Desmarais."

"Em-eric?" My eyes opened wide "That's your real name? You sneaky man. This is news. Where did the extra 'em' come from? It's unique. I like it." I stopped before adding that I also thought it was sexy...like the man himself. With another disconcerting flash, I felt certain I'd heard the name before. I simply didn't know where.

"It's from some Desmarais ancestor from way back. I have this feeling it's the one from New Orleans. Anyway, my great-grandma was pretty cryptic about it, but she's the one who named me."

We lapsed into silence. There was more to the name. We both knew it. And we were doing our darnest to avoid whatever the "more" was.

Eric stretched his arms over his head. "Okay, Theodosia, ready to sift through old books even though we have no idea what we're looking for?"

"Let's hit it. Tell you what, why don't you dig into this tome of history written by a Miss Hannah Chaudret. The pirate's great-great-great whatever. I'm sure it's chock-full of propaganda about how wonderful her family and the island are." I rose and picked the book up from the end table where I'd placed it last night then handed him *Endgate Island: A History.* "Here."

"Looks fascinating. Thanks so much."

"Do I detect a note of sarcasm?"

"Note? You detect an entire symphony." He flipped the book open. "No table of contents or index?"

"Sadly, no."

"What are you planning to read while I slog through this tome? *Dick and Jane Join a Band of Pirates*?"

I squatted down on the floor next to the bookshelf and kicked off my clunky boots, stripped the socks off as well, and wriggled my bare toes in relief of being free from laces and faux leather as I replied, "Cute. And I'm not sure what I'm reading yet. I'm sort of hoping something falls off the shelf and hits me on the head.

However, since my precognitive skills haven't gotten to a kinetic stage, I'm going to use the old-fashioned method of hands-on and peruse each shelf to play a game of find-the-book-not-fitting-with-its-fellows."

I shouldn't have said "cute." I was suddenly less interested in staring at books and more interested in staring at Eric. Then again, "cute" wasn't exactly the right word. Those dark green eyes did shine with an impish quality, but there was strength in his jawline and way too much sensuality in a mouth I wanted to feel on mine. "Not the time or place, Teddie," I muttered to myself. "Books, girl, books."

Eric clicked on the tall lamp and began reading. I pulled out several old novels with copyrights from the 1960s and placed them beside me. Six of the books were gothics and I'd've loved to take the time to dive in and simply enjoy. But I felt a growing sense of urgency to find... something... so they'd have to wait for a quieter time. Instead of reading, I turned each book upside down and gently shook the pages in case a letter, a note, or a memo fell out.

"Jeez," Eric grumbled.

"What? You sound...um...kind of cranky." I turned to face him, shifting my legs into a lotus pose.

"It's this whole uber-pride thing about stuff normal folks wouldn't consider savory, much less admirable."

"Such as?"

"Well, you kind of nailed it with your previous observation. Old Hannah Chaudret makes no bones about her worship for Jacques Chaudret, the first French pirate to settle Endgate—whom she labels a privateer, since it doesn't sound quite so criminal as thief and abductor and killer. Anyway, she adores ol' Jacques—her who-knows-and-who-cares how many great-greats back—who, along with his first mate and navigator and crew, sailed on in and grabbed the island from the natives in the 1700s. Incidentally, his band of merry men? Their last names were Pelletier, Laurent, Prideaux, and Bernard."

"The first families of Endgate. I remember you told me Adler came later. Clearly a carpetbagger and, consequently, a nonentity is my take on it."

"Yep. You know, I've got to say, I loved all the old movies from the 30s and 40s and the whole swashbuckling thing all the action-adventure actors had going, but what they did was so far removed from the reality of piracy they could just as well have been playing Martians. The truth was far more violent and horrible and downright nasty." He shook his head. "Sorry. I'll try to refrain from commentary."

"No problem. You're preaching to the proverbial solo choir, but it's fine. As you can see, I haven't gotten to the reading portion of this enterprise and I'm more than ready to listen."

"Uh-huh. I noticed. But hey. You do look quite fetching in your yoga lotus pose, even if you're not accomplishing anything."

Was he flirting? If so, I liked it. If not, I still liked it, although I wished I knew how to respond. I knew how I'd like to respond, which was physically. But I went with humor. "For your information, I'm accomplishing keeping my body flexible."

"What? You mean climbing ladders and hammering set pieces doesn't do the same thing?"

"Different muscles. Generally more satisfying for getting rid of anger and stress. Hammering nails is awesome therapy. I *need* therapy. I'm beyond stressed trying to figure out why Jenny is missing and pretending I'm not about to fall apart with worry. Also, I am curious as to why someone wrecked those stairs and sent you tumbling. I keep hoping something pops up in one of these books."

"I'm with you on all counts. We need to stay focused on this for now, since we can't do much else to find Jenny."

"Agreed."

We returned to our respective searches, staying silent for the next ten minutes or more.

I changed my position again, stretching my legs out in front of me and pushing my feet against the carton of books I'd brought from Hickory Shadows. Suddenly, I felt a tingle in my right foot...not really a pain, but strong enough to make me stop stretching. I dove inside and pulled out an oversize book. *Broadway Musicals of the 1960s*. There was no reason my antennae were shooting through the roof, but whatever second sight I'd acquired since reading Jenny's e-mail only four days ago was now sending a siren call of "important" at me.

I was about to do the shake-for-papers routine for *Broadway Musicals* when I realized it didn't have the right feel for a book this big. Perhaps it was missing a few chapters?

The book was missing more than a few chapters. A good two hundred pages or more were gone. The book had been hollowed out. Instead of old photos or summaries of productions or biographies of dancers and singers, I found myself staring at what appeared to be a ledger of some kind. An old ledger bound in some kind of vellum or leather, material that had withstood more than a century, although obviously not in this particular book.

I carefully opened the ledger. Faded yet still legible handwriting on the first page showed me what I was reading were financial accounts from the years 1850 to 1865. A chill not coming from any A/C, ceiling, or floor fan washed over me.

Business and finance are *not* my forte, but I didn't require a degree in accounting to read and understand the text in this ledger. Within thirty seconds of scanning page one I discovered a few notifications not financial in nature. They were topics generally found in family bibles, including births, marriages, and obituaries. Those listings were on separate pages for clarity and numbered far less than the accounting. Those dates were 1861 to 1865. The Chaudret family bible had probably been hidden from the Yankees during the Civil War. Whoever had kept this ledger must have planned to transfer the events described into that bible at a later date when the war was over.

The majority of the book concerned trading. Buying and selling and tallying up numbers each month for five years to gauge profit and loss. I began with the first page with a gut awareness I couldn't afford to skip through it, no matter how dull it appeared. I needed to examine each line until I found the reason this ledger was screaming "check this out" at me.

There were entries for seed grain and for pallets, stacks of wood, burlap sacks, plus household goods like fabrics, mason jars, and "consumables." It was fun reading about a butter churn found at a store in New Orleans for five cents along with a pint of cream. Made sense. No cows on Endgate Island, so butter must have been quite a treat.

A variety of items had been bought and sold through the war years. *Hundreds*. There were far fewer names of people, whether it was a listing about a newborn or brides and grooms. In fact, there were almost none. There were also a few death notices. I assumed those were in a real bible somewhere.

Twelve pages into the ledger the cold down my spine became so strong I almost jumped up to turn off the fan.

Bought: March 22, 1860 from estate of Monsieur Pierre Desmarais, Orleans Paris, deceased, by Henri Chaudret. Auction after forfeiture from Desmarais estate. No heirs. Issue: Claim: freemen. Status: Seized assets.

Five house servants (male children—males can read and write). English and French speaking.

Martin (age 35 years), Rebecca (age 32 years), Emeric (age 14 years), Paul (age 10 years), Jilly (age 6 years)

Six field hands: Ben (age 20 years), Sam (age 16 years), Thomas (age 15 years), Tandy (age 15 years), Robert (age 13 years)

I closed my eyes and tried to conquer a growing nausea. I could see them. The little girl, barely out of toddler years. Boys entering adolescence. Their parents, born into slavery themselves, yet never losing hope for a better life for their children. I was no expert on the practice of the slave trade in the years before the Civil War, but if I understood the words in this ledger correctly, it appeared these people had been considered free but had been sold again when the Desmarais estate went under following the death of a nearly bankrupt "Pierre," who had no heirs anyway, so all "assets" were open for disbursement. *Assets.*

I forced myself to continue reading, no matter what details were revealed, but the cold grew worse. It was as if the tower room was forty degrees instead of eighty. I was shivering and began gasping for breath.

"Teddie. What's wrong?" Within seconds Eric was on the floor beside me. I would have loved to have his arms around me, but was at least grateful for his nearness adding a little warmth.

I stated dully, "I wonder if this same information was in the diary."

"What are you talking about?"

"Look at the ages in this ledger. How in *hell* can someone scrawl the word 'bought' and then list an entire family the same damned way he references buying the new butter churn? I'm always amazed, no matter how many years ago, that anyone could think this way."

Eric's tone was tense. "There's more?"

"There's more. This stinkin' ledger. It's too real and it's too striking and painful, even though it was more than a hundred and fifty years ago and they're all gone. Seeing the name of such a young girl…no more than a baby…sent me into a meltdown." I paused before adding, "Eric. There's a reason why this was hidden. I'm not really sure why, but I feel whoever hid it did so in the 1960s."

"Go on."

I pointed first to the Desmarais family's "sales" page and the asterisk by one name—*Emeric*. Then let my finger travel to the bottom of the page to show Eric what I'd found. Another asterisk followed by the words *Lost… June 1865*.

Chapter 13

"Emeric Desmarais? *Lost*? What in hell are they trying to say?" Eric demanded. "*Lost*? Like he's a puppy roaming the neighborhood without his tags? Or somebody's wallet left on the street? Or... oh Lord, I can't even come up with anything dumber."

"It's horrible. Let's figure this out. Eighteen sixty-five. The war ended in the spring. Emeric should have been officially free by then, but I remember reading in a history book there were a ton of slave owners who weren't thrilled with a particular proclamation—and refused to comply. According to this ledger, the Desmarais family had been freed a few years earlier, but resold as assets after Pierre, the original...owner...died. I guess they stayed with him? Jobs were almost nonexistent in a lot of places in the South, so maybe Pierre worked out something with the Desmarais family? It's possible. Anyway, fast-forward a few years and the war is over, but the Chaudrets haven't quite gotten with the program—i.e., freedom. Emeric might well have run off rather than wait around hoping old Henri Chaudret would do the right thing."

We sat in silence, trying to digest words written more than a century and a half ago. Words that impacted our emotions as if the events were happening today. I glanced down at both our hands, resting next to each other on top of the ledger. Black and white.

I sat up straight. "Whoa. Flash. Intuitive-type...not spooky."

"What?"

"I need to go through the records of births, marriages, and deaths in the ledger...at least the few they listed. I'm getting this psychic itch saying we need to check there to find answers."

"Should I get back to the oh-so-enthralling history of the island so you can concentrate?" Eric asked with a mix of sarcasm and worry in his tone.

I still felt chilled. Worse...frightened. "No. Please. Would you mind staying here with me?"

"I'll stay."

"Thanks. I'll try not to faint before I figure this out."

It took only less than a minute to find the next piece of the puzzle.

"Eric, look."

"What am I looking at?"

"Another listing from 1865. Pivotal year. It appears whoever kept this ledger hadn't yet gotten around to shifting notations to the family bible. We have a sad record of deaths of seven boys, I'd guess from the war, and of an old Chaudret patriarch with the first name Beaufort. Underneath Beaufort Chaudret there's another name. Looks like 'Althea' and the month—June—which is damned hard to read because both words have been crossed out."

Eric was quick. "As though someone tried to delete her existence."

"What cardinal sin could she have committed to make the Chaudrets so angry they tried to wipe someone out of history? I haven't found a birth date, so no telling how old she was when they bumped her out of the family."

We stared at each other. Finally, Eric asked, "Are you thinking Althea and Emeric got together? As in, more than on a page in a ledger?"

"Exactly. Talk about their idea of a major sin. If Althea and Emeric, uh, hooked up, it might explain the word 'lost' for Emeric. Maybe it was a euphemism for running away so the Chaudrets wouldn't lose face with their fellow landowners?"

Eric rose and limped over to the edge of the bed. "Let's see if there's anything in Hannah's boring and pompous history book about a relationship between a former slave and a member of the Chaudret family circa 1865. I'm not optimistic, since revealing anything resembling even a friends-only relationship between your friend Althea and Emeric, much less something more, isn't something our snooty author would willingly admit."

I assumed a strong, fake Southern drawl. "Mah, mah, Mister Desmarais. And Ah am shocked at how wild and liberal-minded you are. Such a horrible scandal it would have been. Tsk, tsk, tsk. Shame on you foah even *imaginin'* those two as a couple."

"Uh-uh. You're being quite snarky there, Miz Grant."

I continued musing but without the sarcasm or the accent. "Sadly, and with all snark aside, it's true. As to how these folks would have felt... Things like piracy to Hannah, and many of the islanders, I'll bet, were romantic and sexy. Interracial romance? Their words would have been...uh..."

"Horror? Disgust? Intolerance?"

"*All* the above... along with a whopping big dose of stupidity."

I rose and joined Eric on the bed. My lips felt dry; my heart pounded like a marathon runner hitting the midpoint.

I reached over and touched Eric's hand. It was warm...too much so.

"Eric, one of us has to go ahead and say it. Or, I guess, more properly, ask it."

In a monotone, as if afraid to show emotion that could spiral into feelings too strong to handle, Eric said, "Go ahead."

"Do we believe in past lives?"

Eric winced. "As in 'not a theoretical discussion in a theology class' but as in...us."

"The déjà vu, the odd flashes. Is it possible we were once...other people?"

Eric was silent for a long moment. Finally he asked, "Such as a girl playing piano, wearing a long period-piece dress, and a boy in farm clothes?"

"Yes."

Neither of us was able to come out and say we were now entertaining the possibility we'd once been Emeric and Althea. But the look in Eric's eyes told me he believed it was more than merely speculation and we'd been two people desperately in love in the absolute wrong place and time.

Eric slid his hand away from mine. The chill that washed over me upon losing his touch was as painful as jumping into an icy stream.

Eric softly asked, "Neutral corners?"

I swallowed hard. He was right. There were too many bizarre thoughts and too many conflicting emotions hitting all at once and way too fast. I repeated in agreement, "Neutral corners."

We each took the suggestion literally. I walked away toward the window that overlooked the Laurents' garage, and Eric rose from the bed and headed back to the rocking chair and sat, again propping his foot on the stool for support.

Eric waited another full minute before stating, "I wish I knew who absconded with Marianne's diary, and where he or she stashed it. I'm sure it's chock-full of great stuff. The details we've found in the ledger seem pretty certain in pointing to a link between a possible long-lost ancestor and me, but we really need more information." Eric flipped the old history book open. "Meantime, let's see if something jumps out from the 1860s in old Hannah's book." He smiled. "Please... come help."

I ran across the room and stood behind his chair to peer over Eric's shoulder as we skimmed the self-serving narrative regarding the inhabitants of Endgate Island. "Hold it."

Eric was about to turn a page. "Yes?"

"Check this passage. She says, and I quote, 'In the first ten years following the War Between the States and the Emancipation Proclamation, Endgate Island looked to alternative means for rebuilding its economy.' Then she zips right past the early years of the twentieth century right on to World War One, leaving the reader to inquire, 'what in blazes were alternative means'?"

"Something tells me those means weren't always legal. But it does sound like once those first families on the island lost their free labor for rice farming or harvesting grapes, they might have gone back to the grand old occupation of smuggling. Rum running."

"I wonder how many of the former slaves were able to find work on the mainland. Do you suppose any of them returned?"

"I wouldn't be surprised. Must have been hell all around. Soldiers were looking for work. Farms had been destroyed. Men and women who'd never known freedom suddenly had it dumped in their lap, and then thrust into a job market they weren't equipped for. Most of them weren't literate and had no skills apart from farming. So it makes sense the familiar would seem safe and secure." He paused. "I have to say though, I seriously doubt any of the Desmarais family stayed on the island. I'd imagine they were pretty ticked at being freed and then sold again."

"I share your doubt." I glanced back down at the book and flipped through about five pages. "You're right. Our Hannah skips over about twenty-five years as if they didn't exist."

"Maybe she didn't find documents relating to the early 1900s and wanted to be sure of her facts?"

"Or perhaps she couldn't find anyone willing to talk. Although she might have remembered some of those years herself. What's the copyright date?" We checked the opening pages. "Nineteen-forty," I murmured. "If she was in, oh say, her seventies when she wrote it, she could have lived through those years at an age when she was aware of everything going on."

"And had no desire to include anything that could possibly tarnish what she saw as the shining legacy of Endgate and the first families." Eric slammed the pages together, closing the book, clearly trying to shut out the pain of the history. His family's history. Possibly his *own* history if he'd really once been Emeric.

"Yep." I looked up at the ceiling and tried to stay civil, instead of loudly cursing every first family on the island. "Something tells me with their love of Endgate Island, Hannah and Olivia would have gotten along great, although hopefully Olivia isn't the racist Hannah was."

Eric's cell phone, sitting on an end table by the bed, rang before he could further respond to the gap of years in this particular history of the island.

I perked up. "News of Jenny?"

"We can only pray." Eric grabbed the phone and answered. "Hey. Yeah, it's Eric." Pause. "Oh. Right. Makes sense. Do you want Teddie's help, too?" Another pause. "Okay. See you at the garage as soon as I can clump downstairs."

He hit the "off" button.

"Not Jenny."

"Not Jenny."

I took a deep breath, forcing myself not to break down and just lie on the floor rocking in a fetal position. "So... Teddie's help for what?"

"Boarding up windows around the island. The storm appears to be coming sooner than expected, so any and all able-bodied males are gathering with hammers and lumber."

I managed to smile. "Cool. I'm ready for some manual labor. Could relieve the emotional stress."

Eric sounded amused. "Unless you want to start a one-woman equal opportunity window-boarders fight, you, Miz Grant, get to stay here."

"*Seriously?*"

"Yeah. Michael said he'd love having the help of a superior techie type, but the rest of the macho men on the island feel it's an affront to allow some sweet li'l female to be doin' a man's job. Wanna fight for your right to tack lumber over panes of glass?"

I waved my hand in a dismissive gesture. "Not today. Let the big brave menfolk save the houses. I need a bath and a nap. Then maybe I'll be up for whatever the latest calamity is."

Eric handed me the book. "All yours for a while." He headed for the door but turned back for a second "I'm ready to chuck the boot cast once and for all. I doubt it makes a difference anyway, since word is out we're exploring old houses."

"Do it. You'll be more comfortable, and it'll help strengthen your ankle and you get to quit cutting up clothes to allow room for the boot. Much easier to deal with while boarding windows, too."

"All great points." He paused. "Um. I promise to call if something turns up about Jenny. You do the same, okay?"

"Definitely. Eric, please call even if you simply stumble across a reason she's now been missing more than twenty-four hours." My voice caught. "Damn it. *Twenty-four* hours."

Chapter 14

The attic felt far less inviting after Eric left. But I welcomed the chance to wash up following this morning's excursion through the passageway to the Hickory Shadows cellar.

After I toweled off and hunted through cabinets for a foo-foo lemon body spray, I decided to head back downstairs and see if any of the ingredients of Luc's decadent dessert—like the ice cream and the brandy—were still available. I didn't need the traditional flaming brandy poured over the dish, but the idea of something sweet and cold was more than tempting. I found a pale green sundress that was a complete opposite in style from the jeans I'd worn all day, put the key to the tower room in one of the button-closed pockets in the skirt, and made my way down the maze of halls and stairs until I reached the parlor.

I stopped at the French doors. Someone was playing Rachmaninoff's *Rhapsody on a Theme by Paganini*, the *18th* variation on the piano...and doing a nice job. I quietly opened the doors and slipped inside, hoping not to disturb the musician, who turned out to be Olivia Laurent.

Olivia played the last few chords and I broke into spontaneous applause. She turned and bowed her head in appreciation. "Thank you, Teddie."

"Thank *you*," I stated. "Wow. Beautiful. It also happens to be one of my favorite pieces of music, and I'm not normally a fan of classical. Always been more a girl-group-band-from-the-sixties lady."

Olivia rose from the piano and gestured for me to join her at the sofa. "I love those groups as well, but the songs never sound quite right when it's a piano without other instrumentation. I keep telling Michael to take up electric guitar and get Alex on drums, but they ignore me."

We smiled at each other as I sat next to her. "I have to ask… were—or are you a professional musician?"

"I was. Gave it up when I moved back here about forty years ago now. I still keep in practice, though."

I wanted to try to understand this woman. "I hope I'm not offending you, but how could you bear not to continue with your profession? Didn't you feel trapped here? I'm so sorry. That's probably a rude and way-too-intrusive thing to ask."

She looked up at the ceiling for a moment, as if searching for the right answer, and then stated, "It's fine. Truthfully? It was tough at first. But I adored Cyril and he adored the island, and there was really no way to combine my career with my marriage. So, I made the choice. Never regretted it. He was wonderful about keeping the piano in tune and giving me as much time as I wanted to play." She paused, then added, "In my opinion, wanting more than Jenny thought she'd get has been the biggest issue since she moved here."

"What do you mean?"

"This is not a put-down, really. I know you girls are best friends and I'm honestly not trying to be nasty. But, Teddie, your friend gave up her career in LA. when she married Michael. She had no idea how different things would be for her on the island. It can be a…I guess…insular place. I tried to talk to her and explain how isolated it can be and how much one has to love the island to be happy, but I'm sure it came across as if I didn't want her to marry Michael rather than my actual intention. Consequently, she didn't listen."

I was about to launch into an angry "But Jenny can do no wrong" defense when it struck me Olivia was right. Jenny's feelings and reasons for marriage and moving to the island might have been off base. Didn't mean I loved her any less.

I turned to Olivia. "You're wise. I remember when Jenny called me to tell me that she was going to marry Michael, she sounded so determined. She told me she'd never loved anyone so much, and I'd joked she was in some fairytale world where she pretty much didn't hear a word anyone said to her. It seems there was more truth in my comment than either of us realized."

"Fairytale." Olivia gave a wry smile. "Unfortunately, after Jenny and Michael moved here it wasn't long before she started going to the mainland to see shows or wander around the French Quarter watching the people, which can often turn into more of a show than anything on Broadway. She seemed dissatisfied. The first time I saw her really excited was when she discovered Hickory Shadows and Chittamwood Gardens, which is the house over on Fifth Avenue. Both were vacant. When Michael told her we owned them, she came up with the idea of turning one of them into a theatre and she seemed happy. But something happened about six weeks or so ago. It was as if she simply retreated into her own world and shut everyone out."

I grimaced. "Jenny never did well when she wasn't hip deep into work. But she's a good actress and a good organizer. She can make it work." *If she's found.* "So, let me see if I've got this straight. The Laurents own Hickory Shadows and Chittamwood Gardens. Those two are not in dispute, but the house—or, I suppose—the castle on Tenth Avenue is up for grabs?"

"Correct. We're all in limbo waiting for various legal documents to arrive from archives in New Orleans, although I'm not sure they'll help. It's complicated because the boundaries weren't clearly laid out until the 1800s, and many documents were either lost or taken to parish courthouses for safekeeping. The *big* issue is the Chaudret castle and west beach. There's some difficulty with the original will that makes the place currently up for grabs, and I do mean 'grab.' The greed of some people is overwhelming. You've seen how some of these people behave. Even at what should be polite lunches." She added, with a glint of humor, "I've seen wrestling matches on television that were more genteel."

I laughed, liking her as a real person and not simply Michael's aunt or Jenny's occasional antagonist. "If you don't mind another nosy question, what do you know about the Chaudret family?" *Apart from the obvious*, I thought, *as in, they were pirates and slave holders and thoroughly unpleasant people.*

"Let me first ask, what do *you* know?"

"Very little. I found a history of the island upstairs in one of the bookshelves but it's dry and fairly self-serving."

Olivia's mouth twitched with amusement. "Oh my. You must have found old Hannah's ode to the pirates. Dreadful book. I tried reading it years ago but couldn't make it past the first chapter." Her eyes twinkled. "Hannah was not exactly what one would call a literary genius. If I recall, she died in the late 1930s or early 40s. She was quite old. I didn't come to Endgate until the 1980s and I love this island, but some of the first families who thought they were above everything else because their ancestors were pirates made me a little crazy when I first arrived. To be honest, they still do."

"What's the history of the Laurent family? In connection to the Chaudrets."

"A bit unclear. I've heard the Laurents were on the island *before* the pirates arrived and I've also heard the Laurents came in the late 1700s. It's also been rumored the Laurents were part of Captain Chaudret's crew. At any rate, as to the castle on the west beach, the only thing certain is no Chaudret heirs have turned up in nearly sixty years to stake a claim. It's my understanding the last Chaudret died a few months ago somewhere in north Louisiana." She sighed. "And believe me nothing will be settled today especially with a hurricane coming through. The last thing anyone needs is more sturm and drang right now." She paused then added, "But I'm forgetting my manners. Would you like something to drink? Iced tea or something stronger?"

"Tea sounds great. If anything remotely boozy passes my lips, I'll probably fall asleep right on the floor here. Please don't trouble yourself, though, I can go get it myself."

"Neither of us needs to move. We're *tres* modern here. Technical devices to make life easier." She picked up a cell phone from the sofa end table, hit a number, reached Luc in the kitchen, and made a request. Two minutes later, a young lady of perhaps eighteen I hadn't yet met sauntered into the parlor bearing a tray with two glasses of iced tea, a pitcher of ice with a scooper, lemons, sugar, and a plate of cookies.

My first thought upon seeing the girl was in an island full of attractive people, she stood out as frankly beautiful. Her perfect bone structure would remain for a lifetime, and her dark brown liquid eyes seemed to stare into one's soul.

I gratefully accepted a glass and some kind of sugar cookie. "Looks yummy. Thank you."

Olivia made introductions. "This is Cici Bouvier, Luc's youngest daughter."

My hands were attempting to juggle food and drink, so I kept my greeting vocal. "Great to meet you. I guess you're aware I adore your dad even after only a super-short acquaintance."

"Welcome to the club. He *is* pretty cool, isn't he?" she stated with pride. "I'm working with him this summer before goin' to culinary school in the fall—but honestly? They can't teach me a darn thing, even in Nah'leans, any better than my dad's been doin' since I was about two."

"Sadly, these days it's all about the paper rather than the skill when it comes to education and jobs. Have you decided yet where you're going to be head chef or owner?"

Cici chortled in glee. "Whoa. I like your thinkin'. And sure, I wouldn't mind takin' over one of the touristy restaurants in Nah'leans, but I also have dreams of startin' my own place, maybe in Baton Rouge or up in Lafayette. Perhaps a catering company."

"Or you could always stay near Luc and make the island theatre a total must for every tourist."

"Hmm. Could be fun. Of course, everyone's waitin' to find out if the theatre's a go or not before divin' into menus."

"Good point."

We exchanged a glance that seemed to signal Cici was also worried whether Jenny was okay and could make any theatre a go.

She picked up an empty tray from another end table. "Well, Miz Teddie, it's been a delight meetin' you. Y'all enjoy the tea and cookies. I've gotta head back to the mainland in the next few minutes while Robin is still takin' boats out before the storm hits, but Papa's gonna stay so he'll take care of y'all if you need somethin' else."

"Enjoyed meeting you as well, and thanks."

Olivia Laurent echoed my thanks, then added, "Before you leave, have you heard any news on when the storm is due? It seems whenever I check an app on my phone, they've changed expectations both for time and category. It's really too early in the season for a hurricane, but then, weather is always hard to predict. Robin's probably the one who's most up on the news."

Like an actor responding to a cue, Robin Trahan knocked on the French doors leading to the parlor from the kitchen side.

Olivia motioned for him to come inside. "Robin? What's the word?"

He didn't bother to ask "word on what." "Word is Ah'm done, Miz Livvie. Got all the boats in and tucked away safe, and all Ah can say is if folks are on the island now, they're stayin'."

Cici sounded disappointed. "So I'm not makin' class tonight."

Robin turned to her, "Cici, *no one's* makin' class. Nah'leans is shut down tighter than a shoe on a swollen foot. Everything that *can* be closed is closed."

"Okay. I guess best thing for me then is to help Papa get emergency rations prepped so we can make deliveries round the island rest of the afternoon."

"If you need an extra hand, I'd love to go with you," I volunteered.

"Thanks. I'd really appreciate it," Cici responded with a smile. "It's tough when it's only the two of us, since the men on the island are either out boardin' up windows or checking storm doors for cellars to make sure they're stable. And poor Robin here has to trek back and forth to the mainland fast as he can before the waters get too rough to travel, then check on the other boats so they don't get washed out to sea. A long and full day. Plus, he had to help close down the ferry." She glanced at my dress. "Uh, you might want to wear something less nice, though. If we get caught in an early wave of rain, you're going to be a mess, and your gorgeous dress will be ruined."

I saluted. "Way ahead of you. I'll run upstairs and change into my grubbies. Meet you and Luc... when?"

Robin answered for her. "Ten minutes tops, Miz Teddie. Believe me, it's gonna be a rough night. God help anyone not tucked away safe at home."

Chapter 15

Six years of running to grab trains or buses or dodging traffic on the way to a theatre then coming home to trot up five flights of stairs made my current dash to the tower room easy in spite of nearly zero rest in the last day and a half. I unlocked the door, grabbed a clean pair of cut-offs and a T-shirt from the closet, pulled off the sandals and stuffed my feet into a pair of athletic shoes, strapped my belly bag around my waist, and made it back downstairs in less than five minutes.

Olivia stood in the front hallway. "They're waiting outside. Thank you for helping, Teddie. You've got the island spirit."

I wasn't quite sure how to take her last comment since what I'd seen so far of the island spirit was somewhat less than generous, but I simply responded, "I used to help with delivering meals to the elderly and also hammering roofs on the houses for charities when I lived in Austin. I imagine this is similar…only more urgent. See you in a bit."

Luc, Cici, and a surprise passenger—Alex—were waiting for me in a truck older than I was.

"How many homes are we visiting?" I asked Luc once we were all situated.

"'Bout six families," he answered. "These are the times Ah'm kind of glad the island population is so small. Now, hang on." He pointed to a strap hanging by the door.

"No problem. I've got grabbing poles and rails and even bags on people's shoulders down to a fine art after six years in Manhattan riding subways at hours when empty seats don't exist. What about Cici and Alex? Are they good to go?"

Luc glanced in the rearview mirror where his daughter and Alex seemed relatively safe perched on the edge of the truck bed, then glanced at me. "Better there than a lot 'a other places."

The remark seemed cryptic, but I didn't press him. I sensed romance brewing and it wasn't my business to ask Luc his feelings about his daughter and a Laurent.

Luc put the clutch in, shifted into first gear, and we were off. There was little opportunity for talking since the windows were down and the wind was at beginning-storm levels. Luc was intent on getting the truck and its supplies to families as fast as possible, and consequently kept his focus on avoiding old holes in roads clearly in need of repair. Large and small tree branches were falling and filling those holes, and I inwardly admitted I was more than uneasy about being in the middle of a possible hurricane on what was already a spooky island.

We drove for about seven minutes before coming to the first place on Endgate not labeled "avenue." From what I could see, it had never been labeled anything at all. A row of dilapidated houses mirroring third-world conditions sat at the edge of a large rice paddy

I didn't bother to conceal my dismay.

Luc pulled to a stop in front of the first house. "Not exactly the image of Endgate the first families want to broadcast, is it?"

"This is awful. I guess the rice is grown for mainland companies? And I assume these homes were once slave quarters?"

"Yeah. At least they've got jobs now. And you're right about the slave quarters. The folks who live there now are the descendants of the slaves who never left the island 'cuz there never was a good time or place to go. Stayed and worked the rice fields or the vineyard like they'd always done. Some fared better by workin' at houses for the landowners who managed to make it through the Civil War without losin' much in the way of menfolk, land, or wealth. This part of the island's been called the Quarters for centuries and no one's even bothered to change it. Name's so ingrained now one barely remembers...uh...."

"The adjective that came before 'quarters' for centuries?"

"Yes'm."

Cici yelled, "Come on, y'all. Quit yakkin' and let's get this stuff inside."

Luc and I joined his daughter and Alex at the back of the truck. Alex already had three cases of water on the ground and was lifting a fourth when three children who looked to be middle-school age came racing out of the ramshackle house closest to the truck, circled Cici, and hugged her.

"Miz Cici. We missed you," cried the oldest of the trio, a beautiful girl with huge brown eyes and super-long lashes, who was way too thin and could make good use of the food we'd brought.

Cici reached into the bed of the truck and grabbed two bags. "You too. Now, doncha eat these all at once, y'all. Don't need to be gettin' sick in the middle of a storm. Along with beans and canned veggies and fruit, there's a tin of sugar cookies in one, and some food for Louie. Should keep the pup happy and full today and maybe even a week or two after if y'all don't let him at the bag. Either Papa Luc or I will be back and bring more stuff when it's safe to take the truck out again."

"Louie?" I inquired.

Cici answered, "The sweetest, dumbest canine in five parishes in Louisiana. His arrival on the island is a mystery, but he's pretty much been adopted by all the families in the Quarters here."

A pup of uncertain ancestry, leaning more toward black lab and maybe a short-haired pointer, used his nose to push open the screen door at the front entrance of the house, and then raced toward Cici much in the manner of the kids, meaning with unabashed affection and little grace. For the next minute it was hard to tell individual from individual or dog from person.

I couldn't help but laugh. It was the first time since I arrived on Endgate I'd seen sheer unconditional love expressed. Louie turned to me, another human being to sniff, and within seconds I was on the ground with the mutt sitting on top of me and giving me doggie kisses in between yipping with excitement.

Luc yelled at us from the driver's side window where he was impatiently tapping on the steering wheel. "Hey, kids. We need to get this water and food to the house at the end. Miz Vianca can't come runnin' out here and carry all this herself. Leave the dog alone and let's get on with it."

The children hugged Cici again, checked me out like an alien from one of those alternate planets (New York), hoisted up the cases of water and sacks of food, and hurried back into structures so flimsy I fervently prayed they'd withstand the coming hurricane. If ever an island needed a sturdy concrete shelter, this was it.

Once the dog allowed me to sit up, I gave him a last big squeeze and a pat on his soft head and promised to come by with biscuits once the storm was through.

Cici, Alex, and I dashed back to the truck and barely made it into the bed, which I'd decided would be the most efficient spot for me to help with the jump out and grabbing what needed grabbing, before Luc revved the engine and hauled down the dirt road to visit a lady Luc told me was the ninety-plus-year-old Miz Vianca Giry.

Miz Giry was waiting for us on her porch, rocking in a chair possibly smuggled onto the island with the first settlers. She rose, stood ramrod straight, and waved at Luc. When she spoke, her voice was strong, with a musical cadence and kind of a combined Cajun and Creole accent. "Luc, mah radio broke yesterday and Ah ain't got no powah, so Ah can't charge mah phone. What's the word 'bout the storm? Mah joints be tellin' me it's comin' tonight but they ain't 'xactly givin' me reports of how bad."

"Hey, Miz Vianca, good ta see you. You're prob'ly better n'all those weather folks keepin' busy guessin' what category to put this in. Big whoop, right? There's still gonna be a ton of wind and rain makin' everyone miserable." He gave her a hug. "Ah brought batteries for ya, though, and a cell that's been charge. Should be good for least a day and night."

"Thanks, Luc." She pointed at me as Cici and Alex carried her supplies inside the house. "You Miz Jenny's best friend." It was not a question.

"I am. Teddie Grant. Pleased to meet you, Miz Giry. How did you know about Jenny and me? It was supposed to be a secret. Did Alex tell you?"

"Don' Miz Giry me, chile. Been Miz Vianca or jes Vianca since Ah was 'bout twelve. As to you and Miz Jenny? Well, she been droppin' by here most every week to sit and chat with me. She tole me all 'bout you. We got to be friends fast. Ah used to sing in some clubs in Nah'leans and we recognized the 'Ah gotta perform' need in each othah. Ah think Miz Jenny's funny and she claims same 'bout me. Anyway, Ah'm moren' pleased you made it down here. Ah hope you kin help that chile figure out what she needs to do to be happy."

The words were out of my mouth before I could stop them. "If she's found."

Vianca didn't seem surprised. She stared at me and flatly stated, "She ain't dead. You'll find her. Soon. You jes put your mind to it and it'll come to you where she is."

"Any ideas?"

"No. Wish Ah had a couple, 'cuz believe me, Ah'd tell you. But y'all got a special bond of friendship and once you git somewhere quiet, you let her call your spirit. And then you go get her."

Luc put his hand on my shoulder and patted it in sympathy. "She's right, Teddie."

"Okay."

I wanted to hear more from this woman, who appeared to be one of the few true friends Jenny had on this island. I wanted to be her friend as well. She was clearly "good people" and there was a calm, comfort, and strength about her that must draw everyone she met to her. Sadly, we had more deliveries to make and time was short, which was made clear when rain began to fall.

Alex and Cici came out on the porch, empty-handed now. Alex turned to Miz Vianca. "You sure you don't want to come back with us to Sugarberry Terrace? I hate thinkin' you're out here without power."

She chided him with a mischievous grin, "Now, Mister Alex, don't fret. Ah'll be more comfortable in mah own home. Ah got lanterns and Luc's brought the batteries. Ah'm warm. Ah'll stay dry…and Ah don't have to put up with crazy people Ah don't care to be 'round for more than a minute who'll be campin' out at your house even though they got perfectly good homes themselves. Bunch 'a mooches."

I couldn't help but laugh at Vianca's sharp and valid appraisal of the first families of Endgate Island as Alex responded, "Okay, if you promise you'll use the cell phone? For emergencies."

"Ain't gonna need to use it." She waved at us all but addressed me. "Miz Teddie, Alex tries to boss me 'round because Ah used to be his nanny when he was a young'un and he worries like Ah'm the chile now. But Ah like my house and Ah'm stayin' no matter how bad the storm. Been solid for more n' two hundred years. Now y'all git and Ah'll see you in a day or two once things are calm."

I hugged her and whispered, "Thank you for being Jenny's friend. When I find her, we'll come visit together. We'll bring Jenny's guitar and have a girls-only sing-along."

Her eyes grew moist. She nodded. "Miz Teddie. Hon, I gottta say, there's lotsa talent—and carin'—in Miz Jenny. And *you*. Ah feel it. Now, you git on and help some others who need it more n' Ah do." She paused, then cryptically added, "You gonna be back sooner n' ya think."

We all headed to the truck. I felt a bit more confident Jenny was actually okay thanks to Miz Vianca's own certainty, but I still couldn't help musing it would take more than a day or two for anything to be calm on Endgate Island.

Chapter 16

We needed to deliver goods to three more homes closer to the beach on this side of the island before the wind turned really wicked, so Luc stepped it up and drove with the skill—and the speed—of a professional racer in competition.

The next group of families we visited was better off than the people in the Quarters, but they were still housed in barely-above-poverty-level conditions. After we dropped off water and food to the last house, I turned to Luc.

"Do the owners of this portion of the island, whoever they are in this ridiculous fight, not realize how people live in this section? Do they not care?"

Luc's expression was grim. "Some of 'em care. I swear Mister Michael cares. But this fight is ridiculously complicated 'cause of some ol' will and lawyers from the mainland are forbiddin' everybody from making any changes until a final decision has been made."

I scowled. "Heck, they could at least call in a church group from one of the mainland parishes and have them do mission work repairing these homes without messing up any stupid legal issue."

"Ah agree. And, actually, Cici and Alex been talkin' to a coupla pastors in Nah'leans to help out. Now, not makin' excuses for anyone, but in the last six months we've had horrible weather on the mainland and the island, so it's been tough gettin' equipment and people to get out here to do the work. Wish there was a big ol' bridge to the mainland. Used to be a causeway 'bout a hundred years ago. It kinda disappeared over the years."

"Well, maybe after this storm we could get a few things taken care of for these people. I volunteer to use my skill with a hammer whether or not the men on this island are horrified at my taking a so-called male role in fixing homes. Jeez."

Luc clapped his hands together in delight and agreement. "Ah hope this theatre comes through, Miz Teddie. You're needed on Endgate for more'n bringin' tourists in. Ah swear some of the…well, let's say, fancier folks on this island need a kick in their pants every generation or so."

"After seeing what I saw today, I also volunteer to put on my work boots and do some of that kicking. Or worse. I'm not normally a violent person, but knowing others are allowing families with children to live in the kind of squalor I've just seen…well. My blood is boiling and it's not only from island heat." I took a breath. "Okay, I'm preaching to the choir. I'll be calm now. I promise. So, do we have any more deliveries? Did we bring enough supplies?"

"We're good. Hit everywhere we needed." He glanced out the window at the sky. "Ah'm gonna go back home by way of the beach road instead of through the trees. Wind's pickin' up hard and Ah don't want some big oak crashin' down on us. Which reminds me." He pulled the truck to a stop and stuck his head out the window, shouting to Cici and Alex, "Best come on inside, kids. Don't want y'all slidin' out of the truck or gettin' struck by lightnin'."

Cici and Alex jumped down. I slid over, Alex climbed in next to me, and Cici settled herself on his lap. A nice feeling of camaraderie from finishing our task enveloped the four of us. Alex seemed to have completely forgotten his attitude of the previous day, perhaps because it was clear Cici and I had bonded fast. It was obvious he felt more than friendship for Luc's daughter and it was matched on her part.

"Are there any homes on the west beach road?" I asked no one in particular.

Alex answered, "Of a sort."

"Oh-kay. Can we say…cryptic?"

Cici twisted to face Alex and addressed her dad. "Do we have time to swing by Tenth Avenue? The Chaudret castle? Teddie should see it. By the way, everyone either calls it The Castle or Tenth Avenue, which is slightly confusing unless you realize there are no other homes there. Too darn complicated to bring in the whole *Chateau Sans Frontieres*."

"We're drivin' the west beach anyway to avoid the trees," Luc informed us.

The Chaudret castle was precisely that—a castle. It was totally removed from the old Southern plantation homes one saw while driving down back roads in Mississippi or Alabama. The architecture was clearly French, but from an era nicely suited to the 1500s, perhaps along the coast of Normandy. It was made of stone, with uneven stories and turrets. Dormer openings and evil-looking gargoyles and iron bars on the windows added a spooky medieval touch. I half-expected a moat and wouldn't have been surprised to see ghosts of armored guards marching and circling the area to keep out any and all invaders...living or long dead.

For a brief moment I could see myself in one of the turrets and I felt claustrophobic. I brushed it away, filed it under "another odd vision," and tried to lighten the moment. "Well, call me stunned," I said. "Talk about the perfect setting for a murder mystery...or a murder."

Cici answered for the others in what might best be described as a sardonic tone, "This was the first residence built on the island by Captain Jacques Chaudret and his bride, an English maiden named Grace Sedley. Legend has it she was kidnapped on the high seas right off some fancy boat."

My eyebrows both shot up. "Are you serious? Can we say clichéd on steroids?"

"It does sound like an overdone movie plot, doesn't it?" Cici's eyes sparkled in delight.

"True, though." Luc obviously agreed with his daughter. "Captain Chaudret was a notorious pirate in the seventeenth century and he attacked more 'n one British ship on its way to the Caribbean. Miz Grace was supposedly only 'bout fifteen when Chaudret burned the *Patience* out in the Gulf here. He spared the girl so she could be his wife. Now, why he decided to get married at the ripe ol' age 'a forty-seven has been the big question for centuries."

"Oh man. Fifteen and he was mid-forties? Poor girl. So, what happened to her?"

"She had six children, all boys, and she outlived the ol' scoundrel and became the matriarch of Endgate Island. Legend has it she's the one who named the castle *Chateau Sans Frontieres* after her old Sedley estate somewhere in northern Britain. Seems the Sedleys were originally from Normandy and kept a lot of the French influence. Been said she was determined to keep as much of her own identity as she could to stand up to ol' Jacques. That's the story, anyway. Folks been callin' it Tenth Avenue or The Castle for near four hundred years."

"Did all the Chaudrets stay here on the island?" I asked.

Alex, who'd been silent up to now, jumped into the discussion. "Some of the boys went into the family business—piracy—and some stayed on the island and started the vineyard and several rice plantations. Those who stayed lived in the castle and brought wives in from New Orleans. They pretty much owned the island until World War One."

"Quite a few crew members from the first ships also settled here, but they built normal homes." Cici sneered. "If anythin' built by the first families can be considered normal."

I shot a glance at Alex. "Laurent? Prideaux? Bernard? Pelletier? Adler?"

"Oh, yeah. Quite a legacy, huh?" Alex said sarcastically, then grew serious. "Aunt Olivia keeps insisting Laurents weren't pirates, which is a total crock. They were as swashbuckling as the Chaudrets. At least I can be *mildly* proud of the fact the Laurents didn't get involved in slave trading—although I'm not sure why they skipped that particular profession. I'd like to think it was due to conscience and morality, but the reality is probably because they found a better source of income like smuggling whiskey. And, of course, they saw no problem *owning* slaves for at least two centuries. Makes me sick and really ashamed."

Cici squeezed his arm. "You're *not* your ancestors, Alex. Don't go takin' on their evil just 'cuz you've got their name. You be you and do what's right for your life and the lives of those you love."

"You're a smart woman, Miz Cici," I told her.

"She's just repeatin' words from her proud papa," Luc remarked with a huge smile.

"True. But they're such *wise* words, and I try to live by them," Cici kidded her dad.

"Taught her well, didn't I? Always agree with her daddy. And Alex? You can be a pain in the butt, but you got a good heart and you'll be fine if you let your heart guide you." He turned to me. "Seen enough of the Chaudret chateau, Miz Teddie?"

I took a last look and again felt a tightening in my throat. "Definitely. I'm going to have nightmares for the next week. I assume it's haunted?" I'm not sure why I bothered to ask. I already knew.

All three of my fellows in the truck cab chorused, "Yep."

Luc started driving again but I had one last question. "How long has the castle been vacant?"

Luc thought for a second. "Ah believe since the sixties. Still had some Chaudrets livin'—but no one here on the island. The last boy moved outta state. No idea where. So it's been sittin'."

"But everyone seems to want it," Alex chimed in. "Not only the castle, but the beach and the land right around it. And, believe me, *want* is too mild a word."

Chapter 17

The rain and wind were growing in strength, though the pickup remained fierce. Luc was about to pass Chittamwood Gardens but spotted Michael's van and another truck in front of the house. Michael, Zach Prideaux, George Adler, and Eric were in the process of securing the home. Eric was hammering nails into boards at a window on the second floor while Michael steadied the ladder underneath. I closed my eyes and tried not to scream. The entire enterprise looked ridiculously unsafe.

Luc slid the truck into what passed for a driveway. Alex and Cici jumped out as Alex yelled, "Hey, Dad. The storm's comin' in fast. Time to let it go."

Michael kept both hands on the ladder—thankfully—as he called out, "Last window. Then we'll head home since Sugarberry still needs attention."

Eric hammered in one more nail and made his way down the ladder. No boot cast today to slow him down. My pulse started racing at the mere sight of him. His clothes were filthy and he had a cute patch of dirt on his nose. I had to stifle the impulse to run over to him and kiss it off. I watched as he and Michael headed for Michael's van and Michael shouted over his shoulder to Zach and George to wrap it up..

I slid out of Luc's truck and handed Eric one of the remaining bottles of water we'd tossed into the cab. He ushered me to the porch where we'd stay relatively dry.

"Thanks." He eyed me with what appeared to be admiration. "You look good. So, where have you been off to? Napping in the guest quarters?" he jokingly inquired.

"I'll have you know I've been helping make deliveries before the storm. Oh yeah, and we've also been cruising in front of what has to be the spookiest structure on the island."

"Ah. Of course. The castle on Tenth Avenue."

"You've seen it?"

"Not yet. Remember, I got hurt about two days after I arrived, so I haven't been making day trips. Does it live up to its reputation?"

"Well, I'll tell ya, if we can get a mystery theatre going on the island, the Chaudret chateau gets my vote for the perfect spot. Tourists wouldn't even care if there's a show. Simply walking inside would be worth the price of admission." My lips tightened as my stomach tensed.

"There's more? You have a funny look on your face."

"Eric, I didn't say anything to the others, although something tells me Luc sensed it, but… I had one of those weird flashes I've been getting since I arrived."

"What did you see? Or should I say 'feel'?"

"The latter. It flew by in less than a second, more like an impression than some kind of second sight vision, but I could see myself inside the castle and I was terrified."

"We'll have to check it out once the storm is over. It might be locked down tight, but Michael should have a key."

"We can but ask." I paused before adding with more than a touch of sheer anger, "This island is absurd. There's a huge vacant castle on the beach and less than a mile away people are living in homes I'd classify as third-world huts. It's horrible."

Eric's expression turned grim. "Had no idea. Okay. Let's get through the hurricane intact and then see what we can do to make a difference."

"Let it be known that Luc, Alex, Cici, and I are already recruiting for builders and movers and shakers. Oh. You have to meet Miz Vianca Giry, the oldest living island resident, a friend of Jenny's, a former singer, and probably psychic to boot. I instantly adored her."

"How old is she?"

"Somewhere over ninety. Hmm. You thinking what I'm thinking?"

"She could have a ton of info about the history of the first families… and the slaves they owned."

We high-fived. "We're in sync, Mister Desmarais. Okay, we'll put a visit to Miz Vianca on the agenda as soon as the storm ends. So…you're done here, right?"

"Yeah." Eric grabbed my hand and began to swing it as if we were first graders on our way to school. "So, want to drive back with Michael and me? Zach and George have Zach's truck so there's room for one more in Michael's van."

"Sure." I waved at Luc with my free hand and shouted through the wind to tell him I'd stay with Eric and we'd meet everyone back at the Laurent house in a few minutes.

Michael brought his van around while I helped Eric down the porch steps to the vehicle. Once inside I asked Michael if we needed to shore up Eric's carriage house and whether Luc's house was safe.

"All good, Teddie. Luc and Cici took care of their place early this morning and a team led by Sheriff Guidry took care of the carriage house and a couple of the other places on Fourth and Fifth Avenues this afternoon." He glanced at Eric. "You can stay there if you want, but it's safer if you wait out the storm at the Laurent house. We've got a generator and a ton of food and the makings for margaritas or mojitos."

"I'm sold," Eric declared. "Sugarberry Terrace it is, although I'd like to stop at the carriage house for some clean clothes, if you guys don't mind."

Michael turned the van around and headed toward Eric's place. The wind continued to strengthen but no large trees were falling or being ripped from the ground...yet. When we got to Eric's place, I volunteered to go inside and get whatever he needed. His ankle didn't need the stress.

"You sure?"

"Hey, I'm already soaked. I don't care."

"Okay. I'll be less than a gentleman for the time being since I'm lame. Damn, I hate this. Playing helpless is not my strong suit. Anyway, I've got a bag in the front of the bedroom closet with clothes and toiletries already packed."

"Got it. And I'll get it." I reached over and touched his hand. "Quit trying to be Superman. You're already my hero for getting up on a ladder during killer winds and helping save people's houses."

"I'm now thoroughly embarrassed." He lowered his volume. "But I love the idea of being your hero."

Several bones in my spine melted in response.

Eric gave me his key. I opened the van door and sprinted to the house, unlocked the door, headed to the bedroom, and found the bag just where he told me. I also grabbed the quilt off the bed in case extra blankets were needed during the storm.

I stopped, hit with a feeling so intense I nearly fainted. *Jenny.* I could see her, alive but not moving, lying on a bed on a quilt almost identical to the one I now held.

I scooped up Eric's bag and tore back through the carriage house, nearly sliding off the porch as I ran to Michael's van. "We're not too late, we're not too late, we can't be too late," I kept repeating like a mantra meant to keep desperation at bay.

I could tell Eric knew I'd discovered more than his bag the moment he laid eyes on me. "Teddie? What happened? Are you okay?"

"It's Jenny," I shouted. "We need to go. Now."

Michael turned around and stared at me before shifting the car into reverse. "What?"

"I know where she is."

"Where?" Eric asked.

"Hickory Shadows."

"But you guys were there this morning," Michael argued.

"Well, to be clear, we were in the cellar. Look, Michael, something hit me while I was inside Eric's house. A vibe or vision. Does it matter? When I picked up this quilt, it was like Jenny was sending me a message. Did y'all go there today to board it up?"

Michael shook his head.

Eric immediately said, "It can't hurt to check." He looked at me for a tense second before focusing back on Michael. "Teddie has had some feelings like this and they've led to some interesting discoveries today. And the house isn't far."

Michael put his hand up. "Hey, it's fine. I'm desperate. Any possibility of finding Jenny is worth following, no matter how wacky the source. Hang on, guys, I'm about to break speed records."

He did. We were at Hickory Shadows within two minutes. I had the van door open before Michael completely braked. Eric swung out of the van at the same time Michael was jumping out, and all three of us headed for the porch. Michael and I helped Eric up the steps and still managed to keep a brisk pace even while trying to maintain balance on rain-slicked steps.

The door wouldn't open.

"Damn," I cried. "Anyone have the key?"

Eric put his hand up. "Wait. Take a breath. It's stuck; not locked. Shoulders everyone."

We pushed and the heavy door finally gave and let us in.

Michael turned to me as though I was a prized bloodhound, his voice breaking. "Teddie?" Where is she? It's a huge house. Any ideas?"

"This floor. Bedroom."

We split up so each of us could dart into a room. I took a moment to close my eyes and let whatever mystic visions interested in piercing my consciousness do their magic. Again, it was as if Jenny was calling to me. I abruptly reversed course and headed the opposite direction from both Eric and Michael toward a room at the end of the hall. I opened the door to what had once been a lovely bedroom, with furniture and décor straight out of a set from a Civil War film.

There was a canopied double bed with a huge, ornate headboard taking up half the space. The identical quilt from the carriage house lay under the one occupant. *Jenny*. A small half-filled bottle of pills sat on a nightstand alongside a glass of water. More pills were scattered along the stand.

The room stank of vomit, faintly of Jenny's favorite lemon-scented body spray, and of fear. Evidence that Jenny had lost the contents of her last meals over this twenty-four-hour period was all over the room, from the bed to the bathroom.

I leaned down and lifted Jenny's wrist and felt a pulse. She was weak and not totally conscious, but my best friend was alive.

Chapter 18

I didn't want to leave Jenny's side for even a second, so I yelled, "Eric. Michael," as I lifted Jenny's head and moved a larger pillow underneath so there'd be less chance of choking.

Both men raced into the room.

"Is she...?" Michael breathed out, his voice evincing sheer panic.

"She's alive. Not in great shape though."

Tears flowed down Michael's cheeks. He moved to the side of the bed and cradled Jenny in his arms. She opened her eyes, moaned, and whispered, "Home."

"We've got to get her out of here. Is there any kind of clinic on this island?" I asked.

"There's a first aid station connected to the sheriff's office and what passes as a firehouse," Eric answered. "I was able to get my foot x-rayed there when I fell. Are they even open?"

"The only doctor's stuck on the mainland," Michael answered, plainly frustrated. "We have a nurse practitioner, but I haven't heard from him. I'm not sure there's anyone at the clinic who can really help."

"Well, let's take her to Sugarberry Terrace. *Now.*" I took a deep breath. "Not to be indelicate, but I'd say her own body took care of some serious stomach pumping. She's obviously dehydrated and needs real rest as well."

"What?" Michael finally looked around at the end table. "Oh God. Sleeping pills? Do you think—?"

"No. And don't you think it either. Those are pain pills. Look, we can talk about how she got here and why and who and where later. We need to leave." I glanced out the window. "I've never lived through a hurricane, but I've watched enough weather programs to be pretty sure quiet and a yellow sky means all hell is going to break loose soon, so it's time to haul it and get Jenny to safety. *Now.*"

Michael grabbed his cell phone. "I'm calling the house to tell them we're coming and to get one of the downstairs guest rooms ready." He dialed the house landline and immediately launched into what I thought was way too much information, telling Olivia we'd found Jenny, and he thought she'd taken an overdose of pills, she was in bad shape, but we were on our way and to keep the doors open and ready the guest room.

I scooped up the shoulder bag next to Jenny's side, tossed the spray mist bottle lying on top of her bag inside and then grabbed the bottle of pills and dumped them into my own bag. Eric and I helped lift Jenny into Michael's arms and we hurried out of the bedroom, down the hall, and out to Michael's van as fast as Eric could hobble.

The eerie stillness held for the three minutes it took us to drive to the Laurent house, with Michael nearly crashing the van as he barreled over broken branches.

"Damn. Michael, be careful," I cried.

Eric echoed my concern. "Slow down. Won't help Jenny if we crash."

Michael ignored us both, avoiding a particularly large tree branch by swerving off the road and making a sharp turn around it. He muttered, "I'm going to the back door. There's a wheelchair ramp there left from when we needed it with Cyril and it'll be easier to bring Jenny inside. Teddie, how's she doing?"

The men had placed Jenny on the second row of seats in the van with me able to cradle her head in my lap. She was angled in such as way so she wasn't flat on her back, and I continued to check to be sure she was breathing and couldn't choke. "She's hanging in there. Really," I reassured Michael.

I couldn't tell if he'd heard me. Didn't matter. He shouted, "We're here. Let's go," and had his arms around Jenny, lifting her up almost before I could release my own grip.

"Perfect timing," Eric noted. "I'd say we have about two minutes before the storm really breaks."

Michael carried Jenny into the house. Eric asked if he could help, but Michael told him to go rest his foot while he had the chance, then ran to the parlor. Once we reached the guest room, Michael laid Jenny down on the bed. I found extra pillows to help prop her head up and placed the clean quilt from Eric's bed around her. I figured it would help keep her from going into shock, although I was terrified she already had.

Our arrival had not gone unnoticed. A slew of folks who'd been in the parlor, including Olivia, Zach, Renee, Alex, Monique, Robin, and George, swarmed into the guest room accompanied by gasps and phrases of "you found her," "poor Jenny," "is she alive?" "where was she?" and "Overdose? How dreadful." I couldn't sort out who was saying what, although my senses detected an emotional note not quite in sync or pitch with the words. I didn't have time to analyze it but tucked it away in my brain for later consideration. The only concern now was Jenny.

Michael stepped away from the bed and turned to face the crowd. For a moment the only sound was the rain, pounding and battering against the boarded windows as though determined to break through. I was grateful the heavy downpours had held off until we'd stepped inside the Laurent house but suddenly realized I was soaked from the last wave of water we'd encountered as we'd run inside.

I focused on Michael, who raised his hand for silence. "Okay, everyone, brief report. We found Jenny at Hickory Shadows and rushed back here as fast as we could. She needs a doctor, but until the storm passes we can't get her to the first aid station or the mainland. Now, not to be rude but I want everyone out of this room…except Teddie. Go back to the parlor."

I inwardly applauded Michael finally taking charge and stepping up to protect his wife. The crowd dispersed and presumably went to the parlor, where no doubt Luc had prepared something for the band of storm refugees.

As soon as the doorway was vacant, Cici stepped inside. "Eric told Papa and me you found Jenny and she's really sick. I'm certified in CPR and first aid so thought I might be able to help." She looked at me and at Michael, noticed our wet clothes, and tried to smile. "If nothin' else, I can stay here with Jenny while y'all go change into something dry. We don't need anyone catchin' pneumonia to add to the drama."

Michael and I both meekly left the room. He immediately headed toward the front staircase leading to the main bedrooms, but I turned around and held out my hand to Cici. She took it and we squeezed, sharing a perfect understanding.

"Cici, thank you. I can't begin to tell you what it means having someone in this room we can trust. Well, you probably already know, but I wanted to say it anyway."

"I'll take good care of her." Her tone turned fierce. "And I promise to guard this room like one of those gargoyles we saw at the castle. Now git."

I got.

I snuck through a short hallway from the guest room and circled to the front stairs leading to the tower so I could avoid the mob in the parlor. I wondered if Eric was currently spinning a tale for the curious, or if he'd been able to escape and find a room to change into dry clothes.

A shower sounded like heaven to me, but it's not an activity best enjoyed during a hurricane and the tower room's windows were un-boarded, making the area a less-than-safe space. I changed into jeans and a clean shirt. The way events were unfolding on the island, it appeared I wouldn't be parading around in anything other than work clothes for the next few days, though, I guiltily thought, it would be nice to have Eric see me in something pretty for a change. I didn't bother trying to towel my hair dry. I just pulled it back into a ponytail, found a clean pair of sneakers, and I was done.

I took the stairs two at a time, anxious to check in with Cici and see how Jenny was doing... and to hear what was being said in the parlor. Once I got to the bottom, I tiptoed down the hall to the guest room and peeked in.

"How's she doing?" I whispered.

"She's breathin' better, Teddie. Still kind of in and out though, which worries me."

"Me too. Do you want me to spell you?"

"Nah, I'm good. And you need to get somethin' to eat. I was starvin' by the time we got back from deliveries and you must feel the same, 'specially with the added stress of findin' Jenny."

Jenny must have heard her name. She stirred and threw her arm up as if warding off someone from touching her. She began to cry. I joined Cici by the bedside.

Jenny opened her eyes, but I could tell she wasn't seeing me. Instead she stared straight ahead and cried out one word. A name. "Chaudret."

Chapter 19

Jenny closed her eyes again, leaving Cici and me to stare at each other in astonishment

"Not to sound like a Christmas carol, but did you hear what I heard?" I asked.

"Chaudret."

"As in the first pirate family? As in dudes who haven't been seen on Endgate for like seventy years? Who supposedly died out?"

Cici grimaced. "Well, I'm officially spooked now. Did she get visited by a ghost?"

"Heck, on this island, it wouldn't surprise me."

"I wish Miz Vianca was here."

"Because she's smart, loves Jenny, or has great insight?"

"Oh... all of the above. But mainly 'cause she knows everyone who's been on Endgate since she was born more n' ninety-odd years ago and—"

"Maybe the pirate family didn't all die out?" I conjectured.

"Yeah."

"I'm not sure if it's creepier to believe descendants of the Chaudrets are roaming around the island or if old Jacques himself is hanging out at old houses for the sheer fun of it."

We were interrupted when the door opened and Eric limped inside. He'd traded his soaked shirt and pants for clean, dry jeans and a tee and looked way too good, but was clearly in pain after being on his feet too much today. "Any change?" he asked.

"No and yes," I answered. "Thank God you're here. You're needed not only for some damned fine moral and physical support, but for your mind and common sense. Both of which seem to have deserted me."

"Meaning?"

I told him about Jenny sitting up and breathing out the name "Chaudret" then collapsing again. Eric and I were in sync. He started asking the same questions about how Jenny could have seen a dead Chaudret.

"I did theorize we have a ghost roaming the island," I told him, not quite joking. "After all, the castle is supposed to be haunted."

"I love this fanciful side of you, Teddie Grant, but I'm more apt to go with the idea of an anonymous heir, perhaps one who resembles a portrait of old Jacques, sneaking into Hickory Shadows and scaring the living fool out of Jenny." He paused. "Bastard."

"Damn. It just keeps getting worse. Imagine... living Chaudrets throwing their hat into the 'I own the island' ring. Do you think it's possible?"

"Sure. It's not really a stretch, given this island's size and intermarrying for four hundred years, to imagine more than one member of the Chaudret family is currently living here with a different last name."

"Okay, but what does this have to do with Jenny?" I asked, feeling distinctly lost. "Could she really have discovered a—oh let's say 'Smith' since as far as I can tell there's no one on the island with a Smith surname—um, did she find a John Smith who's really Jacques the twentieth or something? Or to be equal with gender, if a Jane Smith is really Grace Chaudret the who-knows-how-many generations removed?"

"It's as good a theory as anything else," said Eric.

Someone tapped on the door.

Eric made a quick decision. "Ladies? For the time being, I vote we keep this quiet."

"Agreed," Cici and I chorused. We could trust Michael, Alex, and Luc, but the more people who knew Jenny and a Chaudret had something in common meant looking at more people who could slip up and chatter. In which case, the entire island would be speculating and driving her crazy or trying to harm Jenny in order to hide what someone obviously considered a dangerous secret or two.

Eric opened the door and let Olivia inside. "Is she conscious? Everyone's worried."

"She's in and out," I told her. "Where's Michael?"

"I made him sit down and eat. I've never seen him so stressed and upset. We don't need another invalid in the house, especially with too many outsiders camped out in the parlor taking shelter." She glanced at Jenny. "I do wish the doctor hadn't been caught on the mainland earlier today. I'd breathe easier if a medical professional was on hand if she takes a bad turn."

I tried not to wince. The words "bad turn" scared me more than I could express.

Another knock. This time the new arrival was Luc, and the sight of his concerned face reassured me all would be well. He took quick control, motioning first to me. "You go eat, Miz Teddie, before you end up passed out with Miz Jenny. Cici, Ah need you to take over in the kitchen and Ah'll spell you here with Miz Jenny. Mister Eric, get off yo' bad foot once n' fer all, and go eat with Miz Teddie. Ah've got y'all plates in the kitchen so you don't have to deal with the mob in the parlor. Miz Olivia, your guests are asking for you. There's lots 'a curiosity about Miz Jenny and I s'pose they 'spect you to answer."

Olivia, Cici, Eric, and I meekly followed orders from the Laurent chef and let him take over the guard duties. A Doberman inside a gated community was the first image crossing my mind when I saw his expression as he closed the door behind us.

The instant we entered the parlor we were besieged by inquiries about Jenny. My unspoken question, which had nothing to do with my friend, was why these people—who presumably had real live homes on the island—had chosen to camp out at Sugarberry Terrace. I supposed their choice had everything to do with gossip and action, and of course the promise of finding the best food on the island.

My supposition was correct, at least regarding rumor and speculation. Four voices assaulted me within seconds of entering the parlor, all with the same inquiry: "Where did you find Jenny?"

I could smell soup and fresh bread from Luc's kitchen, but getting there meant dealing with a barricade of bodies and questions. So, I held up my hand for silence and responded, "We found Jenny at Hickory Shadows."

Zach was first to counter with, "Why didn't you and Eric see her when you were there in the morning?"

It was a logical, sane question and my brain quit on me before I could come up with a clever response. Eric took over and managed not to lie without getting into the whole truth of exploring the cellar instead of the house. "Because we didn't check the upstairs bedrooms. She was probably unconscious at the time and had no idea we were there."

Renee rudely asked if it was true Jenny had taken pills.

I had no idea how to answer. Did we say we'd found a bottle, half filled, on the nightstand? Did I say "yes, but it was obvious they'd been forced on her"?

Monique noticed my hesitation and followed up on Renee's question. "What are you *not* sayin', Teddie? You don't want to admit your friend tried to kill herself?"

I gasped and had to hold myself back from crossing the room and smacking her face, an action I've never done in my life. I'm slow to anger but these people seemed determined to change my pacifist personality traits with every word they spoke.

Eric replied before I could say or do anything I might regret. "Look, we're still in the dark about what happened. We're lucky we found Jenny and could bring her home before the storm hit." He deliberately tried to lighten the mood. "And discovered Mister Michael Laurent has some mad race-car driver skills. If I'd thought to turn my phone's camera on, heck… we'd've gone viral by now."

It was my turn to back him up. "Eric's right. Um, thanks, everybody, for the interest and care about Jenny, but I'm personally so exhausted I can barely stand, so I'm heading to the kitchen to grab some food."

Two minutes later I was diving into a spicy vegetable gumbo over rice. Eric joined me as I was slathering butter on my second slice of bread. He slid into a chair opposite me and stirred honey and lemon into iced tea.

He growled. "I swear it's like a White House press briefing after a scandal. All details wanted. And I'm not giving them."

"Same here," I said. "Eric, do we rebut the accusations of suicide or leave them hanging in the air? Forget reputation. Which is safer for Jenny?"

Eric shrugged, not as a gesture of indifference, but of honestly not knowing. "Not to be indelicate, but are you positive she *didn't* take those pills? It would be nice to have some evidence one way or another. And she has been horribly unhappy."

We were the only people in the kitchen and the rain and wind made it almost impossible to be overheard, but I was feeling somewhat paranoid, so leaned forward and lowered my volume.

"Eric, those pills were either forced down her throat or dissolved in water and she drank it down because she was simply thirsty."

"Why are you so sure?"

"All emotional, loyal-to-best-friend-type reasons aside, I have clear memories of our sophomore year in college after Jenny had her wisdom teeth extracted and was prescribed pain pills with codeine in them. About thirty minutes after she took one, I found her in the bathroom losing her dinner and her breakfast and every meal from the previous week. Which was when we discovered Jenny Harrison reacts violently to codeine. I grabbed the bottle and the pills when we were at Hickory Shadows. They're in my room now." I glanced up at him. "Eric, the bottle was yours."

"*What?*"

"The label has your name on it. What were you given when you hurt your ankle?"

"Pain pills with codeine." He sounded stunned. "*My* pills? Who would...?"

"I'm assuming they were dissolved in some drink. She didn't willingly put those drugs in her system. Eric, she was forced to take them. They might have been meant to simply knock her out... or someone tried to kill Jenny Harrison Laurent."

Chapter 20

Luc Bouvier had not only found time to bake bread and make gumbo, but he'd stashed a fresh key lime pie into the fridge. It was untouched and uncut, and meant specifically for Miz Teddie Grant, who'd missed out on last night's ice cream. Clearly Luc believed I'd waste away without dessert.

"Eric, want a slice? I'm being generous with the sweets, here, so take advantage before I go full-tilt glutton."

"You're too kind," he said with feigned sincerity, paused for about a second, then grinned. "Pass it over, Grant, before I grab it and lose all sense of decorum."

We spent the next ten minutes devouring the best pie I'd had in my life, relishing the quiet time and pushing away—at least briefly—the raging storm outside and the tension, anger, and general confusion brewing inside. After scraping the last trace of key lime off my plate, I leaned back and sighed.

"I hate to wreck the mood, but we may not have a lot of time safely hiding in here before life breaks and guests interfere, so…"

"So, on to less pleasant things, like why did someone attempt to murder Jenny?"

I inhaled. "Oh my God. I said it to myself earlier. I thought it. And I heard a note in someone's voice when we first came in with Jenny that didn't ring true. As though one of the guests here knew full well what had happened to Jenny. But hearing you say it flat out makes it *true*. Someone tried to kill her. I knew she was in real danger from the moment I arrived on this island and heard she was missing, but I've been pushing it out of my mind. Total denial. Which won't help Jenny."

"Teddie, don't beat yourself up. It's been an insane day. An insane couple of days actually. One discovery after another, although what we found in the ledger doesn't feel like an immediate crisis since the Emeric Desmarais from Endgate Island has been lost since

1865." He shot me a *don't go there* look. "And yes, I'm aware there's something…else…about my ancestor, but I readily admit I'm avoiding diving into what that something is at this point. And I'm sorry, that probably didn't make sense."

"Strangely enough, it did. You're good. Go on."

"Well, we're in the middle of a storm and we all might get blown out to the Gulf or into New Orleans, depending upon which way the wind shifts. We have to take a breath and get some rest and regroup and be ready to investigate…whatever we need to investigate."

"I wish we had a few moments to take those breaths and rest. By the way, what time is it? Feels like it's about two in the morning."

Eric pointed to the giant rooster clock hanging on the wall behind me. "Don't look. You'll go into shock. It's only ten p.m. Two hours before the proverbial witching hour."

"On this island it would more accurately be called the ghosts' hour," I tried to joke as I took another sip of tea. "Speaking of ghosts, I keep trying to figure out what Jenny meant by 'Chaudret'? Oh nuts. Why am I bothering to speculate? She should be more awake soon—I hope—and can tell us why she said it, and why and *how* those pills got into her system, and maybe why somebody didn't want you or Jenny exploring old houses." I paused. "Totally off topic, but is your cell working and is it with you?"

Eric reached into his pants pocket and handed me a fully charged phone with four bars announcing it was still a valid means of communication to the outside world.

"Thanks. I want to call my dad in Texas and tell him I haven't been swept out into the Gulf…yet. Not sure how long we'll all have cell power."

"Want privacy?"

"Nah. Neither of us are big phone talkers, but I don't want him to worry. I'll give him the basics and let him get some sleep."

I called and filled my dad in on the news about the storm, adding if he didn't hear from me in two days to call out the National Guard or send our old German Shepherd, Moxie, over to Endgate Island to hunt me down.

I handed the phone back to Eric, and then took our dishes and glasses to the sink, turned on the hot water, and prepared to clean. It felt good to do something as normal and domestic as washing dishes in a kitchen with a man who had the ability to have my entire being tingle merely by being in the same room with him. I wished he was ready to break down a few barriers, but I had faith the crash was coming.

"There *is* a dishwasher, Teddie," Eric noted with amusement.

He had one arm stretched across the back of the chair next to him, his leg up on another, and a look of amusement—obviously at my expense—on his handsome face. He looked at ease and worlds more approachable than he had when I had met him the other day. I wondered how I had managed to find a man I found so exceptionally attractive—and attractive in all the ways that mattered—on this godforsaken island of all places.

I felt my cheeks flush with heat and kept my gaze firmly on the dishes and away from him. "Yeah, yeah, but I'll feel like I'm helping more doing these by hand. Also, if the power goes out mid-cycle, which is more than likely, Luc would have a major mess to deal with."

"True. Want a super-toweler offer?"

"Normally, yes. But I'm declining because you need to stay off your foot, so I'll make do with the tried-and-true dish rack technique."

Since the water was running and the rain was crashing against the windows and roof, Eric and I gave up trying to talk until the dishes were clean, we were clear of the kitchen, and were heading down the back hallway to the guest room.

Luc stood right outside the door, which he'd left open about three inches.

"Luc, how is she?" I whispered.

"Better. Little more life in her. Ah got her to drink a glass of water and some broth. Michael went in 'bout thirty seconds ago."

Jenny's voice suddenly rose, angry, and louder than the storm. "Get out, Michael. Now. If you're stupid enough to believe I'd actually try to take my own life, then you never should have married me and I sure as hell don't want you around. Didn't you hear me? Get *out*."

Luc, Eric, and I backed away from the door as Michael opened it further and joined us in the hall. He looked devastated. "She hates me."

I privately thought if the man couldn't give my best friend the benefit of the doubt about how pills had gotten into her system then he deserved to be hated, but I didn't voice my opinion. Instead, I tried to sound optimistic and caring when I responded. "Michael, Jenny doesn't hate you. She's confused and she's sick and she nearly died and... Well, she's got a point. Jenny has *never* been suicidal, and she needs your trust. Now more than ever."

Michael stared at me. "Why did she take an overdose if she wasn't trying to kill herself? Can you explain why? I'm serious. Can you?"

We were keeping our voices low but I'd had enough. I pushed open the door and hurried to Jenny's side. She was crying, so I sat on the bed, helped her sit up, gave her a box of tissues and waited while she blew her nose, then scolded her like a mom keeping her child from touching a hot stove, "Enough. You need to tell us what happened. Before things get even further out of control. Okay?"

She hung her head down and sniffed a tear away. "I've missed you, Theodosia."

We hugged each other. "Same here." No other words were necessary.

Luc waved at me. "Ah'll leave her in your hands, Miz Teddie. Ah need to get back to the kitchen before the mob starts whinin' for food. Bet anything the power is gonna go out in 'bout five minutes, so Ah'll be makin' sandwiches fast as Ah can."

He left. Eric broke what had become a tense silence by asking, "Is everyone okay having me in this room at this time? I don't want to intrude."

Jenny motioned for Eric to take the rocking chair close to the window and said, "Stay, Eric. Please."

Michael remained standing at the door, appearing unsure as to whether to stay or go.

I handed Jenny another glass of water and suggested she take a sip before starting her story. She waved it away and stated, with a surprising amount of humor, "Luc has spent the last hour trying to drown me with broth and water. Besides, we need to leave some water for a sponge bath in case I'm too weak to make it to the shower. I stink and I doubt I'll be invited to the best homes until I'm a bit fresher."

"Uh-huh. This *is* the best home on the island, and you're in it and not about to get tossed out. You are so full of it, girl. Now...give."

She inhaled. "Okay. First, a little backstory. I came up with the idea of using one of those huge old mansions as a theatre a couple of months ago. I found out two of them were owned by the Laurents and they'd been vacant for years, so I started exploring to see what kind of shape they were in, if they needed to be renovated, and of course, if they had the right ambiance. About five weeks ago, I found an old diary in the cellar at Hickory Shadows." She glanced at Eric. "The one I told you about with the name Desmarais. The primary reason you're on this damned island."

"And you got in touch with me and told me you hadn't had time to read much of the diary but were intrigued with the possibility I was related to someone who once…lived on Endgate." He didn't say, "who was once a slave on Endgate and might be a lot more than an ancestor," but it was obvious where his thoughts had taken him. "I agreed to come down as soon as I could, which wasn't for another couple of weeks."

"Yep. Then I put the diary in the tower room and a few days later it was gone. I got scared. Why would anyone want an old diary written more than a hundred years ago by some dumb Chaudret daughter? But, stupid me… I go charging off continuing to look at the old houses, especially Hickory Shadows, although I really wanted *Chateau Sans Frontieres* because a spooky old castle would bring folks to the island like nothing else—but we're all still dealing with the whole nagging issue of ownership." She held up her hand for a second. "Hang on. You up on the big first families' fight, Teddie, or do I need to explain?"

"Let's say it's messy. I've heard various stories from multiple sources."

Jenny shot me a sharp look. "I'll bet. Well, I should have let the idea go. But nooooo. I move on to Chittamwood Gardens. It's also got a cellar. I thought a cellar would be perfect for mysteries since you need a ton of exits and trapdoors."

Her breathing seemed shallow but the look on her face was defiant. She was going to finish her story even if she passed out the moment she uttered the last sentence.

I patted her hand, trying to hide my worry. "Don't rush it. Breathe deep and stay calm. Uh, consider it as an observation exercise for Acting 101."

She wrinkled her nose at me. "I don't recall ending up on a bed in my own vomit following a recital of activities on the way to class any time."

"I imagine I'd've remembered," I said dryly. I paused. "Ready?"

"Yeah." She coughed, then resumed the narrative. "Okay. So, I check out the cellar in Chittamwood Gardens. Found some great old steamer trunks and a bunch of cartons and figured I'd ask Alex and Cici to help me put them into Michael's van and bring them back here. I get to the top of the stairs... and the door won't open. I'm banging on it and it won't open—even though I'd had no trouble thirty minutes earlier. It was either locked or blocked. After I got over some initial hysteria and panic, I figured if Hickory Shadows had a passage from the cellar, then Chittamwood Gardens had one. I mean, these crazy pirates built all these shallow tunnels to hide their booty. On a friggin' *island*. Anyway, I remembered where the Third Avenue passage was in relation to the stairs and I found it and kicked through a pile of furniture blocking the entrance. Hauled it home. Gang, I knew there was trouble on Endgate Island."

Eric raised an eyebrow. "Nice title, Jenny."

She beamed. "It is, isn't it? Okay. I came up with a job notice and sent out a mass e-mail so I could bring Teddie down here with no one the wiser as to why I needed her. In retrospect, pretty paranoid and probably not my finest plan."

"It got me here."

"It did."

We looked at each other in perfect understanding.

"So, anyway, That's the backstory. Then, I managed to get Eric to fly down from New York and I asked him to explore the cellar over at Hickory Shadows. He didn't make it halfway down before the stairs collapsed and he's hurt. Yeah. Upped my anxiety by about ten notches, but I still hoped his accident was really accidental... maybe some rotten old wood. Then I kept telling myself maybe I'd misplaced the diary. Yeah. Right. Jenny being delusional." She scowled at Michael. "And my husband didn't seem terribly interested." She stopped. I could sense she was battling the desire to burst into tears or simply embark into one whopping big hysterical breakdown.

Eric prompted her as the silence grew. "Go on. We're at the part where I'm here but injured, Teddie was on her way to the island from Manhattan…so what happened yesterday morning?"

Jenny was clearly beyond exhausted but determined to finish. She took a deep breath but before she could get another word out, we heard a crash and the power went out, plunging Endgate Island into darkness.

Chapter 21

There was silence in the guest room for a good minute following the power outage. Finally, Eric pulled out his phone with its LED light beaming brightly. "I have a feeling the crash we heard was the cell tower hitting more than one power line. But hey. Could all the theatre people have asked for a better setting for scary tales?" he asked. "No offense, Teddie, but looks like Mother Nature has one-upped your efforts in design."

I let my shoulders relax. "Well, She has the advantage of large trees being uprooted and flying around taking down wires. I never seem to have a tech crew willing to attempt a hurricane." I paused and reached down to take Jenny's hand. "How ya doin,' Miz Jenny? Ready for the finale of your story?"

"Ah hell, all things considered, a few lights and the A/C going out are nothing."

Michael spoke for the first time since Jenny had started her recitation of the events of the last month. "We *do* have a generator." He tentatively added, "I guess I need to do a check on it for all the folks still in our parlor so they stay comfortable."

Jenny's answer was a monotone. "If it's more important."

Michael inhaled and finally appeared to find his spine. "No. It's not. And Alex is perfectly capable of connecting it and getting it going." He pulled out a small vanity chair and sank down onto it. "Jenny, I had no idea all this was happening over these last weeks. Why didn't you tell me you were locked inside the cellar? Or you believed Eric's accident was deliberate? Or you were so desperate for help you were afraid to contact Teddie directly instead of a disguised job notice?"

Jenny sniffed. I couldn't tell if it signaled a snub or annoyance or a way to hold back a major onslaught of tears. "I kept quiet because you've been involved with crazy people arguing about who owns what and I didn't want to bother you. And we've, well, we've…"

Eric interrupted before Jenny strayed too far into what could be a marital discussion. "Why don't you two wait for a better time to discuss those issues? Unless you'd prefer Teddie and I stepped out?"

Michael flushed. "Sorry. You're right. Look, if everybody is good with the lack of light, let's have Jenny finish before fifteen people come bursting in here freaking out because some stupid tree crashed."

The door opened and Luc backed in, balancing a tray of sandwiches and a large hurricane lantern and pulling what appeared to be a child's wagon filled with bottled water.

"Wanted to get these to y'all before your guests grab 'em," Luc said. "And Mister Michael? The generator's not workin'. Alex, Cici, Zach, and Robin are messin' with it... not mah area 'a expertise, so Ah have no idea what they're doin'. But don' y'all worry. If we get power, we get power. The good news is the wind seems to be lessenin' a bit. So, y'all stay here with Miz Jenny."

We thanked him and he headed back to the kitchen for more food and water to deliver to anyone who was still up and hungry.

"Michael? Where's everyone staying?" I asked.

"We've got enough bedrooms if our guests don't mind doubling up. At this point, I don't care. My only concern is Jenny."

Jenny came close to beaming at her husband. Finally, Michael was saying what Michael should have been saying for weeks...or perhaps even months.

She grabbed a bottle of water and took a small sip. "Ready to hear the rest?"

There was a chorus of yes from everyone in the room

"Okay then. Yesterday morning I hadn't planned on doing anything but waiting for Teddie to arrive, and was actually checking her room to be sure she had extra bedding and towels and those foo-foo bath sets I knew she'd love." She pointed at me with glee.

"I plead the fifth."

"Uh-huh. Anyway, my cell rings. I didn't check caller ID, just picked it up and answered. And I'm told...of all crazy things...it was about old Miz Vianca. Ooh. I need to introduce you two."

"Met her today. Already love her."

"She is lovable, isn't she?" Jenny acknowledged with a large grin. "Anyway, someone told me Miz Vianca had some documents I'd find interesting about the castle, and this person was calling because Miz Vianca's phone was out but she'd meet me at Hickory Shadows. I thought it was one of the kids in the neighborhood. Teddie, you weren't due to arrive for another two hours, so I got dressed in these now disgusting clothes and grabbed my bag and took off. I left a note on the board by the mudroom in the back by the ramp where we always put stickies."

Michael's voice was grim. "There was no note. I must have checked that damned board fifteen times over the last two days hoping for some clue as to where you were. We never lock doors on the island so it would have been easy for someone to walk off with it."

"We did have a busy little kidnapper, didn't we," Eric commented in a dark tone. "Damn him. Or her. Making calls, setting up traps, stealing notes. Sorry, Jenny, go ahead."

"Where was I? Oh. Note. I left it and went off like Little Red Riding Hood to visit Grandma not realizing the wolf was way ahead of me."

"Nice analogy," I told her as we fist bumped with grim amusement.

"Scary fairy tale. Even scarier when it's real. Anyway, I'm at Hickory Shadows. I grab a bottle of water out of my bag and drink a little, then set it on the counter in the kitchen. I start roaming through the house calling for Miz Vianca until I finally decide I'll call her. No answer—but I was getting suspicious since it rang and I knew the power was on. I went back to the kitchen for more water. I was going to call Michael and see if he could drive to Vianca's place. Anyway, the bottled water. I always use a filter and this had a normal cap on it instead, but I didn't notice. Next thing I'm hallucinating and someone's leading me out of the house into a car and driving toward Tenth Avenue. I swear those bloody gargoyles were laughing at me. I have no idea if I ended up in the castle itself or not. At some point I was back at Hickory Shadows on a bed and sick as a dog." She began to cough.

I handed her a glass of water. "Drink, then tell me if you could see what time it was."

She quickly drank down the full glass. "Crap. I couldn't even tell what *day* it was. No clocks in the room, no phone, and all I could tell from the window was it was sort of light out. Whether it was yesterday or today? No clue. And honestly, I didn't give a damn. I wanted out of there. If I had to guess, I'd say it was this afternoon because the air had kind of a 'before a storm' feel, even inside a house."

"I wonder if you moved more than once while you were out of it? And since you were walking and seeing things, it sounds like you had a little something in your water before the pain pills."

Eric grimly surmised, "Like roofies. Victims walk and talk and don't remember later."

I was so angry I could barely speak. My best friend had been doped with something designed to make her forget. Then she'd been doped with something potentially lethal. "Whoever did this must have realized Eric and I were going to Hickory Shadows this morning and kept you somewhere else overnight. We only explored the cellar, but I'm sure my radar would have sensed you were in that bedroom. Doesn't matter. What happened after you woke up? Do you remember?"

"Things got creepy. Scary creepy." She paused. "I mean, even more than they'd been when I realized someone had either followed me or was waiting for me." She stopped and poured more water for herself before adding, "I'm in the bedroom and the door opens and in walks Jacques Chaudret."

"Oh boy," I said. "Nothing like a pirate ghost making an entrance. At least it explains why you were moaning Chaudret when you woke up here."

"I wish it *had* been old Jacques," she claimed with determined spunk. "We'd have had a great chat and I'd've found out the truth about his marriage to Grace Sedley. But seriously, someone— couldn't tell the gender—was wearing a pirate costume from around the seventeenth century, but believe me, he—or she—was *not* one of the sexy swashbuckling heroes of the movies—and definitely didn't have the charm."

Michael's voice shook. "Could you see a face at all?"

"No. The pirate king or queen had the traditional stocking. Black stocking. Holes for eyes, but I was so terrified I couldn't tell you if they were blue, green, violet, brown, or cat yellow. Next thing I knew there was a glass in my hand and a gun in my face and it was obvious, even with no speaking involved, well... I had a choice. Drink or be shot. I chose the former, praying the nasty pirate would leave and I could do the finger down the throat thing."

Michael was crying. "I'm so sorry. How could I have thought you'd have taken pills yourself? I'm so sorry."

Eric stopped him. "Michael. Let her finish."

Jenny continued, "The pirate left and I immediately felt sick, probably because I wasn't exactly energetic already after whatever was in the first bottle. Anyway, the next thing I knew I was throwing up all over the room."

"Codeine," I stated.

"Aha. That explains why I was having flashbacks to college and the great wisdom teeth disaster. But I was so sleepy and I didn't want to fall down on the floor and hit my head, so I lay down on the bed after my last bout of sick. The last thing I actually remember was pulling out my body mist spray and showering myself with it in the hope someone would come looking for me and get a whiff and find me."

"Which we did."

"Which *you* did, Teddie," came from Michael. "We owe you for saving Jenny's life."

I brushed it aside. "Hey. Best friends forever. Even when dealing with pirates and kidnappers."

Jenny fell back against the pillows piled on the headboard. "I love all of you, and am so grateful you found me, but I'm also past exhausted and I need to rest. Michael, we have a lot to talk about, but tonight's not the night and you need to go help with the generator and make sure everyone is safe and dry and not nuts over lost power. Teddie? Eric? I hate to ask this, but could you guys get some sleeping bags and spend the night in here? I'd feel a lot safer."

Michael wasn't thrilled about being dismissed but obviously didn't want to cause a scene, and he knew Jenny was right. It wasn't the right time or place for them to fight or make up or both. Jenny might be on the road to forgiving him, but it was clear she was at least one good conversation short of trusting him. He told Eric where to find sleeping bags and took off after bestowing a light kiss on Jenny's forehead.

I watched Michael head down the hall and stifled a laugh. It was obvious this was not going to be a romantic evening with Eric Desmarais, assuming he ever wanted to initiate anything more than friendship. Didn't matter. I was about to sit out a hurricane playing guard dog to my best friend, making sure some wacko in a pirate suit didn't get another chance to kill her.

Chapter 22

Eric started to follow Michael down the hall to raid a back closet that held the Laurent family camping gear, including sleeping bags, but I stopped him before he'd gone three steps.

"Eric, could you wait about twenty minutes before bringing the bags?"

"Sure. What's up?"

"Jenny needs a shower worse than a dog who's rolled in a dead carp on the beach. Thankfully, there's this lovely little guest bath. But I really should stay close by in case she passes out."

Jenny, lying on the bed, let out a distinct snort. "Gee, thank you *sooo* much, Theodosia, for publicly announcing I stink…which, yeah, I do. Go away, Eric. When you get back, the air will be fresh and I will be much less cranky. Then again, with power out the water will be cold, so I might be raging furious."

He left, swinging his cell phone ahead of him like a flashlight so Jenny and I could keep the lantern. Jenny told me the antique dresser held some extra T-shirts and jeans, which would work nicely for both of us. It would also save me a trip to Jenny's bedroom to track down nightclothes in the dark, or from having to climb the tower stairs in the dark to hunt for a long tee of my own. I helped her off the bed and to the bathroom. She was much weaker than she'd let on in front of Michael and Eric.

"You gave a nice performance tonight, Jenny Harrison," I noted with a large trace of mirth as I turned the faucets on and gathered the filthy jeans and shirt she handed me, depositing them in a laundry hamper in the corner of the vanity area.

She snickered. "Well, I was sure you'd see through the perky Jenny bit, but I refused to show Michael how much I really wanted to collapse and clam up until at least tomorrow. And, honestly, half my fake energy was sheer anger realizing my husband of less than a year believed I'd tried to off myself merely because he saw pills and me passed out next to the bottle. It's going to be hard to forgive him." She stopped. "On the other hand, Michael is a normal person, and I suppose he had a normal reaction. But still… I'm not happy."

"I could see that. I spotted the ticked-off Jenny underneath the perky Jenny. I'm so sorry. For what it's worth, Michael was frantic once he realized you hadn't gone jaunting off to New Orleans and instead might be hurt and unable to get help."

We stopped talking while Jenny took the shortest shampoo and shower in history. I didn't hear any thuds or slides so I figured she hadn't fainted. A good thing since I wasn't sure I had the strength after this horrible day to pick her up or drag her out and administer CPR.

Once Jenny was clean and dry and back in bed, I changed my own clothes, then peeked out into the hall to see if Eric had returned with the sleeping bags. He was sitting, legs stretched out in front of him, with his bad foot on top of the bags, silent, patient, and ready to crash for the night.

He pointed toward the door. "Am I allowed in?"

"You are. Enter, Mister Desmarais." I gave him a hand up and helped bring in a couple of bags.

"Thank you, Miz Grant. Everyone clean and cozy and ready for sleep?"

Jenny called out, "Clean and cozy here, but will only sleep after you spill the dirt discussed by various guests and Laurent family members."

Eric inquired a bit too casually, "What makes you think any dirt was spread?"

Jenny's tone was pure sarcasm. "Because I've lived in this house for like six months, and I'd lay bets half the refugees from the storm are the same group who apparently have no jobs apart from fighting with Michael about who owns what or sucking up to Michael for whatever." She fell back on the plumped-up pillows. "Enough. I shall cease dissing until I have the energy to be creative."

"Still want to hear the gossip?"

"Well *I* do, even if Jenny poops out on us," I told him.

Jenny groaned. "I'm good for about five minutes. Tops. Give it up, Eric, but make it fast."

"Don't get too excited. There's less talk happening than scurrying to find rooms for the night and not crash into furniture in the dark. However, I heard more than one 'what exactly happened to Jenny?' I'm pretty sure no one noticed me sneaking in and out of the parlor and I didn't volunteer any information. Luc is keeping trays of food coming even with power out. Hungriest bunch of people I've seen since the last opening night party I attended."

I exhaled and let a little Texas girl slip out. "Y'all do realize it's quite possible—wait… switch to probable—that someone in this house right now is the person who abducted Jenny and drugged her and left her for dead? Eric, did anyone come off as guilty or worried?"

"Hard to tell," he said. "What light they have is coming from a couple of hurricane lamps and one or two candles, so everyone in the room looks evil. I didn't hear anyone ask anything marginally different from the original question of 'what happened to Jenny.' I'm not making sense, am I? Possibly because my brain is beginning to resemble a bowl of Luc's gumbo."

Jenny sighed. "I have to say, I'm kind of glad I still have some residual stuff of whatever *wasn't* codeine in the second round, because I doubt I could fall asleep terrified of the possibility someone currently in my own house hates me enough to want me dead. As it is, I'm ready to crash again and smart enough to listen to my common sense. It's what I need."

"This won't really help, but, Jenny? I'd say whatever is going on has nothing to do with you personally. I mean, as a person. It's either something you discovered or were *about* to learn. Something making our pirate kidnapper more than a little anxious. Try not to dwell on it," Eric suggested. "And we *all* need to sleep. The storm's subsiding. Tomorrow we'll probably have power again, even if it's only the generator, and maybe our brains will be working properly and we can figure out what we're missing tonight about means, motives, and opportunities."

"Okay, guys. Time to sleep." I yawned. "Guard dogs and pitiful actresses, all."

Eric and I found spaces for our bags on the floor, leaving room for anyone who needed to get up and use the facilities in the middle of the night. I snuggled inside the bag and let an imp take over to start a round of "good nights."

"Night, Jenny."

"Night, Eric."

"Night, Theodosia."

"Night, Eric."

"Night, Jenny."

"Night, Theodosia."

We were all laughing, trying to figure out who'd drop the "nights" or continue with a gotcha last.

It was a good way to put an end to a day.

Chapter 23

The entire cast of every pirate movie ever made could have marched into the guest room, stomped on my head, poured rum over my entire body, and I'd never have noticed. Once I was out, I was out. Which made me one lousy guard. The only reason I woke around seven was because I'm used to getting up at that hour. The windows were closed with the boards still firmly in place to guard against yesterday's wind and rain, but slivers of sunshine were fighting their way through.

I sat up, quietly wriggled out of the sleeping bag, checked Jenny's breathing to make sure it was even and she hadn't suffered any setbacks in the last seven hours or so, turned back to the door, and discovered we were absent one person from the slumber party. At some point, Eric had taken himself and his sleeping bag and disappeared.

I opened the door a wedge and discovered Eric hadn't gone far. He was right outside the door and he was awake.

"Mornin'," I whispered.

"Morning."

"When did you sneak out? And why?"

"Around three. And before you ask, no, you didn't snore, and Jenny didn't snore, and no one had screaming nightmares." He glanced down the hall as if to check for anyone coming. "But around three, someone tried to get inside. I was stupid. I sat up to see who it was but they were halfway down the hall. I couldn't get out of the bag as fast as I'd've liked, or I'd've hobbled down after them."

"So, you decided to don your 'dragon at the gate' hat and spend the rest of the night in the hall."

"Pretty much. How's Jenny this morning?"

"Breathing easy and still clean. At least I haven't been smelling anything too foul in the room."

Jenny called out from the bedroom, "Yo. I'm awake. You can come back in and talk about me to my face."

I opened the door. "I'll let Eric give you all the news regarding the midnight visitor. You guys chat. I'm going upstairs to take a freezing shower before breakfast. Wait. I smell croissants. The power must be on, right?"

"Michael got the generator going sometime around one," Eric answered. "You two sloths were out cold or you'd have noticed fans blowing again. The good news is the sun is shining and it's moderately cool outside. The hurricane ended up being more of a tropical storm without half the damage we feared. Let's see…the other news is crews from the mainland will be over later to restore electrical power *all* over the island, so life returns to normal. At least in terms of lights and phones and internet service."

"Yeah. Not sure this island can ever be called normal. Okay, I'm gone. Jenny, are you up for joining Eric and me in the kitchen in a bit?"

"Hell yeah. I'm sick of lying around, and I'm starving and ready for some of Luc's marvelous cuisine and about six cups of coffee." She pursed her lips and gave us that defiant look of hers I loved so much. "Plus, I want to make it clear to whoever drugged me and left me to die that my fighting spirit has only been strengthened. Watch out, Endgate islanders."

We agreed to meet in the dining room in about thirty minutes. I left my sleeping bag in the guest room in case more guard duty was deemed necessary tonight, then I headed up the stairs to the tower. I used the twenty minutes to shower in what was blessedly hot water, wash and dry my hair, and dig clean jeans and a shirt out of the dresser. I wanted to believe this day would be spent sipping white wine on the Sugarberry Terrace veranda, but I was realistic enough to assume much of it would be driving around checking on many of the folks I'd met the day before to make sure their houses were intact and the food and water supplies were holding up.

At least I didn't have to worry about hunting for Jenny, although the knot I'd had between my shoulders when she'd been missing was back and, if possible, tighter, since her attempted murderer was roaming around free and unidentified.

Eric and Jenny were seated at the huge dining table along with Alex and a weary-looking Michael. I sank into a chair across from

Eric and nearly burned my tongue in my eagerness to slurp down the *café au lait* the instant it landed in my cup.

"Any word on effects of the storm around the island?" I asked.

"Cici and I made a run and check at about five this mornin'," Alex answered. "Lotsa small trees down, but so far houses are standin' and no major injuries. We didn't check everyone, of course. Mainly folks in the Quarters." He turned to his father. "Not to start a huge fight at breakfast, and yeah, it's problematic because everyone and his dog wants a piece of land in the area, but isn't there *something* our family can do to get living conditions in the Quarters up to...oh, gee, what the heck...the standards of, say, 1950 Somalia?"

"I wasn't aware you were concerned, Alex," was Michael's first response.

Alex turned red. "Well, I am. And I admit I haven't acted like I care about anyone but myself for the last year. I've been a toad. But my own bad behavior doesn't alter the fact that people on this island are living in hell and this family and the other first families are *not*. And we should be doin' something to help."

"I'm with Alex," I stated. "And call me a busybody and yes, I'm a newcomer, but he's right. I was shocked at what I saw yesterday when we were delivering supplies."

Jenny finished a large sip of her coffee before commenting, "Michael, I'm in total agreement. You need to visit some of those folks, including Miz Vianca Giry. It's a disgrace."

Michael held his hand up for quiet. "Before it's everyone-dump-on-Michael time, let me say I *have* visited, I *am* aware, and I agree those homes are a disgrace. I'm more than ready to do whatever is needed to make changes. Now, unfortunately, we're stuck in many ways because it's a toss-up as to who owns the land where the Quarters sits, so we can't just go over there and raze houses and rebuild. Although..." He stopped and thought. A slight smile appeared.

"Yes?" Jenny prompted.

"I doubt it would violate any property laws if a few church groups, funded by...anonymous sources...did some mission work."

Alex was giving his dad a "you're now my hero" look. "We had the exact thought yesterday."

Jenny beamed at Michael. "*You* are getting back in my good graces."

He reached across the table and took her hands in his. "Definitely a perk, Jenny, my love, but I'm dead serious about fixing the Quarters. I'm ashamed of my lack of attention since we moved back to Endgate, but I really believe this is doable."

"Changing the subject but speaking of moving, who all spent the night here?" I inquired. I hoped my question would be taken as an innocent interest in the safety of people during the hurricane, but my ulterior motive was to ferret out who might have snuck into Jenny's room at three a.m. and run before Eric could catch him...or her.

Olivia Laurent opened the French doors to the dining room and heard me. She was impeccably dressed in khaki-colored trousers and a cute matching tunic top, but the effects of lack of sleep were apparent in her voice and the lack of color in her face. "Morning, ladies and gentlemen. Teddie? In answer to your question, we had a full house. Monique, Zach, Renee, George, Robin, Michael, Alex, you, and Eric. I'm honestly not sure who's still here. Cici returned to the Bouvier carriage house around two a.m. and I believe Luc slept in the kitchen." She sat down between Michael and Alex and waved to Luc, who'd entered the dining room from the kitchen entrance the same time Olivia came in through the parlor.

"You're right, Miz Livvie. Ah hunkered down in a sleepin' bag near the doors," Luc told her. "Figured Ah might be needed for Miz Jenny."

Jenny rose and gave Luc a huge hug. "I had a feeling you were close by. Probably the reason I'm so much better today."

Olivia stared at her niece-in-law as Luc poured a cup of coffee for her. "Since no one has seen fit to fill me in on what happened to you, Jenny, would you mind explaining what *did* happen?"

Eric and I exchanged glances. How much would Jenny reveal to Olivia or anyone else who asked? We hadn't talked about it last night. There was no plan of action.

Jenny, always the consummate actress, lied. "It's kind of a mystery, Olivia. I went to visit Miz Vianca, stopped on the way back at Hickory Shadows to make some notes about the place as a possible theatre, and...passed out. I hadn't eaten so it might be I uh...hit my head when I fell? Who knows? Anyway, next thing, I'm sick as a dog and Teddie, Michael, and Eric are bringing me home."

Olivia wasn't finished. "I thought Michael said there were pills involved?"

Michael interrupted. "Misunderstanding, Aunt Livvie. There was a bottle in the room where we found Jenny, but it could have been there for years. I was stupid and frantic and jumped to the wrong conclusions when I saw her lying there."

This whole tap dancing routine was reaching professional levels, but after one more sharp look at Jenny, Olivia began sipping her coffee without pressing for details. All of us fell silent and passed croissants, butter, and homemade jam around as though we hadn't eaten in a month.

Monique, Zach, Renee, Robin, and George arrived while I was pouring my third cup of *café au lait*. All four seemed quite fresh and rested. I checked my wrist. My watch claimed it was 8:00. I wished I'd had those extra hours of sleep. I also wished I could divine if anyone of the guests had snuck into Jenny's room…and what it was someone wanted to keep her from revealing.

As previously stated, the dining table was huge, seating a good twelve people, but it was beginning to feel like an express subway in Manhattan at rush hour. Time to let Group Two dig into a late breakfast and be off. Eric, clearly in sync with me, started to rise the same time I did, but we stopped when Cici Bouvier walked into the room.

Alex Laurent stood and waved. His eyes and smile could have lit the house for years without a single generator.

An air of…I hesitated to call it hostility, but it was far less than cordial…brought a change in the whole atmosphere. I couldn't suppress a wave of unease.

Alex was so busy staring at Cici he didn't notice. Cici did.

Eric and I shared a look. Eric limped over to me and took my hand in his, kept it there, then addressed both Cici and Alex. "Kids? Ready to move out and see what's left of the island?"

Cici released a small breath while Alex, still unaware of the tension, jumped up, shoved his chair back under the table, and joined our group. "See ya, folks. Enjoy breakfast."

Jenny pursed her lips together in a cute pout. "Would love to go, but I'm still feeling puny, so I'd only slow you down. Give Miz Vianca a big hug from me and a bigger one to Louie the dog. Luc, any scraps for the mutt?"

Luc stated, without expression but with enough volume for everyone in the kitchen to hear, "Got some nice bones. And, by the way, Ah'll be hea with Miz Jenny. *All day*. So, call us any time."

Michael chimed in, "Same here. Luc and I will keep Jenny healthy. And Robin's heading off to the mainland soon to get the doctor. I want him to check on Jenny and visit anyone on the island who needs medical attention. Aunt Livvie, would you come help me make some calls?" Olivia nodded, rose, and aunt and nephew left the guests in the dining room and headed toward the parlor, closing the doors behind them.

Eric and I were halfway out the back door of the kitchen when Luc stopped me. "Let me git those bones for the dog, Miz Teddie."

"Thanks, Luc."

Eric released my hand. "I'll meet you outside in the truck, okay?"

"Sure."

Luc had a snack pack prepared and started to hand it to me when the bag slipped out of his hand. I reached down to pick it up and froze at the sound of the voices coming from the dining area. No one could see me, although I'm not sure it would have mattered. It was nearly impossible to identify who was speaking given the mix of male and female pitches, but the overlapping phrases permeated my entire being: "And he's a *Laurent*. How disgustin'. With his little monkey gal."

"Endgate's lookin' at half-breed bastards by next year."

"How precious…the little coon bitch and her mate."

"How humiliating for Olivia and Michael."

I dropped the bag, stood up straight, whirled around, and started to march into the dining room, prepared to do battle. Smack a few folks up the side of the head. For a moment I was blinded by such righteous rage I could barely breathe. This was the crap Eric and Cici and Luc—and all the inhabitants in the Quarters—had been putting up with their entire lives.

Luc stopped me. "Y'all can't do nuthin', Teddie. You're lookin' at centuries of—"

"Stupidity." I growled.

I couldn't meet Luc's eyes. How does one apologize for the bigotry of others?

"They all need their stinkin' mouths washed out with soap. Preferably the kind with bleach—that *burns*," I spat out.

Luc silently picked up the bag for Louie, handed it to me, then reached out and hugged me until I thought my bones would snap. "Best you can do is let my girl and Alex know not everyone on this island feels like some of these…first fam'lies."

I stared at Luc. "What scares me is how far one or more members of the first families will go in expressing their hatred."

Luc shook his head. "Ah know." He paused, "You best be goin', Miz Teddie. Can't do nothing 'bout it now and the kids and Eric are waiting." He attempted to smile. "No need for anyone to know what we've heard. Does no good and causes a world a hurt."

"Okay. You're right… I only wish…"

"Me too."

At least the diatribe of racial epithets had stopped.

It was replaced by the sound of Robin announcing, "If any of you want something picked up on the mainland, speak now. I'm leaving in less than an hour."

I left the kitchen, holding the bag of treats for Louie. Luc was right, I *couldn't* change centuries of racial animus, however badly I wanted to, and it made me literally ill.

But there was one good thing from the last thirty minutes. The warning about Jenny's safety had been given. Whether it would be received was another question. But a glimmer of something… a premonition or second sight or simple intuition snuck into my mind. Someone sitting in that room, currently sipping coffee and pretending all was well, had tried to murder Jenny Laurent less than forty-eight hours ago.

Chapter 24

Alex's old truck was equipped with what Cici informed us were the fiercest tires on either Endgate or the mainland; they could leap broken branches or plough through ditches swollen with rainwater without harm to vehicle or occupants. We tossed our bags into the bed and piled into the cab, with Alex driving, Cici in the middle beside him, and Eric in the passenger seat. I cheerfully sat on his lap, hoping he was as cheerful about the seating arrangements as I was.

Cici waited until we were halfway down the avenue before coming out with the blunt question, "Anyone else smell the tar burning?"

Alex glanced at her, puzzled. "What?"

"Oh, jeez, Alex, I adore you, but you're *so* out of it. I walked into the dinin' room and the crowd of folk shovelin' in my dad's good food for free saw you look at me. They stopped, they stared, and the feathers started flyin'."

Alex's mouth set. He didn't pretend to misunderstand. "I honestly didn't notice. Was it everyone?"

Cici replied with a slight quiver in her voice. "I wasn't takin' a vote, but it seemed the folks who were perturbed cuz you and I are obviously more than friends were Zach and Renee and Monique. Not sure 'bout Miz Livvie. Of course, George is always off in his own world or sniffin' after Monique, so I doubt he cared one way or 'nother. I don't remember if Robin was there."

"My great-aunt Livvie?" Alex looked stricken. "I'd've never imagined her to be some kind of racist."

I tried to reassure him. "It might not be race, Alex, *if* she's even bothered. I wasn't able to tell with the chill in the room given off by the others. Olivia may simply think y'all are too young. Damn. I hope." I tried to hide the fact that I *knew* some of those people were blatantly racist. Overhearing them say those awful things had cut deep, and I knew if *I* hurt, Alex and Cici would be doubly so. I couldn't be the one to tell them—especially after Luc had made it clear he didn't want them to know. Still, it felt deceitful.

I glanced at Eric and knew he had noticed I was hiding something, but I resolved myself to keep quiet on this issue. He didn't need the additional hurt, either.

"Olivia didn't seem too concerned when she saw Teddie holding hands with me," Eric noted after a moment. "And I did that deliberately when I saw the reaction Alex and Cici got. But then, I'm not the Laurent son and heir. Teddie could have nailed it. Not race but age. Olivia doesn't want baby Alex to grow up too fast."

Cici's voice held anger and a trace of fear. "Why in hell should anyone *else* care, though? What flippin' year is this? Eighteen-sixty-something?"

I sat up so straight I bonked my head on the top of the cab. "Ow."

"What?" came from Eric.

"What Cici just said. 'Eighteen-sixty-something' and race. I had a moment of insight, which has now gone poof. Something to do with set attitudes leading to lethal actions." I paused. "Sorry, guys. I'm sure I'm being less than clear. Even to myself. By the way, Alex, where are we going?"

Alex stopped the truck and raised his hands in mock disgust. "I have no idea. I'm merely the chauffeur. Any ideas?"

"Yeah. Let's head to Tenth Avenue," Cici suggested. "Teddie hasn't had a chance to see it apart from a quick drive-through yesterday."

I clapped my hands together in glee. "Our favorite spooky pirate castle? Oh goody. I thought it was locked and secure and no visitors allowed?"

"Well, I was thinkin' more 'bout the beach itself. It sounds weird, but after a storm there's this beauty and a quality... I'd actually call it serenity."

"Let's do it," Eric and I chorused.

Alex started the truck up again and drove to Tenth Avenue, parking behind a retaining wall about fifty yards from the beachfront. He and Cici jumped out and ran down the beach, kicking up sand and generally letting loose, acting more like eight-year-olds than eighteen-year-olds.

I slid down from the truck then gave Eric a hand as he joined me to lessen the stress on his foot.

He nudged my side. "I'd love to join the kids in the frolicking, but I guess we're too old and sedate now."

"Ha. Speak for yourself, Mister Over-Thirty. And don't give me the sedate bit. The only reason you haven't challenged them to a race is the lovely bandage around your ankle."

"Possibly true." He reached his hand out toward me as an invitation. "I can manage a leisurely stroll, though."

"Sounds nice. Mind if I kick off my shoes? This sand screams for bare feet."

"Go right ahead. Natural pedicure, right?"

"Yep."

I got rid of my sandals and we walked down the beach away from the Chaudret castle, amazed at the quiet after yesterday's storm and the lack of debris.

"Must have all swept out to sea," I mused.

"Or to New Orleans," Eric replied. "I guess it's why this side of the island hasn't eroded the way First Avenue has. Faces the mainland, which helps."

"Old Jacques Chaudret was no dummy in terms of building his chateau here. I wonder if he foresaw all the hurricanes for the next four hundred years at the time he settled?"

Eric shook his head. "More likely the old scoundrel knew this was the best place to smuggle in goods from ships he'd robbed than face open sea where the Brits could hunt him down more easily."

We'd reached another retaining wall, smaller than its sister about a quarter mile away. "Care to sit for a spell, Theodosia?"

"Love to."

We sat in silence, staring out at the water and the seagulls, who were busy chattering amongst themselves as they searched for food. My mind was working in clichés this morning, but the sand did sparkle like diamonds under the sunlight, and the small waves flowing over onto the beach seemed easygoing and inviting after yesterday's angry crashes of water.

Alex and Cici were yards ahead of us, but close enough to where I could feel the romance bubbling between them.

I gestured toward the couple enjoying romping in the sand and water without a care. "Think they'll be okay?"

"Yes. I do." He reached out and gently pushed a lock of my hair away from my face then traced his forefinger down my cheek. "Teddie, the kids are great and I'm sure they have a wonderful future ahead of them, but I'm thinking it's time to come out of our neutral corners, be brave, and meet in the ring."

"As in...."

"As in admitting we've got some strong feelings for each other. As in stop avoiding those feelings even if there are probably some good, albeit weird, reasons for not discussing what's obvious. I...care about you. I'm pretty sure you care about me"

My breath caught. I looked into those deep, dark green eyes and saw no trace of imp today. What I saw made my knees weak and my cheeks flush and my heart stop.

He kissed the top of my forehead, then asked, "Care to respond before I continue?" He suddenly looked anxious. "Am I going in the right direction? Should I shut up?"

"Yes. Right direction. 'No' to you shutting up. I'm enjoying listening and looking and being close, and all I ask is don't take your hand away from my face unless it's to hold mine."

"I can do both. Actually, I can do better."

Eric let his hand drop from my cheek and put both arms around me. He mumbled, "Talk later," before he leaned down and put his mouth on mine. He tasted a little like cinnamon and coffee, and I was ready for all the kick of caffeine I could get. If we hadn't been sitting on a beach with Alex and Cici only yards away, we'd've ended up rolling around in the sand scaring the fishes, so we gradually pulled away and sat and grinned at each other like the love-filled idiots we were.

"Nice."

"Nice."

Eric's voice was a soft and sexy as a caress. "I'm not sure if that was too soon since we've only known each other a few days...or too late since we might have known each other centuries ago."

"Doesn't matter. I call it great timing."

I turned my back and snuggled against his chest, feeling safe for the first time since I'd arrived on the island. I could feel his heartbeat against mine, and my one thought was how much I wanted to stay in this one perfect moment forever.

We sat in silence, staring across the water, envisioning a time we could be alone and allow various impulses to take over.

Finally, Eric spoke. "Not to put a damper on things, especially following what was an exceptionally delightful kiss, but I guess it has to be said. This isn't normal and easy." He looked up at the sky for a moment, then back at me. "That's not what I meant to say. Rephrasing...our *feelings* are normal and easy. We can't pretend the *situation* is normal and easy for two reasons." He pursed his lips. "The first is the obvious. I'm black. You're white. Our experiences in life and how others have treated us have been different. I have resentments and anger—and I know you sympathize... hell, even stronger... I *feel* you empathize with your whole heart. And I hope you realize this isn't a put-down, it's life, but you can't ever completely understand, no matter how hard you try to step into my shoes. You've never been a black teenager wondering if the cop following you down the street in your neighborhood is going to ask you where the best coffee shop is or throw you up against a wall and frisk you. Or put a chokehold on you. I guess what I'm saying is we're in for some tough emotional issues."

My heart constricted, imagining what he and every other black kid in Brooklyn—in America—experienced on a nearly daily basis. "Eric, you're right. And we're looking at tough times even when it's only us...together. Then, after trying to conquer our own emotions, we get to add the outside garbage. The haters."

"Exactly." Eric paused, before adding, "Theodosia, I've had friends, performers on Broadway, who've received death threats even in Manhattan because they're in an interracial relationship. And I'm talking *this* past year. Not twenty years ago."

I bit my lower lip, then quietly stated. "Let me step totally out of any neutral corner. I care so much about you. But I'm not stupid, and much as I have never understood the idea of people hating others for no reason...well... I'd have to be wearing blinders not to see it's out there. Hell, I can post rants on social media—and I do—about how wrong it is to hate because of race or faith or gender orientation or who you choose to love, but basically I've been safe in my own world, partly because a lot of my world doesn't deal with people of *any* race. We're too absorbed in platforms and furniture and hammers and nails. Which is great for hiding from a lot of reality. I haven't faced what you've faced. To be honest, I'm scared the lack of shared experiences could keep us apart. If not now, then in whatever future we might share."

Eric softly stated, "Theodosia, don't worry. We're in sync with so many things. You also truly have empathy. That's important. At least for us. Sadly, not for everyone else."

I didn't speak for a long moment. Finally, I asked, "Eric, how do they handle it? Your friends in Manhattan, I mean."

"They talk to each other and keep the communication honest. If they have children, they warn them from an early age there are people who can be mean, vicious, and of course, stupid. One couple does a 'race talk' at least once every six weeks or so. 'Who's feeling what, how are we surviving, what can we do to improve relations, what are we missing?' Seems to work for them."

"Okay. We keep communicating."

We solemnly shook hands as if signing a contract, then Eric leaned forward and kissed my cheek before teasing, "In between a lot of kissing…and a lot more."

"It's a deal." I sat up straight. "Wait. I'm falling behind here. You said race is issue one. What's the other?"

Eric managed only a short hesitation before replying, "Facing who we might have been."

I immediately understood. "Ah. In some ways it's a more complicated issue because we don't know what the fool is really happening with this whole past-lives thing."

"Exactly. How do we deal with the knowledge we may have once known each other and loved each other in another life? Do we ignore the possibility of reincarnation and toss off the feelings of déjà vu as odd coincidences? Do we dig deeper into the past and try to find out what happened in the 1860s to a couple of teenagers named Emeric and Althea?"

I stared into Eric's eyes, wondering if my pulse was going to be this rapid for the rest of my life every time I was near this man. "We dig. I'm no expert, but everything I've heard about reincarnation seems to imply people come back to finish what was left undone."

"Seems to be the prevailing theory. And from what little we read in the ledger, it appears Emeric and Althea were separated before they had a chance to have a life together. I really wonder what Marianne Chaudret's diary has to say about Althea. Could be helpful. But before we dig…."

He kissed me again, stroking my hair and my forehead, then letting his fingers travel down over my eyelids and nose and chin, finally resting in the hollow of my neck. I could feel my toes curl. Finally, regretfully, he released me and whispered, "The good news is I'd say we're ahead of the game in this life."

I could barely breathe, much less speak, but I spotted Cici and Alex approaching and decided I needed to pull myself together and say something. "I agree. After all, we did discuss an issue that could keep us apart if we're not careful or someone decides to harass us into a life of misery thanks to race."

Before Eric could respond, Cici and Alex joined us. Cici, being her wonderful blunt self, remarked, "Heard the last part of y'all's conversation. Sounds like we're all on the same wavelength. We were talkin' 'bout how we deal with bigots who don't seem to like the sight of Alex with me. I'm still feelin' the chill from the kitchen this mornin' when it was clear to everyone Alex and I are far more than friends."

Alex squeezed her hand but addressed me. "And this also slides into me needing to make an apology to Teddie."

"What dreadful thing did you do to me?" I inquired.

"Acted like a complete snotty jerk when you first arrived." He nudged Cici. "Her fault."

Cici lightly whapped his shoulder. "Was not."

"Was too." Alex leaned down and kissed Cici on the forehead, then continued. "I've not been the nicest guy on the planet for the last year. I'd like to explain. Cici and I have been crazy about each other from the time we were about two years old watching Luc cook in the kitchen. We assumed everyone was fine with us and we'd have the biggest island wedding ever once we were old enough. Then, last year, before my great-uncle Cyril passed away, he got into this gigantic huff about Cici and made pronouncements about me not getting a penny of Laurent money or a share of the island unless I found someone, as he put it, suitable."

Cici quickly interjected. "Alex didn't care about the whole stupid inheritance thing, but he was bummed because Mister Cyril was so awful about us, and he was really shocked 'cause we never thought Cyril harbored those kind of feelings. Alex wanted to fight for me, and I told him I didn't want to come between him and his family. I actually spent my last year in high school with some relatives in Chicago to stay away and hope Cyril cooled off about us."

"Which made me totally nuts and angry with the world," Alex added. "But Cici and I had a chance to really talk the night you arrived, Teddie, and came to the conclusion it was only Cyril who had these feelings about us being together. We also decided even if anyone else had problems with us, well, we loved each other and wanted to be together and the rest of the world could go jump in the Gulf." He smiled at me. "Unfortunately, I'd already been a pig to you, and I'd been a pig to Jenny since the day she married my dad." His smile faded. "Cici and I are still determined to get married but *now* I'm wondering about Aunt Livvie."

I stood up and hugged Alex, then Cici. "Well, I say do what your heart says is right. Y'all are too damned perfect together. And Alex? *Ask* her. Olivia, I mean. don't be hostile and get confrontational, but simply tell her you guys felt some itchy vibes floating in the air this morning and you'd like to hear directly from her if you've got her blessing. Hopefully she'll be honest. For what it's worth, Jenny doubtless has already figured out you're a couple and is cheering for you, and if Michael *is* disturbed about you two—and personally I don't think he is because Jenny would never marry a bigot— anyway, I'd say it's the age thing. Most parents want their kids to wait until they're like forty-plus before they have their own families."

"We'll talk to Olivia." Cici fluttered her lashes at Alex. "Of course, I hope she'll say, 'y'all are gorgeous together and wonderful and for a wedding present I want to give you whatever portion of Endgate Island you want.'" She added, "For all its many faults and horrible history, there's a lot of cool stuff here. Like this beach. I'm willin' to fight one old lady for my right to be here with the man I love, just as she did when she married Cyril. Hell, the Bouviers been here a whole lot longer than Olivia, and maybe even the Laurent family."

"Oh. While we're discussing all this, Teddie and I are still trying to wrap our heads around this ownership, heirs, and first families business. Can you explain?" Eric asked. "We've gotten different answers depending on whom we've asked. Lots of legends and rumor and no real facts. And it's looking more and more like it could be the reason behind some of the not-so-nice activity on this island recently, including Jenny being drugged."

"Ah. Ownership. Can we say 'sticky mess'?" Alex replied. "It's complicated. I'll try to summarize and give y'all the quick and dirty. No guarantees I'll succeed."

Chapter 25

Alex cleared his throat and assumed a professorial tone. "It's universally agreed by all combatants in the ownership fight that Captain Jacques Chaudret and his bride Grace were the original settlers on Endgate Island. I'm fairly certain some native tribes were here long before then, but if they were, the pirates either ran them off or…worse. Basically, by the mid-1770s, the island was inhabited by staid old pirates and very colorful birds."

Cici interrupted, "And all the original species of birds are still here, which is one reason I, for one, am in favor of making the area between Tenth Avenue and the Quarters an official sanctuary, unlike certain people who want to use the land for casinos. Or other people who want to slap rental condos all over the beach and open the doors to all the litterin' tourists who want to come for summers and let us clean up later." Her teeth clenched. "Sorry. I tend to get a little…"

"Bonkers?" Alex chuckled. "Strident? Mad as hell?"

"Yeah. Get over it."

He kissed her. "You're so cute. Where was I? Oh. The beginning. Which started with Captain Jacques, who, incidentally, brought a boatload of slaves at one point to ease his poor bride's rough existence in paradise. Now, the first tricky issue comes not long after Jacques built his fortress chateau on Tenth Avenue when word got out this really *was* paradise. Great opportunity for planting sugarcane and rice, plus the nicest beaches in the Gulf. And wham. Population explosion. Not only from other less-than-savory privateers, but French immigrants, too. Families with names like Laurent, Prideaux, Bernard, Guidry, and Pelletier, and Verdery, and a mess of others I don't remember because it doesn't matter, although several out of the original group apparently served on the pirate ships with Chaudret. Confusing. We're talkin' the 1700s, when waves of Europeans were swarmin' over Louisiana and other gulf states. Endgate was so ridiculously out of the way it was overlooked in favor of other islands—and especially the mainland, which probably kept it from the various disasters much of the Barrier Islands have been, and still are, dealing with."

Cici nudged him. "Speaking of going off-topic, geology and geography is fine, but can you jump forward a century or two so Eric and Teddie will have a better idea 'bout who's fightin' whom and maybe why?" She gave him an affectionate tap on his shoulder. "Alex is more an animal person and tends to forget there's people around."

"Considering some people I've met currently residing on this island, Alex is wise to forget they exist, and we'd all do better with four-legged critters," I said. "Back to original settlers and heirs. I have this, uh, weird premonition those folks are more important than any of us realize."

Alex continued, although he was obviously curious as to what I meant by weird premonitions. "Many of the early settlers headed for the mainland, especially after the American Revolution. But those who stayed began documenting boundaries and land ownership. Jumping way ahead to the last sixty years or so, it comes down to the families who've been around for more than two centuries: i.e., the Laurents, the Bernards, the Prideaux, and the Pelletiers, of whom Zach's wife is the last living member."

"Zach is married?" I was astonished. "He sure keeps it quiet. Why didn't he stay at home with his spouse instead of camping out at Sugarberry Terrace last night?"

Cici coughed. "'Cuz she was there too. Renee Pelletier. She never took his name, which is fine, but I swear they've got the most sham marriage I've ever seen. Word has it the only reason they got hitched was to ensure they'd double the ownership rights. Not to mention Renee takes the whole 'my ancestor what's-his-face Pelletier arrived with Captain Jacques Chaudret when they founded the island' like she was on the pirate ship with the guys. Not something I'd personally be proud of. And if I sound nasty and snarky, so be it."

Eric interrupted. "Before we go straying off into marital habits of the islanders, are there any real, live documents to explain who owns what portions of Endgate? I've heard a lot of guesses and pronouncements but not much evidence."

"The debate's been goin' on since I was a little kid," Alex replied. "Of course, and not to be too repetitive, but I have to repeat, the big prize is Tenth Avenue. Cici's right. Everyone wants this portion for a different reason. And it seems every damned week someone comes up with new documentation claiming proof of ownership. No one really cares about First through Sixth. Which makes sense, in a way, because there's nothing in the way of commercial possibilities on the east side of the island. Unless Jenny's theatre takes off, and assuming people are willing to make a ninety-minute boat trip from New Orleans."

"Almost a shame the Chaudret family died out," Eric mused. "I'll wager old pirate Jacques would have everyone under his control and there'd be no dispute. He'd claim the whole island and produce the papers to prove it."

I started to say something, then stopped.

"Teddie? What just crossed over your grave?" asked Cici. "You got a look chillin' me faster than a freezer at a meat plant."

I groaned. "I've told Eric, might as well tell you guys. I've had some strange sort of psychic impressions ever since I walked onto Endgate Island. Well, to be accurate, they started on the plane trip here. Anyway, I've found old ledgers in books hollowed out and no clue they were anything more than books. My feeling about Jenny being in Hickory Shadows and other minor things. And now I keep having this sensation Jacques Chaudret is as important to Endgate Island as he was in sixteen-whatever. Or maybe there's a lost Chaudret who isn't aware he or she is a Chaudret."

"Okay. Slightly convoluted statement," said Eric. "Also scary and spot-on. Can you imagine the uproar if a descendant popped up and made a claim?"

"I think someone is aware of the possibility of this descendant and has gone—and will go—to any lengths to keep anyone from finding documentation proving ancestry." I shivered.

Cici swallowed hard. "Any lengths? I am now sharin' your scary feelin's. Explain?"

"Well, like stealing Marianne Chaudret's diary from Jenny. It's obvious there's something there worth keeping hidden. Moving on to destroying stair steps leading into cellars where other diaries or books with even better info might have been hidden, then becoming desperate enough to grab and drug one Mrs. Jenny Harrison Laurent in what appears to have been an effort to stop her from exploring old houses and finding whatever this someone doesn't want found. My extra sense is screaming this is far from over."

Chapter 26

I stared down at the other end of the beach where the Chaudret chateau stood, proud, defiant, solid, and stable, not one whit disturbed by either last night's storm or our current discussion this morning.

"I'll bet the shade of ol' Captain Jacques is roaming through his castle howling with eerie laughter at all the commotion he started centuries ago."

Eric whispered in an eerie voice, "Or sitting in one of his dank, dark cellars with a huge, rusty lantern at his side, sifting through the coins and jewelry he stole before burning ships in the middle of the gulf. A large bottle of rum at his side."

Cici joined in with, "And there's a skeleton of a large parrot named Butch sitting on the captain's bony shoulder cacklin' and whistlin' sea chanteys while encouragin' him to write his autobiography and host a paranormal TV series. Uh, *Ghost Pirates of the Gulf Islands*."

Alex's eyes twinkled. It was clear he was about to come out with an imaginative vision more outrageous than Cici's spooky parrot, but when his cell phone rang, we knew we were doomed to disappointment. We politely lapsed into silence and let him talk without us in the background.

"Yeah?" Alex paused. "Sure. Now?" He waited. "Okay. Hey, Dad, before you go, is everyone still at the house?" Another pause. "Well, it's about damned time. I thought they'd be camping out for the next week the way they took over last night. Maybe Luc can take a well-deserved break. Okay. See ya in a few."

He clicked off, then announced, "My dad wants us to head over to the south end of the island and see if Robin's back from the mainland. He's supposed to have picked up Doctor Mouton in New Orleans to bring him back to check on Jenny and on a couple of folks in the Quarters who got hit with some debris last night. Should have been back over an hour ago."

We hiked back to Alex's truck. I hated to leave the beach. Apart from it being the setting where Eric and I admitted our feelings for each other, it was the first time in two days I'd felt a sense of peace, which was ironic given its proximity to the Chaudret chateau, a site that howled "perfect setting for a horror movie."

There'd been a lot of talking on the beach. Now, we fell into a comfortable silence, broken only by Alex or Cici playing tour guide and pointing to what appeared to be a fox and some plain gray squirrels, wandering without messing with each other and without fear through an area they instinctively knew was theirs.

"Did I just really see a fox?" I asked with sheer delight.

Alex answered, "Yep. Brought here centuries ago. Some crazy first family probably thought they could raise foxes and have hunts on the island. I wish we had bears here, but we're not big enough. Cat Island, over near St. Francis Parish, is the official federal sanctuary for them, but I keep wanting to cruise by and tell the bears to hang out here. No passport or papers required. But then, one little cub would probably make our fox lunch, so no one would be happy."

"He's cute. Our fox. Or should I change 'cute' to 'fierce' in case he's offended by my observation?"

Alex was clearly amused. "We'll ask his mom, who's hiding right now but is close by making sure we don't mess with her pup. They're affectionate when they're pups—and okay, yeah, cute."

Eric and I spent the rest of the drive straining to look out the window at any other furry creatures who might have ventured out from their homes to take advantage of the sunshine. I spotted several large cats that did not appear domesticated, and many birds I couldn't identify.

Alex pulled up at a different pier from where Robin had docked his boat two days ago when I first stepped on the soil of Endgate Island. I'd had one or two premonitions at the time, mainly caused by Jenny's cryptic job notice and subsequent e-mails, telling me things were wrong on the island. The forewarning had been borne out with Jenny's disappearance and Eric's accident. And now, suddenly, I had a flash making me so frightened I wanted to find the nearest boat and head to New Orleans without a single look back. Something was wrong with Robin.

We climbed out of Alex's truck and I found I couldn't bring myself to talk my heart ached so badly. Alex trotted over to Robin's boat, also tied to the dock, then called out for him, but got no answer. "Doesn't seem to be here. Odd. He hasn't gotten in touch with Dad after leaving this morning around eight or so. Maybe he got sick and headed home without notifying anyone?"

Eric and I walked toward Alex at a slow pace to accommodate Eric's ankle, while Cici began yelling out Robin's name. I stopped her with a soft, "Don't bother."

Cici turned. "What's wrong? You saw something, didn't you?"

My throat constricted but I managed to get out, "Water."

Alex reached into his bag and handed me a bottle. I stopped him. "Thanks, but I was actually referring to the water around the boats."

"Around the boats?" Alex repeated.

"Look under the dock or slip or whatever you call this thing we're on. By the beam."

Alex complied, leaning over and staring into the dark below. He sank to his knees. "Oh damn. Damn. It's Robin." Without another word, he dove in, followed by Eric. The pair grasped the young boatman under the shoulders and swam the three or so feet back to the dock.

Cici and I knelt down and helped lift Robin's body onto dry land. It was clear Robin had been dead for several hours. Eric and Alex climbed back onto the dock and the four of us stood over Robin, offering silent prayers, unable to voice a question as to how or why a young life ended early on this beautiful, sunny day. Or why I hadn't been able to prevent a tragic death. This so-called gift of second sight was pointless if it only led to a parade of horrors and suffering.

Cici's voice trembled. "Do you suppose he slipped and hit his head?"

Alex held her close. "He must've. There's a ton of slick debris on this dock. Hell, even could have been a snake trying to find a safe spot to rest after the hurricane and Robin tripped and couldn't get his balance."

Cici glanced up at me. "What did you see?"

"Nothing clear. I had this impression of a body sliding into the water. But the feeling?" I breathed out and closed my eyes for a moment, then inhaled as I opened them again and said, "Fear. Fear and anger. Not from him. He didn't know."

Cici pulled her cell out of her backpack and dialed the sheriff's number. When Guidry answered, she told him she was at the south pier with Alex, Eric, and me and we'd found Robin's body. She didn't mention a vision by Miz Teddie Grant resulting in checking under the pier. She told the sheriff she'd call Michael since he'd been worried about Robin and sent us here.

She listened for a moment, then responded, "Yessir, we'll stay 'til y'all arrive. You and Mister Laurent both."

She clicked off and the four of us stood in silence. Eric and Alex were both dripping water from the retrieval of Robin's body, and something about the drops falling made his death sadder and more real. Finally, I asked Alex if he had any blankets left from yesterday's supplies still in his truck. He ran back to the bed, pulling a box out and rummaging through it for a few seconds before returning with an army-green fleece blanket. He covered Robin's face and body with it before saying, "I hope I'm not messing with evidence here, in case this wasn't a simple accident, but Teddie's unspoken point is right. Seems indecent to let him lie there without a cover."

We stayed near the body, guarding Robin, although no one could say from what. In less than five minutes Sheriff Guidry arrived, with Michael right behind him in his van. The sheriff asked Alex if he'd mind using his truck to transport Robin's body since the town's one ambulance and one hearse were doing double duty checking for damage after the hurricane and driving people with serious injuries to the island clinic.

Eric was the first to pick up on the last comment. "Did the doctor get back? Wasn't Robin picking him up?"

Guidry replied in the negative. "Doc's not here. Robin never made it to New Orleans. The nurse practitioner was stranded on the island last night with his relatives and he called early this mornin' to tell me he'd pitch in and do whatever was needed. Just grateful everyone on the island escaped with no more than a few cuts or bruises. One broken leg. Oh yeah, Michael here told me y'all found Jenny at Hickory Shadows and it appeared she'd been sick and unable to contact anyone, so if she wants the nurse to check on her, he will." He glanced down at Robin's covered body. "But…this. What in hell happened? How did y'all find him? Alex?"

Alex explained that Michael called, worried, and the four of us arrived at the pier and didn't see Robin and called out for him. All true. The only fib was telling the sheriff "we" noticed a shadow in the water and Alex jumped in and found Robin. No mention of my visions and impressions. It made no difference as far as finding the body, and since Alex, Cici, Eric, and I had been together from about eight a.m. and Robin had clearly been alive then, as corroborated by Michael, who'd been talking to Robin at the Laurent house with Olivia and Luc at his side, no alibis had to be established for any of us.

The sheriff didn't seem to feel there was a problem with how or why anyone thought to look below the dock. Alex, Eric, and Michael gently placed Robin's body in the bed of Alex's truck. The sheriff headed to his own car. Alex waited until he'd started the engine, then the two of them drove in the direction of the middle of the island.

Michael, Cici, Eric, and I watched them go. I pushed down a sudden bout of nausea and tried to take deep breaths to keep the world from spinning. The air around me seemed stale. I couldn't find my voice for what seemed like an absurdly long time.

Finally, when I was able to speak again, I asked, "Do we need to tell him Jenny wasn't sick? Explain she was drugged? Do I say I believe Robin was hit by someone?"

Michael shook his head. "Guidry's a good man, but he has no imagination and he'd be highly skeptical about either the drugging or someone wanting to kill Robin. For now, we're better to keep it to ourselves since we have no proof about…well…anything."

Eric quietly said, "Well, I personally feel we've all had enough for now. I suggest we drive back to your house, Michael, get some rest, eat some lunch, regroup, and hope no more tragic events hit today."

Chapter 27

Eric, nowhere near dry, asked Michael to drop him off at the carriage house. Cici wanted to go back to the Bouvier home, so it fell to Michael and me to provide details concerning Robin's death to Jenny and Olivia, who were waiting in the Laurent parlor. Michael had called from the south pier to tell Jenny Robin's body had been found, but shared nothing else about the circumstances.

Jenny greeted us at the door leading to the front entrance and whispered, "I'd say I didn't invite you down to deal with trouble, but since that's precisely *why* I wanted you here, I'll simply say I'm sorry. Come on inside. Luc made a new pot of coffee, and you and Michael both look like you could use about three cups apiece."

"Gratefully accepted, but if there's something solid to eat to go along with it, I should at least try to get something down. I'm feeling light-headed. It's definitely past lunchtime," I said as I followed her into the parlor. "I have zero appetite, but I'd prefer not passing out and causing a scene. Maybe a little soup?"

"Good idea. No offense, girl, but you look like the proverbial cat-dragged mouse." Jenny turned to her husband. "How about you? Food, I mean."

"I'll wait. But sit for a second so I can tell you and Aunt Livvie about Robin." Michael turned to me. "Would you stay, since you were part of everything?"

We all sat. Michael related the story of the search for Robin once Michael realized Robin was late in returning from the mainland with the doctor. When he got to Alex and Eric's dive into the water, Olivia sat up straighter. She blinked back tears, then asked, "What made the boys look under the pier?"

Again, I saw no reason to say anything about my own impression or vision. I explained we were calling out Robin's name and searching his boat to see if he'd fallen inside and been knocked unconscious or taken ill and I glanced into the water and noticed a shadow and I didn't think it looked right for part of a boat. Olivia stared at me without blinking for a long moment and I fully expected her to jump up and scream, *"Liar. You knew before you looked in the water. The only question is* how *you knew."*

Instead, she began talking about funeral arrangements since Robin's only relative lived in Lake Charles and was in his mid-eighties and probably not up to dealing with burying his grandson.

I have to admit I zoned a little. I was existing in a state of shock following an intense emotional experience and weak from lack of food. Jenny noticed, stood up, and grabbed my hand.

"Okay. Enough for now. Teddie and I shall adjourn to the kitchen for food and a chat."

Olivia had been seated at the piano, but her posture indicated she'd been playing to pass the time and avoid talking to her niece-in-law rather than entertain anyone. She rose and crossed over to sit on the couch. Michael, looking exhausted, sank down beside her.

Once in the kitchen, with coffee in front of me and the smell of gumbo reheating on the stove, Jenny and I relaxed. Our first chance to talk without anyone else in the room or near enough to eavesdrop.

Jenny tore a bite off a roll with more force than needed. "She makes me nuts. She does."

"I presume you mean Olivia?"

"I do. She's subtle about it. But every stinkn' time she looks at me she's inwardly muttering, 'distasteful, crass actress' and biting her tongue before blurting out I'm not the sort the Laurent family had in mind for her nephew Michael's second wife. I gather they still wish he was with wife number one because *she* had the right pedigree. I actually met her. I liked her." She snickered. "But she hated this island like nobody's business, and she and Michael freely admit they got married originally as a buffer against nagging relatives telling them how perfect they were for each other. They were eighteen and just out of high school in New Orleans and practically pushed down the aisle."

"What's her name?"

"Amy."

"Any relatives here or on the mainland aside from Alex?"

"One for sure. Second cousin or once removed cousin. I never get those things straight. Anyway, Amy's folks died a few years ago, but she's alive and well and living in Zurich. And, while we're discussing island gossip, another reason for the early wedding and push to produce an heir was for two solid claims for the west beach. Amy's maiden name was Adler. Second cousin is George Adler. Hence, more claims."

I took a large spoonful of gumbo, waited until I'd swallowed, then remarked, "It's an incestuous little island, isn't it?"

Jenny began shredding her napkin as though it were a member of one of the first families. "You nailed it. The amazing thing is with all the intermarrying, people managed to avoid marrying brothers or sisters—or even first cousins. I guess there were enough families to avoid total incest. Plus, enough outsiders have been brought in from time to time to keep the bloodlines fresh. Including Olivia, although she takes care to keep it quiet she's originally from Illinois. She's worse than Cyril was in terms of this ridiculous snotty island…uh…snobbery."

"When did Michael's parents die?" I asked

"He was young. About five. And they didn't share Cyril or Olivia's idea of 'how cool am I for being a first family of the island.' Didn't care. Thankfully, Michael inherited their genes instead of the itch to become Mister Endgate while being raised by his aunt and uncle."

"Ah yes. Didn't we study the whole nurture versus nature in our psych 101 class freshman year?"

"I'm not sure. Since it was an eight a.m. class and we generally didn't get to sleep until about an hour before, it's like a big black hole in my mind." She paused. "Dang. How did we pass?"

"If I remember correctly, we had a professor who was busy doing a 'publish or perish' routine and gave us multiple choice quizzes anyone with a smidge of common sense could nail."

Jenny chortled. "Common sense? Again, I ask: *how* did we pass?"

We giggled like little kids, which felt great after the shock of seeing Robin's body below the dock less than an hour earlier. The nice feeling didn't last long.

"Speaking of environment, assuming we can figure out why Eric took a spill down rotten stairs, why you were drugged and left for dead, and I'd lay bets Robin was murdered…" I winced. "Sorry. That sounds harsh and unfeeling."

"I get it. It's a shock finding someone dead. So, it appears—what? Someone bashed his head in and dumped him over the side?"

"No clue. I hate these puny little premonition visions. The ones telling me zip before something happens and then not giving really clear pictures of what actually did happen."

"You're giving me a great case of the creeping willies, you know? But, be that as it may, go on…you were saying, speaking of environment?"

"Oh yeah. Sorry. Assuming we find answers and stop evil intent, can you live on this island and be happy?"

"Good question. I keep asking myself the same thing—over and over. If nothing else, I'll have to take at least one trip to LA and one to New York every year to keep sane. I love Michael; I really do, even though I could cheerfully slap him silly for believing I could ever commit suicide. We'll get over it, since he adores me, but we really haven't had a lot of time to sit down and dig into our deepest feelings about things like life and death. At any rate, I still think my idea of the mystery theatre is pretty cool. Michael told me you and Eric managed to avoid specific discussions of exploration in front of our various guests by chattering about interactive productions, right? Pretty much off the cuff?"

"Yep." I rose and deposited my empty bowl in the sink, gave it a quick rinse, then returned to the table.

"Well, I love the concept. It's funny. Remember in college when I always said I wanted to start my own theatre company one day? I never imagined it'd be on a remote island an hour away from New Orleans, but in a way, it's perfect. The whole bloody place is a mystery, and this pirate history thing could be a fantastic draw."

"With a great deal of luck on our side, it'll turn out the Chaudret chateau is really Laurent property, and I can convert it into a theatre. We could give haunted tours." Jenny's expression turned total imp. "Heck, if you keep up with this whole second sight déjà vu thing you got going, you could do séances in the dining room and chat with ol' Captain Jacques himself. Madam Theodosia. Has a nice ring to it."

"Hmmm. It rings of a bordello maybe. If you consider a bordello nice, Miz Laurent. Anyway, my precognition skills have done nothing to persuade Jacques to cough up a few clues as to what is so important someone is willing to kill for it. I have a feeling…yes…a weird, creepy, certainty-type of feeling, it's all to do with who owns what and a missing Chaudret."

Jenny mused, "Sounds like a Renaissance painting. 'A missing Chaudret.'"

I went right with her. "Or a rare vintage of champagne, vines stolen from a ship carrying French aristocrats to Louisiana in 1750."

We were on a roll. Jenny added, "Ship raided, no doubt, by a Laurent, a Pelletier, a Prideaux, and a Bernard. Perhaps an Adler for good measure. Cuttings from the vines hidden in the cellar of Chittamwood Gardens—"

"Stolen back and brought to the castle—"

"And ending up in Hickory Shadows alongside an old diary and several cartons of books."

We fist-bumped across the table, giving each other ridiculous grins.

"Well, it's one idea anyway," Jenny said. "So, forgetting raided ships for the time being, how fast did it take you and Eric to fall madly in love with each other?"

I assumed a look of innocence. "Who's to say we have?"

Jenny howled with laughter, a sound I welcomed even though I scowled at her. "Oh jeez. Theodosia Grant. You're so full of it. The instant I met Eric when I did *Twelfth Night* I've been plotting to get you two together. My own insight or premonition told me you were meant for each other. Only by the time I figured out how to introduce you two, you were running around with ratfink Colin Barrow in Manhattan, and I worried you'd either marry him, or you'd never want to date another director because Colin was such an arrogant jerk. Brilliant? Yes. Gorgeous? Yes. But *so* wrong for you. I was almost glad when weird stuff started happening on Endgate and I had an excuse to bring you and Eric here. So?"

"So?"

"Am I right?"

I couldn't leave her in suspense. She'd had a horrible few days. She'd also succeeded in her matchmaking plans. "You are beyond right. Good job, oh *yenta* woman. Wait, that's too tame. Call it a fantastic job. Thank you. It's funny, I've seen Eric's shows and admired his work, but never would have had the nerve to approach him and say, 'wow, your stuff is great.' But I'm still me. Miss I-Can't-Approach-My-Heroes. Now? Well, I'm somewhere in the clouds about twenty-four-seven—when I'm not worried about whether we'll survive Endgate Island for the next phase of the relationship."

Jenny jumped up and ran around to my side of the table and gave me a huge hug. "Best news in months." She plopped down next to me and sobered. "But…"

"Yeah. Whatever is happening on Endgate concerns him, too. It seems pretty obvious he's descended somehow from a former slave on this island. Which would be simply intriguing, albeit sad, except…" I let my voice trail off. I wanted to tell Jenny that Eric and I believed we might once have been two residents of the island who missed their chance at a happily ever after more than a hundred years ago. But I kept silent. It wasn't a matter of trust. It was a matter of her safety. My gut feeling was the less she knew, the less someone…evil…could get at her through Eric and me.

Jenny whispered, "Eric Desmarais is in danger. And now, I'm horribly afraid, so are you."

Chapter 28

"If anyone of us had any sense we'd steal a boat and steer it directly to New Orleans without a look back."

The voice came from the back door of the kitchen. Eric.

I scooched my chair back so fast it nearly toppled over as I jumped up, ran across the room and hugged him as though we hadn't seen each other for a year.

"Fast," I said with admiration. "You must have taken the shortest shower in history."

"It's actually been an hour. Would have been more, but at least I didn't have to walk once I was clean. The ATV is a terrific mode of transportation. I'm considering getting one for Manhattan. An all-terrain-vehicle doubtless includes riding over taxis midtown during rush hour."

"Probably start a whole trend. I like it." I smiled and ushered Eric to the chair next to me. "There's gumbo and bread left. Want some?"

"Yes. Perfect. It's been a stressful day and I hate to admit I'm starving. Funny how stress makes people either want to avoid food completely or become totally ravenous."

I headed for the cabinet to find another bowl and Jenny headed for the fridge for a pitcher of lemonade. "I won't speak for you guys, but I can't take more caffeine and it's too early to start drinking tequila. Not to mention, I don't think margaritas mix with the aftereffects of a major dosing with drugs. On the other hand, maybe downing massive amounts of alcohol will keep me from angsting about someone trying to kill me."

"Which brings us back to leaving," said Eric. "We all knew you're fierce and tough, but it doesn't keep us from worrying about you."

Jenny waved him off. "In all seriousness, which is a first for me, I'm fine. Hale and hearty and rarin' to go. Eric, you're too thin. You need to eat. Then maybe we can figure out what's next."

She brought the pitcher to the table. I plopped a big bowl of gumbo down in front of Eric, poured glasses of lemonade for us all, then sank back into my chair.

No one spoke for the next few minutes as Eric ate his lunch. Finally, Jenny returned to Eric's comment about grabbing a boat and taking off. "Guys, Eric's right. If we were smart, we'd leave. Sadly, smarts aside, I personally feel if I took off without having answers I'd be nuts forever. And after all, this is now my home and I'd like to be able to live here at least a few years without worrying about getting kidnapped every five minutes."

"Well, I was merely stating what normal, logical people would do in this situation," Eric remarked. "We're all theatre people. We thrive on drama and we thrive on story and theme and digging into motivation. But motivation requires answers, and frankly, not having them is driving me nuts, too. So, I'm staying."

"If you two are going to go all brave and defiant, I can't be the only wimp in the crowd." I paused, then added, "Plus, since something on this island has triggered a weird precognition, déjà vu-ey glitch in my radar, I'd like to understand what and why and whether this is the new normal for Teddie."

Michael had entered the kitchen during my short speech. "Personally, I wish you'd *all* leave."

"Well, *that's* a lovely thing to say," Jenny exclaimed.

Michael put his hands on her shoulder, leaned down, and kissed her. "Not what I meant. I freely admit I'm terrified for everyone in this room. Hell, I'm terrified for people on this island I can't even *identify* who are in danger."

Jenny pulled a chair out for her husband and motioned for him to sit. "And you should include yourself among those people, since at this point we're clueless as to who's doing the terrorizing or why. Still, we can't cut and run. It's *your* home, Michael, and now it's my home, too. I'm staying."

"Resolved," Eric stated firmly. "We're not leaving. But we're not sitting around waiting for the next accident. Or death. We need to figure out—and fast—what's behind the violence."

"I agree. But is there any way we can wait an hour or two before donning our detective caps? If I don't get some rest soon, I swear a giant clue could knock on the door and fling itself at my feet and I'd trip over it on my way to the nearest bed, couch, or sleeping bag."

Eric lifted his right eyebrow with a dramatic flair. "Interesting image. The giant clue. Not *you* tripping over it, which merely sounds painful. Go away, Theodosia. Go to the tower room and do a Sleeping Beauty for a few hours. I need to sleep as well, but I'll head to the carriage house in case Aunt Olivia gets wind of you and me in a compromising position in the attic and a different hell breaks loose."

Michael rose and helped Jenny to her feet. "Well, since Jenny and I are legally wed, we can be as compromising as we want in any room, but damn, a nice nap sounds perfect. You guys head out and we'll be good hosts and do the dishes."

Quick "see you laters," a nice kiss from Eric, and we went our separate ways to recharge. It seemed it took me three times as long to climb the stairs as the last time I'd made the challenge, but once inside the tower room, which was welcoming and peaceful, I decided it was worth the effort. I changed into a loose-fitting tee and flopped onto the bed, fully intending to sleep until welcoming and peaceful changed into disturbing.

I tossed and turned for a good ten minutes. But something kept nagging at me. I sat up and gave the space a long scan and soon had my suspicions confirmed. Someone had been in the room since early this morning. The books weren't placed where they should be. I'm not at all OCD, but I am neat, and I have great organizational skills and memory. After I'd found the ledger with the notes about Emeric Desmarais, I'd rearranged the books on the bottom two shelves and included the books from the carton. Alphabetical by author. The difference now was subtle unless one actually squatted down to check the spines, because the books on those two shelves were almost all the same height. *Almost* being the operative word. And whoever snuck into this room had lined up the books by height. I squatted on the floor and stared at the shelves to be sure my eyes weren't so tired I was imagining things.

There were no books missing. Either the searcher had found what he or she was looking for and gone on their merry way, or there was nothing to be found worth taking. I couldn't tell if anyone had opened the musical theatre book where I'd replaced the ledger. When I checked, I found the ledger still inside, which didn't mean a thing.

I stayed down on the floor doing a second rearrangement while cursing the strange source of the terror on Endgate. The only thing I was sure of was nothing else of value would be found on these shelves. I closed my eyes, hoping for another big hint or even a tiny glint as to where the next clue would appear, but my mind stayed blank. So blank I basically crashed out on the floor and didn't wake for the next two hours.

But what woke me wasn't a soft, sweet, "I've had enough snoozing for the time being, thank you very much" easing out of sleep.

What woke me was the worst vision I'd had since I came to Endgate. It was the one I'd had on the plane. Only now I could identify the man and the scene. And now I knew it was real.

Eric... surrounded by smoke and slipping into unconsciousness.

The carriage house was on fire.

Chapter 29

I grabbed my cell and dialed 9-1-1, hoping my screaming got through to whomever passed for a dispatcher on Endgate Island. I didn't pause to call anyone else. I'd been so tired I'd dumped my carryall bag on the floor when I first came in and it was now blocking the door. I grabbed it, swung it over my shoulder, then took the stairs about three at a time and literally slid down the second set bannister leading to the front entrance. If shimmying down a fire pole at a fire station saved seconds, I figured this was a similar option. I continued yelling, "Fire. Carriage House," on my way down, but again, I didn't know if anyone heard me.

I sprinted the three or four blocks to where Eric was staying and made it to the carriage house in time to watch an explosion demolish the front door. A lethal shard of flaming metal shot like a spear my direction. The porch was now on fire. Obviously, the front entrance was no longer viable. *Windows.* There were windows in the bedroom.

I ran around to the back and was greeted by the sight of smoke but no flames so far. If I'd been at all in control of my emotions, I might have considered the possibility of a backdraft, but it wouldn't have stopped me. *Eric was in there.* I picked up the nearest heavy object on the ground, an empty iron planter, and smashed the window, giving more thanks no bars had ever been hammered into the frame.

The room was filling with smoke but I quickly spotted Eric lying on the floor.

I grabbed a water bottle from my bag and poured the contents of one over Eric's head.

"Wha...?"

"Front room's on fire. We've got to get out."

"Yeah. Was trying to…about five seconds ago when I woke and realized the front room was a furnace, but I fell. I may have snapped the ligament again. Damn."

I helped him up, and though he winced when he put too much pressure on his foot, he gamely began jumping with me toward the window. The door to the bedroom suddenly became a wall of fire. It spread fast, cutting off access.

I unceremoniously dumped Eric back down to the floor as I muttered in a loop, "Drop and roll. Drop and roll. Drop. Roll." Of course, there was no room to roll, but we were better off on the floor than standing near the door.

For a brief second, which was still too long, I found myself mesmerized by the flames. My panic was so strong I couldn't move. The heat doubled, tripled, rose to a level making me dizzy and sick to my stomach.

"We've got to get out," I yelled.

"More water?"

"One bottle. I'm saving it for later. Your lungs need to be cleared of smoke."

He coughed before mumbling, "Can't breathe."

I needed him to stay alert. "Can we move the mattress off the bed and use it as a shield?"

"Yeah. No. Wait. You told me…vision. Trap."

"As in door?"

"Yes. Under the bed. Let's move it. Fast."

We shoved the bed away from the current position in the room to the side not in flames. Eric was right. The outlines of a trapdoor were clearly visible and the little ring to pull and open was intact. I tugged at the ring, praying it would hold and not break off. It stayed solid.

"Are there stairs?" I shouted over the crackling of flames eating away at the side of the bedroom by the window.

"Don't care," Eric shouted back. "Let's go."

No time for chivalry from either of us. I pushed Eric through the hole and jumped down after him. If there'd ever been stairs, they were long gone, but this portion of the house was fairly low and the cellar itself not deep, so we were able to land in dirt without breaking our necks, although Eric's ankle didn't need the extra strain.

We crouched as far away from the trap in the cellar to get away from a house about to collapse above us at any time, not to mention the smoke intent on following us down the trap, which was a scientific impossibility—but my brain didn't care.

My bag was still draped diagonally across my shoulder, so I grabbed the last bottle of water and handed it to Eric. He didn't argue. He drank. He also left a couple of swigs for me. I gulped them down while keeping an eye out for smoke wisping through the trapdoor and entering our immediate vicinity.

I pulled my cell phone out of the bottom of the bag, and muttered, "Let's see if this will bounce off whatever island tower exists from here."

I couldn't get a signal, so a second call for rescue was out, but at least the batteries were working, which meant the flashlight was a go. I lifted it up and surveyed the cellar.

"How long do you suppose we can last in this space before it fills with smoke?"

"Not long. But, Teddie, if this house is like Luc's carriage house and most of the houses on this damned island, there's a passageway leading to a garage or shed. If we can find the opening, we can get out before the roof caves in."

"Good. Okay. Give me a second to get my bearings and try to remember where the door was at the Hickory Shadows cellar. Hopefully, it will be in the same general area."

We could hear crashes and popping and crackling above us. Eric gasped, "Hurry."

I closed my eyes and used my set designing instincts to guide me. If I were going to dig a tunnel under a carriage house, where would I put the door?

I pointed to a steamer trunk resting against a wall. "Behind there."

Eric didn't argue. The trunk was heavier than the bed and hadn't been moved in more than a hundred years. It didn't take kindly to two people determined to slide it across dirt, but with our desperate shoving, it finally moved. There was a padlock on the door, and in my panic I thought we were trapped.

Eric lifted it up and we quickly realized this door was also stuck. With combined shoulders we broke through and began making our way through a passage one could only label as dark, disgusting, and creepy. It wasn't high enough to stand up in, but it was—thankfully—cool and flame-free.

I felt certain we'd made it to the end, but, again, nothing was easy about this rescue. The door, far more solid than the one directly under the bedroom in the cellar, mocked us with whatever lock it had, staying firmly in place, guarding the space from outsiders while keeping escapees from seeing daylight.

"I can't believe this. I have a handy-dandy lock picking kit. I do. I always keep it with me. Don't ask why. But did I throw it in my bag today? Hell no. It's in a *different* bag, sitting neatly on the dresser in the tower room at Sugarberry Terrace. Damn. Damn. And *damn*."

Eric held me and smoothed my hair back. "It's okay. Once the fire is out, we should be able to head back to the house and climb up through the trap into what's left of the bedroom. We're alive and safe. Look. Not a wisp of smoke in this area."

I choked back tears of frustration and fear. We sank down on the dirt floor and hoped someone was currently dousing the house and we'd hear them calling to us.

I sat up straight. "Wait. Something… There's another way out."

"You getting a vision?"

"No. This is strictly set designer Teddie using her knowledge of architecture. Whoever built the house and added traps and tunnels must have included a separate entrance."

"Want to try to crawl back a ways and see if the builders were as smart we hope they were?

Before we could make a move, we heard sounds of wood breaking, and within seconds the sound was followed by the sight of an ax slashing through the huge door. A blonde head peeked through a newly formed opening.

"Hey, guys. Nice to see you. Ready for some fresh air?"

Jenny.

Chapter 30

Eric and I staggered through the broken door and were met not only by Jenny but also Michael, Alex, Cici, Luc, a brawny "real" firefighter, and two preteens from the Quarters who seemed thrilled to be part of this portion of a rescue. Blankets were thrown across our shoulders and a portable oxygen tank attached to Eric after I gasped out I thought he'd inhaled too much smoke.

"Save some for Teddie," Eric croaked before the mask was slapped over his nose and mouth.

I turned to Jenny. "How'd you find us?"

Jenny couldn't hide the fear I knew she'd been experiencing for however long Eric and I had been in the carriage house and the tunnel, but she bluffed with, "Easy."

"Yes? Are you also gifted with second sight these days?"

"Nothing so cool. Remember I've been exploring houses around here for a couple of months. I checked this one out before Eric moved in. I knew there was a trapdoor in the bedroom and also was aware of a tunnel leading to the cellar." Tears began to flow down her cheeks. "I didn't expect this. I'm so sorry. So, so sorry."

"Why? You didn't start the damned fire."

"But I brought y'all down to the island knowing something was wrong. I had no idea it was *this* wrong, but I should've been more…careful. You and Eric need to fly back to Manhattan on the first plane out. Go while you've got the chance."

The firefighter was about to hook me up to a second oxygen tank, but I put my hand up to signal stop. I glared at Jenny. "Right. We'll go. We'll go when you and Michael also go. I mean… this joker is after something, and until we can figure out what, the next person in danger could be Alex or Cici or Luc. Hell, why don't we charter a flippin' plane? Head to Alaska or Siberia or Newfoundland. Someplace *possibly* beyond the reach of a nutcase. Let's face it, the reasons behind the mayhem might not stop simply due to geography."

Jenny groaned. Alex and Cici joined us and Cici immediately told the man with the oxygen tank to ignore me and get the darned thing over my face *now*. So, for a few minutes we were all silent.

Once Eric and I had been released and were declared somewhat fit, with caveats it would be best if we could get to a hospital or clinic on the mainland for a thorough check, the kids and the firefighter left. It appeared the same group of volunteers, plus two other firefighters who'd shuttered windows before the storm, had been working on the actual fire while we'd been below. My frantic 9-1-1 had gotten through as I'd been running down the stairs at Sugarberry Terrace. It sounded as if they'd reached the house about a minute after Eric and I had taken the dive into the cellar. They'd gotten the fire under control, though at this point neither Eric nor I really cared if the bloody thing burned to the ground.

"Home," Jenny decreed. "All of us. Hey. Where's Michael?"

Alex answered. "He decided it would be a good thing to talk to Guidry and emphasize odd things were happening on the island, so the two of them are discussing a week with a near-lethal drugging, arson, and possible murder by drowning. They were at the house about ten minutes ago with the volunteer team. As to now? Anyone's guess."

Jenny added, "You left out a tropical storm, but at least nature was being a pain and not some sinister human type. Come on, everybody, let's go. Alex, would you bring your truck around so Eric won't have to walk?" She squinted at Alex, then at Eric. "You guys are about the same size. Would you mind lending him some clean clothes?"

"Took the idea right out of my mouth." Alex gave a thumbs-up. "I'll be right back with transportation. I've got tons of clothes at home."

Jenny waved him off and mused, "I hope the power's been on long enough for hot showers."

I scowled at no one in particular. "It seems like we spend half our time getting into disastrous, messy, dirty situations and the other half cleaning up so we're not banished from polite company. Why can't the lousy SOB who's behind all this—whatever this is—simply send a threatening note on scented stationery every now and then?"

Eric put his arm around me. "Since you've been playing hero for the last hour or so, I'll pretend you didn't just make a rather ridiculous statement."

"The heroics were mutual, Mister Desmarais."

"Nope. I'd never have made it down to the cellar or found the passage, even if I'd been able to open the trap by myself. I was starting to go down for the count when you did your Superwoman routine and came crashing through the window."

Cici gave me a look of sheer admiration. "Wow. Call me impressed."

"Well, it sounds better than it was. And I had no idea what I was doing. If Eric hadn't seen the trap when he first moved in, well, we'd've both been stuck."

Eric took my hand and pulled me closer to him. "Teddie's spectacular entrance through the window was the stuff of legends. If I hadn't been impressed and entranced before, seeing her dive into the room would have clinched it. Very sexy, Miss Grant."

We all laughed—a good sound and sorely needed.

Alex drove up in the truck less than five minutes later. He helped get Eric into the front seat so he could rest his ankle on top of the glove compartment. I climbed into the back with Cici and Jenny. After sparing a quick look in the truck bed to be sure everyone was secure and wouldn't fall out at the nearest bump, Alex shifted gears and made it to the Laurent house before we had time to settle in.

Once we got to the house, Alex helped Eric inside and to the guest room where Jenny had spent last night. Jenny delivered a mild Bronx cheer. "I'm glad I put clean sheets on the bed and towels in the bath. It appears this is now the official room for all rescued islanders."

Eric waved at Jenny, Alex, Cici, and me, now all standing in the doorway. "Go away, peanut gallery. I love you but I'm going to stand under a shower for about an hour so I can be civilized again and not ruin those sheets." He grabbed my hand. "Although I wouldn't mind a second or two with Teddie before she climbs to the attic."

The others moved out of the way and headed toward the back hall, presumably to the security and comfort of Luc's kitchen. Before they'd gone more than two steps, Jenny turned. "Once both of you are clean and ready to face the world, come on to the parlor. Eric, we'll have a nice stool for your foot and an ice pack or two. And several margaritas for your psyche."

We waited for a moment or two to be sure no one would come popping back into the room. Eric held his arms out and I took a step forward until we were tightly embracing each other. He kissed me, tasting of smoke and dirt, but I didn't care. I'd savor the taste of his mouth on mine forever, as long as it meant he was safe.

I looked into his eyes. "I must tell you, Eric Desmarais, I'd've been royally ticked if we hadn't gotten out of there. I'd like to hang out with you and would far prefer another sixty or so years instead of sixty minutes."

"Exactly my thoughts. And of course, there's not an ounce of romantic ambiance in this room, even with a sturdy bed." He ruefully added, "With the way things are happening, chances are there won't be a good time or place until we're long away from this island. Hopefully alive and well." He gently stroked the top of my hand. "I have to admit there were times today when I began to wonder if Eric and Teddie were going to have to wait for another turn on the reincarnation wheel to be together."

"Do you suppose people get the chance to send a message to their future selves before they die? So they don't waste time trying to determine who they were and what happened to keep them apart in the last life? I have to say, it's confusing."

"It's also a question without any ready answers." Eric smoothed my tangled hair away from my face, then leaned down and gave me another kiss. "To remember me while you're in your tower, princess." We reluctantly parted so we could both get clean and breathe some fresh air. We needed to recharge and prepare to fight for what had become a quest to uncover why terrible things were happening—and a battle to save our lives.

Chapter 31

I shampooed twice to get rid of the scent of smoke and concluded I was developing a split personality—because in between violent waves of fear about what could have happened in the carriage house, I was singing show tunes about how wonderful it was to be in love. I was living a Gothic horror show, yet feeling absurdly happy because I'd become the one-in-a-million lucky human to have found the man I kept defining in my head as my soul mate...clichéd, definitely, but true. Unfortunately, the question as to the two of us surviving Endgate and the murderous lunatic who'd managed to convince everyone on the island he or she was perfectly sane, then proceeding to a somewhat calmer life, was sailing higher in the air than the bubbles drifting off my coconut body wash.

I toweled off, took advantage of the return of full power to blow-dry my hair and use a flat iron to style it in something other than a ponytail, and then looked through the closet for the few dresses or skirts I'd brought. A cotton blue-and-white summery two-piece with lace trim around the collar and sleeves looked like the perfect antidote for the chaos I'd been dealing with since my arrival. I was searching for the white sandals I'd tucked into my suitcase when someone knocked on the door. I froze.

"Theodosia?"

I let myself breathe again. "Jenny. Hang on a sec."

I hurried to the door and unlocked it. Jenny gave me a once-over and whistled approval. "You look gorgeous. Amazing. You found Robin's body this morning and rescued the love of your life this afternoon and could easily grace the cover of a *haute* fashion magazine tonight."

"Uh-huh. Pile it on. And what's your angle, Jennifer Harrison Laurent?"

"Hey. I'm being serious and truthful. Your outfit is perfect and Eric will be drooling and panting more than the dumb dog the kids in the Quarters adopted."

"Well...thanks. I return the compliment. Love your dress. It's got such a cool 1940s look to it. We're both awesome. It's about time we got to wear something other than work clothes or shorts to beat the heat."

"Although it must be said, Theodosia, the shirt you wore at the fire—and the fact that you hadn't paired it with anything else—was attractive. Even the kids helping with the rescue noticed you had great legs. Cici and I were both jealous since we're too short to rock the pants-off look."

I buried my face in my hands in mock embarrassment. "I didn't even realize I hadn't put my jeans on until we were outside breathing real air. Ah well. Can't say I care. It terrifies me even now to imagine thirty seconds wasted on modesty could have been thirty seconds too long before that damned fire burst through into Eric's bedroom." I began to tremble and had to force myself to be calm. "Okay, you did not climb nine million steps to this attic for a chat about couture. What's up?"

"Another dinner party. Wait...misnomer. It's not a party, although dinner will be served. It's the usual suspects coming over with some stupid new plan to distribute parts and parcels of the island. Zach Prideaux and his wife Renee, Monique, and George Adler, who'll drool over Monique and go with whatever everyone else wants. Olivia will be at her queenly spot at the head of the table."

I couldn't suppress a shudder.

"What?"

"Jenny, if what I believe is right, those really *are* the suspects. You've listed the same people who were here last night, any one of whom could have snuck into your room and gotten away before Eric could catch him or her. The only other person who was here was Robin, who is now sadly, but conveniently for someone, deceased. Damn. I keep seeing him lying there on the pier after Eric and Alex pulled him out of the water. It's heartbreaking." I dashed away the tears gathering in my eyes and looked away. I wished I could have foreseen what happened with Robin so I could have done something. *Anything.*

Jenny sank down on the edge of the bed. "Question being, was his death an accident or did some creepy someone bop him over the head and shove him into the water?"

"Likely. My impression was of him on his way *into* the water, so I didn't see anything before then. But, Jenny, someone drugging you was definitely no accident. Maybe it was meant as a prank...or a warning." I began pacing around the room. "What in hell could Robin have done to warrant being murdered? Then again, what in hell have you or Eric done?"

Jenny blinked back tears. "Robin was twenty-four or five. A little wild at times, but a nice guy. Things are so—well—wrong right now on the island. I wish we could grab a boat and head to New Orleans for the night. Or the week. Or month. Or until we figure out who and why." She motioned to me. "Meantime, quit your mouse-in-a-maze activity, come here, and I'll fasten your pendant. Which, by the way, is pretty. I don't remember seeing it before. Family heirloom?"

I crossed over to the bed and let Jenny fasten the clasp behind my neck. "*Somebody's* family. Not mine. I found it at a flea market. Or, to be precise, it found me. It practically jumped into my hand when I was walking by the booth. This is the first time I've worn it, since this is one of the few outfits with the right blue to match the stone. And of course, it doesn't really go with my various show logo sweatshirts and jeans, especially when I'm up on a catwalk in some indie theatre downtown making sure heavy objects don't land on an actor below on stage who's in the middle of some British farce."

Jenny looked wistful. "Sometimes I wonder if I made a mistake not joining you in Manhattan a few years ago. I mean, jeez, live theatre. Good theatre. *Awesome* theatre."

"Jenny, don't go second-guessing your choices. If you'd moved, you might be winning awards, but you'd never have met Michael. And regardless of how dumb he was over the supposed suicide, I foresee at least fifty good years together for you two."

She snickered. "Is this prediction part of your newly acquired second sight giftee?"

"Nah. Merely using my normal eyes. You two are nuts about each other. You light up when the other is in the room."

"I was about to say the same about you and Eric. Talk about fast, Miss Grant."

"Well, it helps push a romance along when a couple is fighting the forces of evil, which seems to be what passes for entertainment on this island. By the way, did you have a chance to look in on Eric before heading up here?"

"I did. He's resilient and stubborn. Exactly like you."

"Meaning?"

"Meaning he's clean, he's wearing a pair of jeans and a crew shirt borrowed from Alex, and he's determined to come to this dinner fiasco because, again like you, he seems to believe the ownership of Tenth Avenue is behind all the bad doin's and hopes someone will let something slip during polite conversation." She paused. "I told him I was thrilled he was feeling better and even if we learned nothing at dinner, Luc and Cici are coming up with exotic dishes so everyone will be happy."

"I keep meaning to ask, why is the Laurent house the central station for *everything*? Dinner parties, hurricane parties, refugee and ownership argument parties."

"The only kind of party you didn't identify is an enjoyable one. And my answer is… a combination of things. For starters, this house is bigger than most of the other houses on Endgate and, apart from the Chaudret castle, more solid during storms. And for whatever reason, Luc has stayed loyal to the Laurents for years—so we have the best cuisine and everyone hangs out here hoping for breakfast, lunch, and dinner. And possibly the most important reason, Olivia dearly loves being hostess whenever she gets the chance, and she definitely makes certain there are lots of chances. By the way, she's *not* the legal heir to any Laurent property."

"She's not? She acts like it."

"Yeah, well, Michael is. Cyril adored Olivia, but according to my loving husband he told him he was making Michael his heir because, and I quote Cyril, 'Livvie is beautiful and talented and smart, but has the business sense of a goat.'"

I had to laugh. "So how does all this work? Financially, I mean."

"Ah. Cyril made certain Olivia has a very nice income for life. He didn't want to ever cause trouble between Michael and Livvie, so some banker in New Orleans is in charge of her trust. She knew all the ins and outs of the will and approved it before Cyril passed away. She's secure. She has money and is still able to play lady of the manor. Now, Miss Nosy, are you ready?"

"Yeah." I glanced around the room, then slumped in surrender. "I doubt there's any point in locking the door. No one's going to sneak up here during dessert, and even if they did, it's been searched so many times now whoever's digging into books should be satisfied and feel it's time to move on. Nothing to see. Then again, I don't want someone sneaking inside and depositing a copperhead or something in the bed. I'll lock it."

I suited action to word and we headed into the hall leading downstairs. Jenny paused at the top. "You may be right believing there's nothing to see in the rest of those books, but I'm going to borrow a glimmer of your psychic powers, Theodosia, and say, with almost total certainty, there's a book or books *somewhere* on this island with answers. If you're up for it, I'd like to check out Chittamwood Gardens tomorrow. Unless I can manage a way to get a key to the chateau?"

"Does either residence include a cellar?"

"Well, Chittamwood Gardens does, but I'm pretty sure all items tucked away below were stored in an attic a few years ago. It's pretty bare. Not clean but not cluttered."

"And *Chateau Sans Frontieres*? I mean for tunnels."

"A veritable rabbit warren of cellars and passages. After all, it was the first smuggler's cave on the island."

I glanced down at my blue and white dress. "I suppose I should enjoy getting to dress up for one night at least, even if I means listening to more talk about the la-di-la first families of the island. Obviously, I'll be back in my grubbies tomorrow since we're exploring again."

"True." Jenny almost snarled. "I do *not* want to go to this stupid dinner party. I *really* do not want to hear what nutty proposal folks have been dreaming up while we've been dealing with drownings and fires and recovering from overdoses of pills."

"I agree, but I don't see a way around you playing second hostess to Olivia's first."

"Yeah, yeah. You're right. Okay. I shall endure. Let's go greet the guests, although it's more than a little scary imagining one or more of them could be our murderer and he or she is sitting at the Laurent table preparing to enjoy Luc's *coq au vin*, with fresh asparagus, and crepes for dessert."

Chapter 32

I stopped at the guest room, now officially Eric's home while on the island, so we could go to dinner together as a couple. Jenny went on ahead, grinding her teeth and grumbling about free-loaders in her house.

Eric opened his door. His eyes widened. "Wow."

"Wow?"

"I agree, not brilliant, but it's the first word that popped into my head. Let me rephrase. Theodosia Grant, you are beautiful. Thank you again for sailing into the fire—literally—to save me, because I'd've been really ticked not to get the chance to be with you. As you noted earlier."

"My pleasure. Thanks for guiding us through the nasty passageway, because I feel the same. I'm afraid to ask... how're your lungs after the great escape?"

"Surprisingly good. I've been coughing a bit, but I lucked out on the smoke inhalation." He softly said, "And I have plenty of lung power for more than breathing." He pulled me close, then lifted my chin to bring my lips up to meet his.

Then he gently released me before we both forgot there was a party to attend.

"To be continued." He moved two deliberate steps back. "Now, let me admire the whole package here." He gave me the "twirl" signal almost like a dad checking out his daughter's attire before prom.

I snorted unattractively, which made him laugh, but I performed a slow pirouette while Eric applauded and whistled. "I'll say it again because you need to hear it. You are beautiful." He spotted the pendant and lifted it away from my neck. "Unusual piece. Suits you." He stopped.

"Yes?"

"Something. This is weird. Is second sight or déjà vu contagious?"

"Not up enough on the topic to speak with even a tiny bit of authority, although I seem afflicted with one or both. Why do you ask?"

"I just got this...um...I'll go with your word, flash. When I touched the pendant."

"Did you *see* something or *feel* something?"

"See. But as though I was looking through someone else's eyes. It's gone now. Tell you what, I'll mention the pendant at dinner and see if the vision returns. Gives me a chance to stare at you without everyone waiting to see if we're going to start rolling on the floor in the throes of heavy passion."

"Ha. Considering who'll be at the table, I'd say they'll be too busy diving headfirst into Luc's cuisine or screaming 'Mine. Mine. I own the castle' like toddlers in a proverbial sandbox. They won't notice anything we do unless it interferes with their dessert."

Eric crooked his elbow. "Care to be my date, Miz Grant?"

"Love to, Mister Desmarais."

We strolled down the hall to the dining room and were waved to our respective chairs by Olivia. Cyril Laurent might have considered his wife to be a ditz when it came to matters of island real estate or financial transactions, but Jenny was right: Olivia was in her element when she was entertaining. The last three days had been stress piled on stress with Jenny's disappearance and dosing with drugs, a storm that thankfully hadn't been up to hurricane standards but was still violent enough to cause flooding in parts of Endgate, the unexpected death of a young man well-liked by the islanders, and the destruction of the Laurent carriage house thanks to arson.

Added to all these disasters was the less-than-polite behavior of several of the guests at this table, who were determined to ask nosy questions with no regard for the health or well-being of anyone involved in the respective disasters. Yet, Olivia remained serene and gracious and in control throughout this last-minute dinner party, which apparently served as a prelude to another fight about land ownership.

Most of the conversation was neutral and light, focusing primarily on food and travel. Eric and I did have to recount our escape from the carriage house, but we glossed over it as not being nearly as scary as folks were saying, pushed the idea of bad wiring, and swung the topic around to what amounted as a guide to Manhattan. We discussed theatre and museums and New York politics and style. Monique and Renee were especially interested in Fashion Week.

"Have you ever gone to any shows?" Monique asked.

"I have. Believe it or not, I even got the chance to model last year. I was helping build the platform for a show by Taft Gibbons, and she decided I was the perfect height and body type to sashay down a runway in a couple of dresses and jewelry she was featuring in her new collection. Great fun, though I wouldn't want to do it all the time because it's not the kind of stress I'm accustomed to. But once was a blast."

Monique gestured toward my pendant. "Is that one of the pieces you wore? It's beautiful. Has an antique feel to it while still bein' unique. Ah just love it."

"It's not from the Gibbons collection," I replied. "I found it at a flea market in Brooklyn. Some colonial matron might have stored it away in an attic until an enterprising estate agent found it along with Revolutionary muskets."

Renee bit her lower lip, possibly in an attempt to keep from commenting on my fanciful excuse as to how the pendant made it to the Bay Ridge Brooklyn street fair last fall. "It's definitely an antique, but probably not from the colonial period. My great-grandmother had a pendant in a similar style, which was made in the mid-1800s. Before the War Between the States."

I resisted the urge to whirl around and shout to Eric, *"This is from the island. Maybe you saw it as Emeric?"* Yeah, that'd be a smooth move, one guaranteed to let the first families know Eric and I were interested in more than setting up a theatre. I focused back on Renee, who was either reading my thoughts or was actually interested in...setting up a theatre.

"So, Teddie, it's been hectic since you arrived, but have you had a chance to come up with anything solid for the Hickory Shadows theatre?"

Her husband, Zach, asked, "Has it been determined Third Avenue is the spot?"

Jenny responded with more than a trace of sharpness in her tone. "Nope. It hasn't. Chittamwood Gardens is also in play...no pun intended. And, of course, the absolute *perfect* venue would be the Chaudret castle."

Silence.

Jenny added, "And before everyone goes ballistic, yes, I'm aware the castle is still up for grabs along with the rest of Tenth Avenue. But I'm stating for the record that it's perfect for a mystery theatre. Plus, if we offered dinners during shows, audiences would love it. Could bring in a lot of revenue for the entire island. And the castle does have a wonderful, huge kitchen."

Olivia held up her hand. "Let's postpone any discussion until we've finished dinner. Luc's cuisine is too good to risk indigestion."

Jenny shot Michael's aunt a look of annoyance and muttered, not quite under her breath, "Fine. You set the agenda, Miss Perfect Hostess." Fortunately, Olivia did not appear to have heard her.

Talk shifted back to safe topics such as museums visited around the world. Monique, surprising me with her knowledge and experience as a global traveler, waxed eloquently about the Hermitage in St. Petersburg, Russia. Renee declared herself a true Anglophile and claimed her favorite was the British Museum, which featured global artifacts found by British explorers, including sculptures from the Parthenon and—what came as a total surprise to me—the Rosetta Stone. Zach also went with Britain, stating the Design Museum in the Kensington area of London was the perfect spot for an architect to become inspired. Even George Adler spoke up to reveal his preference of the Louvre as the ultimate venue for the best artwork on the planet, and unabashedly admitted to loving the Romantics. It was clear there was more to the first families than simply greed over island property.

So, for once, I found myself disagreeing with Jenny. Olivia had been right. It was much nicer to chat about neutral topics and definitely less stressful while eating dinner. I actually started enjoying being around these people for the first time since I'd arrived on the island. A feeling which, sadly, didn't last much past dessert.

After we'd all finished large helpings of Luc's excellent crepes, we adjourned to the parlor for brandy and coffee. Eric and I headed right for the piano bench, which gave us a view of everyone in the room while maintaining a distance on the fringes where we might not be noticed.

The conversation had again shifted, this time to some political operative in New Orleans who was shadier than the island trees. Everyone from Endgate agreed he should be kicked out of office and jailed. I had no idea who this person was and didn't really care, so I took advantage of my spot in the room to eye the guests and play the game of "who might be a killer?"

Might be. Much as I wanted to jump up, point at an individual, and shout like a detective in a 40s film noir movie, *"It was you. You did it,"* nothing had been proven in regard to attempted or real murders. Stairs did rot, and people did fall through them without outside intervention. Robin could have slipped on some oil or debris, hit his head as he landed on the dock, and slid into the water below. The vision I'd had before we found him had only shown Robin's shadow slipping in the water, nothing solid as to how he'd gotten there—although I felt certain there'd been another person with him. The faulty wiring theory Eric and I had raised was not unheard of in an old carriage house, and it *could* have caused the fire.

The most evident, purposeful act was Jenny's drugging. It was deliberate. No possibility of it being accidental. I was willing to admit the person who drugged her might have simply wanted to warn her of the dangers involved in poking through old houses and reading diaries, but the result had been almost fatal.

Then came the all-too-important question: Would the villainous creep doing whatever he or she was doing leave Jenny, Eric, and me alone once they found whatever was so important?

I groaned. Eric glanced at me. "Worried or responding to the three helpings of crepes you had for dessert?"

"Ha. I could've cheerfully devoured two more. My groan was for the former. Worry, anxiety, frustration, and confusion sum up how I'm feeling…at least about accidents and deaths. Other feelings are much nicer because they concern you." Eric put his arm around me and drew me closer, which felt wonderful, but I still couldn't hold back a yawn. "Sorry."

"No problem. I'm right with you. This group better get on with their super, new-and-improved proposals for island-splitting soon because I'm also about to pass out. And to be honest, we're getting the same fish-eye Alex and Cici got this morning merely by being a bit too near each other for *their* comfort. My impression is quite a few first families' descendants would prefer not to have the black guy snuggling up to the white girl. By the way, there's no reason we have to be here for the great family ownership debate, is there?"

As if he'd heard Eric's comment, Zach, at the other end of the parlor by the front French doors, put his coffee cup down on a side table and raised his hand for quiet. "Olivia, this has been a delightful dinner. My compliments to Luc, of course. But we're all tired and edgy, and we need to discuss the proposal Renee and I came up with last night."

Michael stood. "Get to it, Zach. Olivia, Jenny, and I are willing to listen, and I'm sure Monique and George are as well, but I can't imagine what new plan is going to please everyone."

Zach shrugged. "Simple. We do an even split of Endgate. The Laurent family keeps the east beach and pier to Fifth Avenue. Which gives you two choices for your theatre, by the way. Monique takes Sixth Avenue to Tenth. George gets Eleventh through Fifteenth, and Renee and I have Sixteenth through Tenth Avenue. Two less blocks for us, but, of course, we'd get the west beach."

For a moment there was nothing but a stunned silence. Then came a fight to rival congressional ideological debates. No one was listening to anyone else, although I could distinguish a few words and phrases including "stupid," "greedy," and "are you out of your *mind*?"

Eric turned to me, cutting through the noise, "We're definitely not needed, and this is going nowhere. I say let's call it quits for the night and get enough sleep so we can face whatever insanity is in store for tomorrow."

"You'll need it, guys."

I turned around. Jenny had snuck out the front entrance to avoid the mob arguing in the middle of the parlor and was now standing behind the piano.

"Jenny? You still want to check out Chittamwood Gardens?" I asked.

"No. After listening to this argument tonight, it's time we get right to the good stuff and explore the Chaudret castle on Tenth Avenue. It's the grand prize. The big win."

"Yeah, well, what you really mean is you want one Theodosia Grant to try to bond with the ghosts who are no doubt roaming through the icy corridors, right?"

Jenny beamed at me. "Hey, might as well use your spooky new powers as long as they hold out. I'm serious though. This could be our chance to find out why someone is causing mayhem on this island. I'll bet any amount of money our favorite old rogue pirate, Jacques Chaudret, has all the answers—despite being dead for hundreds of years."

Chapter 33

Tenth Avenue on Endgate Island, Louisiana, referred to both the remarkable area bounded by a gorgeous beach, a plot of land inhabited by imported black bears and red foxes, and the castle built in the early 1700s by a pirate for his kidnapped bride. A castle I was connected to, although *how* was a mystery. But connected I was—emotionally, physically, even spiritually, if one considers déjà vu a spiritual event. The question was whether the connection would save me or destroy me. Today might be the day I'd find out.

I headed downstairs early thanks to the scent of croissants coming from Luc's kitchen enticing me out of a deep sleep. I didn't bother with a shower. By the end of our exploration today I figured I'd be grimy, filthy, and downright disgusting, so there was zero point in using up water.

Eric and Jenny were already in the kitchen, sipping coffee and eating croissants.

I glared at them both. "Ah jeez. This is rude, y'all, just darn rude. Couldn't have waited another twenty seconds for me to get down the stairs?"

Eric poured a hot cup for me. "If we'd realized twenty seconds was the maximum time frame, we might have been more polite. Blame Jenny. She said after yesterday's craziness we should let you sleep for another hour or so."

"Are you kidding? The instant I smelled those croissants I was pulling on jeans and was halfway down the stairs." I glanced down at Eric's foot. "You found another boot cast, I see."

"It's the old one. I'd left it in the ATV. Never got touched by the fire. If I were gifted with second sight, I'd say I left it there deliberately, knowing I'd need it again. I do wish I'd've brought more than one pair of jeans and a shirt to the house the night before when we were all sharing the guest room. Thankfully, the clothes I was wearing when we dove in to get Robin's body are in the washer here, so Alex doesn't have to lend me half his closet." He leaned down and rubbed his ankle. "Damn. What a load of disasters in such a short time."

Jenny paused as she slathered butter on a croissant. "You guys suppose we'll find any answers at the castle? Or, more specifically, Teddie, what do *you* think? I mean you're our resident precognitive, since it's obvious Eric has no such abilities—and leaving a boot cast in a vehicle was sheer dumb luck." She wiggled her fingers at Eric. "No offense."

"None taken. I leave all eerie psychic stuff to Teddie." He didn't mention he'd had a couple of signs or portents himself and they appeared to be of another life.

"I'm ignoring both of you," I stated without a shred of truth. "But I admit I'm feeling clueless. I agree gloom and doom have been the buzzwords of the week, but I'm much cheerier because Eric will be clad in his own clothes as soon as the next laundry is done. Now, unless anyone has any objections, I plan to suck down another large cup of coffee and two more croissants and hope Luc has packed a nice lunch for us to eat at the creepy castle while we investigate all the secrets left for us by dead pirates who will probably pop out and scare the fool out of us at every corner. Pass the blackberry jam, would you, Jenny?"

She did. I smeared about a tablespoon on my croissant and the three of us got down to the business of breakfast so we'd be well nourished and ready for exploration. About twenty minutes later, we were in Michael's SUV, with Jenny driving. A picnic hamper filled with sandwiches lay in the backseat along with three boxes of food and paper products Luc had prepared for the detour we planned to take to the Quarters.

Second sight must have jumped from my brain to the residents of the Quarters because they knew we were coming. Jenny barely slid the truck to a stop before six children, Louie the dog, and a couple of tired-looking moms came out to greet us. We unloaded the goods and chatted for a few minutes about how everyone was faring the second day after the storm.

I was on the ground bonding with Louie, providing belly rubs and enjoying canine kisses in return, when I heard Vianca Giry's voice.

"Miz Teddie. Howdy. Ah'm so glad y'all came by today. Y'all want me to git that no-good mutt offa you?"

I looked up at her around Louie's head. "Miz Vianca. Great to see you, too. Thanks for offering, but the dog and I are good. It's actually quite nice after a couple of days of turmoil to be around a warm puppy with no hidden agenda, no malice, and a fun set of floppy ears."

Miz Vianca asked far too sweetly, "Y'all tryin' to say Mister Eric isn't all those things?"

I didn't bother asking how she knew about Eric. Could be island grapevine, intuition, or her own psychic "giftees." I responded with, "Good point. Except, of course, for the floppy ears. He's pretty special and warm and kind and—"

"Y'all need to take care of each other."

I managed to get the dog into a position where he couldn't tackle me and asked, "Why? Specifically? I mean, yeah, it seems a lot of the bad stuff started once Eric arrived, although Jenny told me she's had uneasy feelings for several months. But is there something else?"

"Ah don' wanna sound like a character in a bad voodoo movie, Miz Teddie, but there's evil on this island. Been evil since ol' Jacques Chaudret arrived, and it goes through cycles. Like the bad be restin' for years, then starts up brewin' again. It's bubblin' now, 'bout to boil."

I started to tremble. "I feel it. I've got some kind of weird pull or relationship to that bloody castle. Miz Vianca, do you have any idea why?"

"Ah might. But you've got to find your own way, Miz Teddie. Can't do it for you...or for Mister Eric. He's part of this whole... Ah guess Ah'd call it a quilt. Or more like a big ol' spider web. And Mister Eric...well... He's tied and you're tied. He ain't feelin' much of it yet, and he's avoidin' 'cause there's pain there. But Miz Teddie, y'all gotta take care. Chaudrets are powerful. You gotta be stronger."

I was about to ask her how the Chaudrets could be powerful when they'd died out decades earlier, but we were joined by Eric and Jenny. Jenny informed me the kids were happy with Luc's provisions and we needed to get to the castle. Both Jenny and Eric hugged Miz Vianca, who squeezed Eric's hand and told him to watch out for me.

We arrived at the castle without any damage to the SUV, avoiding ditches deeper than the cellar under the burnt carriage house and after-hurricane debris of unidentifiable objects intent on blocking the road.

"By the way, how do we get inside?" I inquired. "Are we doing a little B & E or crawling through another nasty tunnel?"

"Ha. You unbeliever—I have a key." Jenny chortled. "Michael said the Laurents have had keys for years. Sadly, I think all the first families do."

She parked in a driveway better suited to a modern ranch house in Texas than a castle on an island. Paved, not dirt, with surprisingly few cracks and no gaping holes. We climbed out of the SUV and stood staring at the front of the castle. The sky, which had been sunny and cloudless all morning, darkened.

Clearly, Captain Jacques and his descendants didn't want us here.

Chapter 34

Jenny opened the front door and led us into a huge room with vaulted ceilings, sparsely furnished with the style of chairs I used when I designed *Richard III* for a summer theatre in Vermont two years ago—thrones for royalty more interested in intimidation than comfort. Window seats were pushed up against the tall, stained-glass windows, medieval tapestries covered three different walls in whatever one wanted to label this space. Parlor? Living room? Ballroom? Big honkin' entrance? Stern-faced family portraits of buccaneers and plantation masters decorated the east wall then continued up a winding staircase. My first impression was the place hadn't been updated since 1850. My second impression was the décor appeared more English than French and not a bit "old South." Cleaner lines and less ornate furniture. Perhaps Grace Sedley had wielded more power than one would have imagined from a kidnapped bride, at least in terms of interior design.

My third and most distressing impression was that I'd played in this room under the watchful and disapproving eyes of dead ancestors and live nannies and hadn't been happy. To be honest, I couldn't imagine anyone spending more than ten minutes in this space ever being happy. If I hadn't been on a fact-finding mission, I'd've been out the door and running back to Miz Vianca's about ten seconds after I spotted the family crest on a huge, sword-crossed shield hanging above a fireplace near the entrance to what might be the dining room.

"Did you guys see the portraits? I don't know whether to dissolve in hysterical laughter or cry. There are literally dudes up there with scars over half their faces and eye patches. The only thing missing are parrots. Makes the parlor at Sugarberry Terrace seem positively modern and classy."

They ignored me. I didn't blame them. My humor wasn't at its best today.

Eric took one look at the stairs, glanced down at his ankle, winced, and pointed to the dining area and the table set up to seat at least twenty people. "Shall I explore the gargantuan china cabinet taking up the entire wall next to what I guess is the kitchen? You guys do realize there's no way in hell I'm placing even one toe on those stairs. And while we're standing here, admittedly awestruck, might I ask if you ladies have any idea what we're looking for?"

"Old books, diaries, ledgers, letters, photographs," I responded, trying not to notice the cold racing down my spine.

Eric and Jenny turned and stared at me. "Anything specific?" Eric asked.

"I have no clue. My mouth opened and words came out and sort of streaked by before I knew what I was saying. But it does make sense."

"Books, etcetera?" Jenny asked.

"Yep. Think about it. Written words. Someone stole Marianne Chaudret's diary before you had the chance to read it. Eric and I found out Emeric Desmarais was a former slave who was labeled as 'lost' when we read an old ledger. And there's something weird about the gothic novels we found in the cellar at Hickory Shadows."

Eric sank down onto one of the throne chairs. "I'll bet a large cup of coffee one of those books provides proof positive I once had an ancestor on the island. But if that's true, the Emeric Desmarais living here around the time of the Civil War was a slave, so why should anyone now care... apart from me? Are the accidents and thievery really connected to something centuries past?"

"Miz Vianca compared the events of this week to quilts and webs, and while she didn't get specific, she more than hinted *everything* is connected to the past. I'd say she was definitely referring to your past, Eric, as in ancestors who lived here a long time before any of us knew Endgate Island existed."

"What about you, Teddie?" Jenny asked. "You're the one getting all the vibes, so there must be a reason."

"Me? My ancestors all came from Germany or Scotland, with the Germans heading directly to Galveston and staying in Texas and the Scots hitting Ellis Island long after the Statue of Liberty had been installed. Delivered. Whatever. The Scots ended up in California or something. But I'm talking about my current life."

"Say what?" Jenny inquired.

"Confession time. I've been fighting against believing it, but I'm almost positive I once lived on Endgate Island...more than a hundred years ago." I didn't mention Eric felt the same. It was up to him to decide whether or not to share his feelings with Jenny.

No great surprise: Jenny was thrilled. "My best buddy reincarnated. Call me impressed. Maybe we'll find clues to your past somewhere in this demonic castle."

"My goose bumps agree with you." I rolled my shoulders back. "Okay, troops, I say let's get to it. I'll be brave and athletic and tackle the staircase, even though I swear it should be in a remake of *Vertigo*. Eric, you said you're hitting the dining room?"

"Yeah. And the window seats. They look big enough for storage."

Jenny chimed in with, "There's a library around the other side of this ballroom. I'll check there. With any luck we'll discover someone slipped another diary in among the gothic romances and legal thrillers. Or—this would be cool—a ledger written by Captain Jacques's first mate describing tons of ill-gotten booty from a raid or two. Hey, maybe one of his crew providing true stores about their sex lives throughout the Caribbean islands."

I paused, thought, and stated, "I like it. Give a shout if you find something interesting. Or if the captain or mate pop out from behind a bookshelf."

Jenny giggled. "I'll send them both up to you. You'll bond better. Oh, remember, folks, we're also here to get an idea of how the castle could work if it becomes the site of our uber-awesome-tourist-enticing mystery theatre."

We split up and headed to our respective places of exploration.

The stairs were intimidating, but also provided the first whimsical note seen in the chateau. I was looking at the best bannister and staircase ever invented. Children—and some spunky adults—must have taken advantage throughout the centuries, sliding down while their mamas watched in horror, waiting for the sound of a crash and the wails of pain when bones broke. For a brief second I could feel myself sailing down that bannister in sheer glee, only to be met with the strap of a belt across my bottom for my trouble. I somehow knew it had been worth the spankings and I'd taken that ride every chance I got.

The second floor held bedrooms, a couple of sitting rooms, and a small library. I chose the library to explore first. It boasted one small casement window and bookshelves that lined every wall, kept from dust and weather behind glass. Two tall floor lamps stood behind two fairly comfortable-looking chairs. There were also two end tables, equipped with coasters. Square containers, filled with wooden bookmarks, took up the middle of both tables. Again, I had the impression no one had used this room in years. Decades. What creeped me out though was the nearly pristine quality of the furniture, apart from dust. Pieces should have showed some indication of age, but they were sturdy and solid. Untouched. Perhaps guarded by ghosts?

I sent out a silent hope the last person to use the room had been efficient and organized and consequently categorized the books in such a way as to cut down a search from days to hours. A general uneasiness crept over my body. Something of importance sat on one of these shelves. With any luck, the something would come tumbling down onto my head. Heck, I'd settle for a title screaming "pick me."

I started with the bottom shelf closest to the door, rummaging through dusty books, which turned out to be novels from the nineteenth century. Alcott, Austen, Charlotte and Emily Bronte, Dickens, Dostoyevsky, and Dumas. Familiar classics had been neatly stacked and took up three shelves. The books were in surprisingly great shape, hardbound, with zero human hands touching even the spine in the last sixty or seventy years. Any other day I'd've been in a frenzy of literary madness, plopping in one of the chairs and reading the adventures of the *Count of Monte Cristo*, but nothing here explained why I felt any odd sensations, so I moved on.

The middle shelves held a mix of textbooks. I spotted science, history, and geography books, encyclopedias, along with several novels published in the early 1900s. Three shelves were devoted to children's books, including *Grimm's Fairy Tales*, which, truly, isn't suitable for children unless one wants their kid to grow up with nightmares and some interesting views on society, and quite a few pirate novels. Jacques Chaudret himself would doubtless have enjoyed Robert Louis Stevenson's *Treasure Island* or perhaps Rafael Sabatini's *Captain Blood*. On the other hand, if rumors of his kidnapping the woman who became his bride were true, Jacques might have been less than pleased to note the feminist entry into the genre, one *Fanny Campbell, the Female Pirate Captain*, written by Maturin Murray Ballou in 1844.

Reading titles was fun but wasn't helping me find the one book I needed. Not to mention reading titles could take all morning and afternoon. Time for a new tactic. I sat down in the middle of the room on a rug so old and plush it must have been pirate swag four hundred years ago. I closed my eyes and waited for inspiration. A spooky voice from beyond. A gentle—or a violent—shove pointing me toward the right shelf.

Nothing overly dramatic occurred, but when I opened my eyes, I was inexplicably drawn to the bookcase nearest the one tiny window in the room. I was disappointed when the only books I found were novels. I was secretly hoping for another diary.

I opened a book at random and read a publication date of 1945. I continued checking copyright pages and realized all the books had been released between 1939 and 1965. I'd never heard of a single one, and most of the publishers weren't in existence anymore. It didn't make sense for anything vitally important to have been hidden in the pages, yet my certainty, of *"this is it"* was the strongest I'd experienced since I'd sensed Jenny was on a bed, drugged and sick, in Hickory Shadows on Third Avenue.

There wasn't time to go through all the books without some specific certainty as to which one could hold answers or even provide an idea of what questions needed asking. Although it nearly killed me not to dive in and start reading, I forced myself to pile the books on the floor and mentally measured the size and number of cartons needed to take them back to the Laurents to peruse at leisure.

I'd found everything the small library had to offer. But there was more to uncover in this house. Leaving the books on the rug, I headed into the hall to explore the other rooms on the second floor, the majority of which were bedrooms.

I peeked into the room next door and ducked back out, allowing my sixth sense or second sight to make all decisions. If I didn't feel anything out of the ordinary, there was no point in looking around. Two more bedrooms. Nothing screamed at me, although one room had my senses twitching because it appeared to have been made up in the 1960s for a teenager and then left. There were posters of British rock groups on the wall, a quilt with a red, green, orange, and purple psychedelic pattern on the bed, and hideous red and orange neon-colored drapes hanging from a sturdy curtain rod over the windows. It was obvious that no one had bothered to update for the last sixty years or more. But it didn't feel haunted, so I didn't bother to take a lot of time digging through old dressers or looking through closets.

All the rooms were interesting because of all the antiques and other memorabilia, and any other day I'd've enjoyed looking at the furniture, the handmade quilts and spreads on beds, and the embroidery on rocking chairs. But I found nothing to help explain the danger we'd all been in since arriving on Endgate Island.

Then came the room at the end of the hall.

The door, not opened in decades, or perhaps centuries, stuck. While I didn't have a can of oil-spray in my bag, I did have one of those travel-size bottles of baby oil, since my hands are generally dirty from working on sets and I wash them a lot, so there's always a need for major moisturizing. I put a drop or two on the hinges and rubbed the oil in, gave it a second to work, then tried the door again.

Success. It took a little coaxing using my shoulder and hip, but the door finally gave and I was inside. At first glance, the room was much like the others I'd seen, filled with antique décor and furniture, like the patchwork quilt spread on the four-poster bed, the hope chest in front of the bed, the *petit point* embroidered fabric on the rocking chair, and the huge wardrobe in the corner. A second quilt lay over a window seat, and a beautiful lace runner graced the top of a vanity featuring a mirror so old every image it displayed was distorted.

There were no personal items in plain sight. No jewelry boxes or little odd mementos from trips taken or dances attended. No dolls kept from childhood. No photos in frames. Not a single piece of artwork took up space on any wall. Admittedly, paintings weren't needed. The window faced the beach and provided a view so gorgeous I personally could have gazed at it for the next fifty years or so and never bothered with the wall behind me.

The lack of knickknacks more than hinted someone had been determined to remove any items that could potentially provide an identity. I couldn't get a sense of the girl who'd once used this as her bedroom, except I felt certain she'd inhabited it more than a hundred years ago.

I was about to exit and make the climb to the tower and the turrets but stopped, drawn to the huge wardrobe. I didn't open it. Instead, I glanced down and spotted a glint of what appeared to be a frame peeking out from the side of the wardrobe.

I gently tugged it out and stared at a painting of a young woman done in the style of several portraits I'd passed in the hall on this floor. The painting had been cruelly vandalized, with a gash dissecting her portrait. Thankfully, the damage hadn't destroyed the beauty of the girl or the artist who'd captured what seemed to me to be a feisty and almost impish spirit. A spirit I recognized and identified with.

Her clothing suggested the work had been created during the Civil War era, which gave credence to my suspicions. But the final touch nailing her identity was the pendant around her neck. It was the same sapphire pendant I'd worn last night during dinner at the Laurent house. The pendant Eric said seemed familiar. The pendant I'd bought last fall at a flea market in Brooklyn, New York.

Chapter 35

I grabbed the portrait and my bag and ran from the room, slamming the door behind me. I continued to run, albeit a tad awkwardly, as I tried to hang on to the portrait and not tumble headfirst down the stairs to the first floor. The earlier thoughts of a fun slide down the bannister disappeared, replaced with the urgent need to reach the dining room.

Eric heard my less-than-graceful descent and greeted me at the bottom of the stairs in the main hall.

"Jeez. You took those stairs like an Olympian. What did you find?"

"Where's Jenny? I want to show you guys together. Yo. Jenny."

I sank down on the bottom step, and put the painting on the floor, face down. Eric sat next to me. Jenny ran in from the library and joined us.

"Y'all ready? Okay." I carefully turned the painting over to its correct side and showed them the portrait.

Jenny stared at it for a long moment. "Oh man. She was beautiful. And young. What do you think? Sixteen? Maybe seventeen?"

I answered, "Yeah. Late teens at any rate. Okay, kids. Take a good look at the pendant."

They did. Silence.

Eric spoke first. "It's yours. Unless a jeweler made two pieces exactly alike in the 1860s, which isn't likely."

Jenny nudged me. "You bought yours in New York City, right?"

"Brooklyn. At a flea market in Bay Ridge. And even at the time it seemed there was something a bit strange about how I found it."

"In what way?" Eric asked.

"I didn't make much of it at the time, but it wasn't out front with other necklaces. I was specifically looking for a piece to go with the blue and white dress I wore last night. I wanted an elegant necklace in silver. The man running the stall didn't wait even ten seconds for me to browse. He took one look at me and told me he had the perfect pendant and it would fit my needs exactly."

Jenny's eyes widened. "I'm assuming you weren't wearing the blue dress?"

"You're assuming right. I had on jeans and a sweatshirt. Black and brown. Not even close to matching the blue dress."

"Which begs question number one: How did this particular pendant wind up in Brooklyn more than a century after this portrait was painted?" Jenny asked.

"And the follow-up, which is more mysterious: How, out of the hundreds of people shopping the flea market, did the dealer tag me as the person the pendant was meant for?"

"And another question," Jenny stated before bothering to answer the unanswerable. "Why did someone slash this painting? Why isn't it with the others from this era? I'm pretty good at identifying similar works, and I'd bet anything this was done by the same artist. Who was quite good. There's a sparkle in the girl's eyes not typical for portraits of that time."

Eric traced the frame with his index finger. "We haven't even gotten to what could be the most important question: Do we have any idea who this is?"

"Yeah. I do." I reached over and gently touched the painting. "I have no proof, but I'll bet it's a Chaudret. She's not any old daughter of the fine old family, but one of two daughters who lived here during the Civil War. It looks like the right time period, and it could explain the entry in the ledger I found the other day. Jeez, two days ago. Seems like a year."

Eric leaned over and kissed my forehead. "You're rambling again. Way off point."

"I am?" I bit my lip. "I am. Okay. I believe we are looking at Miss Althea Chaudret, daughter of Henri Chaudret. She seemed to have been missing from all family events after the Civil War but never listed as dead. Along with one Emeric Desmarais, probable runaway."

Jenny stared down at the portrait again. "You believe they're connected, right? As a couple?"

"I'm almost certain. Let me start with the practical. It makes sense. Eric and I talked about it as a possibility when we first found the ledger. The dates are right. And if the daughter of the very white Chaudrets had a romantic relationship with a black slave owned by the same family, it could explain why this portrait isn't gracing the halls with kinfolk and why someone took a knife or scissors and slashed it."

"And the impractical?" Jenny inquired.

"A memory of the day I sat for it. Asking the artist to make sure to get the pendant right because it was my favorite."

"You're talking about Althea," Jenny stated, without the least bit of surprise.

"Yes."

Jenny burst out, "I love it. This is so cool. My best friend lived on this island a hundred-plus years ago. I'm so jealous." Her eyes widened. "Do you suppose I could have been here, too?"

"I haven't gotten any vibes about you in another body, but it's early days," I told her. I glanced at the portrait. "On the other hand, there's something…nah…gone now."

"Well, poo." She suddenly turned to Eric and pointed an accusatory finger at him. "And you."

"What?"

"You're hiding something."

"What makes you think that?"

"Because, Mister Desmarais, you're a fabulously awesome director, but as an actor, you stink."

Eric looked at me. I looked up at the ceiling, feigning innocence. He shrugged and gave up. "Fine. Yes. It seems possible I'm back on the island as well for another run."

"Don't tell me," Jenny chided him. "The guy I thought was your ancestor is really you?"

"It's the working theory," Eric replied drily.

"Well, why aren't you jumping up and down over the sheer thrill of knowing you've been reincarnated?" She chortled with glee. "Apart from the whole nearly-breaking-your-ankle-falling-down-stairs thing."

"Because, Miss Far-too-Delighted, I'm still processing all this. I'm trying to sort out fact from crazy and figure out how I feel." He rose. "Which gets us back to the topic of why someone snuck into the Laurent tower room, stole Marianne's diary, and then went on a one-person destroy-all spree. It's got to have something to do with Althea since they were sisters."

I stood as well. "Until we find the diary, I'm voting for more exploration. Marianne and Althea lived here. I still have the feeling some of those answers are in this house. Much as I hate peeking into more spooky bedrooms, I must now 'woman up' and hit the tower."

Jenny put her hand on my arm. "Wait. Before you go, I want you both to see what I found in the library."

"Okay. Lead on."

Eric and I followed Jenny into the huge main floor library. It was overwhelming, not only due to the size of the room, but because of the number of books gracing the tall shelves and the spiral staircase leading to an easy-access catwalk.

"Wow," Eric and I both exclaimed.

Jenny did a little dance. "In the midst of all the angst about portraits and worry about our safety and well-being, I say with confidence this is the most fabulous room ever and would be ideal for one of the interactive mystery plays. I need to get Michael to call one of his contacts in the area of rare books. I'm amazed these aren't powder at this point, and I'd definitely be happier if someone could move the majority to a space set up in terms of perfect climate control to keep them from falling apart."

"Good thought. So, are these what you wanted to show us?" I asked.

"No. The rare books are as cool as an ice pack, but probably not terribly important in terms of our search for answers. Come here." She led us to a corner of the room. "Check out what's on the top of the desk under the glass."

We did.

"A map. A very old map," I said.

"Yep. At first when I saw it, I was yelling 'Hallelujah' and 'how perfect for treasure hunts for the tourists.' Then I started studying it and realized this shows at least seven different ways to get to this chateau by means of what I assume are tunnels? Passages? Funky hallways? I'll bet next month's rent these tunnels were constantly used by Jacques and his crew for smuggling goods in from ships crashed on the beach or those raided at sea."

Eric and I simultaneously and far too gleefully shouted, "Pirate booty."

The three of us began fist bumping and high-fiving each other.

After the merriment died down a bit, Eric grew practical. "Our romantic, theatrical minds sail right to the land of swashbuckling figures crossing swords in movies, but we forget there are modern-day pirates with automatic weapons terrorizing folks out for pleasure cruises, and they've got to have places to store whatever they've stolen or stash drugs before bringing them into the mainland."

I traced the lines on the ancient map. "I wonder if any of the folks fighting over ownership of the castle have seen this map."

Jenny mused, "Could one of them be sort of a modern-day pirate on the island? Scary thought."

"Possible. It would explain this manic eagerness to get the rights to this particular beach when the east side is as nice," Eric stated.

We continued staring at the map. My breathing turned ragged. "There's something really wrong here."

"You mean more than smuggling and piracy?" Jenny asked.

"Yeah. Map and navigation. Something...very personal. And malevolent." I sighed. "It's gone now."

"Okay, ladies, I say we get back to exploring and see if there's more to uncover," said Eric. "At least you two are on a roll. My contribution has been less than puny. All I've found are sets of very nice glassware and china. Although..."

"Yes?" I prompted.

"Nothing much. I'm borrowing a small page—or perhaps only a small paragraph—from Theodosia the psychic. Hang on a second."

Jenny and I managed to keep quiet.

Eric closed his eyes for a long moment, then opened them, and said, "I feel like I've seen one of the mantel clocks before. It's a pendulum timepiece, clearly antique, and way too familiar—but I can't get a handle on why."

Jenny and I grabbed Eric's elbows and led him out of the library. "Show us."

The clock was in the smaller of the two china cabinets in the dining room, which was still a large piece of furniture. Eric pointed to it and I reached inside and took it out. "Any funky vibes, Teddie?"

"Not really. But I'll keep it in mind for future insights. Maybe some items have to simmer in my mind before any recognition comes through?"

Jenny ran back to the main hall and brought the painting to the dining room. "Well, at least *this* isn't psychic. Look, someone stole the diary, which assumes one will have no qualms about stealing other items related to the Chaudrets. So, I suggest anything we find needs to stay in a room back home with one of us there at all times. Except maybe the map. It's heavy and bulky and if someone has seen it and is already using it for nefarious purposes, it does no good to take it with us."

"Agreed."

I put the clock back in the cabinet. We solemnly shared a three-way handshake.

"And now, guys, I'm going to keep up my schedule of aerobic stepping for the day and head to the tower room."

Eric and Jenny both patted me on the head, pretending sympathy.

I placed my right hand over my forehead and my left arm out to the side in a melodramatic pose. "Do not call me downstairs unless there is a major event taking place. Perhaps an earthquake or a category 6 hurricane. Skydivers parachuting onto the island. Now, if the ghost of Althea Chaudret appears and plops *her* diary into your hands…or should I say *ours*…I'd pull a Quasimodo and swing down from the highest turret."

Chapter 36

My knees were screaming in pain by the time I reached the third floor of the Chaudret castle. I hoped if anything of value had been stored in this tower area, it would be small enough to put in my bag so I wouldn't have to carry it down what now felt like a good half mile of steps.

The climb ended in a square hall. Rooms had been built on each of the four corners, and I pitied anyone who'd been assigned a bedroom up here unless he or she were about ten years old and thoroughly enamored with the ideas of pirates and living in their turrets.

I sank down onto a bench placed outside one of the rooms overlooking the west beach, telling myself I needed to take a short rest after the climb. I was lying. I was avoiding an exploration every part of my psyche was telling me would end in finding something…unpleasant.

My mind's eye returned to the slashed portrait of the girl I knew was Althea. *Me.* Oddly, it was the push I needed to head to the room at the northeast corner of the west wall. As if I owed it to both of us to find answers. The door was heavy and the hinges rusty, but with more help from the bottle of travel moisturizer, I was able to open the door.

I entered emptiness.

The room itself wasn't devoid of furniture, although there weren't many pieces there: a bed, a rocking chair with a floor lamp beside it, a small wardrobe, and a desk. But the feeling of vacancy was so strong I found it hard not to turn and run. It was even hard to breathe. There was nothing on any wall, exactly like the room on the floor below.

The room was cold. And the cold wasn't normal. If ever a space was haunted, this was it. However, instead of some ghostly being with a whispery voice running around rattling chains or tossing objects, there was a lack of *any* presence. Blank. Empty. As if the room had somehow been stripped of all warmth, sound, and feeling.

Worse, I was positive I'd been in this room before. When I crossed from the open doorway to the window, I had a déjà vu moment so strong I couldn't tell if I was living in the past or the present. I shook it off and tried to reclaim my sanity by stepping outside onto the widow's walk and admiring the view of the gulf waters. I breathed in the late-morning air, hoping for the warm breeze to push away a small trace of that eerie chill.

When I felt calm enough to go back inside, I headed for the desk in a manner best referred to as being on autopilot. The only tangible object was a manual typewriter, which gave no clue as to the era when it was last used, although if I had to guess, I'd go with 1950s or 60s. The top drawer on the right-hand side held a stack of blank, yellowed typing paper and an unused typewriter ribbon. Dead ballpoint pens with long-dried ink lay in the middle drawer alongside scattered paper clips and broken pencils with chewed eraser tips. A pack of unopened chewing gum was the big prize in the left top drawer. I hesitated for a moment before opening the bottom drawer, unsure if I wanted to see what was there, run and hide, or find a rope and impress everyone—including myself—by rappelling from the widow's walk to the beach below.

I decided to be a big, brave girl and go with Option One: open the damned drawer. At first glance, there didn't seem to be a reason for all my mental fuss and avoidance. Just a bunch of faded, yellowing pages. About seven in all. Six were blank. The seventh was crumpled and appeared to have been tossed in the drawer when it should have ended up in a wastebasket. I smoothed it out and found a note written in black ink, with the first name appearing as an almost illegible signature. Two sentences had been crossed through.

The note read: *Am sending the manuscript as is, even though the last chapters aren't complete. Can you get to the castle? Please come. If not, call me at Cypress 5568 but ONLY after midnight. Rosalynn.*

The crossed-out sentences were almost impossible to read, but I squinted and held to the light until I finally could distinguish about nine words: *I must get out. My last chapter... own death.*

The paper dropped out of my hands and fell onto the desk. I picked it up and walked out of the room without a glance back. My pace stayed even as I started down the first flight of stairs and remained so until I reached the bottom floor. Sleepwalkers roam from room to room in the same odd fixed tempo, but sleepwalkers generally awaken to reality. I wasn't sure if reality could be found in this particular nightmare.

Eric met me at the bottom of the stairs with a bottle of water in his hand, which he immediately gave to me. "Sit. Breathe. Drink."

I did as I was told in the suggested order, recovering my wits sufficiently to be mildly humorous and ask, "What? No rum? In a pirate's house?"

"Drink the water, Theodosia. One sip from a barrel of rum and you'd be out cold."

I drank. By the time I'd downed the entire bottle, Jenny had arrived.

"Damn, girl, you look like death warmed over."

I narrowed my eyes at my best buddy. "Thank you for the trite phrase, although in this instance it might be better changed to death frozen over."

"Meaning?"

I described the horrible, empty feeling of cold in the turret.

Jenny's tone wavered between horrified and gleeful. "We're talkin' haunted? Really haunted?"

"Yes. Let me just note for the record the room overlooking the west beach could be a poster for 'this way to the ghost.' And I'm trying to be funny because if I let myself remember what I felt inside the space...and I'm sure it was used by Rosalynn, who wrote the note and whoever Rosalynn was apart from a writer... Damn, this is wrong. I'm blocking memories for the time being because my senses were so assaulted if I ever again feel those emotions I will run screaming out of the castle and off this island without a backward glance, and not care a whit about solving any puzzles, mysteries, or reasons for accidents." I took another deep breath. "I apologize for the run-on sentence, but I needed to keep talking before I passed out from shock."

Eric stared at me. "Rosalynn? Who in hell is Rosalynn? What note?"

"Sorry. I'm still kind of...rattled. Let me back up a bit. But don't expect clarity for a while. Where was I?"

"In the haunted room," Jenny prompted. "Which you believe belonged to a writer named Rosalynn."

"Right." I held the note out and stayed silent while Eric and Jenny read through it.

Eric laid the note down by the portrait. "Teddie, are you calm enough to try to figure out who Rosalynn was? Or is? There's a phone number, so we're at least in the twentieth century. She could still be alive."

I perked up. "True. I was so freaked out by the whole ambiance I simply hauled it out of there."

Jenny added, "The phone number begins with the exchange Cypress. Should be a good clue. Eric, do you have your cell?"

He pulled it out of his pocket and handed it to her. She whooped. "Ah the wonders of instant search and broadband available even inside ancient fortresses." She typed in the name of the exchange and Louisiana. We quickly discovered Cypress was used up until the mid-60s when all remaining name exchanges in the state were dropped in favor of the seven-digit system for local calls. Endgate Island was one of the last to use the name, and by 1968 it was no longer in use.

"Seems pretty obvious she didn't write this note after 68," Jenny stated, handing the phone back to Eric, who typed in another question.

"Name exchanges started in the 20s, at least according to this guide," said Eric. "Sounds like we're looking at a span of forty-odd years."

I blinked, holding back tears of frustration. "And all we have is a first name. A pretty first name, but a first name without a last name to accompany it."

Eric glanced at me, then at Jenny. "I'm making an executive decision."

"Yes?" we chorused.

"We're tired and hungry, and Teddie has been up and down those bloody stairs way too many times. The dining room is *not* creepy." He paused. "At least it wasn't last time we were in there, but things change fast on this island. I suggest we adjourn, unpack whatever goodies Luc put in the hamper, spread them out all over the table, eat until we're stuffed, and then see if our investigative skills return."

It was the nicest idea I'd heard all day. And even nicer to enter the dining room and discover Eric was right. If this room had ever been haunted, the ghosts had long departed. We could eat in peace.

Chapter 37

You get three theatre people together in a room—even a room in a spooky castle—and the discussion is going to turn professional. Heck, a theatre person sitting solo at the dinner table is going to bring out their laptop or phone and check reviews or audition notices or find out if a long-running show will move to a different house to make room for a musical version of *Comedy of Errors* from the Royal Shakespeare Company.

So, we ignored the fact that we were breaking bread in a haunted house with some seriously bad juju and sat at one end of the giant dining table, "oohing" and "aahing" over Luc's perfect picnic lunch, and talked theatre. It seemed as though I'd been on Endgate Island for months, not days, and I was surprised to discover—with the aid of Eric's cell—not much had changed on the Manhattan theatre scene. I handed the phone to Jenny, who said she wanted to see who'd taken over several roles in *Phantom of the Opera.*

She squealed. "Yes."

I jumped about three inches out of my chair. "What? Is Captain Jacques Chaudret currently playing the Phantom? Can we say typecasting?"

She scowled at me. "We're not discussing dead pirates. And my 'yes' was because various theatrical awards nominations were announced this week and..." She gave a dramatic drum roll. "One Teddie Grant is listed under nominees for best set design and best lighting design for *Measures of Light.*"

"Are you serious?"

"I am. Take a look." She handed me the phone and I almost fainted for the second time today, but for a much nicer reason. Seeing my name in print—if one could call a website "print"—was an accomplishment anyone would be proud of, but beyond the wonderful recognition, I felt vindicated and free from Colin Barrow's vicious lies.

I jumped out of the chair and did a little dance of joy around the room. "This is so amazing and wonderful. This *almost* compensates for crawling through creepy cellars and haunted towers for the last few days."

Jenny and Eric both congratulated me with true enthusiasm and not an ounce of envy. Admittedly, Jenny had won two television awards and Eric three Off-Broadway awards and been nominated for Broadway, but I had the impression—no, that was too mild, make it the *certainty*—envy was not an option and would *never* be an option for either of them

Jenny grabbed the phone again. "I'm so nosy. Who else got nominated from *Measures of Light*? And before I start looking, I am sick I haven't had the chance to see it." She read aloud the names of actors nominated, then paused and glanced at me. "Interesting."

"Yes?"

"I do not see the name of a certain sleazy director, as in Colin Barrow, anywhere near *Measures of Light* or any other production." She turned red. "Oh hell. Sorry. Should I not have mentioned him?"

"What are we—twelve? Everyone in Manhattan knew I dated Colin, including Eric. Who, incidentally, has *not* been in a monastery the last few years either."

Eric added, "Teddie's breakup with Colin is also not a secret. And we haven't spent a ton of time discussing him because he's... Well, he's..."

"Last season's news," I interrupted before Jenny could come out with what would doubtless be a description that was, if not X, at least R-rated.

"Well, good. May I confess I'm pleased Colin did not receive a nomination? Of course, Teddie can't say it because it would sound petty and extremely snarky, but it's a best friend's prerogative to be allowed to gloat over the *non*-success of her buddy's lousy ex-boyfriend."

Eric and I were both laughing by the time Jenny finished. I shook my finger at her. "Speaking of awards, you get 'most convoluted comment of the week,' Jenny Harrison Laurent. But yeah. If it doesn't get out of this room, I won't offer a peep of protest if y'all want to gloat for the next six weeks." My tone changed to one more somber. "I'll tell you guys though, I'm amazed to see my name there. I figured Colin's poison about my supposedly stealing his ideas would have reached every nominating committee in New York and I'd've been blackballed from the Obie awards, or from ever designing a show anywhere but a junior high school in Boise or Fargo."

Eric patted my hand. "Producers and nominators are smarter than we give them credit for. They take the time to check into nasty allegations before labeling someone guilty. As is clear from this nomination. I'll bet you'll have a lot of great job offers when we get back."

We all solemnly lifted our bottles of water and toasted. "Nice ending to lunch, folks," I said. "I needed this. Not only hearing about a nomination, which will hit me as fact in about ten years, but taking a break from cryptic notes, slashed portraits, and spooky bedrooms."

Jenny took a long swig of her water. "And we should get back to it, I suppose?"

"I have a suggestion," Eric said. "Instead of peeking into more rooms, or heaven forbid, a cellar, or sending Teddie up more stairs, we could look at some of the books. It'll keep us together and help make this less stressful."

My hand immediately popped up. "I vote a big yes. Especially to avoiding creepy spaces under the house. Unfortunately, all the books screaming *'read me'* are still upstairs in the smaller library." I took a long moment and surveyed the room. "I wonder... is there a dumbwaiter system in the castle? One going to the second floor? Obviously some pitiful person *not* in a boot cast and *not* getting over being drugged two days ago—that would be me—has to go upstairs and put the books *into* the dumbwaiter, but at least it would keep the pitiful person—again, me—from having to carry the bloomin' things down stairs and go back up for more."

Eric nodded. "Great idea. Let's check."

Jenny ran back into the kitchen, telling us to stay, and then trotted back within thirty seconds gleefully announcing, "Yes, there is a dumbwaiter, and yes it's big enough to hoist several cartons of books." She added she'd even be willing to bravely climb into the thing herself in order to keep from sending the pitiful person up the stairs again, even though the very idea of getting inside terrified her.

I threw a damp napkin at her. "Do *not* give me the martyr bit, Jenny Harrison. The role is all mine. I shall trudge up the stairs again and gather books and stack cartons and place them in the dumbwaiter and send it down. There is no way we're putting *anyone* in something threatening to crash in the middle of hoisting, which you knew quite well when you volunteered."

Jenny fluttered her lashes at me. Eric suggested before anyone did any climbing we make sure the contraption worked. I rose. "I'll check. Apart from being the only healthy person in the room, I'm the set guru, so I'm supposed to be adept at pulling ropes and sending lifts up two flights before pounding up them myself." I glared at my friends. "Y'all just stay seated. I am woman. I am roaring." Pause. "I am tired."

Eric put his hand over his heart. "You're my hero, Theodosia. Forever and always."

"Yeah, yeah. You can quit smearing the butter and polishing the apple, Desmarais, I'm already committed to the task."

I kissed the man, made my way to the kitchen, checked the dumbwaiter, and silently pronounced it in good working condition. I called for Eric and Jenny to come in and get it going while I made the climb to the second floor for the third and hopefully last time today.

Fifteen minutes later there were four cartons of books sitting on the kitchen floor and I was wondering if any rubbing alcohol could be found in an ancient bathroom for my poor knees.

"Should we dump the books out and start reading?" Jenny asked.

I glared at her. "How would you like to be left in the Hickory Shadows bedroom with a bottle of codeine as nourishment for the next six weeks or so?"

She threw an empty water bottle at me in retaliation for my earlier toss with the napkin. "Not particularly. So, what do y'all want to do with this stuff?"

"Pile them into your truck and head back to your house. Like right now. We also need to pack up the portrait and Rosalynn's note. Eric? Do you want to bring the clock?"

"No. Let's leave it here. We can always come back and take another look. We've got enough to deal with."

We gathered the assorted items, the picnic hamper, and our bags, got everything in the truck in less than five minutes, and took the short route to get to Sugarberry Terrace. I was ready for a rest, but the possibility got shoved to the back of the to-do list when Michael met us at the back with a startling announcement.

"Sheriff Guidry is here. The medical examiner in New Orleans finished the autopsy of Robin Trahan early this morning and has pronounced the manner of death as homicide. Someone murdered him."

Chapter 38

I wish I could say I was surprised to hear Robin's death was not an accident, but I'd be lying. From the moment I'd had the vision of Robin's body in the water, I'd tried to suppress an all-too-swift impression of someone standing over Robin as he knelt on the pier, telling myself it was my imagination. A shadow. Nothing more. He'd slipped.

And now, the shadows had been proven right.

Spending too many hours in a haunted castle making…well, let's call them "intriguing" discoveries…and jogging up and down stairs while trying not to run into ghosts resulted in a huge desire for a nap followed by a dive into the books taken from Tenth Avenue, but the sheriff wanted to hear from anyone who'd been on the dock near the time Robin had died.

"Can we all at least freshen up a bit?" Jenny asked her spouse.

Michael hugged her. "Of course. And I want to hear all about the adventures at the castle, but I guess I need to wait. Guidry is in the parlor talking to Alex and Cici right now, but there's time for y'all to do whatever you need to do. I need to make a run to the dock and see if the medical supplies I ordered this morning have arrived."

Jenny, Eric, and I stored all our findings from the Chaudret castle in the guest room, which was now Eric's residence for as long as he stayed on Endgate Island. It was the most secure spot, complete with locked doors, big closets, and easy access. We hauled the goods inside, then split to get clean and clear our heads. My goal was to answer the sheriff's questions without revealing anything about the abnormal flickers in my mind, which had ultimately led to finding Robin's body.

Because today's eerie encounters were with wisps of ghosts in nearly dust-free bedrooms instead of mud or critters in cellars, I opted to skip the stairs leading to my attic space and do a fast clean downstairs. I splashed some water on my face and combed my hair and hunted in the guest bathroom for the unused toothbrush I was pleased to find in the top drawer. Eric did pretty much the same, and we were prepared to meet with Sheriff Guidry within less than ten minutes.

Alex and Cici, who were still in the parlor, greeted us with hugs. "How was the castle?" Cici asked.

"Bizarre, intriguing, eerie, and possibly edifying, if we get a chance to sit down and figure out what we found," I told her.

Cici's eyes twinkled. "I can't wait to hear all the dirt."

Guidry held his hand up. "Later. Sorry, ladies, but Ah've got an investigation to conduct, and to say Ah'm short-handed is an understatement, since Ah'm the *only* hand. Anyway, Ah need information fast as Ah can git it. Then y'all can tell each other about the ghosts at Chaudret castle." He managed a slight smile. "Word 'round the island is there's more than one."

I smiled back. "No comment for now."

The sheriff turned to business, even producing a small notebook and pen. "Been tryin' to establish a timeline of the other mornin'. Not sure y'all can add much to what Alex and Cici told me already, but we'll see. For starters, Michael called around one and y'all drove to the pier. Right?"

Eric answered. "I'm not precise on the time, but yeah."

"And what happened when y'all got to the pier?"

"Very little, unfortunately. We called out to Robin for about five minutes or so, and of course, there was no answer."

Guidry scribbled something down. "How did you finally determine he was under the pier?"

I stiffened and hoped the sheriff wouldn't notice. "I had this impression of, um, something in the water." I couldn't tell him the impression was in my mind and not in the physical area where Robin had died.

Eric immediately added, "After Teddie told us, Alex and I dove in. It was pretty clear Robin was dead."

Guidry followed up with, "Do you remember anything about the last time you saw him in the morning? Who was with him?"

Eric quietly answered, "Sorry. We were focused on checking on the island folks who might be out of power or water. I honestly can't remember what time he left the house."

"Same here," I said. "I believe it was around eight, though I can't swear to it."

"Well, Ah 'preciate y'all tellin' me what you could. And if somethin' strikes y'all later, give me a call."

Guidry left. Alex, Cici, Eric, and I stood in silence for a moment.

"He's got his work cut out for him," Alex noted.

I bit my lower lip. "Should I have brought up Jenny's drugging or the fire at the carriage house? I mean, I *personally* believe those events and Robin's death are connected, but I have no evidence to support my beliefs, other than gut feelings."

Jenny walked into the parlor as I was asking my question and she was the first to respond. "It's not only you, Teddie. You've got a crowd with you. Michael, Alex, Cici, Eric, Luc, and I all believe it's related. It's obvious whatever's happening on this island is not being caused by the ghost of any old pirate. Instigated, perhaps, but Jacques Chaudret is not serving as drug dealer or arsonist. The sheriff has got an impossible task trying to figure out who snuck up on Robin and bashed him over the head before dumping him in the water. It was perfect timing since everyone was busy dealing with the aftermath of the storm. Who'd notice another person at the pier? And it's even possible the fire was accidental. Oh, by the way, Guidry's not buying my being drugged. For whatever reason. Possibly because he *is* the only law on this island right now, so he's swamped trying to investigate even one incident."

Cici spat in disgust, "There's almost no way to find out who's doing all this until something major breaks. Pointless." She turned to me. "So, moving on, what *did* y'all find at the castle? You brought home stuff. I saw cartons and something in a frame?"

"Wanna check out the booty? We put everything in the guest room." Eric gestured behind him.

Cici vigorously bobbed her head. "Hell yeah. Lead on."

Eric, limping badly, led the way back to the guest room. Jenny, Cici, Alex, and I followed

"Sit," I ordered Eric.

"Woof." Eric sat.

Cici headed straight for the portrait. "Whoa. Who is this? She's beautiful. Why in the hell is there a gash rippin' up the painting from side to side?"

Eric told her we thought it was Althea Chaudret, possibly the same girl who'd been erased from the records of their family in the ledger I'd found in the tower room. He did not mention we felt sure Althea and I shared a personal connection…like our souls.

"Any idea why the family dumped her?"

Eric motioned to me. "Teddie, you tell her. You're the one with the theory."

"Theory?" asked Alex.

"Yeah." I explained my hypothesis regarding a connection between former slave Emeric Desmarais and Althea, a daughter of the Chaudret family. "I have no proof. Strong feelings only. But the slashed portrait and crossed-out entry in the ledger do seem to indicate there was a romance between these two. Jeez. Can y'all imagine? Talk about way more than frowned on. Giant freak-out by the Chaudrets closely followed by tar and feathers is closer to the mark. It seems logical Althea and Emeric figured enough was enough, then took off and headed north."

Jenny added, "Like to Brooklyn, which could explain how a pendant identical to hers ended up in a flea market there."

"Works for me," said Cici. "What's in the cartons?"

"A bunch of books. Probably don't mean a thing, but they kept calling to me," I said. "Also, a mysterious note written by the equally mysterious Rosalynn."

I pulled the note out of the bag and gave it to Alex and Cici.

Cici stared at the note for a long moment. "This is scary. And…I don't know…sad."

"Y'all believe these people have a connection to what's going on now?" Alex asked.

I hesitated for a long moment but finally stated firmly, "Yes, I do."

"What's the next step, then?" Cici inquired. "More houses to tour looking for old paintings?"

"Not today. At least not for me. Welcome to the newly established Sugarberry Terrace Book Club, meeting here and now with a membership of one. I'm reading every damned book in these cartons until I find something."

Chapter 39

Alex and Cici headed out toward the pier to take Alex's boat to New Orleans. Jenny took off to spend some quality alone time with Michael. Eric flopped on the bed in the guest room and I squatted on the floor in front of four small boxes and Althea's portrait.

"Theodosia?"

"Hmmm?"

"Would it be totally lacking in courtesy, not to mention romance, for me to say my ankle is killing me and I'm going take one of those codeine-laden pain pills and try to sleep while you scavenge through books?"

"Smart. Do it."

"You're a nice person, Miz Grant. Beautiful and smart, too, but right now nice tops my list."

I blushed and shot him a soft smile. The pain lines on his face were more pronounced than I had ever seen them. I didn't want him to notice I was more than a little concerned, so I simply said, "Go to sleep. I will hope the soft sounds of snoring will relax me enough to let whatever vibes about these books come crashing down on my psyche and lead me to...whatever."

Eric scooted down the bed until he was at the end nearest the cartons...and me. He kissed me, which was the best action taken in the last few hours, then crawled back before the idea of sleep disappeared in favor of more enjoyable ways to spend the afternoon, even though we both knew this wasn't the time or the place.

I stayed where I was on the floor, slid a box closer, reached inside, and began lifting books out and stacking them in neat little piles around me. It seemed the best way to discover whether any of the books held anything beyond a fun read was to organize alphabetically by author. I willed my intuition to jump out and give me a strong sense of "I found it" as I was dividing the books into smaller piles. If an "I found it" moment sounds odd, I must explain

I'm a huge reader and have on more than one occasion spent long afternoons in Manhattan bookstores soaking in the atmosphere before deciding which books to buy solely based on the vibes I pick up from the books themselves. This was long before I'd ever heard of the existence of Endgate Island, not to mention before my arrival here and subsequent experiences of freaky moments of precognition.

For once, luck or good karma was with me. I sifted through the piles looking for As, Bs, Cs, and Ds. Less than thirty seconds after beginning the search, I found it. No second sight required. It was obvious. The title was direct and simple: *Tenth Avenue*, and the author was Rosalynn Adams. I got a vibe, all right, like nothing I'd sensed before. It was not pleasant. I had to take several deep breaths before I was calm enough to start reading with any sort of focus.

The cover was not especially informative. It was typical of the kind of cheesy covers of gothic romances from the 1960s, featuring the figure of a young woman staring up at a mansion in a woodsy-looking area. I love those covers. They tell you absolutely nothing about where the story takes place, including the country, although most gothics during this period were set in Britain or the United States, with New England generally winning in popularity. Half the romantic suspense novels I read as a teenager were set in coastal towns in Maine, overlooking deadly rocks jutting out of the Atlantic. The young woman on the cover always wore a dress, and the reader could guess at the time period by the length of the hem and whether a hooded cloak completed the ensemble. And you always knew exactly what you were going to get once you opened to Chapter One.

The cover for *Tenth Avenue* displayed a heroine in a simple sheath, circa mid-1960s. The copyright date on the first page was 1965, which squared with the author writing this as a "contemporary" gothic romantic suspense. I was sure, before I even started Chapter One, that Rosalynn Adams was not only the author of this book, but of the note I'd found in the ghastly tower room.

I rose, took the book with me, and headed to the rocking chair, aiming the floor lamp down toward the pages. The book itself was in surprisingly good shape, with an uncracked spine and firm corners.

Possibly because no one ever read it? I silently mused, not wanting to disturb Eric's sleep, as I opened Chapter One and began to read.

According to my new watch with the cartoon face, it was now two a.m. Meaning I'd been sitting in this nearly empty car on the local train for about forty-five minutes. I say nearly empty because there was a grand total of three of us: a guy in ragged jeans who appeared to be making the train his home for the night, a well-dressed middle-aged man reading the Wall Street Journal, *and me.*

I sat up straight, stunned, then forced myself to read the first three chapters, wondering how the liquor supply in the Laurent parlor was holding up. I'm not much of a drinker, but a good stiff whiskey sounded enticing. Two or three would be even better.

The summary of Chapter One was simple, direct, and could have been lifted from my diary, had I chosen to keep one. The heroine, Miss Doree Monroe, was a decorator at a firm in Manhattan, who'd broken up with her boyfriend, the owner of an architectural firm who claimed she'd stolen his designs, only a few days earlier. During the train ride to Washington Heights from midtown, Doree reads the mail she'd tossed into her bag earlier in the morning and finds a frantic letter from her best friend from college, Janet Jefferson. Janet had been married for approximately eight months, and was living on a remote island, Endgate, about an hour's boat ride to New Orleans. Janet, an artist, was looking at houses owned by her husband's family with an eye toward doing some renovating, but felt as if she was in danger, especially after someone stole an antique journal from her room. She begs Doree to come visit and help with the design of a house on Third Avenue, Birchwood Shade.

Janet had already invited an architect friend of hers, also from Manhattan. The friend had been at Endgate approximately two weeks before Doree arrived but was injured while exploring the cellar at the Third Avenue house. Janet additionally notes there's a huge fight regarding the ownership of an intriguing residence on the island. It's called *Tenth Avenue* or, more often, the Candela castle, named for the family who built it.

I stared at Eric, sleeping peacefully after taking the pain meds, and debated whether I should wake him up or read more chapters to see if "Doree's" story continued to mirror my own experiences.

"Keep going, Teddie," I muttered softly. "He's going to need all the rest he can get once he hears this."

Ten chapters later, I'd read about Janet being drugged and found nearly unconscious at Birchwood Shade, and learned Doree and

Rick, the architect, who, incidentally, was black, had discovered what appeared to be a liaison between a former slave named Emeric and Althea, the daughter of a slave-owner, Mr. Peter Candela. Rick believes he's somehow connected to Emeric. The book went into detail about the preparations for a storm with Doree talking about the first families from the island staying at Janet's house. Following the storm, Doree, Rick, Janet's stepson Alan, and the daughter of the Jeffersons' cook, named Celia, find the dead body of a boatman named Bobby…originally from Lake Charles.

And a few chapters later came the kicker:

"Rick. Can we move the mattress off the bed and use it as a shield?"

"No. But, wait. Trap."

"Yeah, we are. Oh, wait, you mean… as in trapdoor?"

"Yes. But it's under the bed so we need to get to it now—fast."

We shoved the bed away from its current position in the room to the side not in flames. Rick was right. The outlines of a trapdoor were clearly visible and even a little ring to pull had been left in place. I carefully tugged at the ring, praying it would hold and not break off, but it stayed solid.

"Are there stairs?" I shouted over the crackling of flames eating away at the side of the bedroom by the window.

"Don't care," Rick shouted back. "Let's go."

There was no time for chivalry from either of us. I pushed Rick through the hole and jumped down after him. If there'd ever been stairs, they were long gone, but this portion of the house was fairly low and the cellar not deep so we were able to land in dirt without breaking our necks, although Rick's ankle didn't need the extra strain.

"Oh my God."

I jumped up and threw the book back on the floor, which woke Eric.

"Teddie?"

"Oh. Damn. Sorry. I didn't mean to shout."

"What's going on?"

"Weirdness piled on top of strange and odd. Plus, bizarre. But…this book…" I was shaking and my breathing was more like gasping.

Eric sat up and reached his hand out for me to join him.

I sat next to him and when I felt I could speak without sounding like I was completely bonkers, told him about Rosalynn Adams and *Tenth Avenue* and the exact similarities of events and people. Then I read aloud the last few paragraphs about the escape into the cellar.

His eyes widened. "What? There's got to be an explanation for all this."

"Right. There *should* be explanations. Really. And thinking logically, I guess the similarity in names isn't terribly, horribly strange. And, yeah, Rosalynn also could have found the same ledger we had, and used the name Emeric and the nickname Rick instead of Eric. Heck, Rosalynn might have been the one who hid the ledger in the 60s musical book and dumped it along with other books in the cellar *at Hickory Shadows*. The storm? Not a biggie. Louisiana has a hurricane every damned five minutes."

"True. But still eerie and really hard to fathom this mirroring. What freaks you out the most?"

"*Everything.* Starting with the hero and the heroine. Rick and Doree. Rick/Eric. Doree/Theodosia. Black guy who's an architect. White girl who's a decorator. Talk about a near match. And neither are from Endgate Island, so she wasn't using characters who were already around. She's bringing them in from New York. The boatman being murdered? Janet being drugged?"

"Teddie, it should be easy to check the history of these things. It's not totally unreasonable to believe a boatman was murdered on this island. Rosalynn Adams might have been a civil rights activist and decided to throw caution to the wind about publishing and make her heroine and hero a biracial couple."

"Maybe. It's a stretch worthy of a yoga master, and it doesn't give me cold chills. But, Eric, what's blowing my mind is my gobsmacked moment of 'where did she come up with this stuff?' Was she psychic? Was she one great guesser? Were all the events incredible coincidences?"

We stared at each other and simultaneously said, "The fire."

I took a deep breath. "We have to find out if a carriage house ever burned down on this island. Specifically, in 1965."

Chapter 40

"What time is it?" Eric asked.

"Let's see. My little cartoon watch and the mantel clock both say eight. You slept and I read through dinner. You hungry?"

"I could use a little something."

"You do what you need to do to fully wake up and I'll see what Luc's got in the kitchen," I told him.

"Sounds good."

Luc Bouvier has a sixth sense for when folks need nourishment, whether physically, or spiritually, or emotionally. He greeted me when I arrived in the kitchen with a hug. "Got some po'boy sandwiches for you and Mister Eric. His has shrimp and yours has double helpin's of avocado with cucumbers and hummus. Figured y'all would be hungry after rootin' though castles all mornin' and Mister Eric still bein' hurt."

"You are the best. Thanks." I glanced at Luc "You've lived here your whole life, right?"

"Most of it. Spent a good deal a' time in New Orleans, too, where Ah was born."

"Do you remember a writer who lived on the island in the 60s? And, by any chance, weird events in say 64 or 65?"

He thought for a moment. "Sixties. Ah was a toddler then, but...define weird?"

"Oh. Like murder?"

"Nope. Mah parents tole me there was some...guess Ah'd call it 'edginess' during the 60s when a Freedom Rider group came through... not the famous one in Mississippi or Alabama. Anyway, some of the first families 'parently got into a snit 'bout the group wantin' to clean up the Quarters. Thank the Lord, no murders."

"What about any fires?"

"Well, Ah believe the ol' LaSalle house in the Quarters burned down round 1983. Bad drought all year. And then that fool Calvin got drunk one night and fell asleep over his whiskey and cigarettes. Bessie, his wife, got him out and neither of 'em had a burn or a scratch, but she divorced him as soon's she could." The corners of his mouth twitched in amusement. "Called Cal the damndest, stupidest, ugliest drunk in the state. But like Ah say, we're talkin' the 80s."

I couldn't hide my own mirth. "Glad to hear they both survived. Was that the only fire?"

"Yeah. Purty much. Ah mean, there's always minor fires in the Quarters. Bad wirin' or cigarettes or even lightnin' strikes, but somethin' tells me you're askin' 'bout somethin' more dramatic?"

"You nailed it. Like the carriage house the other day."

"Nah. Nothin' Ah can remember or heard 'bout. Ah was really young. You need to talk to Miz Vianca. She's lived here her whole life, and her folks before her and her grandparents and great-grandparents. Miz Vianca's always been a wonderful storyteller, plus she's got the best memory of any human on the planet. You want the history of this island for the last three hundred years or so? She'll tell ya."

"Perfect. I adore her anyway, so it'll be a pleasure to have another chance to visit."

He set a tray filled with the sandwiches and a couple of glasses of iced tea into my hands, asked if I needed help getting it down the hall, then went back to cleaning the kitchen when I assured him I was fine. Like every good theatre person, I've done more than one stint waiting tables to squeak by and pay the rent.

I found Eric sitting on the edge of the bed with the Rosalynn Adams book in his hand.

"Have you been reading it?" I asked.

"No. I cleaned up, hoping a shower would wake me and remove cobwebs. I smell better but I'm still in a fog. Anyway, I sat down again and now I can't seem to get beyond the cover."

"I suppose we could simply skip to the end, but I'm terrified I'll miss something important. I'm determined to go through it, chapter by chapter, no matter how spooky and strange it is to read a replay of our lives written before we were born." I grinned at him. "The good news is you do smell delightful."

Eric grabbed me and planted a sweet, if short, kiss on my lips then pulled away and stared at me for a long moment. "It's not only spooky and strange. It's blooming bonkers crazy. Tell you what: I propose we scrap all mention of Tenth Avenue, both the castle and the novel, and Endgate Island for as long as it takes us to eat dinner. And possibly for a couple of hours after."

"You're reading my mind. We can use a break. Big time."

Eric shoved some junk off one of the end tables and put the sandwiches and drinks on the cleared space. We talked about our families. Eric had also lost his mom to a serious illness—when he was fifteen—and we agreed watching a parent die had been the hardest, most painful event in our lives. We talked about what shows we'd like to do in the future, what we'd done in the past, and how we got sucked into theatre in the first place.

"After-school children's program," Eric stated. "The idea was pretty much 'keep the little hellions off the streets and occupied so they don't become felons.' It worked and I loved every minute from the time I was about six through high school. Even did a couple of starring roles, although, as Jenny is so fond of noting, I wasn't exactly the best actor."

I grinned. "But I'll bet you were one darned cute little tyke singing and dancing."

He smirked. "Yeah, yeah. Anyway, I kept hanging out with the director and asking her why she had this group on this side of the stage and another on the other and why she made one character do such-and-such business while another merely sat and did nothing. Mrs. Hamil was fabulous. She didn't poo-poo me or tell me to go learn my lines, which of course, I already had. Nope. She said, 'Eric Desmarais, you have the soul of the director' and let me sit with her and get a glimpse up close and personal into what it took to be the one with the concepts you had to see come alive. Awesome lady. Awesome director." Eric took a swig of tea, swallowed and asked, "You?"

I preened a bit. "Also awesome."

He tapped me on the top of my head. "Cute."

"Yep. Uh, dogs."

He stared at me. "Beg pardon?"

"How I got involved in theatre. Remember? I'm answering the question. Dogs."

"And being extremely annoying and cryptic." He laughed. "Care to explain?"

"Getting there. Now then, when I was six, my family had two dogs. Boo-boo and Princess. I always wanted to help my dad with whatever projects he was doing, which probably drove him nuts, so he decided to keep me busy by having us do a shared doghouse project. I loved it. And I was good at it. I kept building doghouses until my mom kindly explained we only had two dogs and the majority of the time they slept on my bed, so this could be considered a waste of wood."

"How many did you build?"

"The final tally was eight. Anyway, she and Dad found other projects for me to do and then heard about one of the children's theatres in Austin, who were thrilled to have a kid interested in doing all the tech stuff backstage."

"Dare I ask what happened to the doghouses?"

"We gave them to local shelters. Except for the one originally meant for Boo-Boo. It ended up at our neighbor's, whose dog, Duckworth, was one of those weird mutts who loved his doghouse more than his owner's bed, sofa, or even the fine Persian living-room rug. Sweet puppy. Not a brain in his gooney little head. Reminds me a lot of Louie over in the Quarters."

We finished our supper and debated the merits of roaming through Luc's kitchen for the pralines he'd baked earlier in the day, but ultimately decided to hold off until tomorrow.

"Speaking of tomorrow, do we have a plan? Do we *want* a plan?" Eric asked. "Do you want to try to finish the book tonight?"

I stood up and stretched my arms. "I can't read another word. This is the first time I've felt mildly calm and I'd like to keep the feeling. Listen, tomorrow, if we can borrow a vehicle, I want to pay Miz Vianca a visit. Luc said she's like Miss Major Historian on the island, mainly because she's been here forever, has an elephantine memory, and basically loves gossiping about everyone unless sworn to confidence. According to Luc she's rumored to be quite adamant about never breaking a confidence. Also, I really like the woman and want us to be friends."

"Sounds good. Do you want to include anyone else in this excursion or will it be just us?"

"Well, while Jenny, Michael, Alex, and Cici are welcome, we'd probably get more information if it's you and me without a mob."

"Oh?"

"Yeah. When I talked to her the morning of the hurricane, we definitely bonded. I'm not sure our connection would be as strong or she'd be as willing to spill all if anyone else is around. Might be wrong, but it's a strong vibe."

"Since your vibes have had better results than most weather stations, I bow to the connection. I still can't believe you found a painting hidden from the world for probably a hundred years or more."

"I don't even want to go into what I was feeling when I got the urge to look behind the wardrobe. Let's just say I was beyond twitchy."

It was only about ten now, but this whole wacky day made me realize I was now completely exhausted.

"Eric, I'll take the dishes back to the kitchen, but I think I'll go ahead and bid you *adieu* now."

"Do I get a good-night kiss?"

"Want one?" I coyly inquired.

Eric's tone became purely seductive. "A kiss is the least of what I want."

I was tempted to curl up beside him on the bed but settled for leaning down and savoring his mouth on mine for a long moment, imagining more to come.

We drew apart and stared into each other's eyes. Finally Eric asked in a hoarse voice, "So, you'll be heading to the tower, Rapunzel?"

"Once I'm unencumbered by dishes. I will be letting down my hair, right on a real pillow with real sheets. And, no offense to Althea, without a ghostly portrait staring at me all night."

Chapter 41

Eric and I arrived at Miz Vianca's house at eight the next morning. I was worried it was too early, but when we pulled up in Jenny's old Jeep, we spotted the lady herself tending to some plants in her front yard looking remarkably perky after this week's storm.

Vianca rose before we even exited the vehicle and waved us toward the porch.

"Ah figgered y'all'd be back. With questions."

"Yes, ma'am. I hope you can answer one or two."

"Do mah best. Y'all want some coffee? Made Creole style with molasses and chicory and it's good, if Ah do say so mahself. Got some fresh buttermilk biscuits, too. Should be ready"—a timer loud enough to wake half the island rang—"right 'bout now."

We'd skipped breakfast in our hurry to get out of the Laurent house. My mouth watered. "Sounds wonderful. May I help you get everything?"

Miz Vianca glanced at Eric's boot cast. "Well, sure as shootin' Mister Eric ain't helpin'."

Eric protested. "Hey. It's only my foot, not my hands and arms. Everyone keeps calling me helpless."

I waved at him. "Take advantage while you can, Desmarais. Once you're up and running? Fuggedaboudit, Brooklyn dude, you take *all* the chores."

Miz Vianca chided him, "She's right, Mister Eric. Now, Miz Teddie, y'all come on inside and we'll get a tray made up."

I followed her into the tiny, white-glove-clean, ancient house. The front room was sparse. A rocking chair sat by the front window; a loveseat and one other chair faced the combined kitchen and dining area. No clutter or knickknacks; the only things on the walls or tables were photos.

I pointed at the largest, which held a space of honor above the dining table. "Oh my God. Is this the bridge in Selma?"

220

"It is. You got a good eye. Edmund Pettis Bridge. March seventh, 1965." She joined me by the picture. "And there I am smack-dab in the middle there in the hat with all the daisies. Can't tell cause the photo's black n' white, but there was a lot 'a yellow in those flowers."

"What? You were actually at Selma?"

"Ah was. And, hell, Ah still got mah hat, though it looks purty bad now. But it prob'ly saved me from gettin' mah head bashed in back then."

"Well, call me damned impressed. Miz Vianca, I knew you were wonderful, but you're part of *history*. I mean, we all are as people, but this was a *major* historical event. It helped change the world. *You* helped change the world." I impulsively hugged her. "I should ask for your autograph."

She hugged me back. "Mah handwritin's pretty bad, Miz Teddie. Tell ya what...you and your man keep comin' around while y'all on the island and Ah'll be happy. Love young'uns poppin' by to chat and eatin' mah cookin'. Which reminds me, Ah 'spose we'd best be getting coffee and biscuits for Mister Eric 'fore he gets impatient."

We made up a tray and brought it back to the porch. Eric was staring off at the silhouette of the Chaudret castle, about a mile away. He turned. "The damn thing overlooks everything for miles. Talk about ostentatious."

Miz Vianca rolled her eyes. "Mah mama always said Pirate Jacques was compensatin' for somethin'."

Eric and I snickered.

Miz Vianca continued, "She also useta say any fool who hadta steal a woman to marry her steada courtin' like a real man either didn't have what it takes—or smelled damned bad."

We lost it. I barely managed to keep from spilling the entire tray to the ground I was laughing so hard. But I managed to place the coffee and biscuits down on an old card table on the porch and the three of us sat down to breakfast.

Eric took a bite of biscuit and gave a thumbs-up. "Miz Vianca, you and Luc should open a restaurant together. Preferably in Manhattan so Teddie and I could enjoy eating there every day once we're back home."

She beamed. "You're a sweet boy, Mister Eric. And who's ta say Ah won't? Luc's stayin' on this island no matter what, but Ah'm not too old to change." She fluttered her lashes at us. "After all, they say ninety-five is the new eighty."

"I love it."

Minutes later, we all leaned back in our chairs, satisfied.

"Mah manners have disappeared," Miz Vianca exclaimed. "I haven't asked how Miz Jenny is doin'. Any bad effects from those awful drugs?"

Eric answered for both of us. "She's good. Thank you. Tough woman." He reached over and grabbed my hand. "Not as tough as the firefighting rescuer Theodosia here, but not bad for a tiny little actress."

I tapped his shoulder. "Ahem. You forgot to mention Theodosia the stair-climbing aerobics queen."

"No biggie. Any good New Yorker should be able to climb fifty flights without puffing at the end." He leaned back and put his hands behind his head, elbows out.

Miz Vianca poured herself another cup of coffee, took a sip, then held up her hand. "Now, Ah got this notion y'all ain't here just for good coffee. So, ask away. Ah'm ready and willin' to provide any answers I can."

"Not to sound like Alice, but where do I start?" I threw a sharp glance at Eric. "And if you say the beginning, I will steal the last biscuit from your plate."

"Ha. I'd like to see you try." He paused. "But you made a good point. When did the story begin? *Our* stories, as far as Endgate Island is concerned, began about three weeks ago. But something has been going on for years—no, make that centuries—and it seems to be affecting events now."

"Why donch'all start with since you came to the island," Vianca suggested.

"If it's okay, let me first start with the 'why,'" I said. I took my listeners back to the subway train and e-mail on my phone and my fears for Jenny. I told Miz Vianca about the ledger and about the missing diary. "Then we found Jenny nearly dead at Hickory Shadows and Robin was drowned and there was the fire at the carriage house. Yesterday, we searched the castle on Tenth Avenue." I glanced at Eric. He looked back at me, reading my mind as we silently agreed this was something Miz Vianca needed to know. "I discovered a portrait of someone we're guessing is Althea Chaudret.

The painting has a gash running diagonally through the center. But in the portrait she's wearing a dead ringer for a pendant I bought last fall in Brooklyn. This one."

I leaned closer to Miz Vianca so she could examine the necklace, which I'd specifically worn today. She kept silent. "Eric also found a mysterious clock, although we haven't had a chance to examine it and can't explain why it's mysterious. We left it in the china cabinet at the castle. I explored a creepy room at the top of the castle and discovered a note written by someone named Rosalynn, whom we now believe is Rosalynn Adams, author of a gothic romance written in the 60s."

I stopped and swallowed hard. Eric patted my hand, obviously picking up on my nerves. "Want me to tell her?"

"Yeah."

"Teddie read about twenty chapters yesterday and almost all of them mirror the events she's experienced since she got Jenny's message. Events in a novel published in 1965. At this point..."

"Y'all need to find out if some, or any, or all those things happened?"

Eric and I chorused, "We do."

"Well, Ah'm not sure 'bout finding diaries or ledgers, but no Laurent bride—or any *other* bride—been drugged and left for dead while lookin' at houses here. The boatman most used by island folk for the last fifty years is still livin' over in New Orleans. If he was murdered, he's doin' a damned good job disguisin' it. And there's not a carriage house on this island been burned down since before the Civil War. Plenty a' shacks here in the Quarters, but none outside and none to the ground. No mansions burned either."

"So, either Rosalynn Adams time traveled or has one whale of second sight," I mumbled. I thought for a second. "Did you ever meet her, Miz Vianca?"

"Nah, never did. Sorry. You said 65, right?"

"It's the publishing date so yeah. At least approximately."

"Well, as you saw by the photo inside, Ah spent much a mah time in 65 demonstratin' with some folks y'all mighta heard of," she flashed a mischievous grin, adding, "like Reverend King."

Eric's right eyebrow shot up. "You did?"

"She did," I announced with pride. "Miz Vianca is a veteran of Edmund Pettis Bridge." I glanced at her. "Plus many other activities to help bring about civil rights."

Eric echoed my combined astonishment, awe, and admiration. "You're my hero, Miz Vianca." He and I lifted our coffee cups to her.

She smirked at us. "Maght mean more to a toast if there was liquid left in 'em. But thanks. Just did what needed doin' at the time." She turned to me. "Miz Teddie, Ah didn't meet Miz Rosalynn while she was on the island. Wish Ah had. I did hear a few things though, so maybe Ah can help a little."

"What did you hear?"

"Well, Miz Rosalynn was a writer, a' course. Wasn't from the island; came here 'cause one of the Chaudret girls—musta been Katherine—roomed with her in college. Miz Rosalynn did write a book. And then she disappeared without a trace."

Chapter 42

"Just like Althea," I stated.

"Whacha mean, girl?" asked Miz Vianca. She seemed genuinely curious but there was something about the way she asked that made me think she already knew. I filed it under "things to ponder for later."

"Rosalynn Adams. She and Althea both disappeared. I have this romantic notion Althea and Emeric Desmarais took off one fine night and stole a boat, headed north, and lived happily ever after in Brooklyn where someone filched her pendant so I could end up with it, but I have a twitchy premonition I'm romanticizing and it's a crock." I slammed my palm down on the table. "Shoot, all we *really* know is Althea Chaudret was scratched out of the family histories and what I believe to be her portrait was vandalized, then somehow her pendant ended up in a flea market about two thousand miles from Endgate."

Miz Vianca pursed her lips and gave a short, tuneless, whistle. "Ah can't believe y'all found her old portrait. It went missin' and became another of those mysteries been floatin' round the island for a hundred years and more. Ah'd love to see it. See if she matches the picture in m'mind." She paused, then picked up the coffeepot. "Have some more, kids, while Ah tell you a little story. Ah heard a little somethin' 'bout her from what mah great-granny Sally told me growin' up. She knew Miz Althea well. Same age." She added, "The women in mah family live long and—praise the Lord—seem to keep our minds purty sharp. Granny Sally was the smartest woman Ah ever knew."

"What did Granny Sally tell you?" I asked.

"She said Miz Althea was the best of the Chaudrets. They played together when they were kids, even though Granny Sally was Miz Althea's slave."

"What?" I was shocked.

"Yessum. Granny Sally was born sometime 'round 1850 as a slave to the Pelletier family. The Pelletiers been on this island 'most as long as the Chaudrets themselves. Thinkin' on it, could maybe even arrived 'bout the same time. Mah family was originally brought over on a pirate ship in chains back in the late 1600s. Not sure if the Pelletiers were the pirates or the buyers. Didn't much matter, and was probably both since Ah seem to recall some Pelletier was navigator or first mate with ol' Captain Jacques. Anyway, Granny Sally worked in the castle along with my great-great-granny, Sarah, who cooked for the Chaudrets. And Granny Sally and Miz Althea were best friends. When Miz Althea turned twelve, Sally became her personal maid. They never thought…"

She inhaled and looked up at the ceiling.

"What, Miz Vianca?"

"Never occurred to the Chaudrets Miz Sally and Miz Althea would end up real friends. Both gals be sharp enough to get they were born into circumstances without choosin'. Granny Sally tole me once Miz Althea said she didn't want to take anythin' away from what she called the 'awful of Sally bein' a slave,' but Althea herself felt she was in prison in that damned castle. Like she'd been born a hundred years too early for her feelings about people. Ah bet she'da been fightin' with Freedom Riders throughout the 1960s if she'd been around then. Right 'longside Sally, if she'd been alive, too."

Eric quietly asked, "Could your great-granny have known Emeric Desmarais?"

Miz Vianca thought for a moment. "She must've. Ah mean, everyone on the island knew everyone else…jus' like now…slave or free. Granny Sally told me everybody was up in everybody's business then. Again, jus' like now. Lots of intermarryin' and intermigglin' without vows. But 'bout Mister Emeric? She never mentioned him by name, least not as Ah recall, but there was an odd thing… Wasn't odd at the time but now with y'all askin' questions it makes more sense."

We waited.

"When Ah was a little slip of a thing… couldn't've been more than eight or nine at most, and Granny Sally was gettin' close to a hundred…one night she been tellin' me how much she'd loved my great-granddaddy, even though he was picked for her by Mister Pelletier. Anyway, there Ah was, too young to even understand what marriage meant, and Ah confided how much Ah wanted to marry Mister Ezekiel, who worked for the Laurent family back then. Mama said he was way too old for me and Ah'd best knock any lovin' notions clean out of my head." She stopped. She appeared out of breath.

"You okay? Do you need some water?" I asked.

"Ah'm fine. Jus'…memories. Anyways, Ah was all upset and Granny Sally tells mah mama to hush. She says differences in birth shouldn't matter when it comes to who you love, whether it be somethin' to do with age or race or religion or family. She said, 'Like Miz Althea and Emeric.' Sally didn't explain what she meant but, well, she did say the Chaudrets cut Miz Althea out a' their lives in 1865 and everyone on the island talked 'bout it. The name Emeric didn't mean much, but when Ah asked Granny Sally about them all she'd say was, 'different births, different colors. No matter. Love is love. Love for all time.'"

"I'm with Granny Sally," Eric stated

"Count me in, too," I added.

Eric waited a long moment, then quietly surmised, "So, we were right? Althea and Emeric must have run off together."

Miz Vianca's tone was grim. "No one knew for sure. No one does to this day. It's one of those island stories got clammed up more n' a hundred years ago."

My voice sounded hoarse, even to me. "Don't ask me how 'cause it's one of those weird feelings, but I'll bet y'all my lovely pendant Rosalynn Adams knew. She found something a hundred years after the two vanished."

Eric turned to me. "If so, then I'd say we need to track down Miss Rosalynn Adams and ask."

"Any ideas?"

Miz Vianca interjected, "Ah'd start with an online search. Ah got Wi-Fi if y'all want to do it here."

"Vianca Giry, super techie. You're as nosy as we are."

"Yessum, Ah am. Tell you what, y'all take care 'a these dishes and Ah'll get mah laptop warmed up and ready."

We agreed. I gathered up the dishes. Eric, glowering, stated he would be carrying the tray no matter what anyone said, and if I didn't stop treating him like a baby because of one lousy hurt ankle, he'd steal my not-yet-won designer's award in Manhattan *if* I got it, then fly back down to Endgate and hide it in the tower of Tenth Avenue.

As the three of us paraded into the house, I turned to Miz Vianca. "I have to know. What happened to the sexy, older Mister Ezekiel? Did he marry some glamorous woman in New Orleans and leave a certain little girl heartbroken?"

She howled. "Chile, depends on what you call glamorous. Zeke was sixteen years older 'n me. He went off and fought in World War Two, and when he came back, he and I had the biggest, best weddin' this part of the island ever saw. We stayed married and raised six children until the year 2012 when he passed, after fallin' off the roof tryin' to get the damned satellite dish to work right so he could watch his favorite cooking show."

Chapter 43

Ninety minutes later the three of us were frustrated and jazzed on too much Creole coffee. Three smart people with great imaginations, yet we couldn't figure out the best way to find vital information. We had no idea where Rosalynn Adams could be living. Assuming she was still alive. We tried obituaries, paying a fee for a trial subscription to one of those background-checking directories that pull up everything about a person, including their measurements, whether they were involved in an accident last week, or had a criminal record shoplifting candy bars from the local convenience store when they were ten.

Half the problem was we didn't have much to go on. We had Rosalynn's name and the title of one book. We had no idea where Rosalynn had been born or grew up, or even where she'd lived before she came to stay at the Chaudret castle.

The three of us stared at the castle in the distance and prayed for inspiration.

I suggested, "We need other keywords. Type in *Tenth Avenue* along with Rosalynn Adams and Endgate Island, Louisiana. Oh. Check used bookstores."

We waited a few seconds and out came two pieces of information.

The first was there were no copies of *Tenth Avenue* listed on any used bookstore websites or trading or auction sites.

The second was a book titled *Tenth Avenue*, which had indeed been published in 1965 by Sparkleberry Press. We thought this could prove helpful since some of the front pages of the book I'd found had been torn out, including a possible dedication, and finding the name of the publisher could push us forward.

"Sparkleberry Press," Eric and I chimed simultaneously. He added the name to our search.

We quickly learned Sparkleberry Press had gone the way of many family-owned publishing companies in the mid-80s, i.e., bye-bye. Eric was about to move on when I stopped him. "Wait. Check one of the used bookstores again. *Tenth Avenue* isn't available, but if we could find a list of other books by the same publisher, we might find other books by Rosalynn Adams. Or other authors who might have names of editors in their acknowledgments. Editors who might still be around who've actually heard of Miz Adams."

Eric gazed at me with admiration. "Nice work, Miss Grant. Creole coffee makes you sharp."

"Especially when I've had four cups."

We found several old paperbacks released by Sparkleberry Press, but none of them were available in digital format, so we only saw a cover and, in some cases, a back with a blurb.

"Not much help," Miz Vianca sighed.

We each drank another cup of coffee, staring at each other, willing ideas to hit.

I exclaimed. "Oh poo. I'm such an idiot."

"Brilliance has arrived?" Eric inquired.

"I hope. Rosalynn came to the castle at the invitation of her old college roommate. I'm supposing it was one of those, 'hey, want a place to write your novel with free room and board and privacy and ghosts to help with the atmosphere?' kind of things."

"Katherine," came from Miz Vianca. "The last Chaudret."

"Katherine," I repeated. "Thanks. A definite clue. Where is Katherine Chaudret now? Obviously, she's not living at the castle, and no one appears to have inhabited the place even though it's still furnished and made up nicely…well, no one living…in fifty or sixty years, but she should be fairly easy to track down."

Miz Vianca shook her head. "She passed, Miz Teddie."

"Oh no. Um, when?"

"Well, Ah heard only a few months ago. She got married and didn't live on the island. Not for years. Left in 1966. But word went out and there was a small memorial for her."

"Not to sound heartless, but did she have kids we could talk to? They wouldn't be kids, they'd be adults, but they might have heard things about their mom's life on the island. Or what about her husband?"

"No kids," Miz Vianca stated. "And Ah'm pretty sure her husband passed years ago, too. Tryin' to recall where they moved to... Ah'd say... Shreveport sounds raght. He taught at one of the colleges up there." She paused for dramatic effect. "His name was Ruben Steinberg."

Eric's eyebrows and mine lifted at the same time.

Miz Vianca grimaced. "Yeah, marryin' out'a her faith didn't go over well with her folks. Ah remember when Ah came home for visits during the 60s. Big buzz on the island."

"I'll bet. I'm surprised we didn't find her portrait slashed along with Althea's. No wonder her room hasn't been touched."

Miz Vianca firmly stated, "She sure didn't come back visitin' once she married Mister Ruben. They eloped. And her mama and papa didn't live too long after she was married. Katherine had a brother who was like her daddy, slappin' Confederate flags on his trucks and not actin' exactly tolerant. He's one big reason the Quarters hasn't kept up with the years."

"I suppose he's also dead? Otherwise he'd be playing lord of the castle."

"Damn right," Miz Vianca replied. "He died in the 70s, not long after movin' from Endgate to someplace in Florida."

"Interesting mix," I noted with irony. "Folks in one family can produce fine people and bigots. Same generation. So much for environmental influences. Makes one wonder if such a thing as a bad seed exists." I wadded up my napkin for about the third time. "Okay. Enough of the Chaudrets."

"Well, except for Katherine. You've got me thinking," said Eric.

"Yes?"

"Rosalynn and Katherine were roommates at college. Any idea where, Miz Vianca?"

"Oh Lord, lemme think on the past." We stayed silent while Miz Vianca tried to recall conversations with others on the island about the Chaudret family. "Seems there was somethin' durin' one football season 'bout Miz Katherine goin' to the homecoming game with one of the boys on the island. Wait. There was a logo. Ah 'member seeing it on Miz Katherine's sweatshirt. Ah swear she wore it every day it was colder n' seventy. Ah recall it was like a quarter of a moon."

"Wow. Your memory is sharp," I exclaimed.

"Well, it was a pretty logo. The moon. Woulda made a good painting on a wall."

"Crescent City University," Eric announced. "Gotta be. When did she graduate?

"December, but Ah don't know what year. Ah do recall someone talkin' 'bout how she went summer sessions so as to graduate a semester early."

Eric typed in Crescent City University but was shut down by password requirements on their website.

He spent a moment or two cursing at the computer screen.

I patted his shoulder. "Don't worry about it. Might not help even if you *could* log into the site. Some places have a nicely organized list of names. Others don't. But part of our problem is, was Rosalynn Adams in the same class as Katherine?"

A look of horror came over Eric's face.

"What? What did I say? Are you okay? Is your ankle giving you pain?"

"You said 'organized list of names.' Names. Rosalynn Adams. Was it her *real* name? *Tenth Avenue* was a gothic romance featuring a biracial couple written in the middle of some of the worst violence of the 60s. For her own safety, she might have used a pen name."

Eric closed the laptop and stood up. "Enough. I'm making an executive decision to call a halt for the time being. Do you mind?"

"It's fine. Execute. Just do it fast before I grab the computer, drive directly to the Chaudret castle, jog up to the tower room, and drop the damned thing out the window." I winked at Miz Vianca. "I'd buy you another. It'd be worth it."

"Miz Teddie, after this last hour, Ah'd go with you, only Ah'd stand downstairs to make sure the ol' laptop landed on the pavement 'steada some poor ol' piece 'a shrubbery."

Eric waited until we were through being silly. "You ladies done?"

"Yep. Sorry. You were saying?"

"Teddie and I will clean up the kitchen. Then we'll head back to the Laurent house. Miz Vianca gets some rest. Or comes back with us for a lunch made by Luc and one she doesn't have to fix. We get the paperback out and Teddie continues reading from where she left off, which was what? I mean, last event in the book?"

"The fire."

"The fire. Maybe all the mysterious doings on the island will be solved in the next few chapters. If not...."

"Yes?" I inquired.

"Road trip. Well, boat trip. First to New Orleans and every used bookstore in the city, then to the Crescent City campus to hunt down yearbooks and hope a Rosalynn Adams pops up under 'authors I know and love' right next to Katherine Chaudret's senior photo."

"Hey. I haven't even looked at the back of the book. I remember from my college days reading those old paperbacks—during the 60s they often included authors' photos and bios on the last page."

Eric brightened. "We can only hope your misspent youth will come in handy."

Miz Vianca refused to let us clean up, saying she was going to stay at her house and was too full of coffee and biscuits to do justice to one of Luc's lunches. We hugged her good-bye and prepared to leave.

"Miz Teddie? Mister Eric? Ah do have a question for y'all. Remember, kids, Ah ain't psychic, just long-lived with a good memory."

"Go ahead," Eric told her. "Ask away."

"Why y'all so blame determined to find Miz Rosalynn?"

Chapter 44

A long silence followed Miz Vianca's question.

Why *were* we so determined to learn about Rosalynn Adams? Was it to solve the mystery of how a writer in 1965 could predict future events so precisely and include them in a novel? Was it to discover what had happened to her after she wrote a note to an anonymous someone? Someone who might have been able to whisk her off the island before whatever bad things she feared would happen—happened? Was it because we actually believed it would help figure out who was the current perpetrator of the same nasty events paralleled in Rosalynn's novel? Or because she might hold the key to the truth about Althea and Emeric? Was it something I had yet to identify?

All of the above?

I spelled out all my thoughts and questions.

"Can't see the future, Miz Teddie, and don' always have the best grasp 'a the past. But Ah feel certain you're gonna find the answers to—if not all—then most 'a your questions. Now, git back and enjoy a good lunch. If Ah remember anythin' more, Ah'll give you a call."

More hugs and we were off.

After a short, quiet drive, we pulled up behind the Laurent house.

"Teddie, wait."

"Yes?"

"This is *not* an executive decision, it's a suggestion, but how about we skip lunch and borrow one of Michael's ATVs? Do a fun tour of the island? Maybe stop in at Chittamwood Gardens if we get restless—but primarily try to do something for sheer fun?"

"What brought this on? Anything in particular or simply the last few days in their entirety?"

"Probably the whole island experience up to now. I'm calling it an intensity of open claustrophobia."

"Intriguing phrase. 'Open claustrophobia.' Did I create an oxymoron or a paradox or onomatopoeia?" I flicked my fingers and brushed the air away. "Yeah, yeah, I'm aware it's not the latter, but it's such a fun word I had to include it."

"I like it. Heck, I'll take all the fun I can get right now. At any rate, I am a bit punchy and not sure I care about anything regarding gothics or castles. I need a break and I'll bet you do, too. I swear an entire crew of old pirates could walk right up to me with buried treasure and all the secrets of *Chateau Sans Frontieres* and I'd suggest an anatomically impossible area for them to stick any and all treasure. Meantime…break. Recess. A short vacation from insanity and stress." He stopped, leaned over, and kissed my cheek "If I'm pushing and you want to wait 'til later, we can stay here for lunch and rest and read. Tomorrow we can take the ferry to New Orleans for our Rosalynn search. You haven't had the ferry experience yet, right?"

"Only from Staten Island to Manhattan. I love taking the ferry. I always feel like I'm arriving from Europe in the 1800s."

Eric kidded me. "The way things are going I'm not sure we want to spend any more time in the 1800s."

"Ouch. Good point. But I like your idea for the ferry trip tomorrow. And, as to four-wheeling across Endgate today, I agree. We need to do something silly."

We fist-bumped. "Great. It's a plan."

A plan partially derailed the instant we stepped inside the Sugarberry Terrace kitchen and were met by Jenny and Michael Laurent.

"Save me," was Jenny's dramatic greeting. "These people are all wackadoos."

Michael patted his wife's shoulder in sympathy.

Jenny continued muttering epithets, most of which were unintelligible but undoubtedly profane.

"Halt," Eric's baritone rang out.

We all halted.

"We want to hear about the wackadoos, but with a little coherency, Jenny. What in hell are you raving about?"

"Didn't I say?"

Eric and I chorused, "No."

"Oh." She assumed a sheepish look, which I knew was a total crock. "Sorry. Let me explain."

We sat at the table. I pointed at my buddy. "Spill it, Harrison."

"Okay. There's more fighting, *primarily* over the land and castle, but—surprise, surprise—someone had another idea. Remember the split-the-island plan? From yesterday?"

"Yep," I responded. "So, what's the latest?"

"DNA."

"Beg pardon?"

"DNA. They want everyone in contention for Tenth Avenue to get those DNA testing kits and discover who's *actually* related to the Chaudrets."

I rapped my knuckles over Jenny's head. "Excuse me and call me dense, but is there a point? Who cares?"

Jenny glared at me. "Let me break it down for you. Okay. The Chaudret family appears to be no more. I gather there was a son who died in the 70s and a daughter who married and left the island and was disinherited, which wouldn't matter in terms of genetics, but rumor has it she never had kids."

Eric and I again chorused, "Katherine. Died a few months ago, possibly in Shreveport."

Jenny's eyes widened. She shouted, "If you damn well knew, why are you asking?"

"Miz Vianca told us only this morning. But you still haven't explained the DNA issue."

"Oops. Sorry. Can you tell I'm a bit testy?"

I tried not to laugh. "A bit? Okay, pray continue."

"You're *too* kind," she stated sarcastically. "So, Chaudret ownership is like divine right of kings or something. Handed down forever. There's been no will for a good hundred years because the Chaudret land always went to the oldest Chaudret. They were amazingly tolerant in terms of gender, which surprises me considering their other biases, but now there are no Chaudrets. At least not in direct lineage. Monique or Renee… can't recall which, and both of whom happen to be currently sitting in the parlor—and why Sugarberry Terrace is always the meeting place is still a mystery to me—and yes, I'm digressing… Anyway, one of the ladies suggested DNA testing to be performed thanks to all the intermarrying and less legal forms of sharing DNA on Endgate since the first pirates arrived. The assumption is if a tiny Chaudret gene pops up, the person with the gene should rightfully claim the Tenth Avenue parcel as his or her own." She lowered her head and softly banged it on the kitchen table. "Wackadoos."

Eric echoed my earlier comment. "Jenny, does it *really* matter who owns it? If rich folks get a creepy castle with some antiques, who cares?"

She raised her head. "If antiques were the only issue, I'd say take it. Put up a big sign reading 'mine' and I'll put my theatre in Hickory Shadows or Chittamwood Gardens and be happy. The problem is there's more to the prize. You may or may not have been paying attention during the debate the other night, but whoever owns the castle would own what's now an undesignated but generally accepted bird sanctuary, which Michael and I want to keep even if we use the castle for a theatre. Alex would love to start up a chartered fishing boat company and Michael is totally behind him cheering him on. But if Zach and Renee are the owners, they'll slap a giant casino on the beach in five seconds, and if Monique gets it, she'll build tacky rental condos with parking lots—and either way the exotic birds and bees will head for the hills, which is a terrible analogy since there are no hills on this island. Anyway, George Adler is so besotted with Monique he'd do the same if it turned out he's secretly a Chaudret."

I rose from the table and announced, "I never thought I'd want more coffee after this morning, but I'm making a pot. Anyone else?"

Eric and Jenny both gave me a thumbs-up. I was about to bring out all the fixin's when Luc entered the kitchen. He was scowling.

I waved at him. "Hey, Luc. I was going to make coffee and didn't want to disturb you if you were busy elsewhere, but I apologize for rummaging through cans and stuff."

"Ain't you, Miz Teddie. It's the latest crazy talk 'bout the castle. All those folks actin' like they own everything and everybody cuz they might have a drop a blood from a stinkin' pirate. They makin' me as crazy as they are. Hell. Wouldn't surprise me if Cici 'n her mom got more Chaudret genes than any of 'em. All those ol' slave holders, includin' Chaudrets, got around... if ya get my drift."

"We do."

Eric commented, "Whoa. That'd serve 'em right, wouldn't it? Let the descendants of former slaves take their precious land."

"A little justice would be nice for a change," Luc stated. "Cici'd give the castle to Miz Jenny for her theatre and let Alex look after the birds and the fishes and boats." He paused then said grimly, "Some of those folks'd never let it happen. They'd be burnin' crosses and loopin' ropes over trees first." I noticed him tighten his fist for a moment before he pulled himself together. "So, y'all really wantin' coffee? Maybe iced tea, 'stead? It's gettin' mighty hot out."

It took us a moment longer to push aside his probably accurate statement, but eventually decided tea was the way to go. Luc accepted my help in making salads for those of us in the kitchen and sandwiches for the guests in the parlor, giving me a warm smile when I squeezed his hand.

"How do they propose to get a Chaudret DNA sample to compare? Since they're all deceased?"

Jenny looked horrified. "Oh my God. Do you suppose those maniacs would actually try to exhume a grave?"

For a moment we all were stunned into silence by the thought. Then common sense prevailed. "Combs or old toothbrushes?" I mused. "There were personal items in what I think was Katherine's room at the castle. I swore I saw some old toothbrushes still in holders in her bathroom."

Jenny appeared astonished I might be considering this. "Don't tell me, you agree they should do this."

"Of course not. It's only…if they're determined to test, a personal item would be a lot nicer and saner than digging up the coffin of Captain Jacques. Not to mention more legal. Of course, a comb would have to have a hair root that was used by someone like Katherine Chaudret and not her dog or cat. And I have no idea how long spit lasts on a toothbrush. Sorry, I have now come up with something as gross as digging up old pirates."

Luc and I passed around the salads and tea. "Ah'll let y'all do the servin'. The stupidity and greed levels from folks in the parlor is reachin' epic proportions an' Ah'm gonna throw somethin' soon."

"We'll bring this stuff in now," Jenny announced. "Maybe they'll lower the volume a notch with Eric and Teddie in the room so as not to embarrass themselves. Olivia is trying to stay gracious, but even she's becoming frustrated."

We brought trays into the parlor, politely held one out to Olivia so she could take her beverage and sandwich, then set them down on end tables and let Zach, Renee, Monique, and George help themselves. Michael joined us a few minutes later.

Eric and I took what we considered 'our' spots on the piano bench and began to eat. Monique and Olivia were seated in the chairs closest to us. Monique finally broke the tense silence. "So, what have y'all been up to? Are y'all okay after the fire?"

My mouth was full so Eric answered, telling her we'd been checking on residents in the Quarters—semi-true as it was only one resident—and adding we hadn't suffered any residual ill effects from escaping the inferno.

Olivia was clearly concerned. "You two need a break. You should go visit New Orleans, listen to a little Dixieland, drink those ridiculously tall drinks, and watch the interesting characters wander around the French Quarter."

"You're psychic, Miz Olivia. Already in the works," I told her. There was no reason to inform anyone about an itinerary adding used bookstores and a visit to the Crescent City University Alumni Center to the normal touristy activities.

"What'd you say you're planning?" came from Zach, across the room. "Something interesting?"

"A New Orleans spree," Renee answered for me.

"Ah. Good idea," Zach said. "Hasn't been the most pleasant vacation, I suppose."

Eric responded with a distinctly sarcastic tone, "Yeah, falling in cellars, finding dead bodies, and nearly getting burned wasn't quite on my to-do list when I flew down here a couple of weeks ago. To be clear, it's also not a vacation, since the sole purpose was to help Jenny with the mystery theatre, no matter which house is determined to be the final setting."

Silence fell once again, so thick I could practically feel it.

"When are you going to the mainland?" Zach asked in a clear attempt to defuse the situation. I really couldn't understand why Jenny's idea made them all so unhappy.

"Not sure," Eric answered for us, glancing at me with a hidden smile. "We were thinking of taking the evening ferry. Or we might wait 'til tomorrow morning."

"You should probably take a look at Chittamwood Gardens soon, since you haven't yet chosen your theatre," Zach suggested, sounding sincere.

"You'll love Chittamwood," Renee added. "I personally think it's the classiest house on the island. Although it wasn't settled until nearly a century after the other homes. It does need some renovating, however. And a major cleaning." She wrinkled her nose in disgust over what I assumed was the concept of dirt.

"Good thought. We'll check it out this afternoon," I said.

Nods all around, followed by another silence, this time a bit less edgy since folks were eating and being polite by not talking with their mouths full.

Monique, with her perennial lack of tact, asked what we thought about the idea of DNA testing to determine castle ownership. Eric and I looked at each other, then I diplomatically replied, "It's not up to us to weigh in on the issue. Although, if it's the only way to solve this dispute and y'all can get a...sample from a personal item without resorting to less—uh—polite and doubtless illegal methods, it might keep everyone from killing each other. Not to start a big argument again, but are you certain there's no will from sixty or more years ago?"

Michael answered. "If there's a will later than about 1750, no one's seen it. I'm amazed there was even a will made back then, since the pirates weren't exactly concerned with legalities. The island isn't like anywhere else in Louisiana when it comes to law, especially property. Anyway, the Chaudrets just kept handing down the land and the castle to the oldest in each generation. They never envisioned the line dying out."

Assuming it did, I thought. *Wouldn't it be funny if Luc were on to something? If, say, Miz Vianca Giry and her children were the rightful heirs to the old pirate's chateau?*

Chapter 45

Michael was delighted to offer an ATV for our excursion. Eric and I planned to leave right after lunch but ended up helping Luc clean the kitchen and dining area.

Once the kitchen was spotless and the glassware and china had been placed back in their respective cabinets, we headed out to the Laurent garage and found an ATV waiting and ready.

Endgate was an island with enough changes in elevation to allow us to take some dives down sloping roadways and some small "mounds" we could charge up before sailing over ditches still muddy from the storm. We didn't always make a perfect landing, which meant a lot of splashing that was ultimately half the fun, although I wondered if my jeans would ever get clean again.

"This is way too cool," I shouted as we bounced through a ditch covered in brush.

"Want to take the wheel?" Eric yelled back.

"Yeah."

We stopped. Eric turned to me. "I love driving this, but I must admit it's rough on the ankle having to deal with a clutch."

"Oh yeah. Especially when you're changing gears every five seconds on this sucker." I paused. "I warn you, I plan to hold nothing back in bouncing through ditches. None of this boring sedate driving I did the other day when we were heading to Hickory Shadows."

"I have complete confidence we won't flip and land somewhere on the west beach." He turned to me and asked with an almost straight face, "On the other hand, does this vehicle come with helmets?"

I thwapped his shoulder in mock anger.

We spent the next half hour riding through the trees and down the beaches of Endgate Island. As the driver, I couldn't take the time to admire the exotic-looking wildflowers that had miraculously survived the storm, but I marveled at the rich colors of blue, soft yellow, and vibrant reds peeking through broken branches and thick green bushes. I didn't see any wildlife scurrying by, but then again, if I were a wily coyote, savvy muskrat, or too-often-hunted fox and heard one of those demonic human devices cutting through my territory, I'd find the nearest hole and wait 'til it was safe to come out again

The ATV ride was the best idea of that day. I felt every ounce of tension from a week filled with stress and—yes, terror—melt away.

We stopped on the beach for a while to breathe in the air. The storm the other night had had the effect of clearing out toxins, leaving that air fresh and almost invigorating. We found a log perfectly suited for sitting and cuddling close to each other.

Eric suddenly tensed his shoulders. "This is weird."

"What is?"

"Remember when I had the vision about a girl sitting and playing piano and me listening?"

"And we later concluded it must have been Emeric and Althea."

"Right." Eric looked up at the sky for a long moment before turning his gaze back to me. "Another flash. Zipped by—but I got enough. I could swear it's the same two people but much younger. Kids, probably around age ten, playing on this beach, kicking up sand. Not an adult in sight."

I blinked back tears. "Total innocence."

"Exactly. Teddie, we've got to find out what happened. No matter what it takes."

Eric wrapped his arms around me, and we sat in silence, staring out across the water.

Finally, Eric turned me to face him. "Not to break the mood, but I can't help but wonder if there's a way to resolve the issues with the first families and bring a little peace to this island. I'm talking in terms of business."

"What do you have in mind?" I sat up straight. "This place really would be so perfect for tourists."

"There's more than one way to bring revenue to the island. You'd think with all the ideas floating around, the owners could all agree to help this place if people weren't being greedy."

"You talkin' pool resources?"

"Precisely."

I reached down and picked up a handful of sand, then let it slip through my fingers. "You're brilliant. Use the castle as a mystery dinner theatre, put up a few luxury rental condos and a couple of cute stores beyond the beach where they wouldn't bother the wildlife or birdies, build a casino along with the theatre, let Alex get his charter fishing company going, hire folks in the Quarters to come in and work in all areas. Put one large parking area in a place where it wouldn't uproot various little beasties. Oh yeah—the castle could also have ghost tours. Everyone would be happy. The beach would be pristine. The birds and foxes would keep their homes. The ghosts would be the only ones disturbed, which would be perfect since they'd be active and tourists would be thrilled."

"We're geniuses. Seriously, between us we've created a great resort. Suggest it to what Jenny calls the wackadoos as soon as we get back. I'm all for peace."

We fist-bumped approval, then I drew my hand away. "Dang. We forgot something."

"Which is? Sounded like you covered all bases for commerce and entertainment."

"Well, except for the one teensy, tiny little issue. One of these folks is a murderer, and until it's determined *who*, it's probably not in anyone's best interest to make a killer one's business partner. Could be annoying, not to mention dicey, wondering if one is going to get bumped off on any given day."

"I wish I could say you're wrong, but I can't. However, it's still a good idea if we ever find out who our villain is." Eric rose, helped me to my feet, then asked, "Are you ready to check out Chittamwood Gardens and see how it fits into the Endgate Island condo-casino-resort-theatre-wildlife preserve-charter boat-etcetera enterprise?"

"Let's do it. My island radar is telling me there's nothing to be found in there in terms of spooky notes or old books, but I'm still interested as to whether it would work better than Hickory Shadows for an alternate theatre space if our idea gets dissed and tossed. Want me to keep driving?"

"Yeah. Thanks."

Eric navigated us to Fifth Avenue with only a few deviations from the west beach and we pulled up in front of Chittamwood Gardens within about ten minutes.

We surveyed the house outside for a long minute.

"Oh man. This screams bed-and-breakfast," I said.

"My thoughts, too. It has the right feel for an inn. Rockers on the veranda, and there's enough space for little iron café tables, too. The view from the porch is nice since it faces trees and no other houses. Everything looks comfortable and stately and not a bit scary. Wanna go in?"

"Sure." I turned off the ATV.

We climbed the steps leading to the porch, and I gave one of the large rocking chairs a push. Not even a squeak. Perfect condition. The door was unlocked. Jenny had told us there was nothing of value inside, and apart from a diary-stealing thief, she couldn't think of anyone interested enough in the ancient hurricane lamps or old plates and utensils sitting in kitchen cabinets since the 1980s to rob the place.

Renee Pelletier had remarked how messy the house was, and she was right. The hardwood floors needed refinishing and polishing, but they were solid. The walls begged for a new paint job, but there was no mold and the wood beams in the parlor showed no rot or distress. We wandered through ten small rooms I felt would work perfectly for guests if the house became an inn. The only thing to add would be a small connecting bathroom. The kitchen had a cozy feel to it with both tons of counter space and a large island holding a stove with six gas burners in its center and an oven on the side facing the sink.

"Okay. Do you mind if I adopt your executive decision power and say, let's head back to the Laurent house? This place is the ultimate in B&Bs but not so great as a theatre, so I don't see much point in hanging out here much longer," I said.

"Adopt away. I'm embarrassed to admit this after the large lunch earlier, but I could use a tea-time break," Eric responded.

We took a last look around the parlor and then headed back outside.

Before I even realized why, I screamed, "Duck," and dropped to the porch, grabbing Eric's arm and pulling him down with me as something whizzed by and shattered the glass of the front door. We tried to find safety behind the chairs and tables then continued crawling as fast as we could off the side of the porch.

We heard another shot ring out as we hit the ground.

"Really?" I shouted, repeating, "Really? Like being nearly burned to a crisp wasn't enough, you stinkin' *bastard*?" I don't know how I managed to speak, much less shout, because my oxygen had vanished. I couldn't breathe. My skin felt as if someone was bashing me with a poker. A *hot* poker. I fought the urge to vomit and struggled to regain sight.

Eric gently shook me. "Teddie. You've got to focus. Deep breaths."

I forced myself to inhale. My heart was still knocking on my chest begging for release, but I found my voice. I sounded almost normal—at least I thought I did—but normal from about a hundred yards away.

"I hate to ask, but does this place have a cellar with outside doors?"

Eric pointed. "It does. Tornado shelter."

I didn't bother to reply. We scrambled like demented crabs through a line of cypress trees toward the metal double doors we prayed would lead to safety. Luck was with us. The doors were unlocked and we managed to open one wide enough to slip through and slam them shut before the next bullet sailed by. Under the doors were tornado shelter obligatory concrete stairs, and we slithered down them until we reached the cellar.

We stared at each other.

"Damn," Eric exclaimed.

"Yep. The only good thing about this situation is whoever's shooting doesn't appear to have an automatic weapon."

"I'll bet it's a rifle with a scope. Probably for hunting."

Eric pulled his cell phone out and hit the light. "Good illumination."

"Well, we're surprisingly calm, aren't we?" I said in a shaky voice.

Eric responded with his own shaky laugh, "If we ever leave this island, we'll need years of therapy for trauma."

"*If.*"

"Let me see if this stupid phone works underground and call Michael. Maybe he can track down the sheriff."

Within seconds Eric was explaining the situation and a horrified Michael was promising to send what amounted to the cavalry. Our shooter wasn't going to take potshots at a crowd, unless he or she was totally crazy.

Eric hung up. We stayed frozen in place, terrified the killer was outside waiting for another chance to let a bullet fly. We didn't hear anyone else moving. I had a short vision of someone running away from the house and instinctively knew it was over.

About six minutes later we heard honking from two separate vehicles. Then, and only then, we climbed out of the storm cellar to be greeted by Michael, Jenny, Alex, Cici, Luc, and Olivia.

"Can't you stay out of trouble for more than like five minutes?" Jenny scolded me, hugged me, then turned to Eric. "And you, Mister Director and Big Brave Male. Can't you do a better job of taking care of my best friend?" Jenny demanded, then hugged him even harder than she'd squeezed me.

It wasn't a real question and there was no good response. Eric grabbed my hand and drew me into the Jenny-Eric circle for a nice group hug. It felt wonderful

"Any idea who was shooting?" Cici asked.

"None," Eric replied. "We weren't exactly calling out greetings while we hauled it off the porch."

For the first time since I'd met her, Olivia Laurent appeared genuinely distressed and concerned. "I am so sorry. Why is this happening on my wonderful island?"

"Miz Livvie," I said. "Someone seems determined to keep part of Endgate out of the hands of the Laurents and anyone who's in league with the Laurents, like Eric and me. We've all discussed it and we're sure the violence has to do with island ownership."

She swallowed. "I only want things to go back to where they were when I first arrived on the island. Peaceful."

I bit my tongue, wanting to tell her although *her* life had been peaceful, the folks living in the Quarters had been surviving in hellish conditions and might prefer a little progress as opposed to a regression. Instead, I stated, "I'm afraid there's not going to be peace on this island until we get answers on Tenth Avenue. Soon."

Chapter 46

An hour after the insanity at Chittamwood Gardens, the Laurents, except for Olivia, who was resting in her room, Cici, Luc, Eric, and I met in the kitchen for a discussion as to where to go from here.

"Manhattan," I announced. "Kidding." Pause. "I think. Ah heck, it wouldn't solve the original problem that started with Jenny." I stuck my tongue out at her. "No offense."

Jenny flicked her fingers at me in fake dismissal. "None taken. I'll let you off this time since you've been used for target practice today and you did discover a portrait and a book, and you're the only one who has occasional flashes of second sight or insight or near sight or foresight or hindsight or sight-seeing sight or whatever you want to call it. Don't want to piss you off."

"Hush."

I accepted a tall glass of iced tea from Luc. "Thanks. Okay, seriously, folks, does anyone believe someone thought Eric and I looked like a good choice for venison stew and decided to move hunting season to May?"

"No way," said Cici. "Might as well call it what it is—attempted murder. Damn shame the sheriff wasn't around to catch the no-good s.o.b., but last I heard he was trackin' down Robin's next of kin. Doesn't matter. So… who knew y'all would be at the Fifth Avenue house?"

Eric replied, "Every bloody member of the first families who was here at lunch." He raised his hand as if asking for silence before everyone spoke at once to express theories. "And before you ask, there was a good ninety minutes after Teddie and I left the table before we took off in the ATV, which meant lots of time for one or two or five people to head over to Chittamwood Gardens. Although at least they had a helluva wait while we had a lovely time driving through mud holes. We weren't even sure if we were going to end up at the house until we got there."

Jenny growled. "Okay. So, our killer wants Tenth Avenue to the point of obsession."

"Why?" asked Cici. "I mean, what makes you so sure?"

I replied for Jenny. "Combination of things. This push of everyone to grab the castle and surrounding lands is intense to the point of rabid. And there's something…off about it."

"Off?" came from Michael.

"Yeah. I'm sensing a subtext. There's more than greed involved for wanting to build a casino or slap condos around Tenth Avenue." I paused before adding, "Which reminds me, Jenny, and you, too, Michael, before we forget, Eric and I had some ideas for pooling businesses if we ever find our villain and dispatch him or her."

"Great. Tell me later. But, meantime, what's this about the 'off' 'subtext?" Jenny inquired.

"Hard to explain because I'm not sure how much of what I've felt is this premonition déjà vu thing going on and how much is the piling up of accidents that aren't accidents. Truth is, I need to find out who exactly Rosalynn Adams was and why she was afraid." I stood. "Consequently, gang, I'm going to head off to the guest room where I will spend as long as it takes huddled under the reading lamp to finish Rosalynn's book. Maybe I can read what's going to happen *before* it happens for a change."

Eric rose as well. "I suggest everybody rest up. The book might help provide some answers, but we still need to figure out who this woman is and if there's a way to contact her, so a trip to New Orleans is still on for tomorrow. Teddie and I would welcome company for our bookstore tour. What would *really* be helpful is if we could all split into different teams. Alex and Cici? Maybe y'all could check bookstores and Teddie and I could head to the college alum center to look at yearbooks."

"Why the alum center?" asked Alex.

Eric told him our theory we might find information about Rosalynn in a yearbook or a list of alumnae, which could lead to tracking down her current whereabouts. "We figured out Katherine Chaudret must have been at Crescent City University. Long shot, but at this point, we'll take what we can get. I love old bookstores, but we're talking about doing a lot of walking through the city Not to be a wimp, but it would really help if Teddie and I do the driving portion of the investigation."

Alex and Cici declared they were on board, and Michael and Jenny offered to join the kids in checking the bookstores. We all separated to rest or read and decided to keep dinner conversation this evening strictly on topics outside of Endgate Island, no matter who came to the house—including anyone with a loaded rifle, lousy shot or not.

Eric and Jenny stayed in the kitchen to discuss the much lighter topic of the mystery theatre, and while I would have loved to hang out and chat, reading the novel was more important.

Before I headed down the hall to the guest room, I made a suggestion. "Michael, you might consider shutting down what seems to have been the Laurent bed-and-breakfast...and dinner, lately. Apart from the free food issue, which is none of my business, these folks all have motives that makes it *everyone's* business because they hear about all our plans twenty-four/seven."

Michael grimaced. "I'll see if I can get Olivia to understand we don't need to be constantly entertaining the very people who are fighting us for ownership. I'm not sure if she's too caught up in her lady of the manor routine or if she wants to find out what the next crazy idea is out of sheer curiosity. The island has always been a big grapevine of gossip, but now it's dangerous. After this afternoon, though, at least she might be disturbed enough to listen to me."

"Give it your best shot, Michael," Eric urged, adding, "Hell, if nothing else, tell Olivia the food bill will decrease dramatically."

A few minutes later I was on the bed in the guest room, pillows plumped behind me, and a strong light aimed at Rosalynn Adams's book. Again, I was tempted to jump to the end, but terrified I'd miss a helpful clue and discover why someone was determined to sabotage efforts to learn the history of the castle.

The last chapter I'd read before the excursion to the castle yesterday had been about the fire in Rick's house. True to form, Rosalynn's next chapters followed the events as they'd happened to Eric, Jenny, and me, with only minor differences that, in the big picture, changed nothing at all. Her characters explore the castle and discover the portrait of Althea stashed behind the wardrobe. There was nothing written about the pendant. In Rosalynn's book the artist's name had been scratched away along with the gash in the middle of the painting. Rick, Doree, and Janet spot a map of Endgate Island with all tunnels noted. They find an antique mantel clock.

There were no gothic novels, nor did Doree discover anything in the tower room, although….

I sat up. Doree tells the others the tower room felt haunted, but in an odd way. They ask what she means. Her response is, *"I could feel my own spirit in the room, decades from now, trapped and desperate to reach out for someone to hear my voice. Yet at the same time, the room felt horribly empty."*

For a moment, reading those lines, I was back in her room. *Empty.* Exactly the feelings I'd had when I stood there staring down at Rosalynn's note.

I read on. Doree, Rick, and Janet head back to Janet's house and discuss what they need to do next. Doree and Rick decide to head for New Orleans to see if they can find out anything about the artist who painted Althea's portrait. They realize it's iffy at best, but they hope by finding more of the artist's work they will get a lead to a biographer who might have noted something of interest about the people the artist painted during the mid-to-late 1800s, primarily those on Endgate Island. Was the artist himself an islander?

When the trio returns to Janet's house, they decide to delay the trip and have some fun and ask Janet's husband if they can borrow a Jeep to tour the island. They eat lunch with the "suspects" and Doree mentions she and Rick plan to check out a house on Fifth Avenue as a possible bed-and-breakfast.

No big surprise…a shooting incident came next. Rick is able to crawl to the Jeep he and Doree had used to drive to the house and use a walkie-talkie to call for help. I couldn't help but wonder how the author would have dealt with a shooting if she'd set the novel a hundred years earlier.

"They'd've shouted really loudly for help. Or gotten shot and ended the bloody book," I announced to the empty room.

Rosalynn finished the chapter with almost the same words I'd spoken to Olivia. *"There's going to be no peace on this island until we discover who wants Tenth Avenue and why."*

I turned the page, anxious to find out if their trip to the mainland would prove successful in getting the artist's name and finding clues about Althea and why she ran away from home in 1865. Assuming she had.

The next page was blank. Nothing. There were no more pages following the shooting incident. No final chapters. The answers were as empty as the tower room. I slid off the bed and searched through the books I'd stacked on the floor, picking each one up, leafing through them, hoping I'd shake loose pages from *Tenth Avenue*.

There were no extra pages.

I grabbed Rosalynn's book and trotted back to the kitchen. Luc was chopping and dicing, in the throes of creating another culinary masterpiece. He pointed outside. "Veranda."

Jenny and Eric were sitting on the veranda, having an animated discussion about interactive mystery theatres.

Jenny waved at me to sit down with them. "We need help here with your brilliant designs. But before we hand you a sketchpad, did you find out what's going to happen next? Did you find out what happened to Althea? Did you find out anything?"

"Pretty much zip. Well, except Althea's portrait. In the book, Doree and friends find it in the same room in the castle, but as well as the painting being slashed, the artist's name has been scratched out. We might learn something by researching the artist who painted Althea's portrait. But, guys, Rosalynn's story has gone from weird to super creepy and spooky."

"What do you mean?" asked Eric.

"I mean there's no ending. No chapters following Doree and Rick getting shot at. *Tenth Avenue* is missing an ending." I paused. "Not to be overly dramatic, but it appears it's up to us to finish her story."

Chapter 47

Jenny and Eric applauded. "Definitely overly dramatic," Jenny stated with admiration. "But then, look at your audience."

I sank down in one of the chairs next to Eric. "Okay. The drama of our lives aside…. Ooh. What a fun title for a soap? 'The Drama of Our Lives.'"

Eric and Jenny stared at me.

"No? Not buying it? Jeez. Tough crowd. Fine. Moving on. What's the latest with the theatre? Any major decisions, uh, decided?"

Eric answered, "If the Chaudret castle goes to one of the other combatants and they aren't interested in the idea of one nice big resort with theatre and casino and chartered boats, we're opting for Hickory Shadows. It's got clear ownership by the Laurents, and all we'd need to do is add 'theatre' to the end and we're set."

Jenny took over. "Plus, it's perfect for interactive. Large front room, lots of closets for bodies to fall out of, plus a huge kitchen for snacks or something more substantial. Turn the cuisine completely over to Luc and Cici. Hell, it won't matter what happens with the theatre itself—their food will be the draw."

"Assuming Cici wants to stay on the island," I said. "Of course, even if she moves to New Orleans she can come back and help with menus and hiring of kitchen staff if she wants. Which reminds me, as I gaze upon our trio of brilliant creative types with no business sense, who's running and managing this theatre?"

Jenny replied, "Alex."

"Really?"

"Yep. To begin with, he adores Cici and will follow her to the ends of the earth, and hopefully they can persuade each other this is a great opportunity. Plus, Alex happens to be a wiz at organizing and accounting and publicity and all those things a manager has to do. He can work even while getting his degree, since he's planning on

Crescent City University, so it's an easy commute, and half this stuff gets done online these days anyway."

"Cool. I assume y'all have been checking into scripts?"

Eric scowled at me. "Are you serious? Shoot, at this point we could just redo the events of the last couple of weeks."

"Heck, it's more exciting than *Blood on the Bayou*. Plus, no royalties. We simply turn Rosalynn's book into a play." I grabbed a clean glass and poured myself some iced tea. "Okay, let's talk design."

For the next hour we argued and agreed and argued some more, and I sketched and scratched out and tried to come up with ideas for both Hickory Shadows and Tenth Avenue. But my brain wasn't working at optimum creativity. Finally, I pushed away from the table and the sketchpads and announced in mock despair, "Enough. I hate everything I did, and honestly? Another hour of trying to extract awesome ideas from my brain is only going to drain me."

Eric looked at me then at Jenny. "I have a plan. And as the director, you both have to listen and obey."

Jenny snickered. "I knew it. Arrogant. Typical director."

Eric coughed and ignored her. "You're are going to like this. I promise. It's now six. The ferry from Endgate leaves at seven. I propose we grab Michael from wherever he is, see if Alex and Cici are available, and head to New Orleans. Get some dinner at someplace casual, hit one good place for jazz so I don't have to do too much walking from music venue to music venue, drink some giant drinks, spend the night at a hotel, and tomorrow roam through bookstores and the Crescent City University alumnus center."

I jumped up, scraping my chair back. "Perfect."

"Perfect," Jenny echoed.

Jenny picked up her cell, currently lying on the table. "I'll book some rooms at this fabulous bed-and-breakfast. It's a little outside the French Quarter. We can take a cab there to and fro."

We split to get cleaned up and pack overnight bags, agreeing to meet at the garage at quarter to seven so Michael could drive to the pier. Jenny tracked down Alex and Cici in time for them to join the party and we took the ferry, which was relaxing. We checked in at a B&B so fabulous and exclusive it didn't even have a name. Michael and Jenny had one room, Alex and Eric shared, and Cici and I shared.

Cici knew a small restaurant serving what she claimed to be the best Cajun rice and beans in the history of New Orleans along with jalapeno cornbread and banana pudding. An ancient bar provided some of the finest Dixieland jazz in the city, and when it closed at midnight, we found a small club in the Quarter where Eric knew the bandleader, a Mr. Artie Abraham. Eric informed me that Artie had relatives in Brooklyn who happened to own Eric's favorite deli. The two had met numerous times over the years. Artie seemed delighted to see Eric and even asked him to sit in on a few numbers during the next set.

"Damn. If you're ever jobless as a director, you could switch right to musician," I told him. "You play one mean piano, Mister Desmarais."

"I've taken the stage a time or two," he informed me with more than a trace of pride. "You?"

"Vocals only. Yeah, yeah, someone as agile and adept as I am with things like power tools should be able handle a flute or a sax or something, but I'm horrible when it comes to playing an instrument."

Eric grabbed my hand. "Sing anything apart from theatrical musical selections? Like oh… jazz standards?"

"I'm extremely eclectic. Classic rock and 60s protests, too."

"Good enough to perform for a small crowd?"

"Why?"

"I think you need a release from this week, and the crowd needs to see the lovely Teddie Grant perform."

"Love it. I'm not only a techie. I sing with a cabaret group in Manhattan when we have time to get together and rehearse so we don't embarrass ourselves. I'm definitely up for crooning a few tunes for a drunk New Orleans crowd. Hand me a mike and I'm on board."

The band was willing. I figured since it was the last set all anyone could do was boo and kick me out. Eric was back on piano.

I started with the jazz standard "St. Louis Woman," which is brash and bluesy and helped me win over the audience with a song I was sure they'd love. We transitioned into some classic New Orleans tunes, including "Basin Street Blues" and "Bourbon Street."

Shouts of "More!" swept the small room.

Eric swiveled around on the piano bench and motioned to me. I leaned down and brought my face level with his. He asked, "You up for a little romance?"

"Wha'cha got in mind, handsome?" I said flirtatiously. "Though, I suppose we're talkin' musically for the time being?"

"Unless we want to get arrested." He kissed my forehead. "Any favorites?"

"Oh…let's go with Gerswhin. How about 'They Can't Take That Away From Me.'" I smiled. "It can be our mantra."

I sang for another forty minutes or so. Closing time was approaching and I'd gone through a pretty eclectic mix of Broadway, blues, and jazz. I was about to ask Eric what would be a good closer when he rose, drew Artie aside, chatted for about fifteen seconds, then headed to the front of what passed as a stage and took the microphone from its stand.

"I want to thank Artie Abraham and his band for giving Miss Teddie Grant and me the opportunity to perform. Special thanks to all of you. You've been warm and enthusiastic, and we can feel the love up here. Now, I'd like to dedicate the last song of the evening to Miss Grant, if she'll do the honors and sing one more time. With me."

I swallowed nervously, wondering what he had planned.

He turned, held his hand out and brought me to stand beside him, then whispered, "Artie says he's fine with playing a few chords on the piano. We don't need anything else. Teddie, the night we met you mentioned how much you love *Parade*. So, I'm assuming you know 'All the Wasted Time'?"

My heart sang its own song upon hearing that Eric remembered such a tiny part of a conversation with me. "Yes."

It wasn't a song most people had even heard of, including rabid musical theatre fans, but it was an incredibly lovely and intensely personal choice by Eric. The backstory of the couple singing the duet in *Parade* was quite different in terms of what Eric and I had experienced, but the meaning was the same. Years upon years of wasted time, being kept apart, until finally coming together to acknowledge the wealth of caring on both sides.

I barely made it through without dissolving into a puddle. Eric took my hand in his and kept it there. We sang directly to each other, not even caring we still had an audience until the last note sounded.

The cheers and the standing ovation from the still-packed crowd was gratifying. It was the perfect end to an imperfect day.

It was also ridiculously late—or early—and all of us were ready to crash. We hailed a cab back to the B&B, went to our rooms, and for the first time that week, I slept through what was left of the night, until Cici woke me around nine a.m. to announce it was breakfast or bust.

Breakfast at the B&B was beignets and *café au lait*, which was fine with me. I didn't need anything heavy after last night's dinner and several large mojitos. Our group enjoyed the food and coffee but didn't linger. We had work to do.

"Jenny and I are going to scavenge through three used bookstores in the Quarter," Michael stated. "Alex and Cici? You've got some places you want to hit, right?"

"We do," Alex replied.

Eric stood. "And Teddie and I are headed to Crescent City University. I've already called a cab and he's waiting and we're off."

Within less than ten minutes we'd reached the Crescent City University Alumni Association House and were chatting with a student volunteer about accessing yearbooks from the years of 1960 through 1966.

The student, who introduced himself as Jerry, was a bit confused as to our reasons for wanting the yearbooks instead of a directory, but was nonetheless polite. We had our cover story ready, and most of it was true. We'd decided not to get into the whole thing about a gothic novelist who wrote inside a pirate's castle and didn't finish her book. Instead we told Jerry we were trying to find information about Katherine Chaudret but weren't sure when or even *if* she'd graduated. We explained we were planning on setting an interactive theatre in the castle where Katherine once lived and needed to track her down regarding issues of ownership. We skipped trying to explain that tracking her down would involve a séance at this point. It sounded almost as convoluted as it was, but Jerry, a history major, was intrigued and brought out the yearbooks.

Eric and I dove right into the 1965 yearbook, going on what Miz Vianca had told us about the dates when Rosalynn had come to stay at Tenth Avenue. We started with the senior photos. No Rosalynn Adams. We did find Katherine's photo the instant we turned to the page of "C's" which got us all excited and certain at least this was the right year.

"Maybe Rosalynn was a junior? Half my friends in college graduated in different years," I told Eric.

Nothing in the junior photos. Nothing in the sophomore or freshman. Perhaps Rosalynn had been camera shy. Hiding out writing her novel the day pictures were taken.

My cell phone rang.

"Cici?" Pause.

"Yeah," she said. "You guys find anything?"

"Katherine's senior picture, but no Rosalynn. What about you?"

Cici sounded excited. "We managed to unearth a book by Rosalynn Adams, I swear she's like a prodigy or something. The date of publication is 1964, which means she was still in college. Oh. Same publisher as *Tenth Avenue*."

"Cici. That's fantastic. So, is there a bio? Anything we can go on?"

"Yes and no. The title is *Shadow of Blue Harbor Castle*, which I gather is typical of gothics of the era, right?"

"Right. Go on."

"Okay... so, it's set in New England on a coast in Maine. Not in Louisiana or anyplace remotely similar to Endgate Island."

"Do you think it's the same Rosalynn Adams?" I asked.

"Yep," Cici responded. "Has to be. They include the first chapter of her upcoming novel, *Tenth Avenue,* as a teaser at the end of the book. It's her."

"Is there a bio of any kind?"

"There is. But it's sticky—and by sticky I mean we're now stuck. Bio is really thin. Only says the author is currently attending Crescent City U., and Rosalynn Adams is her pen name."

"Wow. Thanks."

I hung up, turned to Eric, and repeated the pertinent points of the conversation. "It seems we've hit a brick wall as concerns one Rosalynn Adams. Real name unknown."

Chapter 48

"You're telling me Rosalynn Adams doesn't really exist," Eric muttered.

"Hang on. She exists. Just not as Rosalynn Adams. Which means we have to go about this from a different angle."

"Ideas?"

"Hand me the 65 yearbook again."

"What are you looking for?" Eric asked.

"Senior class bios. Katherine's little blurb said she was president of her sorority. She was a member of the intramural swim team. Fingers crossed, but if Rosalynn was writing books during college, odds are she was also doing other writing. Like newspaper stories, or poetry if there's a poetry club."

"We have two copies for the 65 edition. Much as I love reading over your shoulder, let's separate for the purposes of time and efficiency and see if anything pops up. I'll start with the As if you'll start with the Ls."

I skimmed through the collection of the seniors, sparing a moment to notice and smile at the hairdos. Sixty-five was a transition year. The long-haired hippie style wasn't quite in, but the pin-curled bob making the girls all look forty instead of twenty was definitely out. The British swingy super-short 'do was popular among this class, possibly because in Louisiana pixie short hair was not only fashionable but also cool in the summer humidity.

I stopped. "I'm so stupid."

"You're not stupid. A little nuts at times, possibly lacking in common sense, but definitely not stupid."

He looked at me and realized I wasn't trying to be funny. "Teddie. You found something." It was not a question.

I couldn't speak for a moment.

"What'd you find? And why are you stupid for finding it?" He reached out and touched my cheek.

"I am stupid because all the clues have been smacking me across my face since I first found the note in the tower. Look." I pointed to the picture of a girl with long, straight hair hinting at the late-60s hippie style. Her eyes sparkled with life; even in the typical "I'm graduating" horrible pose every college yearbook in the world slaps on a page. Her bio was simple and sparse. No mention of a gothic romance novel published the year before. "Feature editor of the *Crescent City University Clarion* and head writer for the drama club's annual production."

Eric dropped his hand from my face and leaned over my shoulder. "Shauna Madison," Eric said aloud. "Pretty name. Pretty girl. You think this is our Rosalynn Adams?"

"Not think. Know."

He glanced at me. "Something tells me this is where the stupid part comes in. Take a deep breath, Teddie. You have zero color and I'm really afraid you're going to faint."

I did as he asked. Then I started to speak but my throat closed up. I coughed and finally managed to get the words out.

"Shauna Madison isn't only Rosalynn Adams. Shauna Madison is me."

Eric looked as if he weren't sure whether to laugh, cry, or run screaming from the building. He went with option four: humor. "Damn, woman, how many bloody lives have you had on Endgate Island?"

"I'm afraid to count." I grabbed Eric's hand like it was a lifeline to sanity. "If I'm right, and I'm pretty positive I am, this means two things."

"Give."

"First, it means Rosalynn Adams, real name Shauna Madison, is dead." I bit my lower lip. "I mean, otherwise if we were sharing space on earth simultaneously, there'd be a serious break in the space/time continuum, right?"

"Very funny." Eric caressed my hand. "Teddie, it's okay. Whatever's happening isn't a typical, everyday occurrence. I think you're fabulous and brave for managing to joke about it."

"Awww, thanks. I guess it's either go with humor or sign myself into the nearest psych hospital after spending a few hours hiding under this table curled up into a fetal position."

"Well, you'd have company. Once we told our friendly shrink we believe we're the resident bodies of at least one soul, they'd be measuring me for a matching straitjacket." He frowned. "Wait. You said two things. What's the other?"

"If I'm Shauna/Rosalynn, it means she didn't get it right while she was here."

"Look, before you get too deep into karmic retribution or the whys of who gets sent back to do what, we need to find out if Rosalynn really is dead. You might be channeling her fear after being in her room and...." He groaned. "Ah hell...I'm not buying it either."

"You're right, though. We need to do more research."

"Then let's get out of here. You okay to walk? Knees relatively stable?"

"Yes and no. I'm shaking and quaking inside, but my legs appear to be in working order."

We returned the yearbooks to Jerry, thanked him for his help, told him we'd been successful in our quest, and went outside. Eric used his cell to arrange for a taxi, then called Cici back to tell her we'd discovered the identity of Rosalynn Adams and ask her to gather everyone back at the B&B for lunch and access to computers with speedy Internet service.

After he hung up, he glanced at me, honest concern showing in his eyes. "You look like there's more. Care to share?"

I cleared my throat so I could speak. "I'm not sure I even want to know what happened to Rosalynn. Shauna. If I'm her, then I died. I don't know how to deal with that. Do I have to relive final moments to understand why I came back? Am I making sense?"

"You are. I get it. I do. I've been pushing away the same thoughts about Emeric. But, look, we've gotten this far in searching for answers to strange questions. And doing an online search should be a picnic compared to the events of the last few days. Heck, it's probably the smartest thing we've done since arriving on Endgate." He paused. "Wow."

"Wow?"

"I'm contemplating recent events. In two weeks, I've personally taken a spill down stairs, Jenny's been drugged, an innocent man died for no good reason, my temporary digs burned to the ground, we were shot at, and you've had close encounters with shades of the past in a tower built by a pirate. Pretty active fortnight."

"Not to mention there was a hundred-and-fifty-odd-years-old diary stolen and the discovery of a painting pointing to some major anger by someone living the same time as the diary was written," I reminded him. "By the way, thank you."

"For?"

"Keeping me sane when I get hit with insights about dead people."

He hugged me. "I'm learning not to question insights striking the lovely Theodosia."

"Wish I could summon them at will."

"Well, if we're into this whole truth thing, I agree. However, I've got an idea. We need a little more down time in New Orleans before heading back. Let's blow off the search for the afternoon and tour a little."

"How's your ankle?"

"Better, but I'd love to take one of the riverboat tours. I realize we'll be back on the ferry later so it might be too much time on the water for one day, but I took a short cruise a couple of weeks ago before I went to Endgate and it was relaxing and fun. Plus, informative about the city. Great views. Good food, although definitely less healthy than what we get from Luc."

"Let's do it." I took the cell from Eric and phoned Cici, who'd turned into our go-to organizer and asked her to tell the others we'd changed plans and to meet us at the Toulouse Street dock if they wanted an excursion. She called back within minutes to tell me Jenny and Michael were heading back to Endgate since they'd taken the tour several times, but she and Alex loved the idea and would be there soon.

Eric, as usual, was right. The riverboat was the needed antidote to the stress of discovering we'd found our author but probably weren't going to learn much else about her. The boat itself provided some great sightseeing in the old engine room, we heard all about battlefields on shore by our animated guide, listened to more jazz, and ate gumbo and hush puppies and bananas foster. The non-vegans dived into crawfish po-boys and oysters and sausage dishes while I scarfed down *calas* (dumplings) as if I hadn't already devoured beignets this morning. It was wonderful.

The cruise took a couple of hours. After disembarking from the riverboat, we hurried back to the B&B for our bags and made it back to the pier with about two minutes to spare for the ferry to Endgate Island.

"Can we stay here?" I begged the other three, not quite in jest. "I mean New Orleans. It's been so nice. An entire day with no one trying to kill us. Damn. What a concept."

We all agreed to call for a moratorium on all scary topics for the trip to the island, which further helped relax me and clear my mind. I hoped tomorrow I could look at this past week with fresh eyes and figure out a way to identify the person or persons behind near-fatal accidents. And while identification was vital for safety, I was oddly more curious about the "why" than the "who." I felt certain all the current nastiness could be traced to events beginning more than a hundred years ago. Possibly the day Captain Jacques Chaudret stepped on Endgate Island and claimed it for his own.

Chapter 49

New Orleans had been a welcome break and could even be considered informative since we'd learned the identity of Rosalynn Adams/Shauna Madison. But there were more discoveries to be made, and after a good night's sleep, feeling safe in the tower room, I was again rarin' to play detective and find answers. Following a long shower and packing a day bag, I headed to the Laurent kitchen around 5:30 a.m. Eric and I had agreed to meet early and head to Chaudret castle before half of Endgate learned of our plans for the day.

Eric greeted me with, "Good morning, gorgeous."

"Back atcha, handsome."

We exchanged a too-short kiss before I slid into a chair and gratefully accepted the steaming cup of coffee Eric placed in front of me. I didn't waste any time.

"I had an 'aha' moment while I was rinsing away the tea tree mint shampoo, which, incidentally, is great for waking one up at ridiculously early hours and isn't bad for getting rid of sinus headaches."

"Interesting, if off topic. You were saying... aha moment?"

"Ah. Yeah. We need to get a good look at the map Jenny found. I barely glanced at it the other day, and it's been one of those itches begging to be scratched."

"Makes sense." He poured coffee into his own mug. "We also need to check the antique clock I found in the china cabinet. It's nagging at me. I've seen it before, but it seemed bigger. I swear I saw one similar when I was a kid. It might not have a damned thing to do with Althea Chaudret or Rosalynn or hauntings or pirates, but my own 'aha moment' is screaming...aha."

"Eric Desmarais. Are you catching my precognition stuff?"

"Oh God, I hope not. I'm not sure the world is ready for a psychic team of Grant and Desmarais, although if you could envision the next numbers for a big lottery win, I wouldn't complain."

"You'll be the first I tell, although most of my visions have been dire predictions of disasters or hints of events, so I wouldn't trust me when it comes to financial gains through psychic means."

"Well, hell. Aren't you totally useless, then," he joked. "Okay, Theodosia, ready for the day's adventure?"

"Yep." I filled up two take-along filtered water bottles, and then tossed in several bags of trail mix, a jar of peanut butter and a large chunk of homemade bread, and some prepacked bags of nuts, raisins, carrots, celery, and apples. I ran through my checklist of exploration items, including a flashlight, the handy can of spray oil, a flat head and a Philips screwdriver, a hammer, and—much to Eric's delight—a set of lock-picking tools.

"Are we robbing the castle?" he inquired. "I thought Jenny gave you the key last night."

"She did, but there are always times when a lock needs pickin'. Sort of like a good fiddle." He laughed and set out.

We borrowed another of Michael's vehicles, this one an old beat-up sedan with plenty of trunk space in case we needed to bring back the huge map for further examination. We considered stopping by Miz Vianca's place to say howdy, but decided to wait until we were through at Tenth Avenue in case we needed to ask her to explain another mystery or two.

We parked close to the castle on the paved driveway in a space obscured from the road and the beach by a line of unidentifiable trees and entered through the back door.

"I hope this is hidden enough to keep our whereabouts a mystery for at least an hour or so. I'm also praying all villains are late sleepers."

"Well, in case anyone's up and roaming apart from ghosts, let's grab the most important items. I'll bring the clock to the dining room," Eric said. "If you need help lifting the map, give me a shout. Glass could be heavy."

"Will do."

Less than five minutes later we'd carried the items of interest to the dining area and placed them on the table. I turned on my flashlight for better viewing.

"Let's start with the clock," Eric suggested.

"You think you might have seen one like it when you were a child, right? How old? I mean, *you*, not the clock."

"Got it. I'm thinking maybe five or six? I keep getting this impression of looking at it on a table and the table was a little shorter than I was. Like I was eye level with the clock." He groaned. "Great. I'm stuck. Any hypnotism techniques to help remember?"

"Only normal meditation while doing yoga poses. But you may be on to something. Sit, close your eyes, breathe deeply, empty your mind of any stress you can, and try to kind of take yourself back to childhood."

"I hope nothing traumatic occurred when I was a little kid or I'll be a basket case for the rest of my life unless you snap me out of it."

He sank down into a chair close to the clock itself, closed his eyes, and began taking slow deep breaths. I remained silent. About two minutes later Eric opened his eyes. "Amazing."

"You remember?"

"I remember."

"Yes?"

"There really was a clock like this at my great-grandmother's house. In Brooklyn. I saw it the day she died. She was ninety-seven. I was five. My mom and grandmother had brought me over to say good-bye. I remember hugging her and then I was sent out of the room since no one thought I needed to be there for the actual passing. I was roaming, looking for something to play with, and I spotted the clock. I thought it was pretty cool. It was inside a cabinet, not on a table, but the shelf was about my height and I really was eyeball to clock face. I was going to try to take it out, but my mother came in and told me Great-Granny had passed and we all needed to pray. All I got. I have no idea what happened to the clock. I never saw it again."

"Pretty amazing you can recall even a little."

"Not sure how much it helps apart from making me less crazy about trying to recall something from thirty years ago."

"It's really a unique piece. But I'm wondering if this could have been part of a set? Let's take this back with us and have Michael, the resident antiques king, take a look."

Eric held his hand up. "Wait. There's more."

"Go on."

"Flickers in the air of memory. Something my grandmother said about it when she came into the room and noticed I was interested. Damn. Why can't five-year-olds put this little flash drive into their brains telling them to remember?"

"Because the flash drive would probably yield a ton of stuff like 'wow. This is great candy.' Or 'really, Mom, I didn't break the lamp. The dog broke it when she tried to turn it on and it was too high. I swear. Can I still have my allowance?' Other useful junk."

"And did the dog really try to turn on the lamp?"

"I seem to recall at least one dog in particular encouraging me to do so. Same thing, right?"

"Something tells me Teddie Grant did not get her allowance that week."

"Nor the next two. Mom sternly informed me I had to pay for the lamp out of my own money. Of course, my allowance at age five was fifty cents. Took me to age seven to realize a dollar would not cover the cost of a thirty-dollar lamp. I did have to help clean up the glass, though."

"Speaking of glass…"

"Ah. Nice transition. Yeah, time to peer under some and check out the map."

I carefully began to study the map, starting at the left side, moving to the right, and hoping for insight into why I felt this map was important. We were calling it a map, but it was more a hodgepodge of blueprint and map of the castle and the rest of what was considered Tenth Avenue. Approximately five blocks worth of Chaudret property.

"Talk about a mass of passages leading to this house. Well, to the cellar. I guess those pirates wanted to be sure of enough storage space." I stopped. "Something's not right."

"What?"

"Spaces missing. I mean, there are places I'm sure exist, but they aren't noted. I'd lay bets this isn't the original map, even though the date at the bottom right says 1866."

"How can you tell?"

"The ink is wrong." I glanced over at Eric. "I have inks down to a fine art. Which sounds weird, but one of my design teachers in college wanted to stress the importance of designs looking authentic if, say, you were doing a Victorian farce and your set had to look like it fit in the late 1800s but you were using twenty-first century materials. We had a couple of weeks of comparing the look of things like maps created using quill pens to those using ballpoint or gel. He brought in antiques so we would immerse ourselves in getting the right look. Anyway, the ink here is ballpoint. The paper is wrong, too. It's too well preserved. The glass would keep parchments for generation upon generation, but this isn't parchment. I'll bet anything this is a copy made in. oh, nineteen-sixty-something, and someone either deliberately or stupidly left out a few 'X marks the spots.'" I pointed to the center bottom of the map. "Here, for example. There's a tunnel marked appearing to lead to what had to have once been a vineyard. But there's nothing to indicate where it began. That makes no sense."

Eric's eyebrow lifted. "Treasure room?"

"But of course. Ready for jewels and gold bullion?"

"Actually, I'd prefer answers."

"Yeah. Me too." I sobered and stared down at the map, waiting for further inspiration. I looked at the clock again and around the dining room at the cabinets still bearing china plates and fine crystal goblets. My first thought was amazement no one had broken in and robbed the place, but I figured the ghosts would scare the fool out of any burglar who tried. My second thought was *goblets. Wine.*

"Eric, do you suppose there's a wine cellar at the start of the tunnel? The Chaudrets had a vineyard for a while. Cellars have barrels for fermenting sometimes, right?"

"I'm no expert, but I've seen big vats in movies with bubbling yeast or something."

"Wine cellar," I repeated. "Now why wouldn't they label it on the map?"

"Super rare vintage?"

"Sounds lovely but I doubt it. Maybe it got converted to storage for your famous pirate pieces of eight?"

"Well, whatever it is, obviously you're itching to explore."

I started to say yes but stopped.

Eric glanced at me. "What?"

"I'm getting a faint vision of Rosalynn/Shauna looking at this map. Except it's the original, not this copy."

"Can you see anything else?"

"Not really. Let me forget past lives and use my expertise in set designing for this one, and imagine where'd I'd build a set for a scary scene in a spooky castle."

Eric stayed silent while I thought and mumbled to myself, coming up with ridiculous ideas like hidden closets inside the hideous gargoyles or a zip line leading from the master bedroom to a bedroom clear across the island where one of Jacques's doubtless many mistresses resided.

Then it hit. "If I were Captain Jacques, a good Frenchman, I'd have built a trapdoor leading to my wine cellar to keep any pesky members of my crew from having easy access."

"It makes sense." He grabbed my hand. "If you're right, even if there's nothing mysterious, we could end up bringing back a few bottles of vintage wine. Time to explore."

Chapter 50

Eric and I took the clock back to the car, locking it in the trunk. We strolled a few yards down to the beach, sat on one of the low retaining walls, ate trail mix, drank water, and breathed the fresh air.

"I would like to announce here and now, if it turns out Jenny can use the castle for her theatre, someone needs to go inside with white sage or a voodoo priestess and dispel the ghosts. I can only stand to be inside about thirty minutes before feeling like I need to go running around the beach in circles like a puppy let loose from its crate. I don't think even paranormal-hungry tourists could deal with the ambiance for more than about five minutes."

"I agree. There's a definite air of downright 'bad' in there." He took another swig of water. "Are we ready to traverse the creepy-crawly tunnel leading to an imaginary wine cellar?"

"Sure."

The entrance to the tunnel was about a half-mile inward from the beach, but Eric stated his ankle was much better and he could handle the distance. There didn't seem to be a good place to move the car where it would be completely hidden, and we didn't need anyone learning we were exploring a space completely removed from actors, audiences, and design. Until there was a tangible piece to add to the puzzle, we preferred not to broadcast our whereabouts—especially to folks with evil intent who might be more than curious. So, we left the sedan where it was.

It took us fifteen minutes to locate the entrance to a small cave. Time had not been kind to this area. Trees toppled from long-past tempests along with others uprooted in the storm from a few nights ago worsened any possibility at finding a smooth path. Once we made it over the trees, we faced machete-worthy brush so thick we circled the cave three times before we were convinced there was something worth hacking away at.

The entrance was small, but once inside, both of us were able to stand upright. About six feet in, there was enough width space for a decent-size wine vat to be wheeled through, making for a less claustrophobic feel. The tunnel floor was made of concrete, so no nasty things came popping out of the ground to welcome us, although I assumed more than one rodent or reptile had called the place home at one time or another for centuries.

The path was long and wound in an arc leading back toward the castle.

After walking for what seemed to be a good half-mile in circles, Eric stated, "I'm completely lost. Do you suppose there's an end? I'm getting a whole rat-in-a-maze vibe."

"Bound to be an end. Soon we shall come upon a wine cellar. I hope. Light and airy and possibly stocked with cases of pirate-era Bordeaux. And a few chests of jewels and gold as well, since this crazy cellar cave was probably built in the first place for hiding, although…"

"Although?"

"The cellar might have both, but I really believe it's the least important thing inside. We're going to find answers and they won't be pleasant."

We stared at each other.

"Maybe we should go back." I started to tremble.

Eric took my hand in his. "Teddie, I agree that whatever we find might not be pleasant. I'm getting a nasty impression the farther down this passage we go. And if you want to head back, I'm with you. But…"

I straightened my shoulders and took as deep a breath as one could in a tunnel. "You're right. We've come this far. If we chicken out now…" I tried to smile. "Heck, we'd probably have to return for *another* life in Chaudret land." I added, "Don't let go, okay?"

"Never."

We turned another corner and suddenly found ourselves in front of a heavy, metal double door. Similar to the type of door one finds at a public storage facility. Disappointing, if one is looking for proof of ancient pirates—but reassuring in assuming whatever was on the other side was still intact. A rusty padlock indicated no one had opened the door in decades.

Eric sighed in frustration. "Great. How do we get in?"

"Oh, ye of little faith. Teddie brought lock-picking tools, remember?"

"And here I thought you were merely being cute, kidding about doing a little B & E." Eric paused. "Should I be asking *why* you learned to pick locks? Was there a felony involved?"

"Oh. Nothing illegal. I promise. More a combination of the sheer thrill of mastering a skill and working for theatres with zero money who send tech people out to find interesting objects to use on stage. And discovering many of those pieces are in places that haven't seen the light of day since they were first locked away. You?"

"Me?"

"Come on, Eric, don't tell me you aren't itching to take one of these handy little tools and go at it with gusto."

"Well, without getting into details, let's say some of my youth was more mis-spent, and yes, I could probably crack this padlock with my eyes closed. I'd be pleased to give it a go, but it'll be faster if you aim the flashlight at the door."

I reached into my bag, handed him the tools, and lifted the light. He was good. Better than I was, and I used to have lock-picking contests with other techies during crew hours in college.

Eric finished the task and, aided by a little oil spritzed on the hinges, had the door unlocked in less than a minute. He started to pull it open just a crack.

"Eric. Wait."

"Why?"

My breath became erratic, coming too fast and then feeling as if it had stopped completely. I put my hand over Eric's arm. "Eric, do you feel it? Don't say anything for a moment, let it simply…"

We didn't speak. Eric closed his eyes and whispered, "He's here."

"Yes."

Eric silently handed me the lock-picking tool kit and I stuffed it back in my bag before we both stepped inside what was, indeed, an old wine cellar. Ten racks filled with bottles lined each side. On the ground next to them were other cases.

"Eric, in an attempt to stay relatively calm regarding what we're about to see, I'm going to make a slightly flippant comment. Ten to one this place wasn't only used for making or storing wine. I'm talkin' bootleg whiskey."

He went right with me in this short avoidance of disturbing topics. "After all, what's a good smuggler to do during Prohibition when he's this close to the Big Easy? I'm sure some of these cases have been here since the 20s."

There was a large barrel on the opposite end of the cellar from the door. "Wine-making vat?" I asked.

"I'd say yes, but I have to admit my knowledge of wine making is right in line with vineyards themselves. As in, less than zero."

I didn't respond. I aimed the flashlight at the barrel and headed toward it like a sleepwalker moving without conscious will.

It wasn't a large cellar. But it felt like hours before we reached the barrel.

"I don't want to look," I said, hearing the hoarseness in my voice.

"I don't either."

He grasped my free hand and held it tightly. I lifted the light and we stared down into a space about ten feet long and six feet wide, hidden from view behind the old barrel.

The clothes weren't much of a clue. Rags by this time, yet enough solid pieces to identify a shirt, with what I'd call poet-style long sleeves, and trousers made of cotton, not denim. We didn't need any clues. We knew.

"Emeric," Eric stated in a flat monotone.

A second set of bones lay close to the first. A white wide headband decorated the skull. Time had been kinder to the garments, but then she hadn't been there as long. The dress was a sheath, with the mini-length so popular in 1965.

"Shauna Madison. Also known as Rosalynn Adams."

Chapter 51

An old musket had been propped against the wall behind the two skeletons. Next to the musket sat a large, padlocked steamer trunk. Eric and I sank down on the trunk close together, unable to speak, barely able to process what we'd found.

Finally, Eric stated, almost casually, "They were shot. There's a big hole in Emeric's shirt. I'm betting it clipped a bone above his heart. Rosalynn could have been shot with the same musket, assuming it even worked after a hundred years, or a completely different weapon, but she was also shot. At least...at least it appears they died of gunshot wounds and weren't locked away down here. Small comfort."

Eric and I were both avoiding using the pronoun "we." While we believed we'd once been Emeric and Shauna, the reality of their deaths was too much to handle. We needed to talk about them in the third person to keep a grip on our sanity.

I brushed away the tears trickling down my face and whispered, "Eighteen."

"What?"

"Emeric was eighteen. Eighteen. And Rosalynn—Shauna—she wasn't much older. Twenty-one? Twenty-two?" Eric put his arm around me and let me cry, although I could tell he wasn't far from letting his own tears fall. "*Why?*"

The newcomer's voice came from inside the metal door and echoed around the room. "Because she read the diary and learned about this cellar."

"Renee? Is that you?"

"Well, who else would it be? Who *else* cares the way I do about the castle? Who really deserves it? I ask you, who? Doesn't matter. You won't be leaving here, so there's no point arguing with you."

It was indeed Renee Pelletier. Coming into view, incongruously wearing an ankle-length pastel blue, lightweight linen dress designed for an afternoon tea party or wedding shower. I say incongruous because apart from exploring dirty tunnels in such an outfit, the primary accessory was the large gun she held in her right hand, which was pointed at us. Eric pushed me behind him as I tried not to be sick.

Eric, who, as a director, was used to dealing with actors and staff who occasionally displayed diva temperaments, attempted to engage Renee Pelletier in a calm discussion.

"Renee, how long have you known about…all this? About the bodies here?"

"Not long," she remarked in a conversational tone. "Not really. Four, maybe five, months. Hadn't seen them though. There was no need to deal with any mess until I was forced to hide proof about remaining members of the Chaudret family. And now, of course, I can accomplish everything at once and finally claim the castle as mine."

She wasn't making a lot of sense. I hoped to get a semi-coherent explanation and asked, "Why yours?"

She stomped her foot in frustration, like a toddler attempting to convince mom to give her the last piece of cake. "*No* one on this island understands. So, let me provide you with the true history of Endgate Island, not the crap dished out by the so-called first families. Philippe Pelletier was the navigation officer on *The Baron* when Jacques Chaudret was captain. The Chaudrets and Pelletiers arrived on the island at the exact same time and originally split the island in equal parts. Jacques grabbed the beach and built the castle. And it stayed Chaudret property until finally, *finally* they died out. When I found out Katherine Chaudret Steinberg was dead and buried and had no children, I was thrilled."

"Oh dear God, why?" I asked.

"Because the will states if no Chaudret is living, *all* of Tenth Avenue will go to the oldest living Pelletier. Me. The will had only been a rumor handed down in our family for several hundred years, but I actually found the document in an old lock safe in Hickory Shadows before my parents sold the place to Cyril Laurent."

Eric and I glanced at each other. I quietly inquired, "Renee, why does this castle mean so much to you?" *So much so you're willing to kill to finally claim ownership,* I left unspoken.

"Because it's taken four hundred damned years to see Grace Sedley finally avenged."

Silence. I wasn't sure I'd heard correctly.

"Grace was Captain Jacques' wife, right?"

Renee almost spat her next words at us. "And yes, she bore him six children, blah, blah, blah—we've all heard it a million times. The wife he abducted when she was only a teenager. Everyone's so stupid. It's so clear how much Grace *hated* Jacques, but islanders want to romanticize the whole pirate-maiden bullshit. And really, the Stockholm syndrome 'I love my kidnapper' theory is also nothing but pure crap. Anyway, during a year when Jacques was off pirating, Grace and my ancestor, Philippe Pelletier, fell in love. When Jacques returned, he learned Madame Valentine Pelletier had died in childbirth, but the Pelletier firstborn child was in great shape. Madame Grace Sedley Chaudret announced she would nurse and help raise him."

I blinked. I was right when I'd said the drama of our lives on this island was straight out of a soap opera.

Eric made an attempt to understand what Renee had told us. "So, the Pelletier family is actually descended from the Sedleys. From Grace."

"Yes. Dammit, aren't you listening? No, of course you're not. You're part of it, and you'll end it."

"I'm sorry to be dense, Renee. I understand you're the last Pelletier and the actual heir, but I'm still not clear as to why the ownership of the castle is so important," I said, even though I could see whatever slight hold Renee had over her emotions had all but disappeared.

"Because the Pelletiers will have control. The Chaudrets are dead and buried and gone. Grace has her revenge."

"Oh-kay. Great. Makes a lot of sense. But I guess what I don't understand is why are *we* the problem? I mean Jenny, Eric, and me? Why have you been trying to drive us off Endgate?" I asked—even as I wished I'd come up with a better phrase than "drive off" since it seemed mild in terms of committing multiple acts of attempted murder.

She was clearly exasperated at what she considered our denseness, but seemed willing to continue to talk, perhaps to convince herself of whatever "right" she was assuming…in more than one meaning of the word. She pointed at Eric. "Are you totally stupid? He's a *black slave's* descendant. It's all in Marianne's diary."

Which you stole before anyone had a chance to read it and possibly save some time and lives, you creep, I thought. I needed to get her mind off Eric, so I quickly said, "We haven't read it. What does it say?"

Renee stared at Eric with simple hatred. "It's not a long story. It comes down to Althea betraying her family and her race and everything she believed to run off with some black bastard who'd gotten her pregnant. Idiot." She actually giggled, and I had to force myself to stare at the gun in order not to tackle her and knock a few teeth out. "Marianne knew Althea was meeting the slave in New Orleans. Marianne helped Althea get to the mainland, then made it back to the island and told her father, Henri, before his slave could get away. Henri Chaudret shot him. Right here." Her eyes became unfocused for a second. "Personally, I'd've left him alive and let him rot."

The sick-to-my-stomach feeling returned in full force. "Why are you sure Eric is Emeric's descendant?" *And wouldn't you really freak out if you knew Eric and Emeric share the same soul?*

Renee stated crisply, "Years later, Marianne got a letter from Althea from New York. Someone from the island wrote Althea and told her Emeric had disappeared the same night and all the darkees were sure he was dead." Her tone dripped with sarcasm and anger. "Althea wrote Marianne how sad, how in despair she was. It was *disgusting*. In her letter she said she'd had the baby and named him Emeric. Made her way north to New York. Called herself Althea Desmarais." She glared at Eric. "Little bastard was too black to pass so she told everyone he was the son of her former mammy and she felt obliged to bring him up after the war."

It was all so terrible and truly tragic. Had Althea gone her whole life wondering what had happened to Emeric?

Eric shifted. The gun twitched in Renee's hand. "Renee, whether I'm a descendant or not, it doesn't matter. It's only sad ancient history."

"But it does," she insisted. "Stinkin' bastard Jacques put in his stupid will that anyone with even a *drop* of Chaudret blood inherits instead of a Pelletier. Illegitimate or not. Nothing 'bout color. Of course, that bastard Jacques *never* imagined there'd be any race mingling." She glanced around the cellar, almost with lust. "But this is *mine*. The castle. The land. It's mine. It's Grace Sedley's. I checked you out, Eric Desmarais. You have no brothers or sisters. Your parents are gone. You're the last remaining possible heir."

She backed up behind the metal door and began to slide it shut, announcing in a sweet tone, "I'm not going to shoot you. You can stay here forever. No one will ever find you."

She slammed the door before we could run across the room and stop her.

"We have been listening to one maniacal nutcase," Eric exhaled.

"You left out racist. And murderer."

"Oh yeah. Those, too."

We sank back down on the trunk and didn't speak for a minute or two, too shocked and disgusted at what had transpired to do anything but try to digest it.

"Do you think she's worked out the whole DNA thing? I mean, if you're descended from Grace Sedley and she's descended from Grace Sedley, y'all are actually related by blood? A tiny drop of blood, but nonetheless…"

"Honestly? No. If she even imagined a relationship, she'd've shot me the minute she met me."

"I'm glad she's not up to speed on genetics, then. Not to mention reincarnation." Tears welled up again and I brushed them away.

Eric took my hand and simply held it for a long moment. His voice became soft and gentle. "We need to let Miss Pelletier get as far from this tunnel as possible. Which means staying here for a few more minutes. Now, I'm as aware there's an escape plan as you, but I still have a ton of questions and need answers before we leave." His tone lightened. "Since most of them are about Rosalynn, I guess I'm hoping you can channel her spirit."

"Questions like why she was also murdered?"

"Yep. For starters anyway."

I thought for a moment. "I'll bet Rosalynn discovered the story about Althea and Emeric when she was staying in the castle. I have no idea if she also realized the past life connection between herself and Althea."

"Why did she write the book? Did Katherine tell her about this story before she came to the island?"

"Wait. Eric, I'm getting another feeling."

"A Teddie vision or a normal guess?"

"Either. Or both. Neither. I'm so confused, I have no idea. Anyway, stand up a second, okay?"

He did. "The trunk?"

"Yeah. Wanna do the honors?" I handed him the lock-picking kit.

Eric quickly worked the padlock on the trunk. There wasn't much inside. Whoever murdered Rosalynn had stowed away her belongings so no questions would arise as to why she wasn't around. A few dresses, jeans, shirts, and underthings fitting the style of the 60s. I felt certain her other dresses, like the designer shift I'd found in the trunk, had been tossed into cartons and taken to Hickory Shadows. I sifted through toiletries, a purse, and a larger carryall bag doubling as a suitcase. A portable radio. Letters stamped with a New York address. And at the bottom, a spiral notebook.

I laid everything out on the floor and closed the lid again. My throat felt tight and sore. I'd had strep a few years ago and this felt the same. As though it would hurt to talk or even swallow. I sank back down on the trunk and stared at the worldly possessions of Rosalynn Adams. Shauna Madison.

Eric put his hand out for the notebook. I gave it to him.

He opened it. "This looks like the rest of the manuscript. *Tenth Avenue*. Guess she never had the chance to type up the pages."

I choked out, "Could you sort of skim them? I don't think I can do it."

"I can, but let's wait 'til we're out of this hellhole. I think Renee's had enough time to haul it off the premises. And you're looking extremely pale."

"The escape plan. You knew I knew there was another way out." I gave him a weak smile.

"Naturally. I figured you weren't panicking or rushing Renee to tackle her and get the gun because we didn't really have reason to worry as long as she didn't shoot us. Now then, what are we looking for?"

I exhaled. "It's kind of ironic. There's a trap leading down here and it's directly above us. I spotted a tiny mark for the kitchen on the map. It might have originally been part of the dumbwaiter system, which makes sense for bringing up wine without having to go all the way around and come through the tunnel. Probably built by our speakeasy whiskey-smuggling Chaudrets. Of course, if I'm wrong, we're in big trouble. I don't think we can pick a nonexistent padlock from the inside."

"I trust your mapping skills. Let's give it a shot. I've had it with this place. It stinks of sadness and lost hopes and plain evil. We'll come back later when we've arranged a way to bring Emeric and Rosalynn out of here and give them a decent burial."

"Agreed."

Eric handed the notebook back to me for safekeeping in my bag. I led him to a spot only a few feet away from where we'd been sitting and pointed the flashlight upward.

"Yes."

A pull like those used for attics dangled within reach of anyone over the height of five four. Eric, at six feet, had no problem grabbing the pull and gently gave it a tug. We didn't need any broken ropes.

It opened easily and revealed a set of stairs. The smugglers were savvy. They'd built them of metal rather than wood and were still in good shape. We climbed up and were soon standing in the Chaudret butler's pantry off the dining room breathing real air.

"I suggest we get out of this place now in case Renee comes back with her little gun, happy she owns the castle since she thinks we've been 'dispatched,' and she decides to tour the place and decorate," Eric said.

I followed him out the kitchen and onto the beach. We needed to hide from Ms. Pelletier. And we still had a ton of questions.

"I think so, too. So, how's your ankle?"

"Okay. Not ready for marathons, but I could walk a good mile or more without trouble. Whatcha got in mind?"

"Not what. Who. Someone who'll take in two refugees who need to stay out of sight until we can reach the sheriff. Someone who lives close enough so we can get there in a hurry. Someone who loves us and who we love, and might be able to provide us with a few more answers. Someone who might also want to hear those chapters and read those letters from Rosalynn."

Eric didn't hesitate. "Miz Vianca Giry."

Chapter 52

Renee Pelletier could have been right behind us. She could have been five feet ahead of us. She could have been hiding behind every tree and bush from the castle to Miz Vianca's house. We didn't stop. We didn't look. We didn't listen. We were on a mission.

Miz Vianca stood on her porch. It was apparent she'd been waiting for us. She motioned to the small table and three glasses of tea, freshly poured.

"Catch your breath, children. Y'all want some mint for your tea?"

"Yes," we said simultaneously.

"Miz Vianca, do you have a phone we can use? I left my cell in the car."

Ninety-five-year-old Vianca Dubois handed me her new smartphone, complete with more apps than the computer I use for designing sets. "You tryin' to get the sheriff?" she asked.

"Yeah."

"Not sure if he's back yet. Went to New Orleans. Somethin' to do with Robin Trahan's murder. Autopsy results 's what Ah heard."

"And I seem to recall the deputy is back at college," said Eric.

"Y'all call Michael. He's one of the few folks out of the first fam'lies with any sense."

"We need to tell Michael and Jenny what's going on anyway." I dialed, got his voice-mail, and left a message to send out the troops to Vianca's, track down Zach and gently try to explain his wife had gone off her rocker, was carrying a nasty gun, and who knew who else she'd be going after?

I sat back and downed my tea. Eric was already on his second glass.

Vianca patted my hand. "Been feelin' evil around all day. Somethin' very wrong. Tell me."

We did.

"You found letters from Miz Rosalynn? Read 'em yet?"

"No. We needed to feel safe and figured anything within half a mile of the castle wasn't exactly sanctuary," Eric said.

I pulled the letters and the notebook out of my bag. "Should I start reading?"

Eric stopped me. "First, what are we trying to learn? And, in a choice between letters and notebooks, which is most likely to have answers?"

"Okay." I took a deep breath. "Why did Rosalynn write the book? While writing, did she find out about Emeric's murder? Did she get a wild hair one day and wander off following the map? Was she murdered because she found Emeric's body? Is there a thread pulling all this together?"

Eric and I looked at each other. "Letters," we chimed simultaneously.

I pulled one out at random.

Dear Shauna,

I'm worried about you. Don't let this quest for answers about the Desmarais family make you crazy, no matter how much you adored old Mr. Rick. I'll try to answer whatever I can for you, but remember, I met Althea Desmarais when she was really, really old. Who's to say if her mind was going by then?

"Oh my God. Rosalynn—I mean Shauna—knew a Rick Desmarais. Eric, who was he to you?"

"Richard, uh, Rick, was my great-great-grandfather. He died long before I was born. Go on."

"Okay."

You were right about the pendant in the portrait. According to Mama, Miss Althea said Emeric Desmarais gave it to her. It was the first item he bought after he got his freedom and was able to work for real wages for a family on the island. It was all Althea had of any value when she arrived in New York in 1866 and stayed with our great-grandparents. The Madisons were big abolitionists and ready to help out a girl with a Negro baby she said she saved right after the War.

Althea had the pendant and a clock she claimed had been one of a set. She refused to sell either piece, so I'm not sure how the clock ended up with the Desmarais family. By the way, there was something odd about it. Grandma once told me she found Althea crying because of the clock. She kept moaning it was the wrong one. As to the pendant? I still have it, passed down from Althea. From your description of the portrait, I'm pretty certain it's Miss Althea wearing it. She must have been really young when the artist painted it. She was only seventeen when she came to New York with the Desmarais baby.

Hope this helps a little. I gather the older Chaudrets aren't terribly forthcoming in answering your questions? Be careful. Sometimes family scandals turn ugly even a century later. I always suspected the baby Althea claimed to have saved on the island wasn't some random child. Why else would the Chaudrets have wanted to do harm to Althea? Enough said. Be careful.

Love, Aunt Susan

I downed another full glass of tea. "Anyone want to take a crack at putting a few pieces together?"

"I'll give it a shot. Starting with 1865. Althea Chaudret, age fifteen or sixteen, falls in love with Emeric Desmarais. Wouldn't surprise me if they even played together as kids and were forced apart once Henri Chaudret realized a slave had a thing for his daughter. Anyway, they managed to get together—in more ways than one—and nature did what nature does. Althea is pregnant. She and Emeric figure the only way for any life for them is to get out and head north."

"They must have hoped an interracial relationship would be more welcomed in New York. Talk about a total fantasy. Poor girl. Ah well. Not the point. Sorry. Go on."

Eric shot me an "are you okay?" look but continued. "They were teenagers and they were in love. Not a time for clear thinking. So, for whatever reason, they agree to meet in the city instead of travel together. Althea and her sister Marianne, whom it seems Althea trusted with the news about the pregnancy, get to New Orleans. Why Marianne decides to turn snitch is a mystery, but she does, and Daddy goes ballistic and grabs his musket. Somehow, he gets Emeric to meet him in the wine cellar, or maybe he shoots him somewhere else and dumps his body down there, but whatever the logistics, Henri kills eighteen-year-old Emeric."

"I wonder how long Althea waited before she realized he wasn't coming." I could feel tears welling up.

"Ah'll bet Marianne found a way to get word to her so'd she leave. Somethin' tells me she didn't want Althea and the baby 'round the island or in Nah'leans anymore n' Daddy Chaudret did," was Vianca's observation.

"Sounds right," Eric said. "We're also in the dark as to how Althea got to New York or whether she had the baby there or in New Orleans, but she ends up in Brooklyn and becomes… what? Maybe a companion to one of the Madisons? Shauna's great-grandparents—if my timeline is correct."

I took over. "Jump forward a hundred years. Nineteen sixty-five. The Desmarais family still lives in Brooklyn. Connected to the Madisons through the years. Shauna has a close relationship with Eric's great-great-grandfather. It's enough to make her curious about the origins of the Desmarais family, especially when by whatever bizarre coincidence she becomes friends with Katherine Chaudret at college and is invited to spend some time at the castle. While there, she discovers the painting of Althea and notices a pendant remarkably similar to one she's seen at the Madison or Desmarais house." I glanced at the other two. "How her pendant ended up at a flea market is beyond me, but I'm not staying up at night worrying about it. It's the same piece of jewelry, though. I've felt an odd connection to it since I first put it on. And Eric, you got this flash of something as well the night I wore it to dinner."

Miz Vianca asked us what had happened at the castle. Eric again took over the play-by-play.

Miz Vianca scowled. "Damn. Knew Miz Renee was plumb crazy. Ah did. *Too* nice in her talkin', while behind her eyes? Not nice. And Ah always said the Pelletiers weren't roarin' with all oars. None of 'em. If what you say is true, it's no wonder. So much anger passed down for hundreds of years from a mad Grace Sedley. And Ah mean mad like angry *and* crazy. Ah told Zach before he married

Renee to watch out. He didn't listen. He never loved her; he's jus' greedy and wanted Pelletier lands to add to Prideaux to try to make a buck. But he ain't no murderer."

"Why did Renee kill Robin?" I asked. "He wasn't even from here. Lake Charles, right?"

"My guess," Eric answered, "is he heard or saw something, whether he knew it or not. Maybe Renee doping Jenny's drink? Or Renee holding a big hacksaw on her way into Hickory Shadows to take care of those stairs in the hopes I'd kill myself when I fell? Could be either. Could be both. Could even be as innocent as Robin seeing Renee try to sneak into the guest room the night we played guard dogs for Jenny. Doesn't matter. Whatever the reason, his death is wrong and sad."

Miz Vianca's phone rang. She answered, listened, and responded, "Ah'm puttin' y'all on speaker."

Jenny yelled, "Yo, guys. What's up? Apart from discovering Renee Pelletier is a cuckoo killer. I've got Michael and Alex out looking for her since Sheriff Guidry seems to be missing in action, and while I normally am not in favor of carrying weapons, the guys grabbed the rifles they use for shooting water moccasins and copperheads and I cheered. If nothing else, they can scare her, hog-tie her, and bring her back. Oh. Olivia is upset. She liked Renee. Considered her a true Southern gentlewoman, and let's face it, Olivia prizes Southern gentility above all else. Maybe Jenny the actress will seem classier now? Sorry. Am I being over-the-top tacky and more than mildly sarcastic?"

"Doesn't matter. Jenny," I raised my volume so she could hear. "Tell the search party to head to the castle. I'd bet anything Renee's squatting somewhere inside salivating because she's convinced she's now the rightful owner to the chateau and Philippe Pelletier and Grace Sedley are doing a ghost happy dance downstairs in the ballroom."

"I'll tell them. Um, want me to come get you guys? Or do you have access to the sedan?"

"It's still parked behind the castle. But we're good for now. Miz Vianca is a far better lady of the manor than Olivia ever could be, and I believe she's about to bring out some homemade hush puppies and grits and salad. Just keep us updated if you hear anything."

"Okay. Hey, I'm sorry again for bringing you guys down here. Really didn't expect you to be stalked and almost killed." We heard an audible sniff followed by the sound of my buddy blowing her nose.

Eric picked up the phone so he didn't have to shout. "Jenny, it was inevitable. Not the stalking and killing, but the connections to Endgate have been too strong to ignore for years."

Vianca brought out the aforementioned foods on a tray and we all took portions. She pointed at Eric. "Clock. The letter from Miz Rosalynn…Ah mean Miz Shauna's…aunt. She talks 'bout a clock. You mentioned somethin' bout a clock the other day."

Eric told her of the similarity in the clock he'd seen, briefly, as a child and the one from the Chaudret castle.

"And the letter. Did Althea say it be the wrong one? Did Ah hear correctly?"

I picked up the letter again and scanned the pertinent section. "You did."

"Where is it now?" Vianca asked. "The clock from the castle?"

"In the trunk of Michael's car. We left it near the beach. Hopefully Renee hasn't driven it into the sea by now. Why?"

"If Ah'm right, it's important."

She refused to say what was behind her interest, so we didn't press. We were too scared Renee was out hunting anyone and everyone who could destroy her plan to live out her days in Tenth Avenue.

We ate in silence, the tension in the air making it tough to enjoy the meal. When we finished, Eric stood. "I'm getting a Teddie premonition."

"Yes?"

"We need to get to the car. Something's going down soon on the beach. Wish I knew what, but things are fuzzy. Miz Vianca, do you have a vehicle we can borrow?"

"Ah do. Come on, y'all."

We left the dishes on the table and hurried to the backyard. An ancient motorcycle, surprisingly clean even after the storm, sat against a shed.

Vianca looked at us, "Either of y'all know how to ride one 'a these?"

"Hell yeah," came from both of us. I gestured toward Eric. "Wanna do the honors?"

"You bet." He climbed on and I quickly followed, wrapping my arms around his waist, feeling secure and safe. After a rushed good-bye, we were off, heading back to the beach on Tenth Avenue. We made our destination in less than five minutes.

Eric stopped the motorcycle. We reluctantly got our feet on solid ground again and were headed toward the parked sedan when Eric began laughing without a trace of humor.

"What?"

"I left the keys to the car—somewhere. Possibly in the cellar?"

I lifted up my bag. "Sounds reasonable. I have to say, I had no idea we'd be in need of picking more locks today than I've done in years. My turn."

I dealt with the trunk and found the clock. I left the map. We didn't need it anymore.

Before I could lift anything up and out of the trunk, we heard the squeal of brakes and a small red sports car stopped about thirty yards away. Eric and I froze as we watched Renee Pelletier gracefully slide out from behind the driver's side, then lift a gun in her right hand and shoot almost casually in our direction.

Déjà vu…again. At least this time we weren't trapped in a wine cellar with the bones of Emeric and Rosalynn lying next to us.

We dropped to the ground and dragged ourselves under the sedan as several bullets flew by, hitting the open trunk.

"I'm so damned glad that woman is a bad shot," Eric growled.

"Any suggestions before her aim gets better?"

He peeked out from under the car. "She's reloading. Let's try to get to the motorcycle before she's up and ready to go again."

We half-crawled and half-ran, hunched over and zigzagging. We reached the motorcycle in time to hear another bullet hit the car. I figured Renee had been too busy popping more bullets into her gun to realize her human targets were no longer hiding beneath a vehicle.

Eric started up the motorcycle again. But instead of riding away from the huntress, he turned the bike and accelerated toward Renee.

"Hang on," he shouted. "We're about to go full-tilt matador."

"What?"

Apparently "full-tilt matador" meant charging the bull…in this case, a woman with a gun. It was crazy, it was risky, and it could well be the only way to stop her. Renee was so startled she let the gun drop to her side, turned, and ran toward the edge of the sand.

Eric didn't let up. He continued to chase her until she was waist-deep in water.

Eric stopped the bike. "Give it up, Renee. Two steps more and you're neck-deep in water and I clearly recall a conversation where you admitted you'd never learned to swim."

"Drop," I yelled.

"What?"

"Now."

Eric didn't ask why. He complied. We dropped to the ground as the deranged woman again sent a bullet flying. This time she succeeded in hitting a tire. Which meant our only weapon—not to mention our means of escape—was now disabled.

Eric turned to me. "You knew she was about to shoot? Insight working overtime? And what now?"

I heard my voice as if from a distance. "Nothing. We'll be okay. Wait."

From seemingly out of nowhere, the cavalry arrived. Cici and Alex and Michael and Zach.

Zach screamed at his wife to drop the gun and to walk back to safety before she drowned.

She stared at him. She seemed confused for a moment, then screamed, "It's mine. The castle's mine. *I'm* the heir, *I'm* the heir. Not him."

Time went into a medley of too slow and too fast. Distorted.

I got up from the sand and began moving forward, but my steps felt as if they were in slow motion, through quicksand. I felt Eric's fingers brush mine, as though desperately trying to stop me moving forward, but I knew I wasn't going to die. Eric wasn't going to die. It had all happened before in another time.

My second sight signaled how events were going to play out. But even knowing the outcome, I will never understand why she decided to end the standoff in such a dramatic fashion. But when Renee gave an odd, winsome little smile, then raised the gun again, it was clear her decision was final.

Chapter 53

Guidry asked for statements from all of us. We gave them. Zach told everyone he wanted to stay on the beach beside Renee's body, now back on dry land, asking for a moment alone.

"I owe her a good-bye. I should have seen this coming. She's always had this belief she owed Grace Sedley some kind of revenge. I thought it was funny. But when Katherine Chaudret died a few months ago, Renee became obsessed. Maniacal, even. I'm so sorry I didn't realize how far gone she was." Zach stared down at the ground, then waved at us to go away.

There wasn't really anything anyone could say. The rest of us split into two groups, piled into the sedan and Alex's truck, then headed back to Sugarberry Terrace. Michael called Olivia to tell her about Renee's suicide and reassure her we were all safe and she should expect family and more company soon.

The kitchen, as always, became the place to sit around the table for a major discussion. Olivia joined us but appeared in shock and simply sat in silence. Luc had pitchers of margaritas ready and sandwiches for those who were hungry. It was time to talk about the hellish events on Endgate Island, not only today, but a week ago when I flew down from Manhattan, nearly three weeks ago when Eric arrived, four months ago when Jenny put in motion her ideas to create a theatre and lost an important diary…and in 1865 and 1965, when personal evils replaced piracy and slavery and wars and ended the reign of the Chaudrets on Tenth Avenue.

Eric and I took turns recounting this morning's events. When we got to our discovery of the skeletons of Emeric and Rosalynn/Shauna, there was a collective gasp of horror from everyone except Vianca and Luc.

Luc poured a margarita into the glass I held out to him. "Luc, you don't seem surprised."

"No, Miz Teddie, Ah'm not. Ah've heard rumors over the years 'bout somethin' bad happenin' at the castle in the 60s. When y'all started lookin' for answers 'bout why a diary was stolen from Miz Jenny and all the accidents kept pilin' on top 'a each other… Well, Ah've been here a long time. I figgered it all went back to those first families, just wasn't sure 'xactly who or why. Not sayin' all of 'em were bad, mind you, but evil keeps comin' out every few generations. Or sometimes even good and evil within the same family."

Olivia managed to say, almost wheezing, "Luc might not be surprised, but I'm in shock. Renee was so elegant and so smart and… Oh Lord in heaven, I'm so sorry. I'm really having a hard time processing this."

Michael reached out and patted his aunt's hand. "We all are. Discovering someone you pretty much grew up with is a murderer is not something you simply ease through in a day or a week. And I hate to say this, but it's true. I'm damned glad I don't have to be terrified every time someone I love steps outside the house. I don't have to worry they won't make it home alive."

Jenny was itching to hear all about the letter to Shauna, so Eric gave her a bullet point summarization, which sent everyone into stunned silence again.

Jenny wiped her eyes. "This is so weird, but it's like I knew her. I mean, all I did was research like mad to find out who Rosalynn Adams really was, but I feel like I lost a friend."

Eric and I exchanged a quick glance. He knew I'd tell Jenny later she really *had* a lost a friend…but reunited with her several decades later. No point in adding to the drama or confusion while Olivia was in the room.

Jenny continued, "How in blazes did Rosalynn end up in the cellar under the castle? Or I guess the question is why? Was she specifically exploring from the map, like you and Eric, and found Emeric's body? I mean bones?" Her voice shook. "Was she forced down there?"

"And who shot her?" asked Cici.

Alex mused, "Couldn't have been another crazy Pelletier trying to become the next heir. Katherine was young and no one at the time knew she wouldn't have kids, so Renee's mother wouldn't have gone off chasing down descendants of Desmarais."

I quietly stated, "I'm sure it was Katherine's father. Wanting to keep the scandal about his great-great-whatever aunt and her black lover from coming out. And before anyone asks, I have no facts. All gut."

We sipped our drinks and wondered if an answer would ever be revealed.

"It doesn't matter," I said. "Not really. The important thing was learning how both Emeric and Rosalynn died, and realizing one had died for love and the other for justice."

"I get the love, but justice?" Cici asked.

"Justice because Rosalynn died determined to bring to light, through her book, the horrors of hatred and racism, in both 1865 *and* a century later. She also was determined to bring some peace to the Desmarais family, since she clearly adored Eric's great-great-grandfather, who simply wanted answers as to his ancestry. She found them, even if they weren't revealed until decades later...like this morning." I stared at my drink and added, "You know, I bet the only person on the island who knew her real name was Shauna was Katherine Chaudret. Shauna might have been afraid someone would find out about her connection to the Desmarais family and she'd be in danger. So Katherine probably introduced her as Rosalynn."

Eric softly added, "I wonder if Katherine's father discovered the truth? Which gave him another reason—in his twisted mind—to murder her and leave her with Emeric. A racist's concept of divine retribution?"

I trembled, physically feeling Shauna's terror as she faced a hundred-year-old musket wielded in hatred by a man carrying a hundred years worth of hatred.

Miz Vianca had stayed silent throughout the discussion. She'd heard the letter. She knew what had taken place in the cellar. Now she spoke up. "Where's the clock, Mister Eric? Ah didn't see y'all bring it inside."

"I was sneaky," he told her. "It's in the guest room. Hang on and I'll get it."

I rose. "I'll bring it. You've been on your ankle way too long today. I need to do a little fresh-up anyway."

Eric had placed the clock next to my bag. I picked up both, then reached inside the bag and pulled out the notebook and took the time to read a little before carrying both articles to the kitchen. I set the clock on the table in front of Vianca.

Vianca assumed the voice of a born storyteller. "There were three clocks. Not two like Miz Althea thought. A slave, Mister Tobias Aubrey, livin' in the Quarters made 'em as gifts. Eighteen-forty-nine, Ah believe. For Althea and Marianne Chaudret at their birth. Pretty bizarre, cuz they were twins. 'parently so different one could hardly tell they were even sisters. Ah'll bet it's why Miz Marianne told her daddy 'bout Miz Althea and Mister Emeric. Hated and loved her sister all at the same time. Anyway, the Chaudrets only wanted two clocks. Didn't care 'bout the third, so old Mister Aubrey kept it. He gave it to mah daddy as a weddin' present years later. Mah granddaughter up in Lafayette has it now."

We all stared at the clock. Eric spoke first. "Why is it important? I've felt this odd connection ever since I saw it and then I remembered my great-grandmother had one. If there were three, then obviously Granny had the one Althea brought with her. But apart from sentimental value, what's the big deal?"

Vianca reached for the timepiece. She jiggled something in the back. "Yep. Thought so. All of 'em had a secret compartment. Althea knew 'bout it, she must've. It makes sense since she was upset and sayin' she had the wrong clock. I'm supposin' there was nothing inside when she took a look once she was up in New York."

This particular clock was *not* empty. The compartment held a piece of paper and a faded photo. Vianca handed both items to Eric. "These are yours, Mister Eric. Your heritage."

He carefully unfolded the paper. "It's a marriage certificate. For Althea Isabella Theresa Chaudret and Emeric Desmarais. Wow. How in hell did they get legally married? I mean, who'd have been brave enough to marry them?"

Vianca's eyes filled with tears. "Take a look at the signin' at the bottom."

Eric handed it to me. "Here. You look. I'm almost afraid to read it."

My eyes widened. "Oh my God. It's signed Reverend Isaiah Giry."

"Mah great-granddaddy," Vianca whispered. "During the war the white minister on the island took off to tend to the Confederate boys fightin'. Someone had to say prayers over the dyin', and Granddad had been minister for years for the slaves. He told me once how proud he'd been to be able to become 'official' right after the war."

I reached over and hugged her. "This is awesome on top of awesome. Talk about connections."

Vianca sniffled enough for me to know this was hitting her as hard as all of us. "Knew from the moment Eric stepped foot on this island we had folks in common from way back."

Eric barely heard us. He was staring at the other item he'd taken out of the back of the clock. The photo. He silently handed it to me.

Two people. A boy and a girl. Teenagers. Dressed to the nines. His suit looked worn and cheap, but it was still a suit, not simply trousers and a shirt. Her dress dripped with lace from top to bottom.

"Anyone have a magnifying glass?" I asked. "Though I'm not sure we need it. It's pretty obvious."

Michael stood up. "There's one in my study. Hang on."

The room fell silent while we waited for him to return. He handed me the glass and I placed it over the photo and watched as the faces came to life. Faces with exact expressions of sheer joy and love.

"Althea. Definitely Althea. Even if I hadn't seen the portrait, I'd recognize her," I said. I didn't add it was like looking in some kind of alternate mirror. One showing a different face while revealing the same soul "And it's Emeric." I paused. "It's *also* Eric. Just younger."

"Wasn't sure if it was my imagination or not. I'm glad you see the resemblance. Proves I'm not crazy."

I passed the photo around. I didn't need to tell anyone to be careful with it. Everyone at the table treated it as though it was the most delicate crystal on the planet.

The conversation broke down into genetics and veered into teasing Eric as to what he wanted to do since it appeared he was the only legitimate heir to Tenth Avenue.

He squeezed another lime into his margarita, then groaned. "I'm definitely not up for this. I'm seeing an attorney as soon as possible and handing it all over to Jenny and Michael. All I ask is you guys bring in as many priests and priestesses of all faiths and rid that damned castle of everything evil from the last four centuries. Jenny can open her theatre without fear of the ghost of Jacques or Grace or Philippe or other Chaudrets getting upset at all the folks coming in for a little entertainment—or freaking out about having their black descendant anywhere near the place. Teddie will design and I will direct whatever Jenny decides and we'll stay until the theatre is up and running—and not a minute later." He glanced at me.

"Uh-huh. Typical director, making decisions for everyone."

Eric, wisely, ignored me and continued, "I *do* want to keep the clock. And Althea's portrait. Hopefully it can be repaired." He stopped. "Wow. Althea Chaudret, a Southern belle from Endgate Island, Louisiana, is my not-sure-how-many-greats-grandmother. How do I begin to process everything?"

Luc handed him another margarita. "This should help."

Everyone raised a glass and toasted to Eric's discovery of his past.

Luc started to clean up the kitchen, shooing us out. Alex and Cici offered to take Miz Vianca home. Olivia rose to her lady-of-the-manor duties and said we all should discuss burial arrangements for two skeletons who needed peace after being dumped behind a wine vat for too many years. It was unanimously decided to leave everything up to her.

After everyone left, Eric and I headed out to the veranda.

He wrapped his arm around my shoulders and I leaned into him, taking comfort in his strength. We let the quiet relax us. It was only one-thirty in the afternoon, but clouds had moved in, promising more rain, and darkening the skies to appear as though it was early evening.

Eric kissed the top of my head. "So, Theodosia, what's with the notebook? Still looking for more answers? Do you believe Rosalynn…you…somehow predicted her own death?"

"Honestly? I do. I mean, Rosalynn's characters were mirror images of nearly everyone on this island who was connected to the castle. But she included thoughts I had and statements only I heard. I guess you could *almost* explain it away if someone else read the book up to where we found it and then carried out the various nasty events. But do you remember how the published version ended with the shooting at Chittamwood Gardens? It was like the Edwin Drood mystery. Something intriguing with no ending. No last chapter."

"Yeah."

"I lied about why I went to get the clock in the guest room. I didn't need to use any facilities. I used the time to skim the last chapter. It was short and I'm a fast reader."

"Uh-oh. I'm not completely sure what you're driving at, but I'd lay bets what you're about to say is...unsettling."

"Unsettling is mild. The chapter in the notebook ended with Doree, the heroine, finding the body of Rick's ancestor in the wine cellar of the castle. A deranged woman enters, claiming ownership of the castle due to Grace Sedley and waves a gun at them. Later the woman shoots herself on the beach in front of the castle. Stop. No final chapter at all. Yet Rosalynn knew. She knew every move the Doree character would make exactly as *I* made them. Like she was inside my mind and my soul."

"You believe she could see into the future?"

"It's the only explanation I can come up with. Did she know she'd come back as Teddie, who had the same thoughts as her fictional character, Doree? I can't be certain. But she nailed future events so perfectly it's uncanny. And I call that unsettling because if I'm truly Shauna, then will I also start being able to predict the future with that kind of certainty? Premonitions and flash visions are one thing. I'm not ready to go full-on psychic."

We heard a cough behind us and turned.

"Miz Vianca. We thought Alex and Cici had taken you home."

"They're waitin' in the truck." She remained standing. "Ah ain't gonna intrude for long but I wanted to say, I'm no fool."

"What do you mean?" I asked. "No one would ever think that."

"Well, you're kind, but some do anyway. But Ah been wantin' to tell you children Ah've known since you and Mister Eric stepped foot on this island you used to be Mister Emeric and Miz Althea. Wasn't sure about Miz Rosalynn 'til today."

Eric raised an eyebrow. "Why didn't you say anything?"

"Cuz it wasn't up to me. You needed to find out yourselves. Was plannin' on steppin' in and tellin' you if you hadn't figured out before you got killed again," she said, not quite in jest.

Eric and I grinned. We rose and entered into a nice group hug. As we all drew away from each other, I said, "Miz Vianca, I love you. But next time a couple of reincarnated souls land on Endgate Island, you might give them a hint or two about their past lives. Could help keep folks safe."

294

She waved her hand in the air. "More fun keepin' secrets." She turned and walked back into the house.

Eric and I sat back down on the top step. He put his arm around me and drew me in close. He kissed me, his lips tasting like tequila and lime. Intoxicating.

When he finally released me, he scooted a few inches away so we could look at each other without getting cross-eyed. "So, Miss Althea-Shauna-Rosalynn-Theodosia, are you ready to finish writing the last chapters in Tenth Avenue?"

"Why is it I'm sure you already have an ending in mind?"

He leaned forward and kissed me again. "Because I do. And it's to provide a happily ever after with you...in all the lifetimes we're lucky enough to share."

ABOUT THE AUTHOR

Flo Fitzpatrick is a multi-published author of mystery and romance (often with splashes of paranormal elements.) Her background is in theatre and dance as a performer, director/choreographer, and teacher. An Army brat, she spent her toddler years in a chateau in France, which helps explain her love of gothic mysteries and romantic settings. Her second novel, was nominated as Best Romantic Suspense by RT Book Review, and optioned for film. When Flo isn't writing, she can found singing with the jazz band, The Usual Suspects.

CONNECT WITH Flo:

www.flofitzpatrick.com

facebook.com/flofitz

twitter.com/flofitzpatrick

linkedin.com/in/flo-fitzpatrick-4b473330/

www.BOROUGHSPUBLISHINGGROUP.com

If you enjoyed this book, please write a review. Our authors appreciate the feedback, and it helps future readers find books they love. We welcome your comments and invite you to send them to info@boroughspublishinggroup.com. Follow us on Facebook, Twitter and Instagram, and be sure to sign up for our newsletter for surprises and new releases from your favorite authors.

Are you an aspiring writer? Check out www.boroughspublishinggroup.com/submit and see if we can help you make your dreams come true.

www.ingramcontent.com/pod-product-compliance
Lightning Source LLC
Chambersburg PA
CBHW020345180626
46812CB00001B/346